Praise for

LIBRARY OF THE DEAD

"THE [...] REVISIT OF
THE AN[...] BETWEEN FREE WILL AND
PREDEST[...]ION: A DANGEROUS SECRET RAISES THE
UNSETTLING SPECTRE THAT WHAT WE IMAGINE IS
FREEDOM MIGHT BE PART OF AN ALL-ENCOMPASSING—
AND TERRIFYING—PLAN."
—Katherine Neville, *New York Times*–bestselling author

"AS COOPER BUILDS THE LAYERS OF
INTRIGUE IT BECOMES CLEAR THAT HE IS NO
ORDINARY THRILLER WRITER, BUT ONE WHO
ASKS BIG QUESTIONS. . . . GRIPPING."
—*The Sunday Telegraph*

"ORIGINAL AND CLEVER."
—*Publishers Weekly*

"EXTREMELY WELL-WRITTEN, IMAGINATIVE,
AND CAPTIVATING."
—*Euro Crime*

"PREPARE TO BE ENTHRALLED BY THIS EPIC THRILLER.
GLENN COOPER'S DEBUT NOVEL IS A MASTERPIECE OF
SUSPENSE. EAT YOUR HEART OUT, DAN BROWN."
—*Peterborough Telegraph*

LIBRARY
of the
DEAD

LIBRARY
of the
DEAD

GLENN COOPER

HARPERCOLLINS PUBLISHERS LTD

Library of the Dead
Copyright © 2009 by Glenn Cooper.
All rights reserved.

Published by HarperCollins Publishers Ltd

First published in Canada by
HarperCollins Publishers Ltd in an
original trade paperback edition: 2009
First Harper Weekend trade paperback edition: 2010
This mass market edition: 2017

No part of this book may be used or reproduced in any manner whatsoever without the prior written permission of the publisher, except in
the case of brief quotations embodied in reviews.

HarperCollins books may be purchased for educational, business, or
sales promotional use through our Special Markets Department.

HarperCollins Publishers Ltd
2 Bloor Street East, 20th Floor
Toronto, Ontario, Canada
M4W 1A8

www.harpercollins.ca

Library and Archives Canada Cataloguing in Publication information
is available upon request.

ISBN 978-1-44345-452-0

Printed in the United States of America
QUAD 10   9   8   7   6   5   4   3   2   1

David Swisher spun the track ball of his BlackBerry until he found the e-mail from the CFO of one of his clients. The guy wanted to find a time to come down from Hartford to talk about a debt financing. Routine stuff, the kind of business he saved for his ride home. He thumb-typed a reply while the Town Car jerked up Park Avenue in stop and go traffic.

A chime announced the arrival of a new e-mail. It was from his wife: *I've got a surprise for you.*

He texted back: *Excellent! Can't wait.*

Outside the window of his limo the sidewalks were busy with New Yorkers intoxicated with the first blush of spring weather. The bleached evening light and the warm weightless air quickened their steps and lifted their spirits. Men with jackets on their thumbs and rolled-up sleeves felt the breeze on their bare forearms, and women in short diaphanous skirts felt it against their thighs. The sap was rising, for sure. Hormones, locked-up like ships trapped in arctic ice, started flowing free in the spring thaw. There would be action tonight in the city. From a high floor of an apartment tower, someone was exuberantly playing Stravinsky's *The Rite of Spring* on a stereo, and the notes wafted down from open windows and fused with the cacophony of the city.

All this was unnoticed by David, who concentrated on his little glowing LCD screen. And he too was unnoticed, veiled by a tinted window—a thirty-six-year-old investment banker, plainly affluent, with a good head of hair, a lightweight wool suit from Barneys, and a scowl plastered on from a day that had done nothing for his career, his ego, or his bank account.

The taxi stopped at his building on Park and 81st, and walking the fourteen feet from the curb to the door he realized the weather was pleasant. By way of celebration he breathed one full measure of atmosphere into his lungs then managed to smile at his doorman. "How're you doing, Pete?"

"Just fine, Mr. Swisher. How'd the markets do today?"

"Fucking bloodbath." He swept past. "Keep your money under your mattress." Their little joke.

His nine room co-op on a high floor cost him a shade under four and three-quarters when he bought it shortly after 9/11. A steal. The markets were nervous, the sellers were nervous, even though this was a gem, a white-glove building, a prewar with twelve-foot ceilings, eat-in kitchen, and a working fireplace. On Park! He liked to buy in at the bottom of a market, any market. This was way he got more space than a childless couple needed, but it was a trophy that got wows from his family, which always made him feel pretty damn good. Besides, it was worth well over seven-five now, even in a fire sale, so all in all a great deal for Swish, he reminded himself frequently.

The mailbox was empty. He called back over his shoulder, "Hey, Pete, did my wife come in already?"

"About ten minutes ago."

That was the surprise.

Her briefcase was on the hall table, sitting on a pile of mail. He closed the door noiselessly and tried to tiptoe, maybe sneak up behind her, cup her breasts in his hands and press up against her rump. His idea of fun. The Italian marble blew his plan when even his supple dress loafers tapped and echoed enough to betray him.

"David? That you?"

"Yeah. You're home early," he called. "How come?"

From the kitchen: "My deposition got pushed."

The dog heard his voice and ran at full throttle from a guest bedroom at the far end of the apartment, its little paws skidding on the marble, sending the poodle crashing into the wall like a hockey player.

"Bloomberg!" David shouted. "How's my little baby!" He put his case down and picked up the white fluff ball, who licked at his face with its pink piston tongue while furiously wagging its bobbed tail. "Don't pee on Daddy's tie! Don't you do that. Good boy, good boy. Honey, was Bloomie walked?"

"Pete said Ricardo walked him at four."

He put the dog down and went for the mail, sorting it into piles in his obsessive kind of way. Bills. Statements. Junk. Personal. His catalogues. Hers catalogues. Magazines. Postcard?

A plain white postcard with his name and address printed in black type. He flipped it over.

There was a typed date: May 22, 2009. And next to it an image that instantly disturbed him: the unmistakable outline of a coffin, about an inch tall, hand-drawn in ink.

"Helen! Did you see this?"

His wife came into the hall, high heels clipping on the stone, perfectly turned out in a pale turquoise Armani suit with a double strand of cultured pearls resting just above a hint of cleavage, her matching pearl earrings playing peekaboo under salon-styled hair. A handsome-looking woman, anyone would agree.

"See what?" she asked.

"This."

She looked it over. "Who sent it?"

"There's no return address," he said.

"It's postmarked Las Vegas. Who do you know in Vegas?"

"Christ, I don't know. I've done business there—I can't think of anyone offhand."

"Maybe it's a promotion for something, like a teaser ad," she suggested, handing it back to him. "Tomorrow there'll be something else in the mail that'll explain it."

He bought it. She was smart and usually figured things out. But still. "It's in bad taste. Fucking coffin. I mean, please."

"Don't let it put you in a mood. We're both home at a civilized time. How great is that? Want to go to Tutti's?"

He put the postcard onto the junk stack and grabbed her ass. "Before or after we fool around?" he asked, hoping the answer was "After."

The postcard bugged David on and off all evening, though he didn't bring it up again. He thought about it while they waited for dessert, he thought about it when they got home right after he came inside her, he thought about it when he took Bloomie for a quick pee outside the building before they turned in for the night. And it was the last thing he thought about before he fell asleep as Helen read beside him, the bluish glow of her clip-on book light faintly illuminating the black edges of the master bedroom. Coffins bothered the hell out of him. When he was nine, his five-year-old brother died of a Wilms' tumor, and Barry's little polished mahogany coffin—sitting on a pedestal in the memorial chapel—haunted him still. Whoever sent that postcard was a shithead, plain and simple.

He killed the alarm clock about fifteen minutes before it would have sounded off at 5:00 A.M. The poodle jumped off the bed and started doing its nutty first-thing-in-the-morning running in circles routine.

"Okay, okay," he whispered. "I'm coming!" Helen slept on. Bankers went into the office hours before lawyers, so the morning dog walk was his.

A few minutes later David said hello to the night doorman as Bloomberg tugged him on his leash into the pre-dawn chill. He zipped his track suit top all the way to his throat before heading north for their usual circuit—up to 82nd, where the dog invariably did most of his business, east to Lex, hit the early-bird Starbucks, then back to 81st and home. Park Avenue was seldom empty, and this morning a fair number of cabs and delivery trucks rolled by.

His mind was perpetually motoring; he found the concept of "chilling" ludicrous. He was always working some angle, but as he approached 82nd Street, he wasn't centered on any particular topic, more an unedited hodge-podge of work-related to-dos. The postcard, thankfully, was forgotten. Making the turn onto the ominously dark tree-lined street, his city-slicker survival skills almost made him alter his route—he briefly considered carrying on up to 83rd— but his trading-floor macho wouldn't let him wimp out.

Instead he crossed over to the north side of 82nd Street so he could keep an eye on the dark-skinned kid milling on the sidewalk about a third of the way down the block. If the kid crossed the street too, he'd know he was in trouble and he would pick up Bloomie and make a run for it. He had run track in school. He was still fast from pickup B-ball. His Nike's were laced nice and tight. So, fuck it, worst case scenario, he'd still be okay.

The kid started walking in his direction on the opposite side of the block, a lanky fellow with a hoodie up so David couldn't see his eyes. He hoped a car would come along or another pedestrian, but the street stayed quiet, two men and a dog, so still, he could hear the kid's new sneakers squeaking on the pavement. The brownstones were dark, their occupants dreaming. The only doorman building was nearer to Lexington. His heart rate ramped up as they drew level. No eye contact. No eye contact. He kept going. The kid kept going, and the gap between them widened.

He allowed himself an over-the-shoulder glance and exhaled when he saw the kid turning onto Park, disappearing around the corner. I'm a fucking wuss, he thought. And a prejudiced one too.

Halfway down the block, Bloomie sniffed at his favorite spot and started to squat. David couldn't understand why he hadn't heard the kid until he was almost on him. Maybe he'd been distracted, thinking about his first appointment with the head of capital markets, or watching the dog find its spot, or remembering the way Helen had flung off her bra last night, or maybe the kid had made an art of urban stealth running. But it was all academic.

David was punched in the temple and went down hard on his knees, momentarily fascinated, more than afraid, by the unexpected violence. The punch made his head soupy. He watched Bloomie finish his poop. He heard something about money and felt hands going through his pockets. He saw a blade near his face. He felt his watch slipping off, then his ring. Then he remembered the postcard, that god-damned postcard, and heard himself asking, "Did you send it?" He thought he heard the kid answer, "Yeah, I sent it, motherfucker."

A year earlier
Cambridge, Massachusetts

Will Piper arrived early to get a drink on board before the others arrived. The crowded restaurant, off Harvard Square, was called OM, and Will shrugged his heavy shoulders at the trendy eclectic Asian ambience. It wasn't his kind of place but the lounge had a bar and the bartender had ice cubes and scotch so it met his minimum requirements. He looked askance at the artistically rough-cut stonework wall behind the bar, the bright flat-screen installations of video art and the neon-blue lights, and asked himself, What am I doing here?

As early as a month ago, the probability of him attending his twenty-fifth college reunion was zero, and yet here he was, back at Harvard with hundreds of forty-seven- and forty-eight-year-olds, wondering where the prime cut of their lives had gone. Jim Zeckendorf, good lawyer that he was, relentlessly cajoled and hounded him and the others via e-mail until they all acquiesced. Not that he signed up for the full monty. Nobody was going to make him march with the class of 1983 into Tercentenary Theater. But he agreed to drive up from New York to have dinner with his roommates, stay over at Jim's house in Weston, and head back in the morning. He'd be damned if he was going to blow more than two vacation days on ghosts from the past.

Will's glass was empty before the bartender was done filling the next order. He rattled the ice to get the guy's attention and attracted a woman instead. She was standing behind him, waving a twenty at the bartender, a splendid-looking brunette in her thirties. He smelled her spiced fragrance before she leaned over his broad back and asked, "When you get him, can you get me a chard?"

He half turned, and her cashmere bosom was at eye level, as was the twenty dollar bill, dangling from slender fingers. He addressed her breasts, "I'll get it for you," then rotated his neck to see a pretty face with mauve eye shadow and red glossy lips, just the way he liked them. He picked up strong availability vibes.

She withdrew the money with a lilting, "Thanks," and inserted herself into the tight space he made by sliding his stool a couple of inches.

In a few minutes Will felt a tap on his shoulder and heard, "Told you we'd find him at the bar!" Zeckendorf had a big grin on his smooth, almost feminine face. He still had enough hair to pull off a curly Jewfro, and Will had a flashback to his first day in Harvard Yard in 1979, a big blond oaf from the Florida panhandle, flopping around like a bonita on the deck of a boat meeting a skinny bushy-haired kid with the self-assured swagger of a local who was bred to wear crimson. Zeckendorf's wife was at his side, or at least Will assumed that the surprisingly matronly woman with thick haunches was the same twiglike bride he last saw at their wedding in 1988.

The Zeckendorfs had Alex Dinnerstein and his girl-friend in tow. Alex had a tight diminutive body and a flawless tan that made him seem the youngest of the roomies, and he flaunted his fitness and panache with an expensive European-cut suit and a fancy pocket handkerchief, white and bright like his teeth. His gelled hair was as straight and black as it was freshman year and Will pegged him as a dyer—to each his own. Dr. Dinnerstein had to keep young for the sweet thing on his arm, a model at least twenty years their junior, a long-legged beauty with a very special figure who almost made Will forget his new friend, who had been left awkwardly sipping at her glass of wine.

Zeckendorf noticed the lady's discomfort. "Will, are you going to introduce us?"

Will smiled sheepishly and muttered, "We haven't gotten that far," eliciting a knowing snort from Alex.

The woman said, "I'm Gillian. I hope you all enjoy your reunion." She started moving away, and Will wordlessly pressed one of his cards into her hand.

She glanced at it and the flicker across her face revealed surprise: SPECIAL AGENT WILL PIPER, FEDERAL BUREAU OF INVESTIGATION.

When she was gone, Alex made a show of patting Will down and hamming, "Probably never met a Harvard man packing heat, eh, buddy? Is that a Beretta in your pocket or are you happy to see me?"

"Fuck off, Alex. Good to see you too."

Zeckendorf herded them up the stairs toward the restaurant then realized they were one short. "Anyone seen Shackleton?"

"You sure he's still alive?" Alex asked.

"Circumstantial evidence," Zeckendorf answered. "E-mails."

"He won't show. He hated us," Alex claimed.

"He hated you," Will said. "You're the one who duct-taped him to his fucking bed."

"You were there too if I recall," Alex sniggered.

The restaurant was buzzing with affluent chatter, a mood-lit museum space with Nepalese statuary and a Buddha-embedded wall. Their table overlooking Winthrop Street was waiting but not empty. There was a solitary man at one end, nervously fingering his napkin.

"Hey, look who's here!" Zeckendorf called out.

Mark Shackleton looked up as if he'd been dreading the moment. His small closely spaced eyes, partially concealed by the bill of a Lakers cap, darted from side to side, scanning them. Will recognized Mark instantly, even though it had been more like twenty-eight years, since he pretty much lost touch with him the minute freshman year was over. The same zero-fat face that made his head look like a deep-socketed, high-domed meatless skull, the same tension-banded lips and sharp nose. Mark hadn't looked like a teenager even when he was one; he just grew into his natural middle-aged state.

The four roommates were an odd-duck sort of grouping: Will, the easygoing jock from Florida; Jim, the fast-talking prep-school kid from Brookline; Alex, the sex-mad premed from Wisconsin; and Mark, the reclusive computer nerd, from nearby Lexington. They had been squeezed into a quad in Holworthy at the northern pole of leafy Harvard Yard, two tiny bedrooms with bunks and a common room with half-decent furniture, thanks to Zeckendorf's rich parents. Will was the last to arrive at the dorm that September, as he'd been ensconced with the football team for preseason training. By then Alex and Jim had paired up. and when he lugged his duffel bag over the threshold, the two of them sniggered and pointed to the other bedroom. where he found Mark stiffly planted on the lower bunk, claiming it, afraid to move.

"Hey, how're you doin'?" Will had asked the kid while sprouting a big southern smile on his chiseled face. "How much ya weigh there, Mark?"

"One forty," Mark answered suspiciously as he struggled to make eye contact with the boy towering over him.

"Well, I register at two twenty-five in my shorts. You sure you want my heavy ass a couple of feet over your head on that rickety old bunk bed?"

Mark had sighed deeply, wordlessly ceded his claim, and the pecking order was thus permanently established.

They fell into the random chaotic conversation of reunionites, excavating memories, laughing at embarrassments, dredging up indiscretions and foibles. The two women were their audience, their excuse for exposition and elaboration. Zeckendorf and Alex, who had remained fast friends, acted as emcees, ping-ponging the banter like a couple of stand-ups extracting laughs at a comedy club. Will wasn't as fast with a quip but his quiet, slowly spoken recollections of their dysfunctional year had them rapt. Only Mark was quiet, politely smiling when they laughed, drinking his beer and picking at his Asian fusion food. Zeckendorf's wife had been tasked by her husband to snap pictures, and she obliged by circling the table, posing them and flashing.

Freshman roommate groups are like an unstable chemical compound. As soon as the environment changes, the bonds break and the molecules fly apart. In sophomore year Will went to Adams House to room with other football players, Zeckendorf and Alex kept together and went to Leverett House, and Mark got a single at Currier. Will occasionally saw Zeckendorf in a government class, but they all basically disappeared into their own worlds. After graduation, Zeckendorf and Alex stayed in Boston and the two of them reached out to Will from time to time, usually triggered by reading about him in the papers or catching him on TV. None of them spent a moment thinking about Mark. He faded away, and had it not been for Zeckendorf's sense of occasion and Mark's inclusion of his gmail address in the reunion book, he would have remained a piece of the past to them.

Alex was loudly going on about some freshman escapade involving twins from Lesley College, a night that allegedly set him on a lifelong path of gynecology, when his date shifted the conversation to Will. Alex's increasingly tipsy clowning was wearing on her and she kept glancing at the large sandy-haired man who was steadily drinking scotch across from her, seemingly without inebriation. "So how did you get involved with the FBI?" the model asked him before Alex could launch into another tale about himself.

"Well, I wasn't good enough at football to go pro."

"No, really." She seemed genuinely interested.

"I don't know," Will answered softly. "I didn't have a whole lot of direction after I graduated. My buddies here knew what they wanted: Alex and med school, Zeck and law school, Mark had grad school at MIT, right?" Mark nodded. "I spent a few years knocking around back in Florida, doing some teaching and coaching and then a position opened up in a county sheriff's office down there."

"Your father was in law enforcement," Zeckendorf recalled.

"Deputy sheriff in Panama City."

"Is he still alive?" Zeckendorf's wife asked.

"No, he passed a long time ago." He had a swallow of scotch. "I guess it was in my blood and the path of least resistance and all that so I went with it. After a while it made the chief uncomfortable that he had a smart-ass Harvard dude as a deputy and he had me apply to Quantico to get me the hell out of there. That was it, and in the blink of an eye I'm staring retirement in the face."

"When do you hit your twenty?" Zeckendorf asked.

"Little over two years."

"Then what?"

"Other than fishing, I don't have a clue."

Alex was busily pouring another bottle of wine. "Do you have any idea how famous this asshole is?" he asked his date.

She bit. "No, how famous are you?"

"I'm not."

"Bullshit!" Alex exclaimed. "Our man here is like the most successful serial killer profiler in the history of the FBI!"

"No, no, that's certainly not true," Will strongly demurred.

"How many have you caught over the years?" Zeckendorf asked.

"I don't know. A few, I guess."

"A few! That's like saying I've done a few pelvic exams," Alex exclaimed. "They say you're the man—infallible."

"I think you're referring to the Pope."

"C'mon, I read somewhere you can psychoanalyze someone in under a half a minute."

"I don't need that long to figure you out, buddy, but seriously, you shouldn't believe everything you read."

Alex nudged his date. "Take my word for it—watch out for this guy. He's a phenom."

Will was anxious to change the subject. His career had taken a few nonsuperlative turns, and he didn't feel much like dwelling on past glories. "I guess we've all done pretty well considering our shaky start, Zeck's a big-time corporate lawyer, Alex is a professor of medicine . . . God help us, but let's talk about Mark here. What have you been up to all these years?"

Before Mark could wet his lips for a reply, Alex pounced, slipping into his ancient role as torturer of the geek. "Yeah, let's hear it. Shackleton is probably some kind of dot-com billionaire with his own 737 and a basketball team. Did you go on to invent the cell phone or something like that? I mean you were always writing stuff in that notebook of yours, always with the closed bedroom door. What were you doing in there, sport, besides going through back issues of Playboy and boxes of Kleenex?"

Will and Zeckendorf couldn't suppress a yuk because back then the kid always did seem to buy a whole lot of Kleenex. But straight away Will felt a pang of guilt when Mark impaled him with a barbed *et tu, Brute?* kind of look.

"I'm in computer security," Mark half whispered into his plate. "Unfortunately, I'm not a billionaire." He looked up and added hopefully. "I also do some writing on the side."

"You work at a company?" Will asked politely, trying to redeem himself.

"I worked for a few of them but now I'm like you, I guess. I work for the government."

"Really. Where?"

"Nevada."

"You live in Vegas, right?" Zeckendorf said.

Mark nodded, clearly disappointed no one had keyed onto his comment about writing.

"Which branch?" Will asked, and when his reply was a mute stare, he added, "Of the government?"

Mark's angular Adam's apple moved as he swallowed. "It's a lab. It's kind of classified."

"Shack's got a secret!" Alex shouted gleefully. "Give him another drink! Loosen his lips!"

Zeckendorf looked fascinated. "Come on, Mark, can't you tell us something about it?"

"Sorry."

Alex leaned in. "I bet a certain someone from the FBI could find out what you're up to."

"I don't think so," Mark replied with a dram of smugness.

Zeckendorf wouldn't let it go and thought out loud, "Nevada, Nevada—the only secret government lab I've ever heard of in Nevada is out in the desert . . . at what's called . . . Area 51?" He waited for a denial but got a good long poker face instead. "Tell me you don't work at Area 51!"

Mark hesitated then said slyly, "I can't tell you that."

"Wow," the model said, impressed. "Isn't that where they study UFOs and things like that?"

Mark smiled like the Mona Lisa, enigmatically.

"If he told you, he'd have to kill you," Will said.

Mark vigorously shook his head, his eyes lowered and turning humorless. There was a reedy dryness in his throat that Will found disquieting. "No. If I told you, other people would kill you."

Consuela Lopez was worn-out and in pain. She was at the stern of the Staten Island ferry, sitting at her usual home-bound spot near the exit so she could disembark quickly. If she missed the 10:45 P.M. number 51 bus, she had a long wait at the bus station at St. George Terminal for the next one. The nine-thousand-horsepower diesel engines sent vibrations through her slight body, making her sleepy, but she was too suspicious of her fellow passengers to close her eyes lest her pocketbook disappear.

She propped her swollen left ankle on the plastic bench but rested her heel on a newspaper. Putting her shoe directly on the bench would be rude and disrespectful. She had sprained her ankle when she tripped on her own vacuum cleaner cord. She was an office cleaner in lower Manhattan and this was the end of a long day and a long week. It was a blessing that the accident happened on a Friday so she'd have the weekend to recover. She couldn't afford to miss a day of work and prayed that she would be fine by Monday. If she was still in pain on Saturday night, she would go to early mass on Sunday and beg the Virgin Mary to help her heal quickly. She also wanted to show Father Rochas the odd postcard she had received and allay her fears about it.

Consuela was a plain-looking woman who spoke little English, but she was young and had a nice figure, and so was always on guard against advances. A few rows away, facing her, an Hispanic youth in a gray sweatshirt kept smiling at her, and although she was initially uncomfortable, something about his white teeth and animated eyes induced her to give him a polite smile in return. That was all it took. He introduced himself and spent the last ten minutes of the journey seated beside her, sympathizing with her injury.

When the ferry docked she limped off, resisting his offer of support. He attentively followed a few paces behind even though she was moving at a turtle's pace. He offered her a ride home but she declined—it was out of the question. But since the ferry was a few minutes late and her egress was so slow, she missed her bus and reconsidered. He seemed like a nice guy. He was funny and respectful. She accepted, and when he left to get his car from the parking garage, she crossed herself for insurance.

As they neared the turnoff to her house on Fingerboard Road, his mood hardened and she became worried. The worry turned to fear as he sped past her street and ignored her protestations. He kept driving mutely on Bay Street until he made a hard left, heading for the Arthur Von Briesen Park.

At the end of the dark road she was crying and he was shouting and waving a folding knife. He forced her out of the car and pulled her by the arm, threatening to hurt her if she called out. He no longer cared about her sore ankle. He pulled her at running speed through the bushes toward the water. She winced in pain but was too frightened to make a noise.

The dark massive superstructure of the Verrazano-Narrows Bridge was ahead of them, like some sort of malevolent presence. There wasn't a soul in sight. In a wooded clearing, he threw her onto the ground and harshly pulled her pocketbook from her grasp. She started sobbing and he told her to shut up. He rifled through her belongings and pocketed the few dollars she had. Then he found the plain white postcard addressed to her with a hand-drawn picture of a coffin and the date, May 22, 2009. He looked at it and smiled sadistically.

"Usted me piensa le envió esto?" he asked. Do you think I sent you this?

"No sé," she sobbed, shaking her head.

"Bien, le estoy enviando esto," he said, laughing and un-buckling his belt. Well, I'm sending you this.

Will assumed she'd still be gone, and his suspicions were confirmed the second he opened the door and dropped his roller bag and briefcase.

The apartment remained in its pre-Jennifer state. The scented candles. Gone. The place mats on the dining room table. Gone. The frilly throw pillows. Gone. Her clothes, shoes, cosmetics, toothbrush. Gone. He finished his whirlwind tour of the one bedroom layout and opened the refrigerator door. Even those stupid bottles of vitamin water. Gone.

He had completed a two-day out-of-town course in sensitivity training mandated at his last performance review. If she had unexpectedly returned, he would have tried out some new techniques on her, but Jennifer was still—gone.

He loosened his tie, kicked off his shoes, and opened the small liquor cabinet under the TV set. Her envelope was tucked under his bottle of Johnnie Walker Black, the same place he had found it the day she did a runner on him. On it, she had written *Fuck You* in her distinctive feminine scrawl. He poured a large one, propped his feet on the coffee table, and for old times' sake reread the letter that revealed things about himself he already knew. A clatter distracted him midway through, a framed picture toppled by his big toe. Zeckendorf had sent it: the freshman roommates at their reunion the previous summer. Another year—gone.

An hour later, hazy with booze, he was flooded with one of Jennifer's sentiments: you are flawed beyond repair.

Flawed beyond repair, he thought. An interesting concept. Unfixable. Unredeemable. No chance for rehabilitation or meaningful improvement.

He switched on the Mets game and fell asleep on the sofa.

Flawed or not, he was at his desk by 8:00 A.M. the next morning, digging through his Outlook in-box. He banged out a few replies then sent an e-mail to his supervisor, Sue Sanchez, thanking her for having the managerial prowess and foresight to recommend him for the seminar he had just attended. His sensitivity had increased about forty-seven percent, he reckoned, and he expected she would see immediate and measurable results. He signed it, *Sensitively, Will*, and clicked Send.

In thirty seconds his phone rang. Sanchez's line.

"Welcome home, Will," she said, oozing treacle.

"Great to be back, Susan," he said, his southern accent flattened by all the years spent away from the Florida panhandle.

"Why don't you come and see me, okay?"

"When would be good for you, Susan?" he asked earnestly.

"Now!" She hung up.

She was sitting behind his old desk in his old office, which had a nice view of the Statue of Liberty thanks to Mohammed Atta, but that didn't irritate him as much as the puckered expression on her taut olive face. Sanchez was an obsessive exerciser who read service manuals and management self-help books while she worked out. She always appealed to him physically, but that sour mug and nasal officious tone with its Latina twang doused his interest.

Hastily, she said, "Sit. We need to have a chat, Will."

"Susan, if you're planning on chewing me out, I'm prepared to handle it professionally. Rule number six—or was it number four?: 'when you feel you are being provoked, do not act precipitously. Stop and consider the consequences of your actions, then choose your words carefully, respectful of the reactions of the person or persons who have challenged you.' Pretty good, huh? I got a certificate." He smiled and folded his hands across his nascent paunch.

"I'm so not in the mood for your BS today," she said wearily. "I've got a problem and I need you to help me solve it." Management-speak for: you're about to get shafted.

"For you? Anything. As long as it doesn't involve nudity or mess up my last fourteen months."

She sighed, then paused, giving Will the impression she was taking rule number four or six to heart. He was aware that she considered him her number one problem child. Everyone in the office knew the score:

Will Piper. Forty-eight, nine years Sanchez's senior. Formerly her boss, before getting busted from his management grade back to Special Agent. Formerly breath-catchingly handsome, a six-plus-footer with I-beam shoulders, electric-blue eyes, and boyishly rumpled sandy hair, before alcohol and inactivity gave his flesh the consistency and pallor of rising bread dough. Formerly a hotshot, before becoming a glib pain-in-the-ass clock watcher.

She just spat it out. "John Mueller had a stroke two days ago. The doctors say he's going to recover but he'll be on medical leave. His absence, particularly now, is a problem for the office. Benjamin, Ronald, and I have discussed this."

Will marveled at the news. "Mueller? He's younger than you are! Fricking marathon runner. How the hell did *he* have a stroke?"

"He had a hole in his heart no one picked up before," she said. "A small blood clot from his leg floated through and went up to his brain. That's what I was told. Pretty scary how that could happen."

Will loathed Mueller. Smug, wiry shithead. Everything by the book. Totally insufferable, the SOB still made snarky comments to his face about his blow-up—insulated, the bastard supposed, by his leper status. Hope he walks and talks like a retard for the rest of his life, was the first notion that came to mind. "Christ, that's too bad," he said instead.

"We need you to take the Doomsday case."

It took almost supernatural strength to prevent himself from telling her to screw herself.

It should have been his case from the start. In fact it was nothing short of outrageous that it hadn't been offered to him the day it hit the office. Here he was, one of the most accomplished serial killing experts in the Bureau's recent history, passed over for a marquee case right in his jurisdiction. It was a measure of how damaged his career was, he supposed. At the time, the snub stung like hell, but he'd gotten over it quickly enough and come to believe he had dodged a bullet.

He was on the homestretch. Retirement was like a glistening watery mirage in the desert, just out of reach. He was done with ambition and striving, he was done with office politics, he was done with murders and death. He was tired and lonely and stuck in a city he disliked. He wanted to go home. With a pension.

He chewed on the bad piece of news. Doomsday had rapidly become the office's highest profile case, the kind that demanded an intensity he hadn't brought to the table in years. Long days and blown weekends weren't the issue. Thanks to Jennifer, he had all the time in the world. The problem was in the mirror, because—as he would tell anyone who asked—he simply no longer gave a damn. You needed raging ambition to solve a serial killing case, and that flame had long ago sputtered and died. Luck was important too, but in his experience, you succeeded by busting your hump and creating the environment for luck to do its capricious thing.

Beyond that, Mueller's partner was a young Special Agent, only three years out of Quantico, who was so imbued with devout ambition and agency rectitude that he likened her to a religious fanatic. He had observed her hustling around the twenty-third floor, speed-walking through the corridors, profoundly humorless and sanctimonious, taking herself so seriously it made him ill.

He leaned forward, almost ashen. "Look, Susan," he began,

his voice rising, "this is not a good idea. That ship has sailed. You should have asked me to do the case a few weeks ago, but you know what? It was the right call. At this point, it's not good for me, it's not good for Nancy, it's not good for the office, the Bureau, the taxpayers, the victims, and the goddamned future victims! You know it and I know it!"

She got up to shut the door then sat back in her chair and crossed her legs. The rasp of her panty hose rubbing against itself momentarily distracted him from his rant. "Yes, I'll keep my voice down," he volunteered, "but most of all, it's terrible for you. You're in the chute. You've got Major Thefts and Violent Crimes, the branch with the second-highest visibility in New York! This Doomsday asshole gets caught on your watch, you move up. You're a woman, you're ethnic, a few years you're an assistant director at Quantico, maybe a Supervisory Special Agent in D.C. The sky's the limit. Don't fuck it up by involving me, that's my friendly advice."

She gave him a stare to freeze mud. "I certainly appreciate this reverse mentoring, Will, but I don't think I want to rely on career advice from a man who is sliding down the org chart. Believe me, I don't love this idea, but we've gone over it internally. Benjamin and Ronald refuse to move anyone from Counterterrorism, and there's no one else in White Collar or Organized Crime who's done this kind of case. They don't want someone parachuting in from D.C. or another office. It makes them look bad. This is New York, not Cleveland. We're supposed to have a deep bench. You've got the right background—the wrong personality, which you're going to have to work on, but the right background. It's yours. It's going to be your last big case, Will. You're going out with a bang. Think of it that way and cheer up."

He took another run at it. "If we catch this guy tomorrow, which we won't, I'll be history by the time this thing goes to trial."

"So you'll come back to testify. By then the per diem will probably look pretty good."

"Very funny. What about Nancy? I'll poison her. You want her to be the sacrificial lamb?"

"She's a pistol. She can handle herself and she can handle you."

He stopped arguing, sullen. "What about the shit I'm working on?"

"I'll spread it around. No problem."

That was it, it was over. It wasn't a democracy, and quitting or getting fired were not options. Fourteen months. Fourteen fucking months.

Within a couple of hours his life had changed. The office manager showed up with orange moving crates and had his active case files packed and moved out of his cubicle. In their place, Mueller's Doomsday files arrived, boxes of documents compiled in the weeks before a sticky clump of platelets turned a few milliliters of his brain into mush. Will stared at them as if they were stinking piles of dung and drank another cup of overstewed coffee before deigning to open one, randomly plucking a folder.

He heard her clearing her throat at the cubicle entrance before he saw her.

"Hi," Nancy said. "I guess we're going to be working together."

Nancy Lipinski was stuffed into a charcoal-gray suit. It was a half size too small and it pinched her waist enough to force her belly to bulge slightly but unattractively over the waistband. She was pint-sized, five feet three inches in stocking feet, but Will's assessment was that she needed to drop some pounds everywhere, even from her rounded soft face. Were there cheekbones under there? She wasn't the kind of hard-body grad Quantico typically spit out. He wondered how she'd passed muster at the academy's Physical Training Unit. They busted it down there and didn't cut the gals any slack. Admittedly, she wasn't unattractive. Her practical collar-length russet hair, makeup, and gloss were all put together well enough to complement a delicately shaped nose, pretty lips, and lively hazel eyes, and on another woman her cologne would have done the trick for him. It was her plaintive look that set him off. Could she really have become attached to a zero like Mueller?

"What are you going to do?" he said rhetorically.

"Is this a good time?"

"Look, Nancy, I've hardly cracked a box. Why don't you give me a couple of hours, later this afternoon maybe, and we can start talking?"

"That's okay, Will. I just wanted to let you know that even though I'm upset about John, I'm going to keep working my tail off on this case. We've never worked together but I've studied some of your cases and I know the contribution you've made to the field. I'm always looking for ways to improve, so your feedback's going to be extremely important to me . . ."

Will felt he had to nip this kind of wretched talk in the bud. "You a fan of *Seinfeld*?" he asked.

"The TV show?"

He nodded.

"I mean I'm aware of it," she replied suspiciously.

"The people who created the show made the ground rules for the characters, and those ground rules set it apart from all the other sitcoms. Do you want to know those rules? Because they're going to apply to you and me."

"Sure, Will!" she said brightly, apparently ready to absorb a lesson.

"The rules were—no learning and no hugging. I'll see you later, Nancy," he deadpanned.

As she stood there, looking like she was deciding whether to retreat or respond, they both heard quick light footsteps approaching, a woman trying to run in heels. "Sue alert," Will called out melodramatically. "Sounds like she's got something we don't have."

Around their shop, information endowed the bearer with temporary power, and Sue Sanchez seemed to get a jazzy rush from knowing something before anyone else.

"Good, you're both here," she said, shooing Nancy inside the cube. "There's been another one! Number seven, up in the Bronx." She was giddy, borderline juvenile. "Get up there before the Forty-fifth Precinct screws it up."

Will threw his arms into the air, exasperated. "Jesus, Susan, I don't know a goddamned thing about the first six yet. Gimme a break!"

Bang. Nancy chimed in brightly, "Hey, just pretend this is number one! No biggee! Anyway, I'll catch you up on the way."

"Like I said, Will," Sue said, cracking an evil grin, "she's a pistol."

Will picked up one of the department's standard-issue black Ford Explorers. He pulled away from the underground garage at 26 Liberty Plaza and navigated the one-ways until he was pointing north, heading up the FDR Drive in the fast lane. The car was detailed and running smooth, the traffic wasn't bad, and usually he enjoyed a nice run out of the office. If he'd been alone, he would have tuned in WFAN and satisfied his sports jones, but he wasn't. Nancy Lipinski was in the passenger seat, notebook in hand, lecturing him as they passed under the Roosevelt Island tramway, its gondola slowly gliding high above the choppy black waters of the East River.

She was as excited as a perv at a porn convention. This was her first serial murder case, the champagne of homicides, the defining moment in her prepubescent career. She pulled the assignment because she was Sue's pet and had worked with Mueller before. The two of them got along famously, Nancy ready and willing to fortify his brittle ego. *John, you're so smart! John, do you have a photographic memory? John, I wish I could conduct an interview like you.*

Will struggled to pay attention. It was relatively painless to get three weeks of data spoon-fed, but his mind wandered and his head was still fogged up from his late night tryst with Johnnie Walker. Still, he knew he could get into the groove in a heartbeat. Over two decades, he had taken the lead in eight major serial killing cases and kibitzed in countless others.

The first was in Indianapolis, during his inaugural field assignment, when he wasn't much older than Nancy. The perp was a twisted psycho who liked to put out cigarettes on his victims' eyelids until a discarded stub broke the case. When his second wife, Evie, got into grad school at Duke, he pulled a transfer to Raleigh, and sure enough, another crackpot with a straight razor started killing women in and around Asheville. Nine agonizing months and five diced-up victims later, he nailed that creep too. All of a sudden, he had a reputation; he was a de facto specialist. They bumped him, messily divorced again, to headquarters to work Violent Crimes in a group headed by Hal Sheridan, the man who trained a generation of agents how to profile serial killers.

Sheridan was a cold fish, emotionally detached and tightly wound to the point where he was the butt of an office joke: if a killing spree broke out in Virginia, Hal would have to be on the hot list. He doled out the national cases carefully, matching the criminal's mind to the mind of his agents. Sheridan gave him cases involving extreme brutality and torture, killers who directed massive rage at women. Go figure.

Nancy's recitations began to penetrate his fog. The facts, he had to acknowledge, were pretty damned interesting. He knew the broad strokes from the media. Who didn't? It was *the* story. Predictably, the perp's moniker, the Doomsday Killer, came from the press. The *Post* nabbed the honors. It's blood rival, the *Daily News*, resisted for a few days, countering with the header POSTCARDS FROM HELL, but soon capitulated and started blaring Doomsday all over the front page.

According to Nancy, the postcards did not have common fingerprints; the sender probably used fiber-free, possibly latex utility gloves. There were a few nonvictim, nonrelated prints on a couple of the cards, and cooperating FBI field offices were in the process of working up postal workers in the Las Vegas to New York delivery chain. The post-cards themselves were plain white three-by-fives available in thousands of retail outlets. They were printed on an HP Photosmart ink-jet printer, one of tens of thousands in circu-lation, fed in twice to print each side. The font was from the standard Microsoft Word pull-down menu. The ink-drawn coffin outlines were probably all done by the same hand using a black Pentel pen, ultrafine point, one of millions in circulation. The stamps were all the same, forty-one-cent American flag designs, one of hundreds of millions in cir-culation, the backs peel-and-stick, DNA free. The six cards were mailed on May 18 and cleared through the central USPS processing center in Las Vegas.

"So the guy would have had plenty of time to fly from Vegas to New York but it would have been a stretch for him to drive or take a train," Will interjected. He caught her by surprise since she wasn't sure he'd been listening. "Have you gotten passenger lists for all direct and connecting flights from Vegas arriving at LaGuardia, Kennedy, and Newark between the eighteenth and twenty-first?"

She looked up from her notebook. "I asked John if we should do that! He told me it wasn't worth the trouble because some-one could have mailed them for the killer."

Will honked at a Camry going too slowly for his liking, then aggressively passed on the right when it didn't yield. He couldn't mask his sarcasm. "Surprise! Mueller was wrong. Serial killers almost never have accomplices. Some-times they'll kill in pairs, like the D.C. snipers or the Phoe-nix shooters, but that's rare as hell. Getting logistical support to set up the crimes? That'd be a first. These guys are lone wolves."

She was scribbling.

"What are you doing?" he asked.

"Taking notes on what you said."

Christ, this isn't school, he thought. "Since your pen is uncapped, take this down too," he said caustically. "In case the killer did do a cross-country dash, check for speeding tickets along major routes."

She nodded, then asked cautiously, "Do you want to hear more?"

"I'm listening."

It boiled down to this: the victims, four males and two females, ranged in age from eighteen to eighty-two. Three were in Manhattan, one each in Brooklyn, Staten Island, and Queens. Today's would be the first in the Bronx. All the M.O.'s were the same. The victim receives a postcard with a date one or two days in the future, each with a coffin drawn on the back, and winds up being killed on the exact date. Two stabbings, one shooting, one made to look like a heroin overdose, one crushed by a car that jumped the sidewalk in a hit and run, and one thrown out a window.

"And what did Mueller say about that?" Will asked.

"He thought the killer was trying to throw us off by not sticking to one pattern."

"And what do you think?"

"I think it's unusual. It's not what's in the textbooks."

He imagined her criminology texts, passages compulsively highlighted with yellow markers, neat marginalia, tiny lettering. "How about the victim profiles?" he asked. "Any links?"

The victims appeared to be unconnected. The computational guys in Washington were doing a multidatabase matrix analysis looking for common denominators, a supercomputer version of six degrees of Kevin Bacon, but so far no hits.

"Sexual assaults?"

She flipped pages. "Just one, a thirty-two-year-old Hispanic woman, Consuela Pilar Lopez, in Staten Island. She was raped and stabbed to death."

"After we finish up in the Bronx, I want to start there."

"Why?"

"You can tell a lot about a killer by the way he treats a lady."

They were on the Bruckner Expressway now, tracking east through the Bronx.

"You know where we're going?" he asked.

She found it in her notebook. "Eight forty-seven Sullivan Place."

"Thank you! I don't have a fucking clue where that is," he barked. "I know where Yankee Stadium is. Period. That's all I know about the fucking Bronx."

"Please don't swear," she said sternly, like a reprimanding middle school teacher. "I have a map." She unfolded it, studied it a moment and looked around. "We need to get off on Bruckner Boulevard."

They rode in silence for a mile. He waited for her to resume her tutorial but she stared at the road stony-faced.

He finally looked over and saw her lower lip quivering. "What? You're mad at me for dropping the F-bomb, for fuck's sake?"

She looked at him wistfully. "You're different from John Mueller."

"Jesus," he muttered. "It took you this long to figure that out?"

Driving south on East Tremont, they passed the Forty-fifth Precinct house on Barkley Avenue, an ugly squat building with too few parking spaces for the number of squad cars packed around it. The thermometer was touching eighty and the street was teeming with Puerto Ricans, toting plastic shopping bags, pushing baby carriages, or just strolling along with cell phones pressed against ears, moving in and out of the grocerias, bodegas, and cheap mom-and-pop stores. The women were showing a lot of flesh. Too many heavy chicks in halter tops and short-shorts, jiggling along in flip-flops, for his liking. Do they actually think they look foxy? he wondered. They made his passenger look like a supermodel.

Nancy was buried in the map, trying not to screw up. "From here, it's the third left," she said.

Sullivan Place was an inconvenient street for a major murder. Cruisers, unmarked vehicles, and medical examiner vans were double-parked in front of the crime scene, choking off the traffic. Will pulled up to a young cop trying to keep one lane passable and flashed his badge. "Jeez," the cop moaned. "I don't know where to put you. Can you swing around the block? Maybe there's something around the corner."

Will parroted him. "Around the corner."

"Yeah, around the block, you know take a couple of rights."

Will turned off the ignition, got out and tossed the cop the keys. Cars started honking like mad, instant gridlock.

"Whaddya doing!" the cop hollered. "You can't leave this here!" Nancy continued to sit in the SUV, mortified.

Will called to her. "C'mon, let's get a move on. And take Officer Cuneo's badge number down in your little book in case he does anything disrespectful to government property."

The cop muttered, "Asshole."

Will was spoiling for a dust-up and this kid would do just fine. "Listen," he said, boiling over with rage, "if you like your pathetic little job then don't fuck with me! If you don't give a shit about it, then take a shot. Go on! Try it!"

Two angry guys, veins bulging, face-to-face. "Will! Can we go?" Nancy implored. "We're wasting time."

The cop shook his head, climbed into the Explorer, drove it down the block and double-parked it in front of a detective's car. Will, still breathing hard, winked at Nancy, "I knew he'd find us a spot."

It was a pocket-sized apartment building, three floors, six units, dirty white brickwork, slapped together in the forties. The hallway was dim and depressing, brown and black ceramic checkerboard tiling on the floors, grimy beige walls, bare yellow bulbs. All the action was in and around Apartment 1A, ground floor left. Toward the rear of the hall, near the garbage shaft, family members crowded together in multigenerational grief, a middle-aged woman wailing softly, her husband, in work boots, trying to comfort her, a fully pregnant young woman, sitting on the bare floor, recovering from hyperventilation, a young girl in a Sunday dress, looking bewildered, a couple of old men in loose shirts, shaking their heads and stroking their stubble.

Will squirmed through the half-open apartment door, Nancy following. He winced at the sight of too many cooks spoiling the broth. There were at least a dozen people in an eight-hundred-square foot space, astronomically increasing the odds of crime scene pollution. He did a quick reconnoiter with Nancy on his heels, and amazingly no one stopped them or even questioned their presence. Front room. Old-lady furniture and bric-a-brac. Twenty-year-old TV. He took a pen from his pocket and used it to part the curtains to peer through each window, a procedure he repeated in every room. Kitchen. Spic-and-span. No dishes in the sink. Bathroom, also tidy, smelling of foot powder. Bedroom. Too crowded with chattering personnel to see much except for plump dead legs, gray and mottled, beside an unmade bed, one foot half inside a slipper.

Will bellowed, "Who's in charge here?"

Sudden silence until, "Who's asking?" A balding detective with a big gut and a tight suit separated himself from the scrum and appeared at the bedroom door.

"FBI," Will said. "I'm Special Agent Piper." Nancy looked hurt she wasn't introduced.

"Detective Chapman, Forty-fifth Precinct." He extended a large warm hand, the weight of a brick. He smelled of onions.

"Detective, what do you say we clear this place out so we can have a nice quiet inspection of the crime scene?"

"My guys are almost done, then it's all yours."

"Let's do it now, okay? Half your men aren't wearing gloves. No one's got booties on. You're making a mess here, Detective."

"Nobody's touching nothing," Chapman said defensively. He noticed Nancy taking notes and asked nervously, "Who's she, your secretary?"

"Special Agent Lipinski," she said, waving her notebook at him sweetly. "Could I get your first name, Detective Chapman?"

Will suppressed a smile.

Chapman wasn't inclined to get territorial with the feds. He'd rant and rave, waste his time and wind up on the losing end of the proposition. Life was too short. "All right, everybody!" he announced. "We got the FBI here and they want everyone out, so pack up and let them do their thing."

"Have them leave the postcard," Will said.

Chapman reached into his breast pocket and pulled out a white card inside a Ziploc bag. "I got it right here."

When the room was clear, they inspected the body with the detective. It was getting toasty in there and the first whiffs of decay were in the air. For a gunshot victim, there was surprisingly little blood, a few clots on her matted gray hair, a streak down her left cheek where an arterial gush from her ear had formed a tributary that tracked down her neck and dripped onto moss-green carpet. She was on her back, a foot from the floral flounce of her unmade bed, dressed in a pink cotton nightdress she had probably worn a thousand times. Her eyes, already bone dry, were open and staring. Will had seen innumerable bodies, many of them brutalized beyond recognition of their humanity. This lady looked pretty good, a nice Puerto Rican grandma whom you'd think could be revived with a good shoulder shake. He checked out Nancy to gauge her reaction to the presence of death.

She was taking notes.

Chapman started in, "So the way I figure it—"

Will put up his hand, stopping him in mid-sentence. "Special Agent Lipinski, why don't you tell us what happened here?"

Her face flushed, making her cheeks appear fuller. The flush extended to her throat and disappeared under the neckline of her white blouse. She swallowed and moistened her lips with the tip of her tongue. She began slowly then picked up the tempo as she assembled her thoughts. "Well, the killer was probably here before, not necessarily inside the apartment but around the building. The security grate on one of the kitchen windows was pried loose. I'd have to take a closer look at it but I'll bet the window frame is rotted. Still, even hiding in the side alley, he wouldn't have gambled on doing the job all in one night, not if he wanted to make sure he hit the date on the postcard. He came back last night, went into the alley and finished pulling the grate off. Then he cut the window with a glass cutter and undid the latch from the outside. He tramped in some dirt from the alley onto the kitchen floor and the hall and right there, and there."

She pointed to two spots on the bedroom carpet, including one smudge that Chapman was standing on. He stepped away like it was radioactive.

"She must've heard something because she sat up and tried to put her slippers on. Before she could finish he was in the room and he took one shot at close range, through her left ear. It looks like it's a small-caliber round, probably a .22. The bullet's still in her cranium, there's no exit wound. I don't think there was a sexual assault here but we need to check that. Also, we need to find out if anything was stolen. The place wasn't ransacked but I didn't see a pocketbook anywhere. He probably left the way he came in." She paused and scrunched her forehead. "That's it. That's what I think happened."

Will frowned at her, made her sweat for a few seconds then said, "Yeah, that's what I think happened too." Nancy looked like she'd just won a spelling bee and proudly stared down at her crepe-soled shoes. "You agree with my partner, Detective?"

Chapman shrugged. "Could very well be. Yeah, .22 handgun, I'm sure that's the weapon here."

The guy doesn't have a fucking clue, Will thought. "Do you know if anything was stolen?"

"Her daughter says her purse is missing. She's the one who found her this morning. The postcard was on the kitchen table with some other mail."

Will pointed at grandma's thighs. "Was she sexually assaulted?"

"I don't have any idea! Maybe if you hadn't kicked the M.E. out we'd know," Chapman huffed.

Will lowered himself onto his haunches and used his pen to carefully lift her nightdress. He squinted into the tent and saw undisturbed old-lady underwear. "Doesn't look like it," he said. "Let's see the postcard."

Will inspected it carefully, front and back, and handed it to Nancy. "Is that the same font used in the other ones?"

She said it was.

"It's Courier twelve point," he said.

She asked how he knew that, sounding impressed.

"I'm a font savant," he quipped. He read the name out loud. "Ida Gabriela Santiago."

According to Chapman, her daughter told him she never used her middle name.

Will stood up and stretched his back. "Okay, we're good," he said. "Keep the area sealed off until the FBI forensics team arrives. We'll be in touch if we need anything."

"You got any leads on this wacko?" Chapman asked.

Will's cell phone started ringing inside his jacket, counter-intuitively playing *Ode to Joy*. While he fished for it he replied, "Jack shit, Detective, but this is only my first day on the case," then said into the phone, "This is Piper . . ."

He listened and shook his head a couple of times before he told the caller, "When it rains, it pours. Say, Mueller hasn't made a miraculous recovery, has he? . . . Too bad." He ended the call and looked up. "Ready for a long night, partner?"

Nancy nodded like a bobble-head doll. She seemed to like the appellation "partner," like it a lot.

"That was Sanchez," he told her. "We've got another post-card but this one's a little different. It's dated today but the guy's still alive."

E rnest Bevin was the link, the go-between. The only cabinet member to serve in both governments. To Clement Atlee, the Labor prime minister, Bevin was the logical choice. "Ernest," Atlee had told his Foreign Secretary, the two of them seated before a hot coal fire at Downing Street, "speak to Churchill. Tell him I'm personally asking for his help." Sweat beaded on Atlee's bald head, and Bevin watched with discomfort as a rivulet ran down his high forehead onto his hawklike nose.

Assignment accepted. No questions asked, no reservations tendered. Bevin was a soldier, an old-line labor leader, one of the founders of Britain's largest trade union, the TGWU. Always the pragmatist, prewar, he was one of the few Labor politicians to cooperate with the Conservative government of Winston Churchill and align himself against the pacifist wing in the Labor Party.

In 1940, when Churchill readied the nation for war and formed an all-party coalition government, he made Bevin Minister for Labor and National Service, giving him a broad portfolio involving the domestic wartime economy. Shrewdly, Bevin struck a balance between military and domestic needs and created his own army of fifty thousand men diverted from the armed forces to work the coal mines: Bevin Boys. Churchill thought the world of him.

Then the shocker. Just weeks after VE day, basking in triumphant victory, the man the Russians called the British Bulldog lost the 1945 general election in a landslide drubbing

by Clement Atlee's Labor Party, tossed aside by an elector-
ate that did not trust him to rebuild the nation. The man who
had said, "We shall defend our island whatever the cost may
be, we shall fight on the beaches, we shall fight on the landing grounds, we shall fight in the fields and in the streets, we
shall never surrender," limped from the grand stage in surrender, depressed and dispirited. Churchill moodily led the
opposition after his defeat, but took most of his pleasure
from his beloved Chartwell House, where he wrote poetry,
painted watercolors, and tossed bread to the black swans.

Now, a year and a half later, Bevin, Prime Minister
Atlee's Foreign Secretary, sat deep underground awaiting
his firmer boss. It was cold, and Bevin kept his overcoat
buttoned over his winter-weight vested suit. He was a solid
man, thinning gray hair swept back and pomaded, fleshy
faced with incipient jowls. He had chosen this clandestine
meeting spot purposely, to send a psychological message.
The subject matter would be important. Secret. Come now,
without delay.

The message was not lost on Churchill, who barged in,
glanced about unsentimentally and declared, "Why would
you ask me to come back to this godforsaken place?"

Bevin rose and with a wave of his hand dismissed the
high-ranking military man who had accompanied Churchill.
"Were you in Kent?"

"Yes, I was in Kent!" Churchill paused. "I never thought
I'd set foot in here again."

"I won't ask for your coat. It's chilly."

"It always was so," Churchill replied.

The two men shook hands dispassionately then sat down,
Bevin steering Churchill to a spot where a red portfolio with
the P.M.'s seal lay before him.

They were in the George Street bunker where Churchill
and his War Cabinet holed up for much of the conflict. The
rooms were constructed in the basement chamber of the
Office of Works Building, smack between Parliament and
Downing Street. Sandbagged, concrete-reinforced, and well

belowground, George Street would probably have survived the direct hit that never materialized.

They faced each other across the large square table in the Cabinet Room, where night or day, Churchill would summon his closest advisors. It was a drab, utilitarian chamber with stale air. Nearby was the Map Room, still papered with the charts of the theaters of war, and Churchill's private bedroom, which still reeked of cigars long after the last one had been extinguished. Farther down the hall in an old converted broom closet was the Transatlantic Telephone Room, where the scrambler, code-named "Sigsaly," encrypted the conversations between Churchill and Roosevelt. For all Bevin knew, the gear still functioned. Nothing had changed since the day the War Rooms had been quietly closed down: VJ Day.

"Do you want to have a poke around?" Bevin asked. "I believe Major General Stuart has a set of keys."

"I do not." Churchill was impatient now. The bunker made him uneasy. Curtly, he said, "Look, why don't you get to the point? What do you want?"

Bevin spoke his rehearsed introduction. "An issue has arisen, quite unexpected, quite remarkable and quite sensitive. The government must deal with it carefully and delicately. As it involves the Americans, the Prime Minister wondered whether you might be unusually well-positioned to assist him personally in the matter."

"I'm in the opposition," Churchill said icily. "Why should I wish to assist him in any activity other than vacating Downing Street and returning me to my office?"

"Because, you are the greatest patriot the nation has ever possessed. And because the man I see sitting before me cares more for the welfare of the British populace than he does for political expediency. That is why I believe you may wish to help the government."

Churchill looked bemused, aware he was being played. "What the devil have you got yourself into? Appealing to my patriotic side? Go on, tell me about your mess."

"That folder summarizes our situation," Bevin said, nodding at the red portfolio. "I wonder if you might read through it. Have you brought your reading glasses?"

Churchill fumbled through his breast pocket. "I have." He wrapped the spindly wire rims around his enormous head. "And you'll just sit there and twiddle your thumbs?"

Bevin nodded and leaned back in the simple wooden chair. He watched Churchill snort and open the portfolio. He watched him read the first paragraph. He watched him remove his glasses and ask, "Is this some kind of a joke? Do you honestly expect me to believe this?"

"It's no joke. Incredible, yes. Fictitious, no. As you read you'll see the preliminary work military intelligence has done to authenticate the findings."

"This is not the sort of thing I was expecting."

Bevin nodded.

Before Churchill resumed reading, he lit a cigar. His old ashtray was still at hand.

From time to time he muttered something unintelligible under his breath. Once he exclaimed, "Isle of Wight of all places!" At one point he rose to uncramp his legs and relight his cigar. Every so often he furrowed his brow and hit Bevin with a quick quizzical stare until, after ten minutes, he had completed the file. He removed his glasses, tucked them away, then took a deep drag on his Havana. "Am I in there?"

"Undoubtedly yes, but I would not know the details," Bevin said solemnly.

"And you?" Churchill asked.

"I haven't inquired."

Suddenly, Churchill became animated, as he had been so many times in this room, his blood boiling with conviction. "This must be suppressed from the public! We are only just awakening from our great nightmare. This will only plunge us into darkness and chaos."

"That is precisely our opinion."

"Who knows about this? How tightly can it be controlled?"

"The circle is small. Besides the P.M., I am the only minister. Fewer than a half-dozen military officers know enough to connect the dots. Then, of course, there's Professor Atwood and his team."

Churchill grunted, "That is a particular problem. You were right to isolate them."

"And finally," Bevin continued, "the Americans. Given our special relationship, we felt we had to inform President Truman, but we've been given assurances that only a very small number of their people have been briefed."

"Is that the reason you've come to me? Because of the Yanks?"

Bevin finally felt warm enough to remove his coat. "I will be completely truthful with you. The Prime Minister wants you to deal with Truman. Their relationship is frosty. The government wants to delegate this matter to you. We don't want to be involved beyond today. The Americans have offered to take full possession of the materials, and after considerable internal debate our inclination is to let them have them. We don't want it. They have all sorts of ideas apparently, but frankly we don't wish to know. There's serious work to be done to reconstruct the country, and we can't take on the distraction, the accountability, should there be a leak—or the expense. Further, decisions must be made regarding Atwood and the others. We are asking you to assume control of this matter, not as the leader of the opposition, not as a political figure, but in a personal capacity as a moral leader."

Churchill had been nodding his head. "Smart. Very smart. Probably *your* idea. I would have done the same. Listen, friend, can you give me assurances that this won't be used against me in the future? I plan on thumping you at the next general election, and it would be bad form to torpedo me beneath the waterline."

"You have my assurances," Bevin replied. "The matter transcends politics."

Churchill got up and clapped his hands together once.

"Then I'll do it. I'll call Harry in the morning if you can arrange it. Then I'll deal with the Atwood conundrum."

Bevin cleared his throat, which had become dry. "I'd rather hoped you could deal with Professor Atwood speedily. He's down the corridor."

"He's here! You want me to deal with him now?" Churchill asked incredulously.

Bevin nodded and rose a little too quickly, as if he were escaping. "I'm going to leave you to it and personally report back to the P.M." He stopped for emphasis. "Major General Stuart will be your logistical aide. He'll attend to you until the matter is resolved and all materials have been removed from British soil. Is that acceptable to you?"

"Yes, of course. I'll take care of everything."

"Thank you. The government is grateful."

"Yes, yes, everyone will be grateful except my wife, who's going to murder me for missing dinner," Churchill mused. "Have Atwood brought in."

"You want to see him? I hadn't thought that was entirely necessary."

"It is not a matter of wanting to see him. I feel I have no choice."

Geoffrey Atwood sat before the most famous man in the world with a look of utter bewilderment. He was fit and sinewy from years of fieldwork but his complexion was sallow and he looked ill. Although fifty-two, present circumstances made him appear a decade older. Churchill noted a fine tremor in his arm when the man lifted a mug of milky tea to his lips.

"I have been held against my will for almost a fortnight," Atwood vented. "My wife knows nothing of this. Five of my colleagues have likewise been detained, one of them a woman. With all due respect, Prime Minister, this is quite outrageous. A member of my group, Reginald Saunders, has died. We have been traumatized by these events."

"Yes," Churchill agreed, "it is quite outrageous. And traumatic. I have been briefed on Mr. Saunders. However, I'm sure you would agree, Professor, that the entire affair is most extraordinary."

"Well, yes, but . . . "

"What were your duties during the war?"

"My expertise was put to good use, Prime Minister. I was with a regiment assigned to the preservation and cataloguing of recovered antiquities and objets d'art looted by the Nazis from museums on the Continent."

"Ah," Churchill replied. "Good, good. And upon discharge you resumed your academic duties."

"Yes. I am the Butterworth Professor of Archaeology and Antiquities at Cambridge."

"And this excavation on the Isle of Wight was your first field project since the war?"

"Yes, I had been at this site before the war but the current excavation was in a new sector."

"I see." Churchill reached for his cigar case. "Do you want one?" he asked. "No? Hope you don't mind." He struck a match and puffed vigorously until the room hazed up. "You know where we are seated, do you not, Professor?"

Atwood nodded blankly.

"Few people outside the inner sanctum have visited this room. I myself had not thought I would ever see it again, but I have been called in, out of semiretirement, as it were, to deal with your little crisis."

Atwood protested. "I understand the implications of my discovery, Prime Minister, but I hardly think that the liberty of myself and my team should be at issue here. If it is a crisis, it is a manufactured one."

"Yes, I take your point, but others might differ," Churchill said with a coldness that disquieted the professor. "There are larger matters at stake here. There are consequences to be reckoned with. We can't have you going off and publishing your findings in some damned journal, you know!"

The smoke made Atwood wheeze and he coughed a few times to clear the phlegm. "I've thought about this night and day since we were taken into custody. Please bear in mind that I was the one who contacted the authorities. I didn't go off and ring Fleet Street, you know. I'm prepared to enter into a secrecy agreement and I'm certain I can persuade my colleagues to do the same. That should put any concerns to rest."

"That, sir, is a very helpful suggestion which I shall consider. You know, in the course of the war, I made many difficult decisions in this room. Life and death decisions . . . " He drifted off, remembering one in particular, the horrific choice to allow the Luftwaffe to fire-bomb Coventry without ordering an evacuation. Doing so would have tipped off the Nazis to the knowledge that the British had broken their codes. Hundreds of civilians died. "You have children, Professor?"

"Two girls and a boy. The eldest is fifteen."

"Well, no doubt they will want to see their father back at the earliest possible moment."

Atwood teared up and became emotional. "You were an inspiration to all of us, Prime Minister, a hero to all of us, and today a personal hero to me. I thank you from the bottom of my heart for your intervention." The man was sobbing. Churchill gritted his teeth at the spectacle of a man letting loose like this.

"Think nothing of it. All's well that ends well."

Afterward, Churchill sat alone, his cigar half done. He could almost hear the echoes of war, the urgent voices, the static of wireless transmissions, the distant crunch of buzz bombs. The plumes and swirls of blue cigar smoke were like ghostly apparitions floating in the underground miasma. Major General Stuart, a man Churchill had casually known during the war, came in and stood erect, parade ready. "At ease, Major General. You've been told this mess is in my lap now?"

"I have been so instructed, Prime Minister."

Churchill put the cigar out in his old ashtray. "You're holding Atwood and his party down in Aldershot, correct?"

"That is correct. The professor believes he is being released."

"Released? No. Take him back to his people. I'll be in touch. This is a delicate matter. One can't be hasty."

The general peered at the portly man, clicked his heels together and saluted smartly.

Churchill gathered his coat and hat and without looking back slowly walked out of the War Rooms for the last time.

July 10, 1947
Washington, D.C.

Harry Truman looked small behind his enormous Oval Office desk. He was neat as a pin, his blue and white striped tie carefully knotted, his smoke-gray summer-weight suit fully buttoned, black wing-tips polished to a high gloss, every strand of thinning hair perfectly combed down.

Midway through his first term, the war was behind him. Not since Lincoln had a new President undergone such a trial by fire. The vagaries of history had catapulted him into an inconceivable position. No one, himself included, would have bet a plug nickel that this plain, rather undistinguished man, would have ever risen to the White House. Not when he was selling silk shirts at Truman & Jacobson in downtown Kansas City twenty-five years earlier; not when he was a Jackson County judge, a pawn of boss Pendergast's Democratic machine; not when he was a U.S. Senator from Missouri, still a patronage puppet; not even when FDR picked him to be his running mate, a shocking compromise forged in the hot sticky back rooms of the 1944 Chicago convention.

But eighty-two days into his vice presidency Truman was summoned urgently to the White House to be informed that Roosevelt was dead. Overnight he was obligated to pick up the reins from a man to whom he had hardly spoken during the first three months of the term. He had been persona non grata in FDR's inner circle. He had been kept out of the loop of war planning. He had never heard of the Manhattan Project. "Boys, pray for me now," he told a gaggle of waiting reporters, and he'd meant it. Within four months the ex-haberdasher would authorize the atomic bombing of Hiroshima and Nagasaki.

By 1947 he had settled into the hard business of governing a new superpower in a chaotic world, but his methodical, decisive style was serving him well and he had hit his stride. The issues had come fast and furious—rebuilding Europe under the Marshall Plan, founding the United Nations, fighting communism with his National Security Act, jump-starting the domestic social agenda with his Fair Deal. I can do this job, he assured himself. Damn it, I'm up to this. Then something from way out of left field landed on his agenda. It was lying before him on his uncluttered desk next to his famous plaque, THE BUCK STOPS HERE.

The manila folder was marked in red letters: PROJECT VECTIS—ACCESS: ULTRA.

Truman recalled the phone call he had received from London five months earlier, one of those vivid events that would remain permanently and exquisitely etched in memory. He remembered what he was wearing that day, the apple he was eating, what he was thinking the moments before and after the call from Winston Churchill.

"I'm pleased to hear your voice," he had said. "What a surprise!"

"Hello, Mr. President. I hope you are well."

"Never been better. What can I do for you?"

Despite the static on the transatlantic line, Truman could hear the constriction in Churchill's voice. "Mr. President, you can do a great deal. We have an extraordinary situation."

"I'll certainly help if I can. Is this an official call?"

"It is. I've been pulled in. There's a small island off our south coast, the Isle of Wight."

"I've heard of it."

"A team of archaeologists has found something there that is frankly too hot for us to handle. The discovery is vitally important but we are concerned we simply don't have the capacity to deal with it in our postwar condition. We can't take the risk of fumbling it. At best it would be a national distraction, at worst a national catastrophe."

Truman could imagine Churchill sitting there, leaning into the telephone, his large frame indistinct in a haze of cigar smoke. "Why don't you tell me what it is your fellows found?"

The unflappable little President listened, his pen poised to jot some notes. After a short while he let the pen fall away unused and began nervously drumming the desk with his free fingers. Suddenly his tie felt too tight and the job felt too big. He had reckoned that the atomic bomb was his trial of fire. Now it seemed like a warm-up to something larger.

Besides the President of the United States, only six other men in the government had Ultra Clearance, a security designation so guarded that its very name was Top Secret. Hundreds, perhaps thousands, had known of the Manhattan Project in its heyday, but only a half dozen were privy to Project Vectis. The only member of Truman's cabinet to have Ultra Clearance was James Forrestal. Truman liked Forrestal well enough personally, but he trusted him absolutely. This was a fellow, like him, who had been a businessman before committing to public service. He had been FDR's Secretary of the Navy, and Truman kept him on in that role.

Forrestal was a cold, demanding workaholic who shared the President's rabid anti-Communist views. Truman had been grooming him for a higher calling. In time Forrestal would assume a newly created position in government, Secretary of Defense, and Project Vectis would stay with him, all-consuming.

Truman cracked the folder's crimson wax seal, an ancient but effective privacy tool. Inside was a memo written by Rear Admiral Roscoe Hillenkoetter, another Ultra insider whom Truman would shortly name to be the first director in a new agency to be called the CIA. Truman read the memo then reached inside and removed a loose bundle of newspaper clippings.

Roswell Daily Record: RAAF CAPTURES FLYING SAUCER ON RANCH IN ROSWELL REGION; and the following day: GEN. RAMEY EMPTIES ROSWELL SAUCER. *Sacramento Bee*: ARMY REVEALS IT HAS FLYING DISC FOUND ON RANCH IN NEW MEXICO. There were a few dozen other national AP and UP stories along the same lines.

Alia jacta est, Truman thought, recalling his boyhood Latin. Caesar crossed the Rubicon declaring "the die is cast," and altered the course of history by defying the Senate and entering Rome with his legions. Truman uncapped his fountain pen and wrote a brief message to Hillenkoetter on a clean sheet of White House stationery. He placed his letter and the other papers back into the folder and retrieved his quaint brass sealing wax kit from the top right desk drawer. He flicked a Zippo, lit the wick of a small jar of kerosene, and began to slowly melt a stick of wax, drip by drip, onto the cardboard until there was a bloodred puddle. The die was cast.

On June 24, 1947, a private pilot flying near Mount Rainier in Washington State reported saucer-shaped objects flying erratically at great speed. Within days hundreds of people across the country had their own sightings and newspapers were awash with flying saucers. The pump was primed for Roswell.

Ten days later, on Independence Day during a fierce thunderstorm, the night sky over Roswell, New Mexico, was lit by a flaming blue object that fell to the earth north of town. Those who saw it swore it wasn't lightning—nothing like it.

The following morning, Mack Brazel, the foreman of the J.B. Foster Ranch, a sprawling sheep farm about seventy-five miles northwest of Roswell, was driving a flock to its watering hole when he discovered a large field scattered with pieces of metal, foil, and rubber. The debris was so dense in places that the sheep refused to traverse the pasture and had to be herded around the site.

Brazel, a sober man with weather-beaten skin, did a quick

look-see and convinced himself this was not like the foil weather balloons he had found in the past. This was something much more substantial. On further inspection he spotted a crisscross of tire tracks leading up to and away from the debris field. Jeep treads, he thought. Who the hell has been on my land? He collected a few fragments of metal and finished his herding. Later that evening he called the Chavez County sheriff, George Wilcox, and told him matter-of-factly, "George, you know all this talk about flying disks? Well, I think I got one splattered all over my land."

Wilcox was well-acquainted with Brazel and knew he wasn't a crank. If that's what Mack said, well, by God, he was going to take it seriously. He placed a call to the local army air field, USAAF Roswell, the 509th Bomb Group, and got the base commander on the horn. Colonel William Blanchard, in turn, mobilized his two top intelligence officers, Jesse Marcel and Sheridan Cavitt, to head out to the ranch the next morning. Then he transmitted a message up the line to his superior officer at the Eighth Air Force in Fort Worth, Brigadier General Roger Ramey, who insisted on receiving a blow-by-blow from the field. The general was a firm believer in the adage, "the shit flows uphill," so he called Washington and gave a preliminary report to an aide to the Secretary of the Army. He stood by for a call-back.

Within minutes his aide informed him that Washington was on the line. "Secretary Patterson?" he asked.

"No, sir," came the reply. "It's the Secretary of the Navy, Mr. Forrestal."

The navy? What in Hades is going on? he wondered before picking up the line.

Sunday morning the heat was already baking the red clay when Mack Brazel met the two intelligence officers and a platoon of soldiers at the ranch entrance. The convoy followed his Ford truck over dusty trails to the scrubby hillside where most of the debris lay. The troops set up a perimeter and shuffled uncomfortably under the scorching sun while

Major Marcel, a thoughtful young man, chain-smoked Pall Malls and poked through the wreckage. When Brazel pointed to the tire tracks and asked if the army had been there earlier, the major took a particularly deep drag and replied, "I sure wouldn't know about that, sir."

Within a few hours the troops had picked through the site, loaded a bunch of debris into their tarp-covered trucks, and driven off. Brazel watched the convoy disappear over the horizon and took a piece of metal out of his pocket. It was as thin as the tinfoil in a pack of cigarettes and just as light. but there was something strange about it. He was a strong man with hands like vises, but as hard as he tried, he couldn't bend it at all.

Over the next two days, Brazel observed army personnel shuttling back and forth to the crash site. He was told to keep his distance. On Tuesday morning he was sure he spotted the star of a brigadier general hurtling by in a jeep. Inevitably, most of the town knew that something was going on up at the Foster Ranch, and by Tuesday afternoon the army couldn't keep a lid on the story any longer. Colonel Blanchard issued an official USAAF press release acknowledging that a local rancher had found a flying disk. It had been recovered by the base Intelligence Office and transferred to a higher head-quarters. The *Roswell Daily Record* blasted out a special edition that evening and the media frenzy was on.

Curiously, within an hour of Blanchard's official release, General Ramey was on the phone with United Press changing the story. It wasn't a flying disk or anything like it. It was an ordinary weather balloon with a radar reflector, nothing to get excited about. Could the press take pictures of the debris? Well, he replied, Washington had clamped a security lid on the whole thing but he'd see what he could do to help them out. In short order he invited photographers into his office in Texas to snap shots of an ordinary foil weather balloon laid out on his carpet. "Here it is, gentlemen. This is what all the fuss was about."

Within a week the story would lose its national legs. Yet,

in Roswell, there were persistent rumblings about strange happenings in the early hours and days after the crash. It was said that the army had indeed been at the crash site before Brazel arrived; there was a disk, largely intact; and that five small nonhuman bodies were recovered early that morning and autopsies conducted at the base.

An army nurse present at the autopsies later talked to a mortician friend in Roswell, sketching drawings on a napkin of spindly beings with elongated heads and massive eyes. The army took Mack Brazel into custody for a while, and afterward he was considerably less talkative. In the days that followed, virtually every witness to the crash and recovery either changed their stories, clammed up completely, or were transferred away from Roswell, some never to be heard from again.

Truman answered his secretary's line. "Mr. President, the Secretary of the Navy is here to see you."

"All right, send him in."

Forrestal, a dapper man whose large ears were his most prominent feature, sat before Truman, his spine ramrod straight, looking every bit the pin-striped banker he had been.

"Jim, I'd like an update on Vectis," Truman began, eschewing small talk. That was fine with Forrestal, a man who used as few words as possible to make a point.

"I'd say things are going to plan, Mr. President."

"The situation down in Roswell—how's that doing?"

"We're keeping the pot stirred just the right amount, in my opinion."

Truman nodded vigorously. "That's my impression from the press clippings. Say, how're the army guys taking to getting their marching orders from the Secretary of the Navy?" Truman chuckled.

"They are not best pleased, Mr. President."

"No, I'll bet they're not! I went for the right man—you. It's a navy operation now so folks'll just have to get used to it. Now tell me about this place in Nevada. How're we doing over there?"

"Groom Lake. I visited the locale last week. It is not hospitable. The so-called lake has been dry for centuries, I would think. It is remote—it borders our test site at Yucca Flats. We will not have a problem with visitors but even if someone purposely sought it out, it is well-defensible geographically, with multiple surrounding hills and mountains. The Army Corps of Engineers is making excellent progress. They are very much on schedule. A good runway has been constructed, there are hangars and rudimentary barracks."

Truman clasped his hands behind his neck, relaxing at the good news. "That's fine, go on."

"Excavation has been completed for the underground facility. Concrete is being poured and the ventilation and electrical work will commence shortly. I am confident the facility can be fully operational within our projected time frame."

Truman looked satisfied. His man was getting the job done. "How's it feel to be general contractor to the world's most secret building project?" he asked.

Forrestal reflected on the question. "I once built a house in Westchester County. This project is somewhat less taxing."

Truman's face crinkled. "'Cause your wife's not looking over your shoulder on this one, am I right?"

Forrestal answered without levity. "You are absolutely correct, sir."

Truman leaned forward and lowered his voice a notch. "The British material. Still high and dry in Maryland?"

"It would be easier to get into Fort Knox."

"How're you going to move the goods across the country to Nevada?"

"Admiral Hillenkoetter and I are still in discussion regarding transport issues. I favor a convoy of trucks. He favors cargo planes. There are pros and cons to each approach."

"Well, hell," Truman piped up, "that's up to you fellows. I'm not gonna manage you to death. Just one more thing. What are we going to call this base?"

LIBRARY *of the* DEAD

"Its official military cartographic designation is NTS 51, Mr. President. The Corps of Engineers has taken to calling it Area 51."

On March 28, 1949, James Forrestal resigned as Secretary of Defense. Truman hadn't spotted a problem until a week or so earlier when the man suddenly became unglued. His behavior began to be erratic, he looked ruffled and unkempt, he stopped eating and sleeping, and was clearly manifestly unfit for service. The word spread that he had suffered a full-blown mental breakdown from job-related stress, and the rumor was confirmed when he was checked into the Bethesda Naval Hospital. Forrestal never left confinement. On May 22 his body was found, a suicide, a bloody rag doll sprawled on a third-floor roof under the sixteenth floor of his ward. He had managed to unlock a kitchen window opposite his room.

In his pajama pockets were two pieces of paper. One was a poem from Sophocles's tragedy, *Ajax,* written in Forrestal's shaky hand:

> *In the dark prospect of the yawning grave—*
> *Woe to the mother in her close of day,*
> *Woe to her desolate heart and temples gray,*
> *When she shall hear*
> *Her loved one's story whispered in her ear!*
> *"Woe, woe!" will be the cry—*
> *No quiet murmur like the tremulous wail*
> *Of the lone bird, the querulous nightingale.*

The other piece of paper contained a single penned line: *Today is May 22, 1949, the day that I, James Vincent Forrestal, shall die.*

T hough he lived in New York, Will was no New Yorker. He was stuck there like a Post-it note that could effortlessly be peeled off and pasted somewhere else. He didn't get the place, didn't connect to it. He didn't feel its rhythm, possess its DNA. He was oblivious to all things new and fashionable—restaurants, galleries, exhibitions, shows, clubs. He was an outsider who didn't want in. If there was a fabric to the city, he was a frayed end. He ate, drank, slept, worked, and occasionally copulated in New York, but beyond that he was a disinterested party. There was a favorite bar on Second Avenue, a good Greek diner on 23rd Street, a reliable Chinese take-away on 24th, a grocery and a friendly liquor store on Third Avenue. This was his microcosm, a nondescript square of asphalt with its own soundtrack—the constant wail of ambulances fighting traffic to get the flotsam of the city to Bellevue. In fourteen months he'd figure out where home was going to be, but he knew it wouldn't be New York City.

It was no surprise that he was unaware that Hamilton Heights was an up-and-coming neighborhood.

"No shit," he replied with disinterest. "In Harlem?"

"Yes! In Harlem," Nancy explained. "A lot of professionals have moved uptown. They've got Starbucks."

They were driving in a torpid rush-hour mess and she was talking a blue streak.

"City College of New York is up there," she added enthusiastically. "There're a lot of students and professionals, some great restaurants, things like that, and it's a lot cheaper than most places in Manhattan."

"You ever been there?"

She deflated a little. "Well, no."

"So how are you so knowledgeable?"

"I read about it in, you know, *New York* magazine, the *Times*."

In contrast to Will, Nancy loved the city. She'd grownup in suburban White Plains. Her grandparents still lived in Queens, off-the-boat Poles with thick accents and old-country ways. White Plains was home but the city had been her playpen, the place where she learned about music and art, where she had her first drink, where she lost her virginity in her dorm at the John Jay College of Criminal Justice, where she passed the bar after graduating top of her class at Fordham Law, where she landed her first Bureau job after Quantico. She lacked the time or money to experience New York to its fullest, but she made it her business to keep a finger on the city's pulse.

They crossed over the murky Harlem River and found their way to the corner of West 140th Street and Nicholas Avenue, where the twelve-story building complex was conveniently marked by a half-dozen squad cars from the Thirty-second Precinct, Manhattan North. St. Nicholas Avenue was wide and clean, bordered on the west by a thin strip of mint-green park, the buffer zone between the neighborhood and the CCNY campus. The area looked surprisingly prosperous. Nancy's smug look said, *I told you so.*

Lucius Robertson's apartment was parkside on the top floor. Its large windows captured St. Nicholas Park, the compact college campus, and beyond it the Hudson River and the heavily forested New Jersey Palisades. In the distance a brick-red cargo barge, the length of a football field, was steaming south under tug power. The sun glinted off an antique brass telescope standing on a tripod, and Will was drawn to it, seized by a boyish impulse to look through its eyepiece.

He resisted and flashed his badge, prompting, "The cavalry's here!" from a precinct lieutenant, a hefty African-American who could hardly wait to take off. The uniformed cops and detectives were also relieved. Their shifts had been stretched and they aspired to make better use of their precious summer evening. Cold beer and barbecues were higher on their agendas than babysitting.

Will asked the lieutenant, "Where's our guy?"

"In the bedroom, lying down. We checked the apartment out. Even had a dog in. It's clean."

"You got the postcard?"

It was bagged and tagged. *Lucius Jefferson Robertson, 384 West 140th Street, New York, NY 10030.* On the flip side: the little coffin and June 11, 2009.

Will passed it to Nancy and checked out the place. The furniture was modern, expensive, a couple of nice Orientals, eggshell walls plastered with gallery quality twentieth century oils. An entire expanse of wall hung with framed vinyl records and CDs. Next to the kitchen a Steinway grand with sheet music stacked high on the closed top. A wall unit crammed with a high-end stereo system and hundreds of CDs.

"What is this guy, a musician?" Will asked.

The lieutenant nodded. "Jazz. I never heard of him but Monroe says he's famous."

A skinny white cop said on cue: "Yeah, he's famous."

After a brief discussion, it was agreed that this situation belonged to the FBI now. The precinct would cover the front and rear of the building through the night but the FBI would take "custody" of Mr. Robertson and watch him as long as they liked. All that was left was to meet their charge. The lieutenant called through the bedroom door, "Mr. Robertson, could you come out, sir? We got the FBI here to see you."

Through the door: "All right, I'm coming."

Robertson looked like a weary traveler, thin and stooped, shuffling out from his bedroom in slippers, loose trousers,

Chambray shirt and a thin yellow cardigan. He was an old-looking sixty-six. The lines on his face were so deep you could lose a dime in a fold. His skin tones were pure black without a hint of brown except on the palms of his long-fingered hands, which were pale, café-au-lait. His hair and beard were close-cropped, more salt than pepper.

He spotted the new faces. "How do you do?" he said to Will and Nancy. "I'm sorry to cause so much fuss."

Will and Nancy formally introduced themselves.

"Please don't call me Mr. Robertson," the man protested. "My friends call me Clive."

Before long the police cleared out. The sun was low over the Hudson and began deepening and expanding like a fat blood orange. Will closed the curtains in the living room and pulled the blinds in Clive's bedroom. There hadn't been a sniper shooting yet but the Doomsday Killer was mixing things up. He and Nancy reinspected every inch of the apartment, and while she remained with Clive, Will swept the hallway and stairwell.

The formal interview was straightforward—there wasn't much to tell. Clive had gotten back into town mid-afternoon from a three-city tour with his quintet. No one had a key to his apartment and to the best of his knowledge nothing had been disturbed in his absence. After an uneventful flight from Chicago, he took a yellow cab directly from the airport to his building, where he found the postcard buried in a week's accumulation of mail. He immediately recognized it for what it was, called 911, and that was that.

Nancy walked him through the names and addresses of the Doomsday victims but Clive shook his head sadly at each mention. He didn't know any of them. "Why would this fellow want to harm me?" he lamented in his gravelly drawl. "I'm just a piano player."

Nancy shut her notebook and Will shrugged. They were done. It was almost eight o'clock. Four hours to go before Doomsday was up.

"My refrigerator's empty 'cause I been away. Otherwise I'd offer you two somethin' to eat."

"We'll order out," Will said. "What's good around here?" Then quickly, "It's on the government."

Clive suggested the ribs from Charley's on Frederick Douglass Boulevard, got on the phone and painstakingly placed a complicated order with five different sides. "Use my name," Will whispered, writing it out for Clive in block letters.

While they waited, they agreed on a plan. Clive wouldn't leave their sight till midnight. He wouldn't answer the phone. While he slept, they would keep vigil in the living room, and come morning they'd reevaluate the threat level and work out a new protection scheme.

Then they sat in silence, Clive fidgeting in his favorite armchair, frowning, scratching at his beard. He wasn't comfortable with visitors, especially straitlaced FBI agents who might as well have beamed into his living room from another planet.

Nancy craned her neck and studied his paintings until her eyebrows suddenly rose and she exclaimed, "Is that a de Kooning?" She was pointing at a large canvas with abstract bursts and smudges of primary colors.

"Very good, young lady, that's exactly what that is. You know your art."

"It's amazing," she gushed. "It must be worth a fortune."

Will squinted at it. To his eye, it looked like the kind of thing a kid brought home to stick on the refrigerator.

"It *is* very valuable," Clive said. "Willem gave it to me many years ago. I named a piece of music after him so we were all square, but I think I got the better deal."

That set the two of them off, jabbering about modern art, a subject about which Nancy seemed quite knowledgeable. Will loosened his tie, checked his watch, and listened to his belly rumbling. It had already been a long day. If not for Mueller's hole in the heart, he'd be on his sofa now, watching TV, swigging scotch. He hated him more and more.

Knuckles were rapping against the front door. Will drew his Glock. "Take him to the bedroom." Nancy wrapped her arm around Clive's waist and hurried him away while Will peeked through the peephole.

It was a police officer holding a huge paper sack. "I got your ribs," the patrolman called out. "If you don't want 'em, me and the guys'll have 'em."

The ribs were good—no, great. The three of them sat in a civilized circle around Clive's small dining room table and ate greedily, scooping up sides of mashed potatoes, mac and cheese, sweet corn, rice and beans and collard greens, chewing and swallowing in quiet, the food too delicious to be spoiled by small talk. Clive finished first, then Will, both of them cross-eyed full.

Nancy kept going for another five minutes, keeping the forkfuls coming. Both men watched with a kind of grudging admiration, politely killing some time by tearing open packets of moist towelettes and fussily cleaning barbecue sauce off each finger.

In high school Nancy had been petite and athletic. She played second base on the softball team and was a winger in varsity soccer. During her first year away from home she started gaining weight, succumbing to freshman syndrome. She packed on pounds in college, and more in law school, and became positively dumpy. Midway through her second year at Fordham she decided she wanted to join the FBI, but her career advisor told her she'd have to get in shape first. So, with crazed determination, she blitz-dieted and jogged herself down to 120.

Assignment to the New York Office was a good news/bad news story. The good news: New York. The bad news: New York. Her GS-10 grade carried a base salary of about $38,000 with a Law Enforcement Availability Pay kicker of another $9,500. Where were you going to live in New York making under fifty grand? For her, the answer was back home in White Plains, where she got her old room back bundled with mama's cooking and special bag lunches. She worked long hours and never saw the inside of a gym. In three years her weight steadily escalated again, padding her small frame.

Will and Clive were watching her like she was a contestant at a hot-dog-eating contest. Mortified, she blushed and laid down her utensils.

They cleared the table and washed up like a little family. It was nearly ten.

Will parted the curtains a few inches with his finger. It was inky dark. Tiptoed, he looked straight down and saw two cruisers at the curb, where they were supposed to be. He let the curtains close and checked the dead bolt on the front door. How determined was this killer? With a police cordon, what would his move be? Would he back off and accept defeat? After all, he'd already murdered an old lady less than twenty-four hours ago. Serial killers weren't typically high-energy types but this guy was killing in bunches. Would he come crashing through the wall of the adjacent apartment? Rappel down from the roof and blast through a window? Blow up the whole damn building to get his victim? Will didn't have a feel for the perp but he was an outlier and the lack of predictability made him very uneasy.

Clive was back in his favorite chair trying to convince himself that time was his friend. He was bonding with Nancy, who seemed entranced by the slow precise cadence of his voice. The two of them were talking about music. It sounded to Will like she knew a fair bit about that subject too.

"You're kidding," she said. "You played with Miles?"

"Oh yeah, I played with them all. I played with Herbie, I played with Dizzy and Sonny and Ornette. I been blessed."

"Who was your favorite?"

"Well, that would have to be Miles, young lady. Not necessarily as a human being, if you know what I'm sayin', but as a musician, my my! That was not a trumpet in his hands, that was a horn he got straight from God. Oh no, that weren't no mortal thing. He didn't make music, he made magic. When I played with him, I thought the heavens was going to open up and angels was going to pour on out. You want me to put on some Miles right now so I can show you what I mean?"

"I'd rather hear some of *your* music," she replied.

"You are trying to charm me, young Miss FBI! And you are being successful." He said to Will, "You know your colleague here is a charmer?"

"This is our first day together."

"She's got a personality. You can go far with that." He pushed himself up from the chair and made his way to the piano, sat on the stool and made a few fists to loosen his joints. "I got to play soft now, on account of the neighbors, you see." He began to play. Slow, cool music, obliquely tender, with haunting hints of melodies that disappeared into the mist to return anew down the line. He played for a good long time with his eyes closed, occasionally humming a few bars of accompaniment. Nancy was mesmerized but Will kept up his guard, checking his watch, listening through the notes for taps or scratches or thumps in the night.

When Clive finished, when the last note faded to nothingness, Nancy said, "Oh my God, that was beautiful. Thank you so much."

"No, thank you for listening and for watching over me tonight." He sank back into his easy chair. "Thanks to both of you. You're making me feel real safe and I appreciate that. Say, chief," he said to Will, "am I allowed to have a nightcap?"

"What do you want? I'll get it for you."

"Over in the kitchen cupboard to the right of the sink, I got a nice bottle of Jack. Don't you go puttin' no ice in it."

Will found the bottle, half full. He unscrewed the top and sniffed. Could someone have poisoned it? Is that how this was supposed to go down? Then, an inspired thought: I need to protect this man *and* I could use a drink. He poured himself two fingers and downed it fast. Tasted like bourbon. A nice little buzz started. I'll wait for half a minute to see if I die, if not, the man gets his nightcap, he thought, impressed with his own logic.

"Find it, chief?" Clive called out from the other room.

"Yeah. Be right there."

Since he'd survived, he brought out a glass and handed it to Clive, who sniffed his breath and remarked, "Glad to see you helped yourself, my man."

Nancy glared at him.

"Quality control, like a Roman food taster," Will said, but Nancy looked horrified.

Clive started sipping and talking. "You know what, Miss FBI, I'm going to send you some CDs of my group, the Clive Robertson Five. We're just a bunch of old-timers but we still got our thing going on, if you know what I'm sayin'. We still cookin' with gas, though my man, Harry Smiley, on drums, he passes plenty of gas too."

Almost an hour later he was still talking about life on the road, keyboard styles, the music business. His drink was finished. His voice trailed off, his eyes fluttered closed, and he began to softly snore.

"What should we do?" Nancy asked quietly.

"We've got an hour till midnight. Let's have him stay right there and wait this out." He got up.

"Where're you going?"

"To the bathroom. You okay with that?"

She nodded sullenly.

He hissed at her. "What? Did you think I was going to get another drink? For Christ's sake, I needed to make sure it wasn't poisoned."

"Self-sacrifice," she observed. "Admirable."

He took a leak and came back angry.

He strained to control his volume. "You know, partner, you need to get off your high horse if you want to work with me." He demanded, "How old are you?"

"Thirty."

"Well, sweetheart, when I got into this game, you were in junior high, okay?"

"Don't call me sweetheart!" she hissed.

"You're right, that was inappropriate. In a million fucking years you'd never be my sweetheart."

She responded with a full blast of whispered fury. "Well

that's good news because the last time you dated someone in the office you almost got fired. Way to go, Will. Remind me never to take career advice from you."

Clive snorted and half stirred. They both went mute and glared at each other.

Will wasn't surprised she knew about his checkered past; it wasn't exactly a state secret. But he was impressed she had brought it up so quickly. It usually took him longer to push a woman to her boiling point. She had balls, he'd give her that.

He had taken the transfer to New York six years earlier, when Hal Sheridan finally kicked him out of the nest after convincing the H.R. group in Washington that he could handle a managerial assignment. The New York office thought he was an acceptable candidate for Supervisor of Major Thefts and Violent Crimes. He was sent back to Quantico for a management course, where they crammed his head with everything a modern FBI supervisor needed. Sure he knew he wasn't supposed to screw the admins, even the ones in another department, but Quantico never put a picture of Rita Mather in their training manuals.

Rita was so perfectly luscious, so fragrant, so inviting, and so allegedly spectacular in bed that essentially he had no choice. They hid their affair for months, until her boss in White Collar Crimes didn't ante up the raise she was expecting and she asked Will to intervene. When he demurred, she blew up and outed him. A huge mess ensued: disciplinary hearings, lawyers up the wazoo, H.R. into overdrive. He came within a hairsbreadth of termination but Hal Sheridan intervened and brokered a quiet demotion to let him finish out his twenty. On a Friday, Sue Sanchez reported to him; on the Monday, he reported to her.

Of course he considered resigning but, oh, that pension— so near and dear. He accepted his fate, took his mandatory sexual harassment training, did his job adequately, and kicked up his drinking a notch.

Before he could retort to Nancy, Clive stirred, his eyes blinking open. He was lost for a few moments then remembered where he was. He smacked at his dry lips and nervously checked the fine old Cartier on his wrist. "Well, I ain't dead yet. Okay if I go pee on my own without federal assistance, chief?"

"Not a problem."

Clive saw that Nancy was upset. "You all right, Miss FBI? You look mad. You're not mad at me, are you?"

"Of course not."

"Must be mad at the chief then."

Clive rocked himself upright and painfully straightened his arthritic knees.

He took two steps and abruptly stopped. His face was a mixture of puzzlement and alarm.

"Oh, my!"

Will whipped his head around, scanning the room. What was happening?

In a fraction of a second he ruled out a gunshot.

No shattered glass, no impact thud, no crimson spray.

Nancy cried out, "Will!" when she saw Clive tipping past his balance point and nose-diving the floor.

He fell so hard his nasal bones pulverized on impact and splattered the carpet with an abstract pattern of blood resembling a Jackson Pollock painting. If it had been captured on canvas, Clive would have been pleased to add it to his collection.

Peter Benedict saw his reflection and marveled at the way his image was chopped up and scrambled by the optics of the glass. The front of the building was a deeply concave surface, soaring ten stories over Wilshire Boulevard, almost sucking you in off the sidewalk toward the two-story disk of a lobby. There was an austere slate courtyard, cool and empty except for a Henry Moore bronze, a lobulated and vaguely human conception off to one side. The building glass was flawlessly mirrorlike, capturing the mood and color of the environs, and this being Beverly Hills, the mood was usually bright and the color a rich sky blue. Because the concavity was so severe, the glass also caught the images from other panes, tossing them like a salad—clouds, buildings, the Moore, pedestrians, and cars jumbled together.

It was wonderful.

This was his moment.

He had reached the pinnacle. He had a scheduled and confirmed appointment to see Bernie Schwartz, one of the gods at Artist Talent Inc.

Peter had fretted about his wardrobe. He'd never done a meeting like this and was too sheepish to inquire about dress codes. Did agents wear suits in this day and age? Did writers? Should he try and look conservative or flashy? Buttoned-down or casual? He opted for a middle ground to play it safe—gray pants, white oxford shirt, blue blazer, black loafers. As he drew closer to the disk, he saw himself, undistorted, in a single mirrored pane and quickly looked away, self-conscious of his bony litheness and receding hairline, which he usually hid under a baseball cap. He did know this—the younger the writer, the better, and it appalled him that his balding nut made him look way too old. Did the world have to know he was pushing fifty?

The revolving doors swept him into chilled air. The reception desk was fabricated from polished hardwoods and matched the concavity of the building. The flooring was concave too, made of thin planks of curved slippery bamboo. The interior design was all about light, space, and money. A bank of starlet-type receptionists with invisible wire headsets were all saying, "ATI, how may I direct your call."

"ATI, how may I direct your call?"

Over and over, it took on the quality of a chant.

He craned his neck at the atrium, and high up on the galleries saw an army of young hip men and women moving fast, and yes, the agents did wear suits. Armani Nation.

He approached the desk and coughed for attention. The most beautiful-looking woman he had ever seen asked him, "How may I help you?"

"I have an appointment with Mr. Schwartz. My name is Peter Benedict."

"Which one?"

He blinked in confusion and stammered. "I—I—I don't know what you mean. *I'm* Peter Benedict."

Icily, "Which *Mr. Schwartz*. We have three."

"Oh, I see! Bernard Schwartz."

"Please take a seat. I'll call his assistant."

If you hadn't known Bernie Schwartz was one of the top talent agents in Hollywood, you still wouldn't know after seeing his eighth-floor corner office. Maybe a fine art collector, or an anthropologist. The office was devoid of the typical trappings—no movie posters, arm-around-star or arm-around-politician photos, no awards, tapes, DVDs, plasma screens, trade mags. Nothing but African art, all sorts of carved wooden statues, decorative pots, hide shields, spears, geometric paintings, masks. For a short, fat, aging Jew from Pasadena, he had a major thing going for the dark continent. He shouted through the door to one of his four assistants, "Remind me why I'm seeing this guy?"

A woman's voice: "Victor Kemp."

He waved his left hand in a gimme sign. "Yeah, yeah, I remember. Get me the folder with the coverage and interrupt me after ten minutes, max. Five, maybe."

When Peter entered the agent's office, he felt instantly ill at ease in Bernie's presence, even though the small man had a big smile and was waving him in from behind his desk like a deck officer on an aircraft carrier. "Come in, come in." Peter approached, faking happiness, assaulted by primitive African artifacts. "What can I get you? Coffee? We got espresso, lattes, anything you want. I'm Bernie Schwartz. Glad to meet you, Peter." His light thin hand got squashed by a small thick hand and was pumped a few times.

"Maybe a water?"

"Roz, get Mr. Benedict a water, will ya? Sit, sit there. I'll come over to the sofa."

Within seconds a Chinese girl, another beauty, materialized with a bottle of Evian and a glass. Everything moved fast here.

"So, did you fly in, Peter?" Bernie asked.

"No, I drove, actually."

"Smart, very smart. I'm telling you, to this day I won't fly anymore, at least commercial. Nine/eleven is still like yesterday to me. I could've been on one of those planes. My wife has a sister in Cape Cod. Roz! Can I get a cup of tea? So, you're a writer, Peter. How long you been writing scripts?"

"About five years, Mr. Schwartz."

"Please! Bernie!"

"About five years, Bernie."

"How many you got under your belt?"

"You mean just counting finished ones?"

"Yeah, yeah—finished projects," Bernie said impatiently.

"The one I sent you is my first."

Bernie closed his eyes tightly as if he were telepathically signaling his girl: Five minutes! Not ten! "So, you any good?" he asked.

Peter wondered about that question. He'd sent the script two weeks ago. Hadn't Bernie read it?

To Peter, his script was like a sacred text, imbued with a quasimagical aura. He had poured his soul into its creation and he kept a copy prominently displayed on his writing desk, three-hole-punched with shiny brass brads, his first completed opus. Every morning on his way out the door, he touched the cover as one might finger an amulet or stroke the belly of a Buddha. It was his ticket to another life, and he was eager to get it punched. Moreover, the subject matter was important to him, a paean, as he saw it, to life and fate. As a student, he had been deeply moved by *The Bridge of San Luis Rey*, Thornton Wilder's novel about five strangers who perished together on a collapsing bridge. Naturally, when he started his new job in Nevada he began to dwell on the notions of fate and predestination. He chose to craft a modern take on the classic tale where—in his version—the strangers' lives intersected at the instant of a terror attack. Bernie got his tea, "Thank you, honey. Keep an eye out for my next meeting, okay?" Roz cleared Peter's line of sight and winked at her boss.

"Well, I think it's good," Peter answered. "Did you have a chance to look at it?"

Bernie hadn't read a script in decades. Other people read scripts for him and gave him notes—coverage.

"Yeah, yeah, I got my notes right here." He opened the folder with Peter's coverage and scanned the two-pager.

Weak plot.

Terrible dialogue.

Poor character development, etc., etc.

Recommendation: pass

Bernie stayed in character, smiled expansively and asked, "So tell me, Peter, how is it you know Victor Kemp?"

* * *

A month earlier, Peter Benedict walked into the Constellation with a hopeful spring to his step. He preferred the Constellation over any casino on the Strip. It was the only one with a whiff of intellectual content, and furthermore, he had been an astronomy buff as a boy. The planetarium dome of the grand casino had a perpetually shifting laser display of the night sky over Las Vegas, exactly as it would appear if you stuck your head outside while someone turned off the hundreds of million of lightbulbs and fifteen thousand miles of neon tubing that washed out the heavens. If you looked carefully, came often enough, and were a student of the subject, over time you could spot each of the eighty-eight constellations. The Big Dipper, Orion, Andromeda—a piece of cake. Peter had found the obscure ones too: Corvus, Delphinus, Eridanas, Sextens. In fact, he only lacked Coma Berineces, Berineces' Hair, a faint cluster in the northern sky sandwiched between Canes Venatici and Virgo. One day he would find that too.

He was playing blackjack at a high-stakes table, minimum bet per hand $100, maximum $5,000, his baldness covered by a Lakers baseball cap. He almost never exceeded the minimum but preferred these tables because the spectacle was more interesting. He was a good, disciplined player who usually ended an evening a few hundred up, but every so often he left a thousand richer or poorer, depending on the streakiness of the cards. The real thrills flowed his way vicariously, watching the big money players juggling three hands, splitting, doubling down, risking fifteen, twenty grand at a time. He would have loved pumping out that kind of adrenaline but knew it wasn't going to happen—not on *his* salary.

The dealer, a Hungarian named Sam, saw that he wasn't having a good night and tried to cheer him up. "Don't worry, Peter, luck will change. You will see."

He didn't think so. The shoe had a count of minus fifteen, highly favoring the house. Yet, that knowledge didn't change his play, even though any reasonable card-counter would have backed off for a while, come back in when the count climbed.

Peter was an odd duck of a counter. He counted because he could. His brain worked so fast and it was so effortless for him that having mastered the technique, he couldn't *not* count. High cards—ten to ace—were minus one; low cards—two through six—were plus one. A good counter only had to do two things well: keep a running tally of the total count as the six-deck shoe was dealt out, and accurately estimate the number of undealt cards in the shoe. When the count was low, you bet the minimum or walked away. When it was high, you bet aggressively. If you knew what you were doing, you could tilt the law of averages and consistently win; that is, until you were spotted by a dealer, the pit boss, or the eye-in-the-sky and booted and banned.

Peter occasionally made a count-based decision, but since he never varied his bet, he never capitalized on his inside knowledge. He liked the Constellation, enjoyed spending three- or four-hour stretches at the tables, and was scared of getting kicked out of his favorite haunt. He was part of the furniture.

That night there were only two other gamblers at his table: a bleary-eyed anesthesiologist from Denver in for a medical convention, and a nattily dressed silver-haired exec who was the only one putting serious money into play. Peter was $600 down, pacing himself and languidly drinking a comped beer.

With a few hands to go before the shoe got reshuffled, a young rangy kid, about twenty-two, in a T-shirt and cargo pants, planted himself into one of the two empty chairs and bought in for a grand. He had shoulder-length hair and a breezy western charm. "Hey, how's everybody doing tonight? This a good table?"

"Not for me," the executive said. "You're welcome to change that."

"I'd be pleased to be of any assistance I can," the kid said. He caught the dealer's name tag. "Deal me in, Sam."

Betting the minimum, the kid turned a quiet table into a chatty one. He told them he was a student at UNLV majoring in government and, starting with the doctor, asked everyone where they were from and what they did for a living. After blathering about a problem he was having with his shoulder, he turned to Peter.

"I'm local," Peter offered. "I work with computers."

Prompting, "Cool. That's cool, dude."

The executive told the table, "I'm in the insurance business."

"You sell insurance, dude?"

"Well, yes and no. I run an insurance company."

"Awesome! High roller, baby!" the kid exclaimed.

Sam reshuffled the shoe and Peter instinctively started to count again. After five minutes they were well into the new shoe and the count was getting high. Peter puttered along, doing a little better, winning a few more hands than he lost. "See, I told you," Sam told him cheerfully after he won three hands in a row. The doctor was down two grand, but the insurance guy was out over thirty and he getting testy. The kid was betting erratically, without any apparent feel for the game, but he was only down a couple hundred. He ordered a rum and coke and fiddled with the swizzle stick until it accidentally dropped out of his mouth onto the floor. "Oops," he said quietly.

A blonde in her late twenties in tight jeans and a lemon and lime tube top approached the table and took the empty chair. She put her expensive Vuitton bag under her feet for safekeeping and plonked down $10,000 in four neat stacks. "Hello," she said shyly. She wasn't gorgeous but had a dynamite body and a soft, sexy voice and she stopped the conversation dead. "I hope I'm not barging in," she said, stacking her chips.

"Hell, no!" the kid said. "We need a rose among us thorns."

"I'm Melinda," and they amiably dispensed their minimalist Vegas-style introductions. She was from Virginia. She pointed to her wedding band. Hubby was at the pool.

Peter watched her play several hands. She was fast and sassy, betting $500 a hand, making border-line draws that were paying off pretty well. The kid lost three hands in a row, leaned back in his chair and said, "Man, I am hexed!"

Hexed.

Peter realized the count was plus thirteen with about forty cards left in the shoe.

Hexed.

The blonde pushed a stack of chips worth $3,500 forward. Seeing this, the insurance guy stepped up and bet the max. "You're giving me courage," he told her. Peter stuck to his $100, the same as the doc and the kid.

Sam quickly dealt and gave Peter a strong nineteen, the insurance guy fourteen, the doc seventeen, the kid twelve, and the blonde a pair of jacks—twenty. The dealer was showing a six. She's a lock, Peter thought. High count, dealer probably draws and busts, she's sitting pretty with her twenty.

"I'm going to split these, Sam," she said.

Sam blinked and nodded as she put up another $3,500.

Holy shit! Peter was dumbstruck. Who splits tens?

Unless?

Peter and the doc stood pat, the kid drew a six and stayed on eighteen. The insurance man busted out with a ten and spat out in disgust, "Son of a bitch!"

The blonde held her breath and clenched her fists until Sam dealt her a queen on one hand and a seven on the other. She clapped and exhaled simultaneously.

The dealer flipped his hole card, revealing a king, and drew a nine.

Bust.

Amidst her squeals, Sam paid out the table, shoving seven grand in chips her way.

Peter hastily excused himself and started for the men's room in turmoil. His mind was grinding. What am I thinking? he said to himself. This is none of my business! Let it go!

But he couldn't. He was overwhelmed with moral outrage—if *he* didn't take advantage, why should they?

He pivoted, went back toward the cluster of blackjack tables and made eye contact with the pit boss, who nodded and smiled at him. Peter sidled up and said, "Hey, how're you doing?"

"Just fine, sir. How can I help you this evening?"

"You see that kid at the table over there and the girl?"

"Yes, sir."

"They're counting."

The corner of the pit boss's mouth twitched. He'd seen a lot but he'd never seen one player turn in another. What was the angle? "You sure about this?"

"I'm positive. The kid's counting and signaling her."

"Thank you, sir. I'll handle it."

The pit boss used his two-way to call the floor manager, who in turn got security to play back the tape of the table's last couple of hands. In retrospect the blonde's stepped-up bet did look suspicious.

Peter had returned to the table just as a phalanx of uniformed security men arrived and laid hands on the kid's shoulders.

"Hey, what the fuck!" the kid shouted.

Players at other tables stopped and stared.

"You two know each other?" the pit boss asked.

"I never saw her in my life! That's the goddamn truth!" the kid wailed.

The blonde said nothing. She just picked up her pocketbook, gathered her chips, and tossed a $500 tip to Sam.

"See you, fellows," she said as she was led away.

The pit boss made a hand signal and Sam was replaced by another dealer.

The doc and the insurance guy looked at Peter with glazed astonishment. "What the hell just happened here?" the insurance man asked.

"They were counting," Peter said simply. "I turned them in."

"No you did not!" the insurance guy howled.

"Yeah, I did. It ticked me off."

The doc asked, "How'd you know?"

"I knew." He felt uncomfortable with the attention he was getting. He wanted to scram.

"I'll be damned," the insurance guy said, shaking his head. "I'm going to buy you a drink, friend. I'll be damned." His blue eyes sparkled as he reached into his wallet and pulled out a business card. "Here, take my card. My business runs on computers. If you need any work, just call me up, all right?"

Peter took the card: NELSON G. ELDER, CHAIRMAN AND CEO, DESERT LIFE INSURANCE COMPANY.

"That's very nice of you, but I have a job," Peter muttered, his voice barely audible above the repetitive melodies and clanging of the slots.

"Well, if things change, you've got my number."

The pit boss approached the table. "Look everyone, I apologize for what happened here. Mr. Elder, how are you tonight, sir? All of you are eating and drinking on the house tonight and I got tickets to any show you want. Okay? Again, I'm very sorry."

"Sorry enough to reverse my losses tonight, Frankie?" Elder asked.

"I wish I could, Mr. Elder, but that I cannot do."

"Oh, well," Elder told the table, "you don't ask, you don't get."

The pit boss tapped Peter on the shoulder and whispered, "The manager wants to meet you." Peter blanched. "Don't worry, it's all good."

Gil Flores, the floor manager of the Constellation, was sleek and urbane, and in his presence Peter felt scruffy and self-conscious. His armpits were damp, he wanted to leave. The manager's office was utilitarian, equipped with multiple flat-screen panels getting live feeds from the tables and slots.

Flores was drilling down, trying to figure out the hows and the whys. How did a civilian spot something his guys didn't and why did he turn them in? "What am I missing here?" Flores asked the timid man.

Peter took a sip of water. "I knew the count," Peter admitted.

"You were counting too?"

"Yes."

"You're a counter? You're admitting to me you're a counter?" Flores's voice was rising.

"I count, but I'm not a counter."

Flores's polish rubbed off. "What the fuck does that mean?"

"I keep the count—it's kind of a habit, but I don't use it."

"You expect me to believe that?"

Peter shrugged. "I'm sorry but it's the truth. I've been coming here for two years and I've never varied my bets. I make a little, lose a little, you know."

"Unbelievable. So you knew the count when this shithead does what?"

"He said he was hexed. The count was thirteen, you know, a code word for thirteen. She joined the table when the count was high. I think he dropped a swizzle stick to signal her."

"So he counts and decoys, the chick bets and collects."

"They probably have a code word for every count, like 'chair' for four, 'sweet' for sixteen."

The phone rang and Flores answered it and listened before saying, "Yes, sir."

"Well, Peter Benedict, it's your lucky day," Flores announced. "Victor Kemp wants to see you up in the penthouse."

The view from the penthouse was dazzling, the entire Strip snaking toward the dark horizon like a flaming tail. Victor Kemp came in and extended his hand, and Peter felt his chunky gold rings when their fingers entwined. He had black wavy hair, a deep tan and gleaming teeth—the sleek, easy looks of a headliner at the best club in town. His suit was a shimmery blue that caught the light and played with it, a fabric that seemed unearthly. He sat Peter down in his cavernous living room and offered him a drink. While a maid fetched a beer, Peter noticed that one of the wall monitors at the far end of the room had a shot of Gil's office. Cameras everywhere.

Peter took the beer and considered doffing his cap but kept it on—damned if he did, damned if he didn't.

"An honest man is the noblest work of God," Kemp said

suddenly. "Alexander Pope wrote that. Cheers!" Kemp clinked his wineglass against Peter's beer flute. "You have lifted my spirits, Mr. Benedict, and for that, I thank you."

"You're welcome," Peter said cautiously.

"You seem like a very clever guy. May I ask what you do for a living?"

"I work with computers."

"Why am I not surprised to hear that! You spotted something an army of trained professionals missed, so on one hand I'm pleased you are an honest man but on another I am displeased at my own people. Have you ever considered working in casino security, Mr. Benedict?"

Peter shook his head but said, "That's the second job offer I've had tonight."

"Who else?"

"A guy at my blackjack table, the CEO of an insurance company."

"Silver hair, slim fella in his fifties?"

"Yes."

"That would be Nelson Elder, a very good guy. You're having quite a night. But, if you're happy with your job, I've got to find some other way to thank you."

"Oh. No. That's not necessary, sir."

"Don't sir me! You call me Victor and I will reciprocate by calling you Peter. So, Peter, this is like you just found a genie in a bottle but because this isn't a fairy tale you only get one wish and it's got to be, you know, realistic. So what's it going to be, you want a girl, you want a credit line, some movie star you'd like to meet?"

Peter's brain was capable of processing a tremendous amount of information swiftly. In a few seconds of thought he worked through various scenarios and outcomes and out popped a proposition that, for him, was high impact.

"Do you know any Hollywood agents?" he asked, his voice quavering.

Kemp laughed. "Sure I do, they all come here! You're a writer?"

"I wrote a script," he said sheepishly.

"Then I'm gonna set you up with Bernie Schwartz, who's one of the biggest guys at ATI. Will that work for you, Peter? Does that float your boat?"

Joy-soaked, he exulted, "Oh yeah! That would be unbelievable!"

"Okay, then. I can't promise you he'll like your script, Peter, but I will promise you that he'll read it and meet with you. Done deal."

They shook hands again. On his way out, Kemp put his hand on Peter's shoulder in a fatherly way. "And don't be counting cards on me now, Peter, you hear? You're on the side of righteousness."

"Isn't that interesting," Bernie said. "Victor Kemp *is* Las Vegas. He's a prince of a man."

"So what about my script?" Peter asked, then stopped breathing to await the answer.

Crunch time.

"Actually, Peter, the script, as good as it is, needs a bit of polishing before I could send it out. But here's the bigger thing. This is a big budget film, you got here. You got a train blowing up and a lot of special effects. These kind of action films are getting harder and harder to make unless they've got a built-in audience or franchise potential. And you've got a terrorism angle which is the real killer. Nine/eleven changed everything. I can tell you that very few of my projects that got cancelled back in '01 have been resurrected. Nobody wants to make a terrorism picture anymore. I can't sell it. I'm sorry, the world has changed."

Exhale. He felt light-headed.

Roz came in. "Mr. Schwartz, your next appointment is here."

"Where's the time gone!" Bernie sprang to his feet, which made Peter levitate too. "Now, you go and write me a script about high-stakes gambling and card counters and throw in some sex and laughs and I promise I'll read that. I'm so happy we were able to meet, Peter. You give my regards to

Mr. Kemp. And listen, I'm glad you drove. Personally, I won't fly anymore, at least commercial."

When Peter got back to his small ranch house in Spring Valley that night there was an envelope sticking out from under his welcome mat. He tore it open and read the handwritten letter under the porch light.

> Dear Peter,
>
> I'm sorry you struck out with Bernie Schwartz today. Let me make it up to you. Come over to Room 1834 at the hotel tonight at ten.
>
>   Victor

Peter was tired and dispirited but it was a Friday night and he had the weekend to recover.

The check-in desk at the Constellation had a room key waiting for him and he went straight up. It was a big two-bedroom suite with a great view. The coffee table in the living room sported a fruit basket and a bottle of iced Perrier-Jouet. And another envelope. There were two cards inside, one a voucher for $1,000 of merchandise in the Constellation shopping plaza and the other a $5,000 line at the casino.

He sat down on the sofa, stunned, and looked down onto the neon landscape.

There was a knock at the door.

"Come in!" he called out.

A female voice: "I don't have a key!"

"Oh, sorry," Peter said, sprinting for the door, "I thought it was housekeeping."

She was gorgeous. And young, almost girlish. A brunette with an open, fresh face, firm ivory flesh pouring out of a clingy black cocktail dress.

"You must be Peter," she said, shutting the door behind her. "Mr. Kemp sent me to say hello." Like many in Vegas, she was from somewhere else—her accent had a hillbilly twang, dainty and musical.

He blushed so brightly his skin looked like it was made of red plastic. "Oh!"

She slowly walked toward him, backing him up toward the sofa. "My name is Lydia. Am I okay?"

"Okay?"

"If you'd prefer a guy, that's cool. Didn't know for sure." She had a charming ditziness about her.

His voice got squeaky from laryngeal constriction. "I don't like guys! I mean, I like girls!"

"Well, good! 'Cause I'm a girl," she purred with practiced artifice. "Why don't you sit yourself down and open that bottle of champagne, Peter, while we figure out the kind of games you'd like to play."

He reached the sofa as his knees were buckling and went down hard on his rump. His brain was swimming in a sea of juices—fear, lust, embarrassment—he'd never done anything like this before. It seemed so silly, yet . . .

Then, "Hey, I've seen you before!" Now Lydia was genuinely excited. "Yeah, I've seen you tons of times! It just hit me!"

"Where? At the casino?"

"No silly! You probably don't recognize me because I'm not in that stupid uniform. My day job is at the reception desk at McCarran Airport, you know—the E.G. and G terminal."

The rouge drained from his face.

This day was too much for him. Too much.

"Your name's not Peter! It's Mark something. Mark Shackleton. I'm good with names."

"Well, you know how names are," he said shakily.

"I get it! Hey, none of my beeswax! What happens in Vegas stays in Vegas, honey. If you want to know the truth, my name's not Lydia."

He was speechless as he watched her strip off her black dress, showing all her black lacy gear underneath, talking a mile a minute as she went. "That is so cool! I've always wanted to speak to one of you guys! I mean how crazy must it be to commute to Area 51 every day. I mean it's like so top secret it basically makes me hot!"

His mouth fell open a little.

"I mean I know you're not allowed to talk about it but please, just nod if we've really got UFOs we're studying out there cause that's what everybody says!"

He tried to keep his head still.

"Was that a nod?" she asked. "Were you nodding?"

He composed himself enough to say, "I can't say anything about what goes on there. Please!"

She looked bummed then brightened up and started to work again. "Okay! That's cool. Tell you what, *Peter*," she said, swinging her hips, slowly approaching the sofa, "I'll be your personal UFO tonight—unidentified fucking object. How would that be?"

Will had a devastating hangover, the kind that felt like a weasel had woken up warm and cozy inside his skull then panicked at its confinement and tried to scratch and bite its way out through his eyes.

The evening had begun benignly enough. On his way home he stopped at his local dive, a yeasty smelling cave called Dunigan's, and downed a couple of pops on an empty stomach. Next up, the Pantheon Diner, where he grunted at the heavily stubbled waiter who grunted back at him and without exchanging any fully formed phrases brought him the same dish he ate two to three days a week—lamb kebabs and rice, washed down, of course, with a couple of beers. Then before decamping to his place for the night he paid his wobbly respects to his friendly package store and picked up a fresh half gallon of Black Label, pretty much the only luxury item to adorn his life.

The apartment was small and spartan, and stripped of Jennifer's feminizing touches, a truly bleak uninteresting piece of real estate—two sparse white-walled rooms with shiny parquet floors, meager views of the building across the street, and a few thousand dollars worth of generic furniture and rugs. Truth be told, the apartment was almost too small for him. The living room was fourteen by seventeen, the bedroom ten by twelve, the kitchen and bathroom each the size of a good closet. Some of the criminals he had put away for life wouldn't see the place as a major upgrade. How had he put up with sharing the flat with Jennifer for four months? Whose bright idea was that?

He hadn't intended to drink himself stupid but the heavy full bottle seemed to hold so much promise. He twisted off the top, cracking its seal, then hoisted it by its built-in handle and glugged a half tumbler of scotch into his favorite whiskey glass. With the TV droning in the background he sofa-drank, steadily sinking into a deep dark hole as he thought about his effing day, his effing case, his effing life.

Notwithstanding his reluctance to take on the Doomsday case, the first few days had been, in fact, rejuvenating. Clive Robertson was killed right under his nose and the audacity and perplexity of the crime electrified him. It reminded him of the way big cases used to make him feel, and the kicky pulses of adrenaline agreed with him.

He'd immersed himself in the tangle of facts, and though he knew that epiphanous moments were the stuff of fiction, had a powerful urge to drill down and discover something that had been missed, the overlooked link that would tie together two murders, then a third, then another, until the case was cracked.

The distraction of important work had been as soothing as butter on a burn. He started by running hot, pounding the files, pushing Nancy, exhausting both of them in a marathon of days bleeding into nights bleeding into days. For a while he actually took Sue Sanchez's words to heart: Okay, this would be his last big case. Let's ride this sucker out and retire with a big old bang.

Crescendo.

Decrescendo.

Within a week he'd been burnt out, spent and dispirited. Robertson's autopsy and toxicology reports made no sense to him. The seven other cases made no sense to him. He couldn't get any feeling for who the killer was or what gratification he was getting from the murders. None of his initial ideas were panning out. All he could fathom was a tableau of randomness, and that was something he had never seen in a serial killer.

The first scotch was to dull the unpleasantness of his afternoon in Queens interviewing the family of the hit-and-run victim, nice solid people who were still inconsolable. The second scotch was to blunt his frustration. The third was to fill some of his emptiness with maudlin remembrances, the fourth was for loneliness. The fifth . . . ?

In spite of his pounding head and hollow nausea, he stubbornly dragged himself into work by eight. In his book, if you made it to work on time, never drank on the job, and never touched a drop before happy hour, you didn't have a booze problem. Still, he couldn't ignore the searing headache, and as he rode the elevator he clutched an extra large coffee to his chest like a life preserver. He flinched at the memory of waking, fully clothed, at 6:00 A.M., a third of the mighty bottle empty. He had Advil in his office. He needed to get there.

Doomsday files were stacked on his desk, his credenza, his bookcase, and all over the floor, stalagmites of notes, reports, research, computer printouts, and crime scene photos. He had carved himself walking corridors through the piles—from door to desk chair, chair to bookcase, chair to window, so he could adjust the blinds and keep the afternoon sun out of his eyes. He made his way through the obstacle course, landed hard on his chair, and hunted down the pain relievers, which he painfully swallowed with a gulp of hot coffee. He rubbed his eyes with the heels of his hands, and when he opened them Nancy was standing there, looking at him like a doctor.

"Are you all right?"

"I'm fine."

"You don't look fine. You look sick."

"I'm fine." He fumbled for a file at random and opened it. She was still there. "What?"

"What's the plan for today?" she asked.

"The plan is for me to drink my coffee and for you to come back in an hour."

Dutifully, she reappeared in precisely one hour. His pain and nausea were subsiding but his thinking was still milky. "Okay," he began, "what's our schedule?"

She opened the ubiquitous notebook. "Ten o'clock, telecon with Dr. Sofer from Johns Hopkins. Two o'clock, task force press conference. Four o'clock, uptown to see Helen Swisher. You look better."

He was curt. "I was good an hour ago and I'm good now." She didn't look convinced, and he wondered if she knew he was hung over. Then it dawned on him—she looked better. Her face was a little thinner, her body a little sleeker, her skirt didn't pinch as much at the waist. They had been constant companions for ten days and he'd only just realized she was eating like a parakeet. "Can I ask *you* a question?"

"Sure."

"Are you on a diet or something?"

She blushed instantly. "Sort of. I started jogging again too."

"Well, it looks good. Keep it up."

She lowered her eyes in embarrassment. "Thanks."

He quickly changed the subject. "Okay, let's take a step back and try to see the big picture," he said foggily. "We're getting killed with details. Let's go through these, one more time, focusing on connections." He joined her at the conference table and moved the files onto other files to give them an uncluttered surface. He took a clean pad and wrote on it, *Key Observations,* and underlined the words twice. He willed his brain to work and loosened his tie to encourage blood flow.

There had been three deaths on May 22, three on May 25, two on June 11, and none since. "What does that tell us?" he asked. She shook her head, so he answered his own question. "They're all weekdays."

"Maybe the guy has a weekend job," she offered.

"Okay. Maybe." He entered his first key observation: *Weekdays.* "Find the Swisher files. I think they're on the bookcase."

Case #1: David Paul Swisher, thirty-six-year-old investment banker at HSBC. Park Avenue, wealthy, all-Ivy background. Married, nothing obvious on the side. No Enron skeletons in his closet as far as they knew. Took the family mutt for a pre-dawn walk, found by a jogger just after 5:00 A.M. in a river of blood—watch, rings, and wallet missing, left carotid cleanly sliced. The body was still warm, about twenty feet out of range of the nearest CCTV camera located on the roof of a co-op on the south side of 82nd Street—twenty goddamned feet and they would've have had the killing on tape.

However, they did have a glimpse of a person of interest, a nine-second sequence time-coded at 5:02:23–5:02:32, shot from a security camera on the roof of a ten-story building on the west side of Park Avenue between 81st and 82nd. It showed a male walking into the frame from 82nd turning south on Park, pivoting then running back the way he came and disappearing down 82nd again. The image was poor quality but FBI techs had blown it up and enhanced it. From the suspect's hand coloration they determined he was black or Latino, and from reference calculations, they figured he was about five-ten and weighed 160 to 175 pounds. The hood of a gray sweatshirt obscured his face. The timing was promising since the 911 call came in at 5:07, but in the absence of witnesses they had no leads on his identity.

If not for the postcard, this would have been a street mugging, plain and simple, but David Swisher got a postcard. David Swisher was Doomsday victim one.

Will held up a photo of the hooded man and waved it at Nancy. "So is this our guy?"

"He may be David's killer but that doesn't make him the Doomsday Killer," she said.

"Serial murder by proxy? That'd be a first."

She tried another tack. "Okay, maybe this was a contract murder."

"Possible. An investment banker is bound to have enemies," Will said. "Every deal has a winner and a loser. But David was different from the other victims. He was the only one who wore a white collar to work. Who's going to pay to murder any of the others?" Will flipped through one of the Swisher files. "Do we have a list of David's clients?"

"His bank hasn't been helpful," Nancy said. "Every request for info has to go through their legal department and be personally signed off by their general counsel. We haven't gotten anything yet but I'm pushing."

"I've got a feeling he's the key." Will closed Swisher's file and pushed it away. "The first victim in a string has a special significance to the killer, something symbolic. You said we're seeing his wife today?"

She nodded.

"About time."

Case #2: Elizabeth Marie Kohler, thirty-seven-year-old manager at a Duane Reade drugstore in Queens. Shot to death in an apparent robbery, found by employees at the rear entrance when they got to work at 8:30 A.M.. Police initially thought she'd been killed by an assailant who waited for her to arrive to steal narcotics. Something went wrong, he fired, she fell, he ran. The bullet was a .38 caliber, one shot to the temple at close range. No surveillance video, no useful forensics. It took police a couple of days to find the postcard at her apartment and connect her with the others.

He looked up from her file and asked, "Okay, what's the connection between a Wall Street banker and a drugstore manager?"

"I don't know," Nancy said. "They were nearly the same age but their lives didn't have any obvious points of intersection. He never shopped at her drugstore. There's nothing."

"Where are we with her ex-husband, old boyfriends, co-workers?"

"We've got most of them identified and accounted for," she replied. "There's one high school boyfriend we can't find. His family moved out of state years ago. All her other exes—if they don't have an alibi for her murder, they've got one for the other murders. She's been divorced for five years. Her ex-husband was driving a bus for the Transit Authority the morning she was shot. She was an ordinary person. Her life wasn't complicated. She didn't have enemies."

"So, if it weren't for the postcard, this would have been an open and shut case of an armed robbery gone bad."

"That's what it looks like, on the surface," she agreed.

"Okay, action items," he said. "See if she had any high school or college yearbooks and have all the names entered into the database. Also, contact the landlord and get a list of all her present and former neighbors going back for five years. Throw them into the mix."

"Done. You want another coffee?" He did, badly.

Case #3: Consuela Pilar Lopez, thirty-two-year-old illegal immigrant from the Dominican Republic, living in Staten Island, working as an office cleaner in Manhattan. Found just after 3:00 A.M. by a group of teenagers in a wooded area near the shore in Arthur Von Briesen Park, less than a mile from her house on Fingerboard Road. She'd been raped and re-peatedly stabbed in the chest, head, and neck. She had taken the ten o'clock ferry from Manhattan that night, confirmed by CCTV. Her usual routine would have been to take the bus south toward Fort Wadsworth, but no one could place her at the bus station at the St. George Ferry Terminal or on the number 51 bus that ran down Bay Street to Fingerboard.

The working hypothesis was that someone intercepted her at the terminal, offered her a ride, and took her to a dark corner of the island, where she met her end under the loom-ing superstructure of the Verrazano-Narrows Bridge. There was no semen in or on her body—the killer apparently used a condom. There were gray fibers on her shirt, which ap-peared to have come from a sweatshirt type of fabric. At postmortem, her wounds were calibrated. The blade was four inches long, compatible with the one that killed David Swisher. Lopez lived in a two-family house with an extended group of siblings and cousins, some documented, some not. She was a religious lady who worshipped at St. Sylvester's, where stunned parishioners had packed the church for a memorial mass. According to family and friends, she had no boyfriend, and the autopsy suggested that even though she was in her thirties she had been a virgin. All attempts to connect her with the other victims proved fruitless.

Will had spent a disproportionate amount of time with this particular murder, studying the ferry and bus terminal, walking the crime scene, visiting her house and church. Sex crimes were his forte. It hadn't been his career aspiration—no one in his right mind wrote on his Quantico application: *One day I hope to specialize in sex crimes.* But his first big cases had serious sexual angles, and that's the way you got pigeon-holed in the Bureau. He did more than follow his nose, he burned hot with ambition and educated himself to expert grade. He studied the annals of sex crimes sedulously and became a walking encyclopedia of American serial perversion.

He'd seen this kind of killer before, and the offender profile came to him quickly. The perp was a stalker, a planner, a circumspect loner who was careful about not leaving his DNA behind. He'd be familiar with the neighborhood, which meant he either currently lived or used to live on Staten Island. He knew the waterfront park like the back of his hand and calculated exactly where he could do his business with the least chance of being happened upon. There was an excellent chance he was Hispanic because he made his victim feel comfortable enough to get into his car and they were told that Consuela's English was limited. There was a reasonable chance she knew her killer at least by limited acquaintance.

"Wait a minute," Will said suddenly. "Here's something. Consuela's killer almost definitely had a car. We ought to be looking for the same dark blue sedan that crushed Myles Drake." He jotted: *Blue Sedan*. "What was the name of Consuela's priest again?"

She remembered his sad face and didn't need to check her notes. "Father Rochas."

"We need to make up a flyer of different models of dark blue sedans and have Father Rochas pass them out to his parishioners to see if anyone knows anyone with a blue car. Also cross-run the list of parishioners with the DMV to get a printout of registered vehicles. Pay particular attention to Hispanic males."

She nodded and made notes.

He stretched his arms over his head and yawned, "I've got to hit the john. Then we've got to call that guy."

The forensic pathologists at HQ had pointed them toward Gerald Sofer, the country's leading expert in a truly bizarre affliction. It was a measure of their frustration in Clive Robertson's death that they had sought his consultation.

Will and Nancy had frantically administered CPR on Clive's pulseless body for six minutes until the paramedics arrived. The following morning they hovered over the M.E.'s shoulder as the coroner laid Clive's body open and started the search for a cause of death. Besides the crushed nasal bones there was no external trauma. His heavy brain, brimming so recently with music, was thin-sliced like a bread loaf. There were no signs of a stroke or hemorrhage. All his internal organs were normal for his age. His heart was slightly enlarged, the valves normal, the coronary arteries had a mild to moderate amount of atherosclerosis, especially the left anterior descending artery, which was seventy percent occluded. "I've probably got more blockage than this guy," the veteran M.E. rasped. There was no evidence of a heart attack, though Will was advised that a microscopic exam would be determinative. "So far, I don't have a diagnosis for you," the pathologist said, peeling off his gloves.

Will waited anxiously for the blood and tissue tests. He was hoping a poison or toxin would show up but was also interested in his HIV status since he'd done mouth-to-mouth on Clive's bloody face. Within days he had the results. The good news: Clive was HIV and hepatitis negative. The bad: *Everything* was negative. The man had no reason for being dead.

"Yes, I did have a chance to review Mr. Robertson's autopsy report," Dr. Sofer said. "It's typical of the syndrome."

Will leaned toward the speaker phone. "How's that?"

"Well, his heart wasn't all that bad, really. There were no

critical coronary occlusions, no thrombosis, no histopatho-
logical evidence of a myocardial infarction. This is perfectly
consistent with the patients I've studied with stress-induced
cardiomyopathy, also know as myocardial stunning syndrome."

Sudden emotional stress, fear, anger, grief, shock could
cause sudden devastating heart failure, according to Sofer.
Victims were people who were otherwise healthy, who experienced a sudden emotional jolt like the death of a loved
one or a massive fright.

"Doctor, this is Special Agent Lipinski," Nancy said. "I
read your paper in the *New England Journal of Medicine*.
None of the patients with your syndrome died. What makes
Mr. Robertson different?"

"That's an excellent question," Sofer replied. "I believe the
heart can be stunned into pump failure by a massive release of
catecholamines, stress hormones like adrenaline that are
secreted by the adrenal glands in response to a stress or a
shock. This is a basic evolutionary survival tool, preparing
the organism for fight or flight in the face of life-threatening
danger. However, in some individuals the outpouring of these
neurohormones is so profound that the heart can no longer
pump efficiently. Cardiac output drops sharply and blood
pressure falls. Unfortunately for Mr. Robertson, his pump
failure combined with his moderate blockage in his left coronary artery probably led to poor perfusion of his left ventri-
cle, which triggered a fatal arrhythmia, possibly ventricular
fibrillation and sudden death. It's rare to die from myocardial
stunning but it can occur. Now as I understand it, Mr. Robertson was under some acute stress prior to his death."

"He had a postcard from the Doomsday Killer," Will said.

"Well, then I'd say, to use laymen's terms, your Mr. Robertson was literally scared to death."

"He didn't look scared," Will remarked.

"Looks can be deceiving," Sofer said.

When they were done, Will hung up and drank the last of
his fifth cup of coffee. "Clear as fucking mud," he muttered.
"The killer bets he's going to kill the guy by scaring him to

death? Gimme a break!" He threw his arms into the air, exasperated. "Okay, let's keep going. He kills three people on May twenty-second and he takes a breather over the weekend. May twenty-fifth our unsub's busy again."

Case #4: Myles Drake, twenty-four-year-old bicycle courier from Queens, working the financial district at 7:00 A.M. when an office worker on Broadway, the only eyewitness, is looking out her window and notices him on the sidewalk of John Street slinging his backpack and mounting his bicycle just as a dark blue sedan jumps the curb, plows into him and keeps on going. She's too high up to see the license plate or credibly identify the make and model. Drake succumbs instantly from a crushed liver and spleen. The car, which unquestionably sustained some front-end damage, remains unlocated, despite extensive canvassing of body shops in the tristate area. Myles lived with his older brother and was, by all accounts, a straight-arrow. Clean record, testimonials to his work ethic, etc. No known connections to any other victims either directly or indirectly, though no one could say for sure that he'd never been to Kohler's Duane Reade on Queens Boulevard.

"Nothing to link him with drugs?" Will asked.

"Nothing, but I remember a case when I was in law school of bike couriers supplying cocaine to stockbrokers on the side."

"Not a bad thought—our drug theme." He wrote: *Test backpack for narcotics residue.*

Case #5: Milos Ivan Covic, eighty-two-year-old man from Park Slope, Brooklyn, middle of the afternoon, plunges out of his ninth floor apartment and makes an ungodly mess on Prospect Park West, near Grand Army Plaza. His bedroom window is wide open, apartment locked, no signs of a break-in or robbery. However, several framed black-and-white photos of a young Covic with others, family presumably, are found shattered on the floor by the window. There is no suicide note. The man, a Croatian immigrant who had worked for fifty years as a cobbler, had no living relatives and was so reclusive there was no one who could attest to his mental state. The apartment was covered in only one set of finger-prints: his.

Will leafed through the stack of vintage photographs. "And there's no ID on any of these people?"

"None," Nancy replied. "His neighbors were all inter-viewed, we put out feelers among the Croatian-American community, but nobody knew him. I don't know where to go. Any ideas?"

He pointed his palms toward the heavens. "I got nothing on this one."

Case #6: Marco Antonio Napolitano, eighteen-year-old, recent high school graduate. Lived with his parents and sister in Little Italy. His mother found the postcard in his room and the coffin image sent her into hysterics. His family looked for him unsuccessfully all day. Police found his body later in the evening in the boiler room of their tenement with a needle in his arm and heroin works and tourniquet beside him. Autopsy showed an overdose but the family and his closest friends insisted he wasn't a user, which was borne out by the absence of needle tracks on his body. The kid had a couple of juvies, shoplifting, that sort of thing, but this wasn't a major bad guy. The syringe had two different DNAs, his and an unidentified male's, suggesting someone else had shot up with him using the same works. There were also two sets of fingerprints on the syringe and the spoon, his and another's, which they ran through IAFIS and came up empty, ruling out about fifty million people in the database.

"Okay," Will said. "This one's got possible linkers."

Nancy saw them too, perked up and said, "Yeah, how about this? The killer's an addict who murders Elizabeth, trying to knock off her Duane Reade for narcotics. He's got a gripe against Marco and overloads a syringe, and a score to settle with Myles, who's his supplier."

"What about David?"

"He's more like a mugging for cash, which also fits with an addict."

Will shook his head with an exasperated smile. "Pretty

damned soft," he said, writing: *Possibly an Addict???* "Okay, home stretch. Our man takes a two-week break then starts up again on June eleventh. Why the pause? Is he tired? Busy with something else in his life? Out of town? Back in Vegas?"

Rhetorical questions. She studied Will's face as his mind churned.

"We've run down all the eastbound moving violations issued on major routes between Vegas and New York during the intervals between the postmarked dates on the cards and the dates of the murders and we've got nothing of interest, correct?"

"Correct," she replied.

"And we've got passenger manifests for all direct and connecting flights between Vegas and metropolitan New York for the relevant dates, correct?"

"Correct."

"And what have we learned from that?"

"Nothing yet. We've got several thousand names that we're rerunning every few days against all the names in our victims' databases. So far, no hits."

"And we've done state and federal criminal background checks on all the passengers?"

"Will, you've asked me that a dozen times!"

He wasn't going to apologize. "Because it's important! And get me a printout of all the passengers with Hispanic surnames." He pointed toward a stack of files on the floor near the window. "Pass me that one. This is where I came in."

Case #7: Ida Gabriela Santiago, seventy-eight-year-old killed by an intruder in her bedroom with a .22 caliber bullet through her ear. As Will suspected, she hadn't been raped, and aside from the victim and her immediate family, there were no unaccounted fingerprints anywhere. Her purse had indeed been stolen and remained unrecovered. A footprint from the earth below her kitchen window showed a size twelve distinctive waffle pattern that matched a popular basketball sneaker, Reebok DMX 10. Given the depth of the print and the moisture content of the soil, the lab techs estimated the suspect weighed about 170, roughly the same weight as the Park Avenue suspect. They had searched for connections, especially with the Lopez case, but there were no recognizable intersects between the lives of the two Hispanic women.

That left Case #8: Lucius Jefferson Robertson, the man who was literally scared to death. There wasn't much more to say about him, was there? "That's it, I'm fried," Will announced. "Why don't you sum it up, partner?"

Nancy earnestly flipped through her fresh notes and glanced at his Key Observations. "I guess I'd have to say that our suspect is a five-ten, 170-pound Hispanic male who's a drug addict and a sex offender, who drives a blue car, has a knife, a .22 caliber and a .38 caliber gun, shuttles back and forth to Las Vegas either by car or air, and prefers to kill people on weekdays so he can kick back on weekends."

"One heck of a profile," Will said, finally cracking a smile. "Okay, so bring it all home. How does he pick his victims and what's with the fucking postcards?"

"Don't swear!" she said, playfully swatting her notebook in his direction. "Maybe the victims are connected and maybe they're not. Each crime is different. It's almost like they're deliberately random. Maybe he chooses the victims randomly too. He sends postcards to let us know the crimes are connected and that he's the one who decides if someone's going to die. He reads about the Doomsday Killer in the papers, watches the wall-to-wall cable coverage, it's a real power trip for him. He's very clever and very twisted. That's our man."

She waited for his approbation, but instead he stuck a pin in her balloon.

"Well, you're a real hotshot, Special Agent Lipinski, aren't you?" He stood up and marveled how fine it was to have a clear head and a stomach that could take food. "There's only one thing wrong with your synthesis," he said. "I don't believe a word of it. The only archcriminal I know who's capable of all this evil brilliance is Lex Luthor, and last time

I checked, he was in a comic book. Take a break for lunch. Come get me for the press conference."

He shooed her away with a wink and studied her as she retreated. She's definitely looking better, he thought.

As the case dragged into the summer, the Doomsday press updates had been stretched to weekly. Originally there were daily briefings, but that level of newsworthiness was not sustainable. Yet, the story had legs, strong legs, and was proving to be a bigger ratings draw than O.J., Jon Benet, and Anna Nicole put together. Every night on cable the case was dissected down to a molecular level by talking heads and a legion of ex-FBI and law enforcement officers, lawyers, and pundits who weighed in breathlessly with their pet theories. Of late, a common theme was emerging: The FBI was not making progress, ergo the FBI was inept.

The news conference was in the New York Hilton ballroom. By the time Will and Nancy took their positions near a service entrance, the room was three-quarters full with press and photographers and the bigwigs were settling in up on the dais. On signal, the TV lights switched on and the live feed went out.

The mayor, a natty and imperturbable man, took the podium. "We are six weeks into this investigation," he began. "On a positive note, there have been no new victims in ten days. While there have been no arrests at this time, law enforcement professionals from New York City, New York State, and federal agencies have been working diligently, and I believe productively, in running down multiple leads and theories. However, we cannot deny that there have been eight related murders in this city, and our citizens will not feel entirely safe until the perpetrator is caught and brought to justice. Benjamin Wright, Assistant in Charge of the New York Office of the FBI, will take your questions."

Wright was a tall lean African-American in his fifties with a pencil mustache, close-cropped hair, and professorial wire-rimmed glasses. He stood and smoothed the creases from his double-breasted suit jacket. He was at ease in front of cameras and spoke crisply into the bank of microphones. "As the mayor said, the FBI is working in concert with city and state law enforcement officials to solve this case. This is far and away the largest criminal investigation of a serial killing in the history of the Bureau. While we do not have a suspect in custody, we continue to work tirelessly and I want to make this very clear—we will find the killer. We are not resource-constrained. We are throwing everything we've got at this case. It's not a matter of manpower, it's a matter of time. I'll take your questions now."

The press swarmed like a disturbed hive of bees, anticipating that nothing new was forthcoming. The network and cable reporters were civil enough, leaving it to their lower-paid ink-stained brethren from the papers to throw the bricks.

Q. Was there any more information on Lucius Robertson's toxicology tests?

A. No. Some tissue testing would take a few more weeks.

Q. Did they test him for ricin and anthrax?

A. Yes. Both were negative.

Q. If everything was negative, what killed Lucius Robertson?

A. They didn't know yet.

Q. Wasn't this lack of clarity bound to trouble the public at large?

A. When we know the cause of death we will make it known.

Q. Were the Las Vegas police cooperating?

A. Yes.

Q. Were all the fingerprints on the postcards accounted for?

A. Mostly. They were still tracking down some post office letter handlers.

Q. Did they have any leads on the hooded man at the Swisher crime scene?

A. None.

Q. Did the bullets from the two gunshot victims match any other crimes on file?

A. No.

Q. How did they know this wasn't an Al-Qaeda plot?

A. There was no indication of terrorism.

Q. A psychic from San Francisco had complained the FBI wasn't interested in speaking with her despite her insistence that a long-haired man named Jackson was involved.

A. The FBI was interested in all credible leads.

Q. Were they aware that the public was frustrated in their lack of progress?

A. They shared the public's frustration but remained confident in the ultimate success of the investigation.

Q. Did he think there would be more murders?

A. He hoped not but there was no way of knowing.

Q. Did the FBI have a profile on the Doomsday Killer?

A. Not yet. They were working on it.

Q. Why was it taking so long?

A. Because of the complexities of the case.

Will leaned over and whispered into Nancy's ear, "Colossal waste of time."

Q. Did they have their best people assigned to the case?

A. Yes.

Q. Could the media talk to the Special Agent in charge of the investigation?

A. I can answer all your questions.

"Now it's getting interesting," Will added.

Q. Why couldn't they meet the agent?

A. They would try to make him available at the next press conference.

Q. Is he in the room now?

A. —

Wright looked at Sue Sanchez, who was seated in the first row, his eyes pleading for her to control her guy. She looked around and spotted Will standing off to the side; the only thing she could do was fix him with a death stare.

She thinks I'm a loose canon, Will thought. Well, it's time to start the iron rolling. I'm the Special Agent in charge. I didn't want the case but it's mine now. If they want me, here I am. "Right here!" He raised his hand. He'd faced the press dozens of times during his career and this kind of stuff was old hat—he was anything but camera-shy.

Nancy saw the horrified look on Sanchez's face, and as a reflex almost grabbed him by the sleeve. Almost. He bounded toward the podium with a wicked bounce to his step as the TV cameras swung to stage left.

Benjamin Wright could do nothing except: "Okay, Special Agent Will Piper will answer a limited number of questions. Go ahead, Will." As the two men crossed, Wright whispered, "Keep it short and watch your step."

Will smoothed his hair with his hand and stepped up to the podium. The alcohol and its by-products were fully out of his system and he was feeling good, even feisty. Let's mix it up, he thought. He was photogenic, a big sandy-haired man with broad shoulders, a dimpled chin, and superbly blue eyes. Somewhere a TV director in a control room was saying, "Get in close on that guy!"

The first question was—how do you spell your name?

"Like the Pied Piper, P-I-P-E-R."

The reporters edged forward on their chairs. Did they have a live one? A few of the older ones whispered to each other, "I remember this guy. He's famous."

How long have you been with the FBI?

"Eighteen years, two months, and three days."

Why do you keep track so precisely?

"I'm detail oriented."

What's your experience with serial killings?

"I've spent my entire career working these cases. I've been agent-in-charge of eight of them, the Asheville Rapist, the White River Killer in Indianapolis, six others. We caught all of them, we'll catch this one too."

Why don't you have a profile of the killer yet?

"Believe, me, we've been trying, but he's not profilable in a conventional way. No two murders are alike. There's no pattern. If it weren't for the warning postcards, you wouldn't know the cases were connected."

What's your theory?

"I think we're dealing with a very twisted and very intelligent man. I have no idea what's motivating him. He wants attention, that's a certainty, and thanks to you he's getting it."

You think we shouldn't be covering this?

"You don't have a choice. I'm just stating a fact."

How are you going to catch him?

"He's not perfect. He's left clues, which I'm not going to go into for obvious reasons. We'll get him."

What's your bet? Is he going to strike again?

"Let me answer that this way. My bet is that he's watching this on TV right now, so I'm saying this to *you*." Will stared straight into the cameras. Those blue eyes. "I will catch you and I will put you down. It's only a matter of time."

Wright, who was hovering, practically hip-checked Will away from the mikes. "Okay, I think that's it for today. We'll let you know the time and location of our next briefing."

The press rose to their feet and one voice, a female reporter from the *Post,* rose above the others and screamed out, "Promise us you'll bring the Pied Piper back!"

Number 941 Park Ave was a solid cube, a thirteen-story brick prewar, its two lower floors clad in fine white granite, the lobby done up tastefully in marble and chintz. Will had been there before, retracing David Swisher's last steps from the lobby to the precise spot on 82nd Street where the blood had drained from his body. He had walked the walk in the same predawn darkness, and lowering himself on his haunches, right on the spot—still discolored despite a good scrubbing from the sanitation department—had tried to visualize the last thing the victim might have seen before his brain went off-line. A section of mottled sidewalk? A black iron window grate? The rim on a parked car? A thin oak rising out of a square of compacted dirt?

The tree, hopefully.

As expected, Helen Swisher rubbed Will the wrong way. She had played too hard to get these past weeks with her telephone tag, her scheduling problems, her out-of-town travel. "She was a victim's wife, for Christ's sake," he had vented to Nancy, "not a goddamned suspect! Show some fucking cooperation, why don't you?" Then, while he was in the middle of being blessed out by Sue Sanchez over his Al Haig, "I'm in charge here" performance at the press conference, wifey rang his mobile just to let him know he needed to be punctual as her time was extremely limited. And the topper—she greeted them at Apartment 9B with a faraway look of condescension, like they were carpet cleaners there to roll up one of the Persians.

"I don't know what I can tell you that I haven't already told the police," Helen Swisher said as she led them through a palladium arch into the living room, a formidable expanse overlooking Park Avenue. Will stiffened at the decor and furnishings—all this fineness, a lifetime's salary shoveled into one room, decorators-gone-wild heirloom furniture, chandeliers and rugs, each the price of a good car.

"Nice place," Will said, his eyebrows arched.

"Thank you," she replied coolly. "David liked to read the Sunday paper in here. I've just put it on the market."

They sat and she immediately began fiddling with the band of her wristwatch, a signal they were on the clock. David sized her up quickly, a miniprofile. She was attractive in a horsey kind of way, her looks enhanced by perfect hair and a designer suit. Swisher was Jewish, she wasn't, probably a Wasp from old money, a banker and a lawyer who met, not through social circles, but on a deal. This gal wasn't a cold fish, she was frozen. Her lack of visible grief didn't mean she wasn't attached to her husband—she probably liked him fine—it was simply a reflection of her ice-in-the-veins nature. If he ever had to sue someone, someone he really hated, this was the woman he'd want.

She made eye contact exclusively with him. Nancy might as well have been invisible. Subordinates, such as the law associates at Helen's white-shoe firm, were implements, background features. It was only when Nancy opened her notebook that Helen acknowledged her presence with a dimpling scowl.

Will thought it was pointless to start with manufactured sympathy. He wasn't selling and she wasn't buying. Right out of the box he asked, "Do you know any Hispanic men who drive a blue car?"

"Goodness!" she replied. "Has your investigation become that narrowed?"

He ignored the question. "Do you?"

"The only Hispanic gentleman I know is our former dog walker, Ricardo. I have no idea if he owns a car."

"Why former?"

"I gave David's dog away. Funnily enough, one of the EMTs that morning from Lenox Hill Hospital took a shine to him."

"Can I get Ricardo's contact information?" Nancy asked.

"Of course," she sniffed.

Will asked, "If you had a dog walker, why was your husband walking it the morning he was killed?"

"Ricardo only came in the afternoon, while we were at work. David walked him otherwise."

"Same time every morning?"

"Yes. About five A.M."

"Who knew his routine?"

"The night doorman, I suppose."

"Did your husband have any enemies? The kind who might want him dead?"

"Absolutely not! I mean, anyone in the banking business has adversaries, that's normal, but David was involved in standard, generally amiable transactions. He was a mild person," she said, as if mildness was not a virtue.

"Did you receive the e-mail of the updated victims' list?"

"Yes, I looked at it."

"And?"

Her face contorted. "Well, of course neither David or I knew anyone on that list!"

There he had it, an explanation for her lack of cooperation. Apart from the inconvenience of losing a reliable spouse, she loathed the association with the Doomsday case. It was high-profile but low-rent. Most of the victims were anonymously underclass. David's murder was bad for her image, bad for her career, her Waspy partners whispering about her while they peed in their urinals and putted on their greens. On some level she was probably angry at David for getting his neck slashed.

"Las Vegas," he said suddenly.

"Las Vegas," she countered suspiciously.

"Who did David know from Las Vegas?"

"He asked the same question when he saw the postmark, the night before he was killed. He couldn't recall anyone offhand and neither can I."

"We've been trying to get his client list from his bank without success," Nancy said.

She addressed Will. "With whom have you been dealing?"

"The general council's office," he said.

"I know Steve Gartner very well. I'll call him if you like."

"That would be helpful."

Will's phone started to play its inappropriate tune and he unapologetically answered it, listened for a few seconds then rose for privacy and moved toward a cluster of chairs and sofas in a far corner, leaving the two women uncomfortably alone.

Nancy self-consciously flipped through her notebook, trying to look importantly occupied, but it was clear she felt like a warthog next to this lioness. Helen simply stared at the face of her watch as if doing so would magically make these people disappear.

Will clicked off and strode back. "Thank you. We've got to go."

That was it. Quick handshakes and out. Cold stares and no love lost.

In the elevator, Will said, "She's a sweetheart."

Nancy agreed. "She's a bitch."

"We're going to City Island."

"Why?"

"Victim number nine."

She almost pulled a muscle snapping her neck to look up at him.

The door opened at the lobby.

"The game's changed, partner. It doesn't look like there's going to be a victim number ten. The police are holding a suspect, Luis Camacho, a thirty-two-year-old Hispanic male, five-foot-eight, 160 pounds."

"Really!"

"Apparently he's a flight attendant. Guess what route he flies?"

"Las Vegas?"

"Las Vegas."

Confluence.

The word had been rattling around his mind, and when he was alone it would occasionally roll off his lips and make him tremble.

He had been preoccupied by the confluence, as had his brethren, but he was convinced he was more affected than the others, a wholly imagined position since one did not openly discuss such matters.

Of course, there had long been an awareness that this seventh day would come, but the feelings of portent had dramatically escalated when in the month of Maius a comet appeared, and now, two months later, its fiery tail persisted in the night sky.

Prior Josephus was awake before the bell rang for Lauds. He threw off his rough coverlet, stood and relieved himself in his chamber pot, then splashed his face with a handful of cool water from a basin. One chair, one table, and a cot with a straw pallet on a hard earthen floor. This was his windowless cell; his white tunic of undyed wool and his leather sandals were his only earthly possessions.

And he was happy.

In his forty-fourth year he was already balding and a little fat, owing to his affection for the strong ale that poured from the barrels of the abbey brewery. The baldness on his dome made it easier to maintain his tonsure, and Ignatius, the barber surgeon, made fast work of him every month, sending him on his way with a pat to his raw pate and a brotherly wink.

He had entered the monastery at age fifteen, and as an oblate was restricted to the remotest parts of the monastery until his initiation was complete and he advanced to full membership. Once inside, he knew he would live here forever and die within its walls. His feelings of love for God and his brotherly bond with the members of his community—his famulus Christi—were so strong he often wept with joy, tempered only by the guilt of knowing how fortunate he was compared to the many wretched souls on the isle.

He knelt by his bed and, following the tradition that St. Benedict himself had begun, began his spiritual day with the Lord's Prayer in order that, as Benedict had written, "the thorns of scandal that are wont to arise" would be cleansed from the community.

> *Pater noster, qui es in caelis:*
> *sanctificetur Nomen Tuum;*
> *adveniat Regnum Tuum;*
> *fiat voluntas Tua . . .*

He finished, crossed himself, and at that moment the abbey bell chimed. Suspended in the tower by a heavy rope, the bell had been fashioned almost two decades earlier by Matthias, the community blacksmith and a dear friend of Josephus, long dead from the pox. The melodious clang of the clapper between the beaten iron plates always reminded Josephus of the hearty laugh of the ruddy-cheeked blacksmith. He wanted to dwell for a moment on his friend's memory but the word *confluence* invaded his thoughts instead.

There were chores to be done before Lauds, and as the prior of the community he was charged with overseeing the work of novices and young ministers. Outside the dormitory it was pleasantly cool, inky dark, and when he breathed the moist air through his nose it tasted of the sea. In the stables, the cows were laden with milk, and he was pleased the young men were already attending to their udders by the time he arrived.

"Peace be with you, brother," he quietly said to each man, touching them on the shoulder as he passed. Then he froze, realizing there were seven cows and seven men.

Seven.

God's mysterious number.

The Book of Genesis alone was ripe with sevens: the seven heavens, the seven thrones, the seven seals, the seven churches. The walls of Jericho crumbled on the seventh day of the siege. In Revelations, seven spirits of God were sent forth into the earth. There were exactly seven generations from David to the birth of Christ, the Lord.

And now they were on the verge of the seventh day of the seventh month of Anno Domini 777, confluent with the advent of the comet that Paulinus, the abbey astronomer, had warily named Cometes Luctus, the Comet of Lamentation.

And then there was the matter of Santesa, wife of Ubertus the stonecutter, nearing the end of her worrisome term.

How could everyone appear so placid?

What, in the Lord's name, would tomorrow bring?

The church at Vectis Abbey was a grand work in progress, a source of immense pride. The original timber and thatch church, built nearly a century earlier, was a sturdy structure that had held up well to the harsh coastal winds and the lashings of sea storms. The history of the church and the abbey were well known, as some of the older ministers had personally served with some of the founding brothers. Indeed, in his youth one of their number, the ancient Alric, now too infirm to even leave his cell for mass, had met Birinus, the exalted Bishop of Dorchester.

Birinus, a Frank, came to Wessex in the year 634, having been made a bishop by Pope Honorius with a commission to convert the heathen West Saxons. He soon found himself an arbiter of a civil war in this godforsaken land and endeavored to forge an alliance between the loutish West Saxon king, Cynegils, and Oswald, King of Northumbria, an entirely more agreeable sort, a Christian. But Oswald would not ally himself with a nonbeliever, and Birinus, sensing a glorious opportunity, persuaded Cynegils to convert to Christianity, personally pouring baptismal water over his filthy hair in the name of Christ.

A pact with Oswald followed, then a long peace, and Cynegils in gratitude gave Dorchester to Birinus as his episcopal see and became his benefactor. Birinus, for his part, embarked on a campaign to found abbeys in the tradition of St. Benedict throughout the southern lands, and when the charter for Vectis Abbey was established in 686, the year of the great plague, the last of the Isles of Britannia came to the bosom of Christianity. Cynegils bequeathed to the Church sixty hides of good land near running water on this island enclave, an easy sail from the Wessex shores.

Now it was up to Aetia, the present Bishop of Dorchester, to keep the silver flowing from royal households to Church interests. He had impressed on King Offa of Mercia the spiritual benefits of funding the next phase of glory for Vectis Abbey—its conversion from wood to masonry—to praise and honor the Lord. "For after all," the bishop had murmured to the king, "prestige is measured not in oak, but in stone."

In a quarry not far from the abbey walls, Italian stonecutters had been laboring for the past two years, chiseling blocks of sandstone and oxcarting them to the abbey, where the cementarii mortared them in place, slowly erecting the church walls using the existing timber structure as a frame. Throughout the day the incessant metallic clanging of chisel on stone filled the air, silenced only during the Offices, when the ministers filled the Sanctuary for quiet prayer and contemplation.

Josephus swept back through the dormitory on his way to Lauds and gently opened the door of Alric's cell to make sure the old monk had made it through the night. He was heartened to hear snoring, so he whispered a prayer over the curled body, slipped out and entered the church through the night stair.

Fewer than a dozen candles lit the Sanctuary, but the light was sufficient to prevent mishaps. High above, in the dark, Josephus could make out the shapes of fruit bats darting among the rafters. The brothers were standing on either side of the altar in two opposing ranks, patiently waiting for the abbot to arrive. Josephus sidled next to Paulinus, a small nervous monk, and had they not heard the heavy main door creaking open, they might have exchanged a furtive greeting. But the abbot was approaching and they dared not speak.

Abbot Oswyn was an imposing man with long limbs and large shoulders who had spent much of his life a head taller than his brethren, but in his later years he seemed to shrink as a painful curving of his spine stooped him. As a result of his malady his eyes were permanently cast downward at the earth and in recent years he found it nearly impossible to gaze up toward the heavens. Over time his disposition had darkened, which had inarguably cast a pall over the fraternity of the community.

The ministers could hear him shuffling into the Sanctuary, his sandals scraping the floorboards. As usual, his head was sharply lowered and the candlelight glinted off his shiny scalp and his snowy white fringe.

The abbot slowly climbed the altar stairs, grimacing at the effort, and took his place atop the altar under its canopied ciborium of polished walnut. He placed his palms flat on the smooth cool wood of the tabula and with a high, nasal voice intoned: *"Aperi, Domine, os meum ad benedicendum nomen sanctum tuum."*

The monks prayed and chanted in their two ranks, calling and responding, their voices melding and sonorously filling the Sanctuary. How many thousands of times had Josephus given voice to these prayers? Yet today he felt a particular need to call out to Christ for his mercy and forgiveness, and tears formed when he called out the last line of Psalmus 148.

"Alleluja, laudate Dominum de caelis, alleluja, alleluja!"

The day was warm and dry and the abbey was a beehive of activity. Josephus strode across the freshly scythed lawn of the cloisters quadrangle to make his morning rounds, checking on the critical functions of the community. At last count there were eighty-three souls at Vectis Abbey, not counting the day laborers, and each one expected to see the prior at least once in the day. He was not given to random inspections; he had his routine and it was known to all.

He started with the masons to see how the edifice was progressing, and noted ominously that Ubertus had not reported for work. He sought out Ubertus's eldest son, Julianus, a strapping teenage lad whose brown skin gleamed with sweat, and learned that Santesa's labor had begun. Ubertus would return when he was able.

"Better it is today than tomorrow, eh? That's what people are saying," Julianus told the prior, who solemnly nodded his agreement and asked to be informed of the birth when it occurred.

Josephus went on his way to the cellarium to check on meat and vegetable stores, then the granary to make sure the mice hadn't gotten into the wheat. At the brewery, he was obliged to sample from each barrel, and as he seemed unsure of the taste, he sampled again. Then he went to the kitchen adjoining the refectory to see if the sisters and their young novices were in good cheer. Next he toured the lavatorium to see if fresh water was properly flowing into the hand-washing trough, and then the outhouses, where he held his nose while inspecting the trench.

In the vegetable gardens, he checked how well the brothers were keeping the rabbits away from the tender shoots. Then he skirted the goat meadow to inspect his favorite building, the Scriptorium, where Paulinus was presiding over six ministers hunched at tables, making fine copies of *The Rule of St. Benedict* and the *Holy Bible*.

Josephus loved this chamber above all because of its silence and the nobleness of the vocation that was practiced within, and also because he found Paulinus to be pious and learned to a fault. If there were a question on the heavens or the seasons or any natural phenomenon, then Paulinus was ready with a thorough, patient, and correct interpretation. Idle conversation was frowned upon by the abbot, but Paulinus was an excellent source of purposeful discourse, which Josephus greatly valued.

The prior crept into the Scriptorium, taking great care not to interrupt the concentration of the copyists. The only sounds were the quills pleasantly scratching on vellum. He nodded to Paulinus, who acknowledged him with a hint of a smile. A greater show of camaraderie would not have been appropriate, as outward displays of affection were reserved for the Lord. Paulinus gestured him outside with the crook of his finger.

"Good day to you, Brother," Josephus said, squinting in the midday glare.

"And also to you." Paulinus looked worried. "So, tomorrow is the day of reckoning," he whispered.

"Yes, yes," Josephus agreed. "It has finally come."

"Last night I watched the comet for a long while."

"And?"

"As midnight approached its beam became bright and red. The color of blood."

"What does this mean?"

"I believe it to be an ominous sign."

"I have heard the woman has begun her labor," Josephus offered hopefully.

Paulinus folded his arms tightly across his habit and pursed his lips dismissively. "And you suppose that because she has given birth nine times before, this child will be delivered to the world quickly? On the sixth day of the month rather than the seventh?"

"Well, one might hope so," Josephus said.

"It was the color of blood," Paulinus insisted.

The sun was getting high, and Josephus made haste to complete his circuit before the community assembled back in the Sanctuary for prayers at Sext. He rushed past the Sisters' Dormitory and entered the Chapter House, where the rows of pine benches were empty, awaiting the appointed hour when the abbot would read a chapter of *The Rule of St. Benedict* to the assembled community. A sparrow had gotten in and was urgently flapping overhead, so he left the doors open in hopes it would find its freedom. At the rear of the house he rapped his knuckles on the entrance to the adjoining private chamber of the abbot.

Oswyn was sitting at the study table, his head hovering over his Bible. Golden shafts of light shone through the glazed windows and struck the table in a perfect angle to make the holy book appear to be glowing fiery orange. Oswyn straightened himself enough to make eye contact with his prior. "Ah, Josephus. How are things at the abbey today?"

"They are well, Father."

"And what progress on our church, Josephus? How is the second arch on the eastern wall?"

"The arch is nearing completion. However, Ubertus the stonecutter is absent today."

"Is he not well?"

"No, his wife has begun her labor."

"Ah, yes. I recall." He waited for his prior to say something more, but Josephus remained silent. "You are concerned by this birth?"

"It is perhaps inauspicious."

"The Lord will protect us, Prior Josephus. Of this, you can be assured."

"Yes, Father. I was wondering, nevertheless, whether I should venture to the village."

"Toward what end?" Oswyn asked sharply.

"In the event a minister is required," Josephus said meekly.

"You know my views on leaving the cloisters. We are servants of Christ, Josephus, not servants of man."

"Yes, Father."

"Have the villagers sought us out?"

"No, Father."

"Then I would discourage your involvement." He pushed his bent body up from the chair. "Now, let us go to Sext and let us join with our brothers and sisters to praise the Lord."

* * *

Vespers, the sunset Evening Office, was Josephus's dearest of the day since the abbot allowed Sister Magdalena to play the psaltery as accompaniment to their prayers. Her long fingers plucked the lute's ten strings, and the perfection of pitch and precision of cadence were testament, he was sure, to the magnificence of Christ Almighty.

After the service, the brothers and sisters filed out of the Sanctuary and made toward their respective dormitories, past the blocks of stone, rubble, and the scaffolding left for the day by the Italians. In his cell, Josephus tried to clear his mind for a period of contemplation but was distracted by small sounds in the distance. Was someone approaching the walls? Was news of the birth forthcoming? At any moment he half expected the guest bell to be rung.

Before he knew it, Compline was upon him and it was time to reconvene in the church for the last service of the day. Because of his preoccupations, his meditation had been unsuccessful, and for this transgression he prayed for forgiveness. When the last strains of the last chant were uttered, he watched the abbot carefully descending from the high altar and thought that Oswyn had never appeared older or more frail.

Josephus slept fitfully, roiled by disturbing dreams of bloodred comets and infants with glowing red eyes. In his dream, people were gathering in a village square, summoned by a bell ringer with one strong arm and one withered one. The bell ringer was distraught and sobbing, and then, in a start, Josephus awoke and realized the man was Oswyn.

Someone was thumping at his door.

"Yes?"

From the other side of the door he heard a young voice. "Prior Josephus, I am sorry to wake you."

"Enter."

It was Theodore, a novice who was charged this night with attending the gatehouse.

"Julianus, the son of Ubertus the stonecutter, has come. He pleads that you go with him to his father's cottage. His mother is having a hard labor and may not survive."

"The child has not yet been born?"

"No, Father."

"What hour is it, my son?" Josephus swung his feet onto the floor and rubbed his eyes.

"The eleventh."

"Then it will soon be the seventh day."

The path to the village was rutted from the wheels of ox-carts, and in the moonless dark Josephus almost turned his ankles. He labored to keep up with the long sure strides of Julianus so he could more readily follow the lad's hulking black shape and stay on the path. The cool light wind carried the sounds of chirping crickets and calling gulls. Ordinarily, Josephus would have relished this night music, but tonight he hardly noticed.

As they neared the first cottage of the stonecutters' village, Josephus heard the bell ringing back at the abbey, the call for the Night Office.

Midnight.

Oswyn would be told of his foray, and Josephus was quite sure he would not be pleased.

Being the middle of the night, the village was eerily active. In the distance Josephus could see oil lamps glowing from open doors of tiny thatched cottages and torches moving up and down the lane, signs of people out and about. As he drew closer it was clear that the center of activity was Uber-tus's cottage. Villagers milled outside it, their torches casting fantastic elongated shadows. Three men were crowding the door, peering in, their backs forming a phalanx blocking the entrance. Josephus overheard feverish chattering in Italian and snippets of Latin prayer the stonecutters had over-heard in the church and stolen like magpies.

"Make way, the Prior of Vectis is here," Julianus declared, and the men withdrew, crossing themselves and bowing.

A scream erupted from inside, a woman in agony, a cur-dling horrible cry that almost pierced the flesh. Josephus felt his legs weaken and uttered, "Merciful God!" before forcing himself to cross the threshold.

The cottage was crowded with family and villagers, so packed that for Josephus to enter two had to leave to make room. Seated by the hearth was Ubertus, a man as hard as the limestone he cut, slumped, his head in his hands.

The stonecutter cried out, his voice thin from exhaustion, "Prior Josephus, thank God you have come. Please, pray for Santesa! Pray for us all!"

Santesa was lying in the best bed surrounded by women. She was on her side, her knees up against her bulging belly, her shift pulled high, exposing mottled thighs. Her face was the color of sugar beets, contorted and almost lacking humanity.

There was something animalistic about her, Josephus thought. Perhaps the Devil had already taken her for his own.

A plump woman he recognized as the wife of Marcus, the foreman of the cementarii, seemed to be in charge of the birthing. She was positioned at the foot of the bed, her head darting in and out from under Santesa's shift, blathering in Italian and barking orders to Santesa. The woman's hair was braided and bobbed to keep it out of her eyes, her hands and smock covered in pink, gelatinous material. Josephus noted that Santesa's belly was glistening from reddish ointment and that the bloody foot of a crane was on the bed. Witchcraft. This, he could not condone.

The midwife turned to acknowledge the presence of the minister and simply said, "It is breeched."

Josephus edged up behind her, and the midwife suddenly lifted the shift to let him see a tiny purple foot dangling from Santesa's body.

"Is it a boy or a girl?"

The woman lowered the shift. "A boy."

Josephus gulped, made the sign of the cross and fell to his knees.

"In nomine patre, et filii, et spiritus sancti . . ."

But as he prayed, he wished with all his might for a still birth.

* * *

On a raw November night, nine months earlier, a gale blew outside the stonecutter's cottage. Ubertus stoked the fire for the last time and went from cot to cot checking on his off-spring, two or three to a mattress except for Julianus, who was old enough for his own pallet of straw. Then he crawled into the master's bed beside his wife. She was on the verge of sleep, drained after another long day of heavy toils.

Ubertus tugged the heavy woolen coverlet to his chin. He had carried the cloth with him from Umbria in a chest of cedarwood, and it served him well in these harsh climes. He felt Santesa's warm body beside him and laid a hand on her softly heaving chest. The urge was there and his hardness would have to be satisfied. By God, he deserved some plea-sure in this difficult, earthly world. He slid his hand down and pulled her legs apart.

Santesa was no longer beautiful. Thirty-four years and nine children had taken their toll. She was puffy and hag-gard and she chronically scowled from the pain of rotting molars. But she was nothing if not dutiful, so when she became aware of her husband's intentions, she sighed and whispered only, "It is the time of the month to take note of the consequences."

He knew precisely what she meant.

Ubertus's mother had borne thirteen children; eight boys and five girls. Only nine of them had survived to adulthood. Ubertus was the seventh son, and as he grew he carried this mantle. If ever he had a seventh son, that boy, by legend, would be a sorcerer, a conjurer of dark forces: a warlock, some said. Everyone in their hillside village knew about the lore of a seventh son of a seventh son, but no one, truth be told, had ever met one.

In his youth, Ubertus had been a lady's man and exploited the dangerous image of the potential locked within his loins. Perhaps he had used his status to bait Santesa, the prettiest girl in the village. Indeed, he and Santesa had teased each other over the years, but after the birth of their sixth son, Lucius, the teasing stopped and their sexual unions took on an air of gravity. Each of the next three births was the source of considerable trepidation. Santesa sought to foretell the sex of the babies by pricking her finger with a thorn and letting a drop of her blood fall into a bowl of springwater. A sinking drop indicated a boy, but sometimes the drop sank and sometimes it floated. Blessedly, each child had been a girl.

Ubertus rammed himself in. She caught her breath and whispered, "I pray it will be another girl."

At her bedside, deep into the night, the situation was becoming more grave despite Josephus's urgent prayers. Santesa was too weak to scream and her breathing was shallow. The tiny protruding foot was getting darker, the color of the deep blue clay the abbey potters favored.

Finally, the midwife declared that something must be done or all would be lost. There was heated debate, then a consensus: the baby must be forcibly extracted. The midwife would reach in with both hands, grab each leg and pull as hard as was necessary. This maneuver would in all likelihood destroy the baby, but the mother might be spared. To do nothing would condemn both to certain death.

The midwife turned to Josephus for his blessing.

He nodded. It must be done.

Ubertus stood beside the bed, looking down on this catastrophe. His hugely muscled arms hung weakly at his side. "I beseech you, Lord!" he cried out, but no one was sure whether he was praying for his wife or his son.

The midwife began her traction. It was apparent by the strain on her face that she was exerting great effort. Santesa muttered something unintelligible but she was beyond pain.

The midwife loosened her grip and withdrew her hands to wipe them dry on her smock and catch her breath. She regripped the legs and began again.

This time there was movement. It emerged slowly. Knees, thighs, a penis, buttocks. Then suddenly it was free. The birth canal yielded to the large head, and the boy was wholly in the hands of the midwife.

It was a large baby, well-proportioned, but clay-blue and lifeless. As every man, woman, and child in the room watched in awe, the placenta squirted out and thudded onto the ground. With that, the baby's chest spasmed and it inhaled. Then another breath. And within moments the blue boy was pink and squealing like a piglet.

At the moment life came to the boy, death came to his mother. She took her last breath and her body went still.

Ubertus roared in grief and grabbed the infant from the midwife.

"This is not my son!" he screamed. "It is the Devil's!"

He moved fast, dragging the placenta along the dirt floor, using his shoulders to force his way through the crowd and out the door. Josephus was too stunned to react. He sputtered but no words came out of his mouth.

Ubertus stood in the road holding his son in his stone-hard hands and he wailed like an animal. Then, as torch-bearing villagers looked on, he grabbed the umbilical cord and swung the baby high over his head as if he were wielding a sling.

He brought the small body crashing down hard onto the earth.

"One!" he shouted.

He swung it over his head and smashed it down again.

"Two!"

And over and over: "Three! Four! Five! Six! Seven!"

Then he dropped the bloody broken carcass onto the lane and numbly shuffled back into the cottage.

"It is done. I have killed it."

He couldn't fathom why no one was paying him any mind.

Instead, all eyes were on the midwife, who was hunched over the lifeless Santesa, frantically groping between her legs.

There was a shock of ginger hair showing.

Then a forehead.

And a nose.

Josephus watched in amazement, scarcely believing his eyes. Another child was springing from a lifeless womb.

"Mirabile dictu!" he muttered.

The midwife grimaced and pulled the chin free, then a shoulder and a long thin body. It was another boy, and without any prodding it instantly began breathing, strong, clear breaths.

"A miracle!" a man said, and this was repeated by everyone.

Ubertus stumbled forward and glassily took in the spectacle.

"This is my *eighth* son!" he cried. "Oh, Santesa, you made twins!" He warily touched its cheek as one might touch a boiling pot.

The infant squirmed in the hands of the midwife but did not cry.

Nine months earlier, when Ubertus had finished planting his seed, his spray had shot through Santesa's womb. That month, she had produced not one but two eggs.

The second egg fertilized became the baby who now lay shattered on a cart path.

The first egg fertilized, the seventh son, became the ginger-haired boy who now held every soul in the room spellbound.

As an only child growing up in Lexington, Massachusetts, Mark Shackleton was rarely frustrated. His
doting middle-class parents satisfied every whim and he
grew up with only a passing relationship with the word no.
Nor was his inner life disturbed by feelings of frustration,
since his quick, analytical mind sliced through problems
with an efficiency that made learning nearly effortless.

Dennis Shackleton, an aerospace engineer at Raytheon, was
proud that he'd passed on math genes to his son. At Mark's
fifth birthday party, a family affair in their tidy split-level,
Dennis produced a clean sheet of tracing paper and announced, "Pythagorean Theorem!" The skinny boy grabbed
a fat crayon and felt the eyes of his grandparents, aunts, and
uncles follow him as he approached the dining room table,
drew a big triangle and underneath it wrote: $a2 + b2 = c2$.
"Good!" his father exclaimed, pushing his heavy black
glasses up the bridge of his nose, "Now what's this?" he
asked, jabbing a finger at the long leg of the triangle. The
grandfathers chuckled as the boy screwed up his face for a
moment then exploded with: "The hippopotamus!"

Mark's earliest frustrations came as a teenager when he
became aware that his body had not developed as robustly
as his mind. He felt superior—no, he *was* superior—to the
jocks and the goofballs who populated his high school, but
the girls couldn't see beyond skinny legs and a pigeon chest to
the inner Mark, a soaring intellect, scintillating conversation-
alist, and budding writer who constructed elaborate science

fiction stories about alien races conquering their adversaries with superior intelligence rather than brute strength. If only the cute girls with pillowy chests would talk to him instead of giggling when he gangled through the halls or eagerly pumped his hand into the air from the front row of class.

The first time a girl said no to him, he vowed it would be the last. In his sophomore year, when he finally mustered the courage to ask Nancy Kislik to a movie, she looked at him strangely and coldly said, "No," so he shut down that part of himself for years. He threw himself into the parallel universe of Math Club and Computer Club, where he was coolest of the uncool, first among equals. Numbers never said no to him. Or lines of software code. Not until well after grad school at MIT, when he was a young employee at a database security company, flush with stock options and a convertible, and dated a plain Jane systems analyst, did he mercifully score for the first time.

Now, Mark paced nervously in his kitchen, kinetically transforming himself into his alter ego and nom de plume, Peter Benedict, man about town, gambler extraordinaire, Hollywood screenwriter. An entirely different sort of man than Mark Shackleton, government employee, computer geek. He took a few deep breaths and knocked back the last of his lukewarm coffee. *Today's the day, today's the day, today's the day.* He psyched himself up, praying almost, until his reverie was halted by the hated reflection in the glass of the deck sliders. Mark, Peter, it didn't make a difference. He was slight, balding, and bony-nosed. He tried to shake it but an unpleasant word crept in: pathetic.

He had begun work on his screenplay, *Counters,* shortly after his meeting at ATI. The thought of Bernie Schwartz and his African masks made him queasy but the man had virtually commissioned a script about card counters, hadn't he? The ATI experience had been gut-wrenching. He loved his rejected script with the kind of affection lavished on a firstborn but had a new plan now: he'd sell the second script then use it as leverage to resurrect the old one. He swore he would never let it die on the vine.

So he threw himself into the project. Every evening when he got home from work and every weekend he pecked out the action sequences and the lines of dialogue, and in three months it was done—and he thought it was more than good, that it was maybe even great.

As he conceived it, the film would be first and foremost a vehicle for major stars who, he imagined, would approach him on the set—the Constellation?—and tell him how much they loved the lines he had put on their lips. The story had it all: intrigue, drama, sex appeal, all set in the high-stakes world of casino gambling and cheating. ATI would sell it for millions and he would trade his life in an underground lab in the middle of the desert, with his life savings of about 130 grand, for the glittering world of a screenwriter, living in a grand house high in the Hollywood Hills, taking calls from directors, attending premiers, klieg lights sweeping the horizon. He wasn't fifty yet. He still had a future.

But first Bernie Schwartz had to say yes. Even the simple act of calling the man was complicated. Mark left for work too early and returned too late to connect with Bernie's office from home. Outside calls from work were impossible. When you worked deep underground in a bunker, there was no concept of popping outside to make a call on a cell phone, even if mobiles were permitted, which they weren't. That meant he literally had to take sick days to remain in Las Vegas to phone L.A. Too many more absences and his superiors were bound to ask questions and force him to get evaluated by the medical department.

He dialed the phone and waited till he heard the chant, "ATI, how may I direct your call?"

"Bernard Schwartz, please."

"One moment, please."

For the past couple of weeks the music on hold had been a Bach harpsichord work, soothing in a mathematical sort of way. Mark saw the musical patterns in his head and it helped relieve the stress of calling this loathsome but essential little man.

The music stopped. "This is Roz."

"Hi, Roz, this is Peter Benedict. Is Mr. Schwartz there?"

A pregnant pause, then, frostily, "Hello, Peter, no, he's away from his desk."

Frustration. "I've called seven times, Roz!"

"I'm aware of that, Peter. I've talked to you seven times."

"Do you know if he's read my script yet?"

"I'm not sure if he's gotten to it."

"You said you were going to check when I called last week."

"As of last week he hadn't."

"Do you think he'll read it this week?" he pleaded.

There was silence on the line. He thought he could hear the rapid-fire clicking of a ballpoint pen. Finally, "Look, Peter, you're a nice guy. I'm not supposed to say this, but we got the coverage of *Counters* from our readers and it wasn't good. It's a waste of your time to keep calling here. Mr. Schwartz is a very busy man and he's not going to represent this project."

Mark gulped and squeezed the phone so hard it hurt his hand.

"Peter?"

His throat was tight and it burned. "Thank you, Roz. I'm sorry I bothered you."

He hung up and let his knees buckle him onto the nearest chair.

It started as a tear from his left eye, then his right. As he wiped away the moisture, the pressure rose from below his diaphragm reached his chest and escaped his larynx as a single low rumbling sob. Then another and another until his shoulders were heaving and he was crying uncontrollably. Like a child, like a baby. No. *No.*

The desert sky turned coronation purple as Mark numbly walked into the Constellation, his right hand curled around a wad of cash in his pants. He plowed through the crowded lobby with a tunnel vision that blurred the periphery and set a clear path toward the Grand Astro Casino. As he crossed the threshold he hardly noticed the din of voices, the clanging and goofy musical tones of the slots and video poker machines. Instead, he heard blood throbbing in his ears, like a pulsing, heavy surf. Uncharacteristically, he paid no attention to the points of light on the planetary dome, with Taurus, Perseus, and Auriga directly overhead. He bore left through the valley of the slots and passed beneath Orion and Gemini on his way to Ursus Major, the Great Bear, where the high-stakes blackjack room beckoned.

There were a half-dozen $5,000 tables to choose from, and he picked the one where Marty, one of his favorite dealers, was working. Marty was a New Jersey transplant, his wavy brown hair pulled back into a neat little ponytail. Marty's eyes lit up when he saw him approaching. "Hey, Mr. Benedict! I got a nice chair for you!" Mark sat down and mumbled hello to the four other players, all men, all deadly serious. He pulled out his wad and traded it for $8,500 in chips. The stake was the largest Marty had ever seen from him. "Okay!" he said loudly, catching the ear of the pit boss nearby. "I hope you do real well tonight, Mr. B."

Mark stacked his chips and stared at them stupidly, his mind gummy. He bet the $500 minimum and played automatically for a few minutes, breaking even until Marty reshuffled and started a fresh deal. Then his head cleared as if he'd taken a whiff of smelling salts and he began to hear numbers pinging in his head like an audible beacon in the fog.

Plus three, minus two, plus one, plus four.

The count was calling out to him, and hypnotically he allowed himself for once to link the count to his bets. For the next hour he ebbed and flowed, retreating to the minimum bet on low counts and jacking the wager on high counts. His stack grew to $13,000, then $31,000, and he played on, hardly noticing that Marty was gone, replaced by some sourface named Sandra with nicotine-stained fingertips. A half hour later he hardly noticed that Sandra was shuffling more frequently. He hardly noticed that his stack had grown to over $60,000. He hardly noticed that his beer hadn't been refreshed. And he hardly noticed when the pit boss sidled up behind him with two security guards.

"Mr. Benedict," the pit boss said. "I wonder if you could come with us?"

Gil Flores moved back and forth with quick little steps like one of the Siberian tigers in Siegfried and Roy's old act. The meek humiliated man sitting before him could almost feel plumes of hot breath on his bald pate.

"What the fuck were you thinking of," Flores demanded. "Did you think we wouldn't spot this, Peter?"

Mark didn't answer.

"You're not talking to me? This isn't a fucking court of law. It's not like you're innocent till proven guilty. You are guilty, my friend. You basically fucked me up the ass and I do not like my sex that way."

A blank, mute stare.

"I think you should answer me. I really think you'd fucking better answer me."

Mark swallowed hard, a dry, difficult swallow that produced a comical *gulp*. "I'm sorry. I don't know why I did it."

Gil ran his hand through his thick black hair, mussing himself in exasperation. "How can an intelligent man say 'I don't know why I did something'? To me, that doesn't make any sense. Of course you know why you did it. Why did you do this?"

Mark looked at him finally and started to cry.

"Don't be crying at me," Flores warned. "I'm not your fucking mother." That said, he tossed a box of tissues into Mark's lap.

He dabbed his eyes. "I had a disappointment today. I was angry. I felt angry and this is how I reacted. It was stupid and I apologize. You can keep the money."

Flores had almost been mollified until the last concept, which threw him into a tizzy. "I can keep the money? You mean the money you stole from me? This is your solution?

To let me keep that which already fucking belongs to me!"

Mark winced at the shouting and needed another tissue.

The desk phone rang.

Flores picked it up and listened for a while. "You sure about this?" After a pause, he continued, "Of course. Absolutely."

He put the phone down and moved in front of Mark, making him crane his neck. "Okay, Peter, this is how we're going to handle this."

"Please don't report this to the police," Mark begged. "I'll lose my job."

"Would you please shut your mouth and listen to me. This is not a conversation. I'm going to talk and you're going to listen. That's the asymmetry that your actions have brought upon you."

A whisper. "Okay."

"Number one: you're permanently banned from the Constellation. If you walk into this casino again you will be arrested and we will seek your prosecution for criminal trespass. Number two: you are leaving with the $8,500 you walked in with. Not a penny more, not a penny less. Number three: you violated a trust and a friendship so I want you to get the fuck out of my office and out of my casino right now."

Mark blinked at him.

"Why are you still here?"

"You're not going to call the police?"

"Were you not listening to me?"

"And you're not going to have me banned at other casinos?"

Flores shook his head in amazement. "Are you giving me ideas? Believe me, I could think of a lot of things I'd like to do to you including sending you to an orthopedic surgeon. Get lost, Peter Benedict." He spit out the last words: "You are persona non grata."

From the penthouse, Victor Kemp watched the stoop-shouldered man push himself out of a chair and shuffle out the door, and on other video feeds he followed him, accompanied by security as he made his way back into the casino, where he scanned the planetarium dome a final time in a last-ditch effort to spot Coma Berineces, through the lobby, and out into the parking lot and the authentic night sky.

Kemp freshened his drink and spoke out loud in a rich tenor to the colossal empty living room: "Victor, you will never make a buck trusting people."

Mark slowly drove his Corvette down the Strip in stop-and-go traffic. It was three hours till midnight and the town was getting busy as people were settling on the evening's entertainment. He was heading south, the Constellation in his rearview mirror, but he had no particular destination. He tried not to think about what had just happened. He was cast out. Banished. The Constellation was his home away from home and he could never return. What had he done?

He didn't want to be alone in his house, he wanted to be in a casino bar, with giddy action and loopy slot-machine jingles to distract him. Thank God Flores hadn't put the word out and blasted his photo to every casino in the state. He had caught a break. So, the question he mulled as he jerked down the Strip was: where should he go? He could drink anywhere. He could play blackjack anywhere. What he needed was a place with the right atmosphere to suit his peculiar temperament—a place like the Constellation, which had an intellectual component, albeit a token one.

He passed Caesars then the Venetian, but they were too fakey and Disneylike. Harrahs and the Flamingo left him cold. The Bellagio was too flash. New York New York, another theme park. He was running out of Strip. The MGM Grand was a possibility. He didn't love it but he didn't hate it either. At the corner of Tropicana he almost made a left to swing into the MGM parking lot. But then he saw it and knew it was going to be his new place.

Of course, he had seen it before, thousands of times, since after all it was a Las Vegas landmark. Thirty stories of black glass, the Luxor pyramid rose 350 feet into the desert sky. An obelisk and the Great Sphinx of Giza marked the entrance, but the true marker was at the apex, a spotlight pointing straight upward, piercing the darkness, the brightest beacon on the planet, putting out an insane forty-one gigacandela of luminosity, more than enough to blind an unsuspecting pilot making an approach into McCarran. He drove toward the glass edifice and drank in the mathematical perfection of the triangular faces. His mind filled with the geometrical equations of pyramids and triangles, and then a name tenderly slipped from his lips.

"Pythagoras."

Before Mark settled into the sedate bar at the casino-level steakhouse, he gave the property a once-over as if he were a prospective house buyer. It wasn't the Constellation but it punched a lot of tickets. He liked the bold hieroglyph designs on the gold, red, and lapis carpets, the towering lobby recreation of the temple statues of Luxor, and the museum quality mock-up of Tutankhamen's tomb. Yes, it was kitschy but this was Vegas, for heaven's sake, not the Louvre.

He drank his second Heineken and pondered his next move. He had located the high-limit rooms behind frosted glass partitions to the rear of the casino floor. He had money in his pocket and knew that even if he refused to acknowledge the count in his head he could still spend a few diverting hours at the tables. Tomorrow was Friday, a workday, and his alarm would sound at five-thirty. But tonight there was something titillating about being in a new casino; it was like a first date, and he was feeling shy and stimulated.

The bar was nearing capacity, clumps of diners awaiting tables, couples and groups spouting animated conversation and throaty laughter. He had chosen the empty middle stool in a row of three and as the alcohol took effect wondered why the stools on either side of him remained unoccupied. Was he radioactive, tainted? Did these people know he was a failed writer? Had they heard he was a card cheat? Even the bartender had treated him coolly, hardly making the effort for a decent tip. His mood darkened again. He drank the last of his beer fast and tapped the bar for another.

As the alcohol soaked into his brain he had a paranoid notion: what if they also knew his *real* secret? No, they were clueless, he decided contemptuously. You people have no idea, he thought angrily, no fucking idea. I know things you'll never know in your whole fucking insignificant lives.

To his right a busty woman in her forties leaning hard on the bar shrieked like a girl when the fat guy standing next to her touched the back of her neck with an ice cube. Mark swiveled to take in the little drama, and when he swiveled back a man was occupying the stool to his left.

"If someone did that to me I would split their lip," the man said.

Mark looked at him, startled. "I'm sorry, were you talking to me?" he asked.

"I was just saying, if a stranger did that to me, it would be all over, you know what I mean?"

The fat man and the lady with a cold neck were pawing each other, having a jolly time.

"I don't think they're strangers," Mark said.

"Maybe not. I'm just saying what I would have done."

The man was thin but extremely muscular, clean-shaven and black-haired, with soft fleshy lips and oily skin the color of hazelnuts. He was Puerto Rican with a strong island accent, casually dressed in black slacks and loose-fitting tropical shirt open to the breastbone. He had long manicured fingers, a square gold ring on each hand, and shiny gold chains around his neck. At most he was thirty-five. He extended a hand, and Mark had to grab it out of politeness. The ring seemed to weigh as much as the appendage. "Luis Camacho," the man said. "How you doin'?"

"Peter Benedict," Mark replied. "I'm doing okay."

Luis pointed emphatically at the floor. "When I'm in town, this is my favorite place. I love the Luxor, man."

Mark sipped his beer. There was never a good time for small talk, especially tonight. A blender whirred loudly.

Undeterred, Luis continued, "I like the way the rooms have sloping walls, you know on account of the pyramid. I think that's pretty cool, you know?" Luis waited for a reply, and Mark knew he had to fill the void or perhaps risk getting a split lip.

"I've never stayed here," he said.

"No? Which hotel you stayin' at?"

"I live in Vegas."

"No shit! A local! I love that! I'm here like twice a week and I almost never meet locals outside of the people who work here, you know?"

The bartender poured something thick from the blender into Luis's glass. "It's a frozen margarita," Luis declared proudly. "You want one?"

"No thanks. I've got a beer."

"Heineken," Luis observed. "Nice beer."

"Yep, nice beer," Mark replied stiffly. Unfortunately the beer was too fresh to excuse himself gracefully.

"So what kind of work do you do, Peter?"

Mark glanced sideways and saw that a comical frothy moustache had appeared on Luis's lip. So who would he be tonight? Writer? Gambler? Computer analyst? Like a slot machine, the possibilities rolled around until the wheels stopped. "I'm a writer," he answered.

"No shit! Like novels?"

"Films. I write screenplays."

"Wow! Have I seen any of your movies?"

Mark fidgeted on his stool. "They haven't been produced yet but I'm looking at a studio deal later this year."

"That's great, man! Like thrillers? Or funny comedies?"

"Thrillers mostly. Big budget stuff."

Luis took large slushy pulls on his drink. "So where do you get your ideas from?"

Mark gestured broadly. "All around. This is Vegas. If you can't get ideas in Vegas, you can't get them anywhere."

"Yeah, I see what you mean. Maybe I could read something you wrote. That would be cool."

The only way Mark could think to change the conversation was to ask a question himself. "So what do you do, Luis?"

"I'm a flight attendant, man. For US Air. This is my route, New York to Vegas. I go back and forth, back and forth." He moved his hand one way then another to illustrate the concept.

"You like it?" Mark asked automatically.

"Yeah, you know, it's okay. It's like a six hour flight so I get to overnight in Vegas a few times a week and stay here, so yeah, I like it pretty well. I could get paid more but I got good benefits and shit and they treat us with respect most of the time."

Luis's drink was spent. He waved the bartender over for another. "You sure I can't get you one, or another Heineken, Peter?"

Mark declined. "I've got to take off soon."

"You play the tables?" Luis asked.

"Yeah, I play blackjack sometimes," Mark answered.

"I don't like that game so much. I like the slots. But I'm a flight attendant, man, so I gotta watch out. What I do is limit myself to fifty bucks. I blow through that, I'm like done." He tensed a little then asked, "You bet big?"

"Sometimes."

Another margarita was served up. Luis seemed overtly nervous now and licked his lips to keep them moist. He took his wallet out and paid for his drinks with Visa. The wallet was slim but stuffed, and his New York driver's license slid out with the credit card. He absently let the license sit on the bar and placed his wallet over it and took a large gulp of his fresh margarita.

"So, Peter," he said finally. "You feel like betting big on me tonight?"

Mark didn't understand the question. It disoriented him. "I don't know what you mean."

Luis let his had move across the polished wood until his pinky touched Mark's hand ever so slightly. "You said you never saw what the rooms here look like. I could show you what mine looks like."

Mark felt faint. There was a legitimate chance he was going to pass out, fall right off the bar stool like a drunk in a slapstick. He could feel his heart start to pound and his breathing become rapid and shallow. His chest felt like it was mummy-wrapped. He straightened his spine and pulled his hand away, sputtering, "You think I—"

"Hey, man, I'm sorry. I thought, you know, that maybe you dug guys. It's no big deal." Then, almost under his breath, "Anyway, my boyfriend, John, would be happy I struck out."

No big deal? Mark thought violently. No fucking big deal! Hey, asshole, this is a major big deal, you fucking faggot! I don't want to hear about your fucking boyfriend! Leave me the fuck alone! This broadside blared inside his head as a cascade of visceral sensations piled on, dizziness, rising nausea, full-blown panic. He didn't think he'd be able to stand up and walk away without hitting the ground. The sounds of the restaurant and casino disappeared; he could only hear thumping in his chest.

Luis seemed alarmed by Mark's wide eyes and crazy stare. "Hey, man, chill, you know. You're a nice guy. I don't want to stress you out. I'm just going to hit the john, then we can just talk. Forget about the room thing. Cool?"

Mark didn't respond. He sat motionless trying to get his body under control. Luis grabbed his wallet and said, "Be right back. Watch my drink, okay?" He lightly patted Mark's back and tried to sound soothing. "Chill, okay?"

Mark watched as Luis disappeared around the corner, his slender hips packed tightly into his slacks. The sight distilled all his emotions into one: rage. His temperature soared. His temples burned. He tried to cool himself by chugging the rest of his cold beer.

After a few moments he thought he might be able to stand and he gingerly tried out his legs. So far, so good. His knees held. He wanted to leave fast, without a trace, so he hastily threw a twenty down on the bar, then another ten to make sure. The second bill landed on a card. It was Luis's license. Mark looked around then furtively picked it up.

Luis Camacho
189 Minnieford Avenue, City Island, New York,
    10464
Date of birth 1-12-77

He threw it back down on the bar and almost ran out. There was no need to write it down. It was already memorized.

After he left the Luxor, he drove home to his subdivision on a quiet six-unit cul-de-sac. The patio house was a pleasant off-white stucco with an orange tile roof. It sat on a small plot with rug-sized lawns. The backyard had a deck off the kitchen and a privacy fence for sun bathing. The interior was decorated with a bachelor's insouciance. When he was in the private sector earning a big high-tech salary in Menlo Park, he'd purchased expensive contemporary furniture for a modern apartment, minimalist pieces with sharp angles and splashes of primary colors. That same furniture in a Spanish-style ranch looked off, like rancid food. It was a soulless interior almost completely devoid of art, ornaments, and personalized touches.

Mark couldn't find a comfortable spot. He felt raw, his emotions a roiling acid bath. He tried to watch TV but after a few minutes turned it off in disgust. He picked up a magazine then threw it down on the coffee table, sending it sliding into a small framed photograph, which toppled. He picked it up and looked at it: the freshman roommates, twenty-fifth reunion. Zeckendorf's wife had it framed and sent it as a memento.

He wasn't sure why he had displayed it. These people meant nothing to him now. In fact, he'd despised them once. Especially Dinnerstein, his personal tormentor, who turned the ordinary traumas of being a socially backward freshman into exquisite torture with his constant ridicule and opprobrium. Zeckendorf wasn't much better. Will had been different from the others, but in a way he wound up being more disappointing.

In the photo, Mark stood woodenly, faking a smile, with Will's big arm over his shoulder. Will Piper, golden boy. Mark had spent the entire freshman year enviously watching how easily things came to him—women, friends, good times. Will always displayed a gentlemanly grace, even to him. When Dinnerstein and Zeckendorf ganged up on him, Will would defuse them with a joke or bat them away with his bear paw of a hand. For months he had fantasized that Will would ask to room with him sophomore year so he could continue to bask in his reflected glory. Then in the spring, right before midterms, something happened.

He had been in bed one night, trying to sleep. His three roommates were in the common room, drinking beer and playing music too loudly. In frustration, he shouted through the door, "Hey, you fuckers, I've got an exam tomorrow!"

"Did the dipshit call us fuckers?" Dinnerstein asked the others.

"I believe he did," Zeckendorf confirmed.

"Need to do something about that," Dinnerstein fumed.

Will turned the stereo down. "Leave him alone."

An hour later the three of them were beyond drunk: loose-jointed, room-heaving, inebriated—the kind of state where bad ideas seem good.

Dinnerstein had a roll of duct tape in his hand and was sneaking into Mark's bedroom. Mark was a heavy sleeper and he and Zeckendorf had no problem taping him to the top bunk, looping the film around and around until he looked like a mummy. Will watched from the doorway in a stupor, a stupid grin on his face, but did nothing to stop them.

When they were satisfied with their handiwork, they kept on drinking and laughing in the common room until they crashed out on the floor.

The next morning, when Will opened the bedroom door, Mark was cocooned to the bed, immobile in a gray wrap. Tears were streaming down his red face. He turned his head to Will. There was hatred and betrayal in his eyes. "I missed my exam." Then, "I peed myself."

Will cut the tape away with a Swiss Army knife and Mark heard him mutter a thick apology through his hangover, but the two of them never spoke again.

Will had gone on to fame and renown doing admirable things, while he had labored a lifetime in obscurity. Now, he remembered what Dinnerstein had said about Will that night in Cambridge: the most successful profiler of serial killers in history. The man. Infallible. What could people say about him? He clenched his eyelids tightly.

The darkness triggered something. Ideas started forming, and given the speed of his mind, they were forming quickly. As fast as the ideas crystallized, another part of his brain tried to melt them so they would wash away harmlessly.

He shook his head so vigorously it hurt, a dull, pounding pain. It was a primitive impulse, something a very young child might have done to shake evil things out of his head. *Stop thinking these thoughts!*

"Stop it now!"

Shocked, he stood up, realizing he had just shouted out loud.

He went outside onto the deck to calm himself by scanning the night sky. But it was unseasonably cool and swarms of wispy clouds obscured the constellations. He retreated to the kitchen, where he drank another beer while sitting uncomfortably at the dinette on a high-backed chair. The more he tried to squelch his mind, the more he left himself open to swirling feelings of anger and disgust rising like brackish floodwater.

Day from hell, he thought. Fucking day from hell.

It was after midnight. He suddenly thought of something that would make him feel better and dug his cell phone from his pocket. There was only one way to medicate this epidemic of a day. He took a breath and retrieved a number from the phone's address book. It rang through.

"Hello?" A woman's voice.

"Is this Lydia?"

Sweetly, "Who wants to know?"

"It's Peter Benedict, from the Constellation, you know, Mr. Kemp's friend."

"Area 51!" she squealed. "Hi, Mark!"

"You remembered my real name." This was good.

"Of course I do. You're my UFO buddy. I stopped working at McCarran, if you've been looking for me."

"Yeah. I noticed you weren't there anymore."

"I got a better day job in a clinic right off the Strip. I'm a receptionist. They do vasectomy reversals. I love it!"

"That's cool."

"So what's up with you?"

"Yeah, well I was wondering if you were free tonight?"

"Honey, I'm never free, but if the question is whether I'm available, I wish I were. I'm just heading over to the Four Seasons for a rendezvous then I've got to get my beauty sleep. I need to be at the clinic early. I'm sorry."

"Me too."

"Oh, sweetie! You call me back soon, you promise? Give me a little more notice and we can definitely hook up."

"Sure."

"You say hello to our little green friends, okay?"

He sat for a while longer and, thoroughly defeated, let it happen, succumbing to the emerging plan that was galvanizing in his mind. He'd need to find something first. What had he done with that business card? He knew he'd kept it, but where? He went searching, urgently covering all the usual places until he finally found it under a pile of clean socks in his dresser.

NELSON G. ELDER, CHAIRMAN AND CEO, DESERT LIFE INSURANCE COMPANY

His laptop was in the living room. Eagerly, he Googled Nelson G. Elder and started absorbing information like a sponge. His company, Desert Life, was publicly traded and had been tanking, its stock near a five-year low. The Yahoo message boards were awash in investor vitriol. Nelson Elder was not beloved by his shareholders and many had graphic suggestions about what he could do with his $8.6 million compensation package. Mark visited the company's website and clicked through to the corporate securities filings. He scrolled though screens of legalese and financials. He was an experienced small-time investor, familiar with corporate documents. Before long he had a comprehensive understanding of Desert Life's business model and financial condition.

He slapped the laptop shut. In a flash the plan rushed in, fully formed, every detail in vivid clarity. He blinked in recognition of its perfection.

I'm going to do it, he thought bitterly. I'm going to fucking do it! Years of frustration had built up like hot, gassy magma. Fuck the lifetime of inadequacies. Fuck the truckloads of jealousies and yearnings. And fuck the years of living under the weight of the Library. Vesuvius was blowing! He looked again at the reunion photograph and stared icily at Will's ruggedly handsome face. *And fuck you too.*

Every journey begins somewhere. Mark's began with a furious rummage through one of his kitchen drawers, the overstuffed one where he kept a grab bag of old computer components. Before he collapsed onto his bed, he found precisely what he was looking for.

At seven-thirty the next morning he was softly snoring at fifteen thousand feet. He rarely slept on his short commute to Area 51, but hadn't gotten to bed until very late. Below him the land was yellow and deeply fissured. From the air, the ridge of a long low mountain range resembled the spine of a desiccated reptile. The 737 had only been airborne for twelve minutes on its northwesterly course and it was already starting its approach. The plane looked like a stick of candy against the hazy blue sky, a white body with a nose-to-tail cheerful red stripe, the colors of the long defunct Western Airlines coopted by the defense contractor EG&G for its Las Vegas shuttle fleet. The tail numbers were registered to the U.S. Navy.

Descending toward the military field, the copilot radioed, "JANET 4 requesting clearance to land at Groom Lake, Runway 14 left."

JANET. Radio call sign for Joint Air Network for Employee

Transport. A spook name. The commuters called it otherwise: Just Another Non-Existent Terminal.

On wheels down, Mark awoke with a start. The plane braked hard and he instinctively pushed against his heels to take the pressure off his seat belt. He raised the window shade and squinted at the sun-baked scrubby terrain. He felt cramped and uncomfortable, sick to his stomach, and wondered if he looked as strange as he felt.

"Thought I was going to have to nudge you."

Mark turned to the fellow in the middle seat. He was from Russian Archives, a guy with a fat tush named Jacobs. "No need," Mark said as matter-of-factly as he could. "I'm good to go."

"Never saw you sleep on the flight before," the man observed.

Was Jacobs really from Archives? Mark shrugged it off. Don't be paranoid, he thought. Of course he is. None of the watchers had fat asses. They were nimble sorts.

Before they were permitted to go subterranean, deep into the cool earth, the 635 employees of Groom Lake Building 34—commonly called, the Truman Building—had to endure one of their two dreaded rituals of the day, the S&S, aka strip 'n' scan. When the buses dropped them off at the hangarlike structure, the sexes split toward separate entrances. Inside each section of the building were long rows of lockers reminiscent of a suburban high school. Mark walked briskly to his locker, which was halfway down the long corridor. Many of his coworkers were perfectly happy to dawdle and make it through scanning at the last possible moment, but today he was in a hurry to get underground.

He spun the combination lock, stripped down to his briefs, and hung his clothes on hooks. A fresh olive jumpsuit with SHACKLETON, M: embroidered on the breast pocket was neatly folded on the locker bench. He threw it on; the days were long gone when employees could wear street clothes into the facility. Every item a Building 34 employee brought on the commute had to be left in the lockers. Up and down the line, books, magazines, pens, cell phones, and wallets were shelved. Mark moved fast and got himself near the front of the scanning line.

The magnetometer was flanked by two watchers, humorless young men with buzz cuts who waved each employee through with a clipped military gesture. Mark waited, next up for the scan. He noticed that Malcolm Frazier, Chief of Operational Security, the head watcher, was nearby, checking on the morning scan. He was a fearsome hunk of a man with the grotesquely muscular body and rectangular head of a cartoon-book villain. Mark had exchanged few words with Frazier over the years, even though the watchers had input into some of his protocols. He would duck behind his group director and let her run interference with Frazier and his lot. Frazier was ex-military, ex-special ops, and his surly testosterone-seeped visage scared him silly. As a habit, Mark avoided eye contact, and today in particular he lowered his head when he felt the man's penetrating gaze upon him.

The scan had a singular purpose: to prevent any photographic or recording devices from entering the facility. In the morning, employees went through the scanners clothed. At the end of the day, they went back through buck naked since scanners couldn't detect paper. Underground was sterile ground. Nothing came in, nothing came out.

Building 34 was the most sterile complex in the United States. It was staffed by employees who had been selected by a cadre of Department of Defense recruiters who didn't have the slightest clue about the nature of the work for which they were recruiting. They only knew the skill set that was required. At the second or third round of interviews they were allowed to reveal that the job involved Area 51, and then only with the permission of their superiors. Inevitably the recruiters were then asked, "You mean the place they keep aliens and UFOs?" to which their authorized reply was, "This is a highly classified government installation doing critical work on national defense. That is all that can be disclosed at this time. However, the successful applicant will be among a very small group of government employees who will have full knowledge of research activities at Area 51."

The rest of the pitch went something like this: you will be a member of an elite team of scientists and researchers, some of the best minds in the country. You will have access to the most advanced hardware and software technology in the world. You will be privy to the highest level of classified data in the country, information that only a handful of high officials in the government even know exists. To partially compensate you for leaving your high-paying corporate jobs or your academic tenure track positions, you will receive free housing in Las Vegas, federal income tax abatement, and subsidized college tuition for your children.

As recruiting pitches went, this one was solid gold. Most recruits were intrigued enough to throw their hat into the ring and enter the screening and profiling phase, a six- to twelve-month process that can-opened every aspect of their lives to the scrutiny of FBI Special Agents and to profilers from the DOD. It was a punishing process. For every five recruits who entered the funnel, only one passed through the other end with an SCI, or Sensitive Compartmented Clearance, in Special Intelligence.

SCI-eligible recruits were invited to a closing interview at the Pentagon with the Associate General Counsel of the Office of the Navy. Since its founding by James Forrestal, NTS 51 had been a navy operation, and within the military these traditions died hard. The navy lawyer, who personally had no knowledge of Area 51 activities, presented a service contract and walked the applicant through the details, including the dire penalties that would result from breach of any provisions, especially confidentiality.

As if twenty years of imprisonment at Leavenworth weren't bad enough, once inside, the rumor mill deliberately would grind down new employees with tales of loose lips becoming dead lips at the hands of shadowy government operatives. "Now, can I be told about the nature of my work?" the navy lawyer was typically asked. "Not on your life," was the rejoinder.

Because once the contract was understood and verbally accepted, a further security clearance was required, a Special Access Program, or SAP-NTS 51, this one even tougher to obtain than an SCI. Only when the final hoops were cleared, the SAP granted, and the contract duly executed, was the newbie flown out to the base at Groom Lake and told the jaw-dropping truth about the operation by the head of Personnel, a dead-pan navy rear admiral, who sat at his desk in the desert like a duck out of water and wished he had a hundred bucks for every time he heard, "Holy shit, I never expected anything like that!"

Mark breathed easier when he passed through the scanner without triggering an alert, the watchers and Malcolm Frazier none the wiser. Elevator one was waiting at ground level. When it was filled with the first dozen men, the doors shut and it dropped six stories through multiple layers of hardened concrete and steel until it slowed and stopped at the Primary Research Laboratory. The Vault was another sixty feet lower, meticulously temperature and humidity-controlled. A multi-billion-dollar upgrade to the Vault in the late 1980s added giant earthquake and nuclear blast-resistant shock absorbers, technology purchased from the Japanese, who were on the cutting edge of earthquake mitigation.

Few employees had reason to visit the Vault. However, there was a tradition at Area 51. On his or her first day, the executive director would take the newbie down a special restricted elevator to the Vault level to see it.

The Library.

Watchers with sidearms would flank the steel doors trying to look as menacing as they could. The codes were entered and the thick doors silently swung open. Then the newbies would be led into the enormous, softly lit chamber, a place as quiet and somber as a cathedral, and stand in absolute awe at the sight before them.

Today, only one other member of Mark's Security Algorithms Group was on the elevator, a middle-aged mathematician with the unlikely name of Elvis Brando, no relation to either. "How ya doing today, Mark?" he asked.

"Pretty good," Mark replied, a wave of nausea hitting him hard.

The underground was bathed in harsh fluorescence. The lightest sounds echoed off uncarpeted floors and asylum-blue walls. Mark's office was one of several on the perimeter of a large central room that doubled as a group conference area and bench space for lower-level techs. It was small and cluttered, and compared to his aerie at his last private-sector job in California, with its campus views of manicured lawns and reflecting pools, a closet. But space was tight underground and he was lucky he didn't have to share. The desk and credenza were cheap and veneered but his chair was an expensive ergonomic model, the one creature comfort the lab didn't skimp on. There was lot of rump time in Area 51.

Mark booted his computer and logged onto the network with a password and dual fingerprint and retinal scans. The jaunty insignia of the Department of the Navy adorned the welcome screen. He looked through the common room. Elvis was already hunched over his work station in an office cater-corner to his. No one else in the department had made it through screening yet, and most important, his group director, Rebecca Rosenberg, was on vacation.

As it happened, he didn't have to worry about excessive scrutiny. Aboveground and below, he was a loner. Coworkers generally let him be. He didn't dish gossip or engage in banter. At lunch he would find a spot on his own in the vast commissary and grab a magazine from the rack. Twelve years ago, when he first arrived at the base, he had made some awkward efforts to mingle. Early on someone asked him if he was any relation to Shackleton of Antarctica and he'd said yes to bolster himself, launching into a laughable family history involving a great-uncle from England. It didn't take long for a database geek to run the genealogy and expose his lie.

For twelve years he had come to work, done his job and done it well. At grad school and at a succession of high-tech companies in Silicon Valley, he had established a reputation as one of the preeminent database security experts in the country, an authority in protecting servers from unauthorized access. It was the reason he was heavily recruited for Groom Lake. Reluctant at first, he was eventually seduced by the allure of doing something secret and vital, as a counterpoint to the dullness and predictability of his rootless life.

At Area 51, he wrote ground-breaking code to inoculate their systems from worms and other intrusions, algorithms that would have been widely adopted by industry and government as new gold standards—had he been able to publish them. Within his group the buzzwords were public and private key security systems, secure socket layers, Kerberos tokens, and host intrusion detection systems. It was his responsibility to constantly monitor the servers for unauthorized access attempts from within the complex as well as from without—probes by external hackers.

Also, the watchers fed his group quarantine lists, one for each employee—names of family members, friends, neighbors, spouse's coworkers, etc., that were personal no-gos. One of Mark's flypaper algorithms would detect an employee who attempted to access information from their quarantine list, and it was a matter of faith that detection would lead to unpleasant consequences. There was institutional memory of an analyst from the late 1970s who tried to look up his fiancée, and the poor fellow was allegedly still in a hole in federal prison.

Mark was seized by a sharp intestinal cramp. He gritted his teeth, rushed from his office and fast-walked down a corridor to the nearest men's room. Soon, back at his desk feeling relieved, he held something tightly in his left hand. When he was sure there were no prying eyes, he unclenched his fingers and dropped a bullet-shaped piece of gray plastic, about two inches in length, into the top drawer of his desk.

Returning to the common room, he moved like an invisible man among people loudly chatting about weekend plans, who now filled the room. In a walk-in supply closet, he found the soldering set and nonchalantly returned with it to his office, where he quietly shut the door behind him.

With Rosenberg out, the chance of someone interrupting him was close to zero, so he pressed on. There were rubber-banded bundles of computer cables in his lower desk drawer. He selected a USB lead and, using a small pair of pliers, gently broke off one of its metal connectors. He was ready for the gray bullet.

A minute later the job was done. He had successfully soldered the metal connector onto the bullet, and by doing so fabricated one fully functional four-gigabit flash memory stick, capable of storing three million pages of data, a device more lethal to the security of Area 51 than if he had smuggled in an automatic weapon.

Mark returned the memory stick to his desk and spent the rest of the morning writing code. Earlier that morning, during the brief drive to the airport in Las Vegas, he'd worked it out in his head, and now his fingers fairly smoked the keyboard. It was a camouflage program, designed to conceal that he was about to take down his own impenetrable host intrusion detection system. By lunchtime he was done.

When the common room and adjoining offices cleared out for lunch, he made his move and activated the new set of code. It worked perfectly, as he knew it would, one hundred percent audit-proof, and when he was satisfied that he couldn't be detected, he logged onto the primary United States database.

Then he entered a name—*Camacho, Luis, DOB 1/12/1977*—and held his breath. The screen lit up. No joy.

Of course, he had other ideas up his sleeve. Next best, he figured, would be Luis's *boyfriend*, John. He assumed correctly that finding him would be trivial. Cloaked by his camouflage program, he opened an NTS 51 portal into a customized database that consolidated billing records of all U.S. telephone service providers.

When he cross-tabbed the first-name John with the address 189 Minnieford Avenue, City Island, New York, out popped a full name—John William Pepperdine—and a social security number. A few keystrokes later he had a date of birth. Piece of cake, he thought. Armed with the data, he reentered the primary U.S. database and clicked on the search icon.

He gasped, scarcely believing his luck. The result was outstanding. No, perfect!

He had his anchor.

Okay, Mark, move it, he thought. You got in, now get the hell out! People in his department would be arriving back from lunch soon, and he wanted to stop walking the tight-rope. He carefully wiggled his newly soldered memory stick into a USB port on his computer.

It took only seconds to download the forward-looking U.S. database to the flash drive. When it was done, he expertly covered his tracks, taking his camo program down and simultaneously restarting the host intrusion detection system. He finished the operation by snapping off the metal connector from the gray bullet and resoldering it to the USB cable. When all the components were restashed in his desk, he opened his door and as casually as possible sauntered to the supply closet to return the soldering iron.

When he turned away from the closet shelf, Elvis Brando, a squarish overbearing man, was blocking his way, close enough that Mark could smell chili on his breath.

"Skipped lunch?" Elvis challenged.

"I think I've got a stomach bug," Mark said.

"Maybe you should go to Medical. You're sweating like a pig."

Mark touched his damp forehead and realized his jump-suit was soaked through the armpits. "I'm all right."

When there was half an hour until quitting time, Mark paid another visit to the men's room and found an empty stall. He pulled two items from his jumpsuit pocket—the bullet-shaped flash drive and a crumpled condom. He slid the plastic bullet into the condom and shed the jumpsuit. Then he clenched his jaw and shoved the greatest secret on the planet up his rear end.

* * *

That night he sat on his sofa and lost track of time while his laptop burned his crotch and stung his eyes. He trolled the pirated database, shuffling it like a deck of cards, doing cross-checks, verifications, writing lists by hand and revising them until he was satisfied.

He worked with impunity, though even if he'd been online, his computer had hack protection the watchers couldn't penetrate. His hands and fingers were the only parts of his body in motion, but when he finished he was almost breathless from the exertion. His own audacity electrified him—he wished he could brag to someone about his brazen cleverness.

When he was a boy he would run and tell his parents whenever he got a good grade or solved a math problem. His mother was dead from cancer. His father had remarried an unpleasant woman and was still bitterly disappointed at him for leaving a good company for a government job. They hardly talked. Besides, this wasn't the kind of thing you could tell a living soul.

Suddenly, he had an idea that made him giggle with delight.

Why not?

Who would know?

He closed the database, locked it with password protection, then opened the file containing his first screenplay, his Thornton Wilderesque ode to fate that had been trashed by the little Hollywood toad. He scrolled through the script and started making changes, and each time he hit Find and Replace he squealed excitedly, like a naughty little boy with a wicked secret.

When Will was young, his father would take him fishing because that's what fathers were supposed to do. He'd be woken before dawn with a poke on his shoulder, throw on clothes and climb into the pick-up truck for the drive from the panhandle town of Quincy down to Panama City. His father would hire a 26-footer by the hour from a working-class marina and chug south about ten miles into the Gulf. The journey, from his dark bedroom to the sparkling fishing grounds would occur with scant exchange of words. He would watch him pilot the boat, his bulky frame tinged orange by the rising sun and wonder why even the natural beauty of a warm morning boat ride on calm shimmering waters did not bring joy to the man's face. Eventually, his father would stub out a cigarette and say something like, "Okay, let's get these lines baited up," then lapse into sullen silence for hours at a time until a snapper or a wahoo hit the tackle and orders had to be barked.

Crossing City Island Bridge and gazing out toward East-chester Bay, he found himself thinking about his old man the moment the first marina came into view, an aluminum forest of masts bobbing in the stiffening afternoon breeze. City Island was a small, curious oasis, a part of the Bronx from a municipal perspective, but geo-culturally, quite a bit closer to Fantasy Island, a speck of land that led visitors to free associate about other places and other times because it was so unlike the city on the other side of the causeway.

To the Siwanoy Indians, the island had been for centuries a fertile fishing and oyster ground, to the European settlers, a ship building and maritime center, to the current residents, a middle-class enclave of modest single-family houses mixed with fine Victorian sea-farers mansions, its coastline dotted with yacht clubs for wealthy off-islanders. With a rabbit-warren of small streets, some almost country lanes, myriad ocean dead-ends, the incessant infantile cries of gulls and the briny smell of the shore, it was evocative of vacation spots or childhood haunts, not metropolitan New York.

Nancy could see he was slack-jawed over the place. "Ever been here before?" she asked.

"No, you?"

"We used to come here for picnics when I was a kid." She consulted the map. "You need to take a left on Beach Street."

Minnieford Avenue was hardly an avenue in the classic use of the word, more like a cart path, and it was another poor spot for a major crime scene investigation. Police and emergency vehicles and media satellite trucks clogged the road like a thrombosis. He joined the long single-file of hopelessly stuck cars and complained to Nancy they'd have to walk the rest of the way. He was blocking a driveway and was expecting a fracas from a thick-limbed fellow in a wife-beater who was giving him the once-over from his steps, but the guy just called out, "You on the job?"

He nodded.

"I'm NYPD, retired," the man offered. "Don't worry. 'I'll watch the Explorer. I ain't going nowhere."

The jungle drums had beaten loud and fast. Everyone in law enforcement and their uncles knew that City Island had become ground zero in the Doomsday Killer case. The media had already been tipped off which ratcheted the hysteria. The small lime-green house was surrounded by a throng of journalists and a cordon of cops from the 45th Precinct. TV reporters jockeyed for angles on the crowded sidewalk so their cameramen could frame them cleanly against the house. Grasping their microphones, their shirts and blouses fluttered like maritime flags in the stiff westerly winds.

When he spotted the house he had a mental flash of the iconic photographs that would blanket the world should it prove to be the place where the killer was captured. Doomsday House. A modest 1940's-era two-story dwelling with warping shingles, chipped white shutters and a sagging porch with a couple of bicycles, plastic chairs and a grill. There was no yard to speak of – a spitter with good lung power could lean out the windows and hit the houses on either side and to the rear. There was just enough paved space for two cars – a beige Honda Civic was crammed between the house and the neighbor's chain-link fence, an older red BMW 3-series was parked between the porch and the sidewalk, where a patch of grass might otherwise have been.

He wearily checked his watch. It was already a long day and it wasn't going to end anytime soon. He might not get a drink for hours and he resented the deprivation. Still, how superb would it be to wrap the case up here and now and coast to retirement, reliably hitting the barstool by 5:30 every night? He quickened his pace at the thought, forcing Nancy into a trot. "You ready to rock and roll?" he called out.

Before she could answer, a babelicious reporter from Channel Four recognized him from the news conference and shouted to her cameraman. "To your right! It's the Pied Piper!" The video cam swung in his direction. "Agent Piper! Can you confirm that the Doomsday Killer has been captured?" Instantly, every videographer followed suit and he and Nancy were surrounded by a baying pack.

"Just keep walking," he hissed, and Nancy tucked in behind and let him plow through the scrum.

The kill zone was in their faces the instant they walked inside. The front room was a bloody mess. It was taped off, perfectly preserved, and Will and Nancy had to peer through the open door as if they were viewing a cordoned museum exhibit. The body of a thin open-eyed man was half-on,

half-off a yellow love seat. His head was lying on an armrest, well and truly caved in, his brown hair and scalp
cleaved, a crescent of dura mater glistening in the last
golden rays of the sun. His face, or rather, what was left of
it, was a swollen pulpy mess with exposed shards of ivory
bone and cartilage. Both his arms had been shattered into
sickeningly unnatural anatomical positions.

He read the room like a manuscript – red splatter all
over the paint, teeth scattered on the carpet like popcorn
from a messy party – and he concluded that that the sofa
was where the man had died but not where the attack had
begun. The victim had been standing near the door when the
first strike landed, an upwardly arcing swing that glanced
off his skull and splashed blood onto the ceiling. He had been
struck again and again as he reeled and spun around the
room, unsuccessfully fending off a hail of blows from a
blunt instrument. He had not gone easily, this one. Will
tried to interpret the eyes. He had seen that wide-eyed stare
countless times. What was the final emotion? Fear? Anger?
Resignation?

Nancy was drawn to another detail in the diorama. "You
see that?" she asked. "On the desk. I think it's the postcard."

The Commanding Officer of the precinct was a young
turk, a spit-and-polish captain named Brian Murphy. His
athletic chest proudly bulged under his crisply-ironed blue
shirt as he introduced himself. This was a career-altering
collar for him, and the deceased, one John William Pepperdine, surely would have been irritated at how much ebul-
lience his passing had engendered in this policeman.

On their drive over, he and Nancy had fretted about the
45th Precinct trampling another crime scene but they needn't
have, because Murphy had taken personal charge of this one.
Fat, sloppy Detective Chapman was nowhere to be seen. He
complimented the captain on his forensic awareness and it
had the same effect as stroking a mutt while cooing "good
dog." Murphy was now his friend for life and he giddily
briefed them how his officers, responding to a neighbor's

911 about shouts and screams, had discovered the body and the postcard and how one of his sergeants had spotted the blood-soaked perpetrator, Luis Camacho, wedged behind the oil tank in the basement. The guy wanted to confess on the spot and Murphy had the good sense to videotape him waiving his Miranda rights and giving his statement in a dull monotone. As Murphy disdainfully put it, it was a fruit-on-fruit crime.

Will listened calmly but Nancy was impatient. "Did he confess to the others, the other murders?"

"To be honest with you, I didn't go there," Murphy said. "I left that for you guys. You want to see him?"

"As soon as we can," he said.

"Follow me."

He smiled. "He's still here?" Instant gratification.

"I wanted to make it easy for you. You didn't want to go hauling around the Bronx, did you?"

"Captain Murphy, you are a fucking all-star," he said.

"Feel free to share your opinion with the Commissioner," Murphy suggested.

The first thing he noticed about Luis Camacho was that he was a dead-match of their physical composite: dark-skinned, average height, slight build, around 160 pounds. He could tell from the stiffening of her lips that Nancy pegged him too. He was sitting at the kitchen table, hands cuffed behind his back, tremulous, his jeans and swooshed Just Do It T-shirt starched with dry blood. Oh, he did it, all right, he thought. Look at this guy, wearing another man's blood like something out of a tribal ritual.

The kitchen was tidy and cutesy, a collection of whimsical cookie jars, pasta shapes in acrylic tubes, place mats with hot air balloons, a baker's rack stacked with floral china. Very domesticated, very gay, Will thought. He loomed over Luis until the man reluctantly locked eyes.

"Mr. Camacho, my name is Special Agent Piper and this is Special Agent Lipinski. We're with the FBI and we need to ask you some questions."

"I already told the cops what I did," Luis said just above a whisper.

Will was redoubtable in interrogation. He used his tough-guy size to threaten then counter-balanced it with a soothing tone and gentle Southern drawl. The subject was never completely sure what he was up against and Will used that as a weapon. "We appreciate that. It's definitely going to make things easier for you. We just want to broaden the investigation."

"You mean the postcard John got? Is that what you mean by broaden?"

"That's right, we're interested in the postcard."

Luis shook his head mournfully and tears started streaming. "What's going to happen to me?"

Will asked one of the cops flanking Luis to wipe his face with a tissue. "Ultimately, that'll be up to a jury, but if you keep on cooperating with the investigation, I believe that's going to have a positive impact on the way things play out. I know you already talked to these officers but I'd appreciate it if you'd start off by telling us about your relationship with Mr. Pepperdine and then tell us what happened here today."

He let him talk freely, tweaking the direction from time to time while Nancy took her usual notes. They had met in 2005 in a bar. Not a gay bar but they had they found each other efficiently enough and they had started dating, the temperamental Puerto Rican flight attendant from Queens and the emotionally-blocked Episcopalian bookstore owner from City Island. John Pepperdine had inherited this comfortable green house from his parents and he had let a succession of boyfriends move in with him over the years. With his 40th birthday in the rear-view mirror, John had told friends that Luis was his last great love, and he had been correct.

Their relationship had been tempestuous, infidelity an ongoing theme. John had demanded monogamy, Luis was incapable. John regularly accused him of cheating but Luis's job, with its constant travel to Vegas, carried a certain carte blanche. Luis had flown home the evening before but rather than return to City Island, he went to Manhattan with a businessman he had met on the flight who bought him an expensive meal and took him home to Sutton Place. Luis had crawled into John's bed at four AM and didn't awake until one that afternoon. Hung over, he had shakily descended the stairs to make a pot of coffee, expecting to have the house to himself.

Instead, John had stayed home from work and had camped out in the living room, an emotional wreck, almost incoherent and sobbing with anxiety, his hair uncombed, his complexion pasty. Where had Luis been? Who had he been with? Why hadn't he picked up his urgent phone and text messages? Why, of all days, had he abandoned him yesterday? Luis shrugged the tirade off, wanting to know what the big deal was. Couldn't a guy go out after work and have a couple of drinks with friends? It was beyond pathetic. You think I'm pathetic, John had shouted. Look at this you son of a bitch! He had run off to the kitchen and had come back with a postcard pinched between his fingers. It's a Doomsday postcard, Asshole, with my name on it and today's date!

Luis had looked at it and had told him it was probably a sick joke. Maybe the idiot clerk John had recently fired was getting back at him. And anyway, had John called the police? He hadn't. He was too frightened. They had argued back and forth for a while until Luis's cell phone had gone off on the hall table with its campy "Oops I Did it Again" ring tone. John had leapt for it and had cried out, Who the fuck is Phil? Answer, truth be told, was the guy from Sutton Place, but Luis had dodged the truth unconvincingly.

John's emotions had red-lined and, according to Luis, the normally mild-mannered fellow had lost it, grabbing the aluminum soft ball bat that he had abandoned by the front door a decade earlier after tearing an Achilles tendon in an adult-league game in Pelham. John had wielded it like a lance, pushing the end into Luis's shoulders, screaming obscenities. Luis had screamed back at him to put it down but the jabbing continued, inflaming Luis beyond his ability to control what would happen next when somehow the bat wound up in his hands and the room began to get painted with blood.

Will listened with rising discomfort because the confession had the ring of authenticity. Still, he didn't bring papal infallibility to the table. He'd been duped before, and God-willing, he was being duped now. He didn't wait for Luis to stop crying before aggressively and suddenly asking, "Did you kill David Swisher?"

Luis looked up, startled. His instinct was to wave his arms in protest which made his wrists chafe against the handcuffs. "No!"

"Did you kill Elizabeth Kohler?"

"No!"

"Did you kill Marco Napolitano?"

"Stop!" Luis sought out Nancy's eyes. "What's this guy talking about?"

By way of a response, Nancy continued the battery, "Did you kill Myles Drake?"

Luis had stopped crying. He snorted his nose dry and stared at her.

"Did you kill Milos Covic?" she asked.

Then Will, "Consuela Lopez."

Then Nancy, "Ida Santiago."

And Will, "Lucius Robertson."

Captain Murphy grinned, impressed at the rat-a-tat.

Luis shook his head vigorously. "No! No! No! No! You guys are crazy. I told you I killed John, in like self-defense, but I never killed these other people. You think I'm the fuck-ing Doomsday Killer? Is that what you think? Come on! Get real, Man!"

"Okay, Luis, I hear you. Take it easy. You want some water?" Will asked. "So how long have you been flying the New York-Las Vegas route?"

"Almost four years."

"Do you have a diary, some kind of flight log handy?"

"Yeah, I've got a book. It's upstairs, on the dresser."

Nancy hurried out the door.

"You ever mail any postcards from Vegas?" Will demanded.

"No!"

"I heard you say loud and clear that you didn't kill these people but tell me this, Luis, did you know any of them?"

"Of course not, Man!"

"That includes Consuela Lopez and Ida Santiago?"

"What? Because they're Latinos, I should know them? What are you, some kind of an idiot? You know how many Spanish there are in New York?"

He didn't break stride. "You ever live in Staten Island?"

"No."

"Ever work there?"

"No."

"Got any friends there?"

"No."

"Ever visited there?"

"Maybe once, for a ferry ride."

"When was that?"

"When I was a kid."

"What kind of car do you drive?"

"A Civic."

"The white one out front?"

"Yeah."

"Any of your friends or relatives drive a blue car?"

"No, Man, I don't think so."

"You own a pair of Reebok DMX 10s?"

"Do I look like I'd wear some jive-ass teenage sneakers, Man?"

"Did anyone ever ask you to mail postcards from Las Vegas?"

"No!"

"You admitted you killed John Pepperdine."

"In self-defense, Man."

"Did you ever kill anyone else."

"No!"

"Do you know who killed the other victims?"

"No!"

He abruptly halted the interview, went looking for Nancy and found her on the upstairs landing. He had a bad feeling and her crimpled mouth confirmed his fears. She was wearing a pair of latex gloves, leafing through a black 2008 day planner. "Problems?" he asked.

"If this diary is legit, we've got big problems. Except for today, he was in Las Vegas or in transit during every other murder. I can't believe it, Will. I don't know what to say."

"Say fuck. That's what you should say." He leaned wearily against the wall. "Because this case is completely fucked."

"Maybe the diary's been doctored."

"We'll check the records with his company, but we both know this guy's not Doomsday."

"Well, he killed Victim Nine that's for sure."

He nodded. "Okay, Partner, here's what we're going to do." She put Luis's diary down and opened her notebook to take down his instructions.

"You don't drink, do you?"

"Not really."

"Good, consider yourself designated. We're going to clock out and go off duty in about five minutes. Your assignment is to take me to a bar, talk to me while I get drunk then drive me home. Will you do that for me?"

She looked at him disapprovingly. "If that's what you want."

He knocked back his drinks quickly, shuttling the waitress between the booth and the bar. Nancy watched him slip the bonds of sobriety while she moodily sipped a diet ginger ale through a bendy straw. Their table at the Harbor Restaurant overlooked the bay, the calm waters blackening as the sun began to set. He had spotted the restaurant before they made it off the island, muttering "That place's bound to have a bar."

He wasn't drunk enough to miss the fact that Nancy was uncomfortable having an after-work drink with her superior, a guy who happened to have a reputation as an office scoundrel and a souse. She was literally squirming with discomfort.

She wasn't talking so he amused himself by doing a boozy

profile. She probably felt like an enabler, helping him lube up as fast as he could.

And she was probably falling for him. He could see it in her eyes, especially the first thing in the morning when she came into his office. Most women succumbed eventually. It wasn't boasting, just a fact.

Right now she probably hated him for who he was and wanted him simultaneously. He did that to women.

In the small glow of a kerosene table lamp, his body compressed and softened like an unfired clay mold left outdoors on a scorching day. His face sagged, his shoulders rounded and he slumped on the shiny vinyl banquette.

"You're supposed to talk to me," he slurred. "You're just sitting there, watching me."

"Do you want to talk about the case?" she asked.

"Fuck no, anything but."

"What then?"

"How about baseball?" he suggested. "You like the Mets or the Yankees?"

"I don't really follow sports."

"That so. . ."

"Sorry." Through the windows she watched the running lights of a powerboat crawling past at headway speed until it was out of sight. His head was lowered; he played with the ice cubes in his drink, sending them into a vortex with his finger and when the glass was empty he crudely waggled his wet finger at the young waitress.

He tried to sharpen Nancy's blurring features by scrunching his forehead. "You don't want to be here, do you?"

"Not particularly."

He made her flinch when he banged the table with the heel of his hand, too hard and too loudly for decorum, turning heads. "I like your honesty." He scooped up some nuts and crunched at them, then brushed the salt off his greasy palms. "Most women aren't honest with me till it's too late." He snorted as if he'd just said something humorous. "Okay, Partner, tell me what you'd be doing tonight if you weren't babysitting me."

"I don't know, helping with the dinner, reading, listening to music." She apologized, "I'm not a very exciting person, Will."

"Reading what?"

"I like biographies. Novels."

He feigned interest. "I used to read a lot. Now I mostly watch TV and drink. Want to know what that makes me?"

She didn't.

"A man!" he cackled, " A goddamned 21st century male Homo sapiens!" He slammed more nuts into his mouth, truculently folded his arms across his chest and curled his mouth into a toothy shit-eating grin. From Nancy's stony reaction, he knew he was going too far but he didn't care.

He was getting good and drunk and too bad if she didn't like it. The waitress had a small gold crucifix which swung and knocked against the top of her deep cleavage when she put down another scotch. He leered at her. "Hey, you wanna come home with me to watch TV and drink?"

Nancy had enough. "I'm sorry, we'll take the check, " she said as the waitress scurried off. "Will, we're leaving," she announced sternly. "You need to go home."

"Isn't that what I just suggested?" he drawled.

The Ode to Joy rang from his jacket. He groped until he was able to extract the phone from his pocket. He squinted at the caller ID. "Shit. I don't think I should talk to her right now." He handed it to Nancy. "It's Helen Swisher," he whispered as if the caller were already listening.

Nancy pushed the talk button. "Hello, this is Will Piper's phone."

He slid from the booth and weaved toward the men's room. By the time he returned, Nancy had paid the bill and was waiting for him beside the table. She decided he wasn't too wasted to hear the news. "Helen Swisher just got David's client list from his bank. He had a Las Vegas connection after all."

"Yeah?"

"In 2003 he did a financing for a Nevada company called Desert Life Insurance. His client was the CEO, a man named Nelson Elder."

He had the appearance of a man trying to steady himself on the deck of a storm-tossed boat. He swayed unsteadily and loudly pronounced, "Okay, then. I'm gonna go out there, I'm gonna talk to Nelson Elder and I'm gonna find the goddamned killer. How's that for a plan?"

"Give me the car keys," she demanded. Her anger pierced his inebriation.

"Don't be sore at me," he implored. "I'm your partner!"

Out in the parking lot their senses were clobbered by warm gusts of salty wind and the pungent bouquet of low tide. Ordinarily, this one-two punch might have made her dreamy and carefree but she looked like she was in a dark place as she listened to her partner shuffling behind her like Frankenstein's monster, drunkenly mumbling.

"Going to Vegas, Baby, going to Vegas."

It was harvest time, perhaps Josephus's favorite season, when the days were pleasantly warm, the nights cool and comfortable, and the air was filled with the earthy smells of newly scythed wheat and barley and fresh apples. He gave thanks for the bountiful proceeds from the fields surrounding the abbey walls. The brothers would be able to restock the dwindling stores in the granary and fill their oaken barrels with fresh ale. While he abhorred gluttony, he begrudged the rationing of beer that inevitably occurred by midsummer.

The conversion of the church from wood to stone was three years complete. The square, tapering tower rose up high enough for boats and ships approaching the island to use as a navigational aide. The squared-off chancel at the eastern end had low, triangular windows that beautifully illuminated the sanctuary during the Offices of the day. The nave was long enough not only for the present community, but the monastery would be able to accommodate a greater number of Christ's servants in the future. Josephus often sought forgiveness and did penance for the pride that bubbled up in his chest for the role he played in its construction. True, his knowledge of the world was limited, but he imagined the church at Vectis to be among the great cathedrals of Christendom.

Of late, the masons had been hard at work finishing the new Chapter House. Josephus and Oswyn had decided the Scriptorium would be next and that the structure would have to be greatly expanded. The Bibles and rules books they produced, and the illustrated *Epistles of St. Peter* written in golden ink, were highly regarded and Josephus had heard that copies made their way across the waters to Eire, Italia, and Francia.

It was mid-morning, approaching the third hour, and he was on his way from the lavatorium to the refectory for a chunk of brown bread, a joint of mutton, some salt, and a flagon of ale. His stomach was rumbling in eager anticipation, as Oswyn had imposed a restriction of only one meal a day to strengthen the spirit of his congregation by weakening the desires of their flesh. After a prolonged period of meditation and personal fasting, which the frail abbot himself could scarcely afford, Oswyn shared his revelation with the entire community which had dutifully assembled in the Chapter House. "We must fast daily as we must feed daily," he declared. "We must gratify the body more poorly and sparingly."

So they all became thinner.

Josephus heard his name called. Guthlac, a huge rough man who had been a soldier before joining the monastery, caught up with him at a run, his sandals slapping on the path.

"Prior," he said. "Ubertus the stonecutter is at the gate. He wishes to speak with you at once."

"I am on my way to the refectory for supper," Josephus objected. "Do you not feel he can wait?"

"He said it is urgent," Guthlac said, hurrying off.

"And where are you going?" Josephus called after him.

"To the refectory, Prior. For my supper."

Ubertus was inside the gate near the entrance to the Hospicium, the guest house for visitors and travelers, a low timber building with rows of simple cots. He was rooted to a spot on the ground, his feet unmoving. From a distance Josephus thought he was alone, but as he approached he saw a child behind the mason, two small legs visible between his tree-trunk legs.

"How may I help you, Ubertus?" Josephus asked.

"I have brought the child."

Josephus didn't understand.

Ubertus reached behind and pulled the boy into sight. He was a barefoot, tiny lad, thin as a twig with bright ginger hair. His shirt was dirty and in tatters, exposing a ladder of ribs and a pigeon chest. His trousers were too long, hand-me-downs that he had not yet grown to fit. His fine skin was parchment white, his staring eyes green like precious stones, and his delicate face as immobile as one of his father's blocks of stone. He was tightly pressing his blanched pink lips together, and the effort to do so tensed and puckered his chin.

Josephus had heard about the boy but never laid eyes on him. He found him an unsettling sight. There was a cold madness about him, a sense that his small raw life had not been blessed by the warmth of God. His name, Octavus, the eighth, had been bestowed on him by Ubertus the night of his birth. Unlike his twin, an abomination who was better destroyed, his life would be blissfully ordinary, would it not? After all, the eighth son of a seventh son is but another son even if born on the seventh day of the seventh month of the 777th year after the birth of the Lord. Ubertus prayed he would become strong and productive, a stonecutter like his father and his brothers.

"Why have you brought him?" Josephus asked.

"I want you to take him."

"Why would I take your son?"

"I cannot keep him any longer."

"But you have daughters to care for him. You have food for your table."

"He needs Christ. Christ is here."

"But Christ is everywhere."

"Nowhere stronger than here, Prior."

The boy dropped to his knees and stuck his bony finger into the dirt. He began moving it around in little circles, carving a pattern in the soil, but his father reached down and yanked him by his hair to stand him up. The boy flinched but did not make a sound, despite the ferocity of the tug.

"The boy needs Christ," his father insisted. "I wish to dedicate him to religious life."

Josephus had heard talk of the boy being a strange one, mute, seemingly absorbed in his own world, completely without interest in his brothers and sisters or other village children. He had been wet-nursed, although he'd fed poorly, and even now at five years of age he ate sparingly and without gusto. In his heart, Josephus was not surprised at how the boy had turned out. After all, he had witnessed this child's remarkable entrance into the world with his own eyes.

The abbey had taken in children with regularity, though it was not an actively encouraged practice since it strained resources and drew the sisters away from other tasks. Villagers were particularly keen to deposit mentally and physically deformed children at their gates. If Sister Magdalena had her way, they would all have been denied, but Josephus had a soft spot for the most unfortunate of God's creatures.

Still, this one was disquieting.

"Boy, can you speak?" he asked.

Octavus ignored him and only looked toward the ground at the pattern he had made.

"He cannot speak," Ubertus said.

Josephus gently reached for his chin and lifted his face. "Are you hungry?"

The boy's dark eyes wandered.

"Do you know of Christ, your savior?"

Josephus could detect not a flicker of recognition. Octavus's pale face was tabula rasa, a blank tablet with nothing writ.

"Will you take him, Prior?" the man implored.

Josephus let go of the boy's chin and the youth fell to the ground and resumed making patterns in the soil with his dirty finger.

Ubertus had tears running down his chiseled face. "Please, I beg of you."

Sister Magdalena was a stern woman whom no one could recall smiling, even when she played her psaltery and made heavenly music. She was in her fifth decade of life and had lived half of it within the abbey walls. Underneath her veil was a mound of gray braids, and underneath her habit was a tough virgin body as impenetrable as a nutshell. She was not without ambitions, well aware that under the Order of St. Benedict a woman could ascend to the position of abbess should the bishop so wish. As the most senior sister at Vectis this was not out of the question, but Aetia, the Bishop of Dorchester, barely acknowledged her when he visited for Easter and Christmas. She was certain her private musings on how she might better lead the abbey were not vainglory but simply her desire to make the monastery more pure and efficient.

She often approached Oswyn to inform him of her suspicions of waste, excess, or even fornication, and he would patiently listen, sighing under his breath, then later take up the matter with Josephus. Oswyn had been inexorably hobbled by his spinal infirmity, and his pain was a constant thing. Sister Magdalena's complaints about the flow of ale or the lustful glances she imagined, aimed at her virgin charges, only added to the abbot's discomfort. He counted on Josephus to deal with these worldly issues so he might concentrate on serving God and honoring Him by completing the rebuilding of the abbey in his lifetime.

Magdalena was known to have no love for children. The filthy particulars of their conception troubled her and she found them altogether needful. She disdained Josephus for allowing them sanctuary at Vectis, particularly the very young and disabled. She had nine children under the age of ten in her care and found that most of them did not sufficiently earn their keep. She had the sisters work them hard, fetching water and firewood, washing plates and utensils, stuffing mattresses with fresh straw to combat the lice. When older they would have time for religious study, but until their minds were tempered by toil she considered them only good for simple hard labor.

Octavus, Josephus's latest mistake, infuriated her.

He was incapable of following the most basic commands. He refused to empty a pot or throw a log onto the fire in the kitchen. He would not go to bed without being dragged to it or arise with the other children without being pulled from the pallet. The other children sniggered at him and called him names. At first Magdalena believed him to be willful and beat him with sticks, but in time she tired of the corporal punishment since it had no effect whatsoever, not even eliciting a satisfying cry or a whimper. And when she was done, the boy would invariably retrieve her stick from the wood pile and use it to scratch his patterns onto the dirt floor of the kitchen.

Now, with the autumn about to turn to winter, she ignored the boy completely, leaving him to his own devices. Fortunately, he ate like a small bird and made little demand on their stores.

On a cold December morning, Josephus was leaving the Scriptorium on his way to mass. The first wintry storm of the season had blown over the island during the night and left behind a coating of snow sparkling so brightly in the sunshine it stung his eyes. He rubbed his hands together for warmth and tread rapidly up the path as his toes were getting numb.

Octavus was squatting beside the path, barefoot in his thin clothes. Josephus frequently saw him in the abbey grounds. He usually paused to touch the boy's shoulder, say a fleeting prayer that whatever malady he possessed might be healed, then quickly went on with his business. But today he was afraid the boy might freeze if left unattended. He looked around for one of the sisters but there was no one in sight.

"Octavus!" Josephus exclaimed. "Come inside! You must not be about in the snow without shoes!"

The boy had a stick in his hand and, as usual, was drawing patterns, but this time there was a hint of excitement on that blank delicate face. The snowfall had created a vast clean surface for him to scratch upon.

Josephus stood over him and was about to lift Octavus up when he stopped short and gasped.

Surely this could not be so!

Josephus shielded his eyes from the intense glare and confirmed his initial fear.

He bounded back to the Scriptorium and moments later returned with Paulinus, whom he dragged furiously by the sleeve, despite the protestations of the thin minister.

"What is it, Josephus?" Paulinus cried. "Why will you not say what is the matter?"

"Look!" Josephus answered. "Tell me what you see."

Octavus continued to work his stick on the snow. The two men towered over him and studied his etchings.

"It cannot be!" Paulinus hissed.

"But surely it is," Josephus countered.

There were letters in the snow, unmistakable letters.

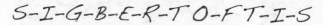

S-I-G-B-E-R-T O-F T-I-S

"Sigbert of Tis?"

"He is not done," Josephus said excitedly. "Look: Sigbert of Tisbury."

"How can this boy write?" Paulinus asked. The monk was as white as the snow and too scared to shiver.

"I do not know," Josephus said. "No one in his village can read or write. The sisters have certainly not been teaching him. In truth, he is considered feeble-minded."

The boy kept working his stick.

18 12 782 Natus

Paulinus crossed himself. "My God! He writes numbers too! The eighteenth day of the twelfth month, 782. That is today!"

"Natus," Joseph whispered. "Birth."

Paulinus stamped his feet through the snow writings, eradicating the numbers and letters. "Bring him!"

They waited for the monks to leave the Scriptorium for mass before seating the boy atop one of the copying tables. Paulinus put a sheet of vellum in front of him and handed him a quill.

Octavus immediately began to move the quill over the parchment and did not seem at all bothered that there was nothing to see.

"No!" Paulinus exclaimed. "Wait! Watch me." He dipped the quill into a ceramic pot of ink and gave it back to him. The boy continued to scratch but this time his efforts were visible. He seemed to take notice of the tight black letters he was forming, and a guttural noise emanated from deep in his throat. It was the first sound he had ever made.

Cedric of York 18 12 782 *Mors*

"Again, the date. Today," Paulinus muttered. "But this time he writes 'Mors.' Death."

"This is surely sorcery," Josephus lamented, stepping backward until his rump bumped against another copying table.

The ink ran dry and Paulinus took the boy's hand and made him dip the quill himself. Expressionless, Octavus started writing again but this time it began as gibberish.

呼延. 18 12 782 *Natus*

The men shook their heads in confusion. Paulinus said, "These are not normal letters but once again here is the date."

Josephus suddenly caught himself and realized they were to be late for mass, an inexcusable sin. "Hide the parchments and the ink and leave the boy in the corner. Come, Paulinus, let us make haste to the Sanctuary. We will pray to God to help us understand what we have seen and beg for him to cleanse us of evil."

That night, Josephus and Paulinus met in the chilly brewery and lit a fat candle for light. Josephus felt the need for an ale to calm his nerves and settle his stomach, and Paulinus was willing to humor his old friend. They drew a pair of stools close to one another, their knees almost knocking.

Josephus considered himself a simple man who understood only the love of God and the Rules of St. Benedict of

Nursia that all ministers of God were obliged to follow. However, he knew Paulinus to be a sharp thinker and a learned scholar who had read many texts concerning the heavens and the earth. If anyone could explain what they had seen earlier, it was Paulinus.

Yet Paulinus was unwilling to offer an explanation. Instead he suggested a mission, and the two men schemed about how best to accomplish it. They agreed to keep their knowledge of the boy secret, for what good could possibly come in upsetting the community before Paulinus could divine the truth?

When Josephus had drained the last of his ale, Paulinus reached for the candle. Just before he blew it out he told Josephus something that had been on his mind.

"You know," he said, "there is nothing to say that in the case of twins, the seventh son to be born of a woman is, by necessity, the seventh son that God had conceived."

Ubertus rode through the countryside of Wessex on the mission that Prior Josephus had pressed on him. He felt an unlikely servant for the task but was beholden to Josephus and could not refuse him.

The heavy, sweating animal between his legs warmed his body against the crisp chill of the mid-December day. He was not a good rider. Stonecutters were used to slow speeds in an ox-drawn cart. He gripped the reins tightly, pressed his knees against the belly of the beast and held on as best he could. The horse was a healthy animal that the monastery kept stabled on the mainland, just for this kind of purpose. A ferryman had rowed Ubertus from the shingled beach of Vectis to the Wessex shore. Josephus had instructed him to make haste and return within two days, which meant the horse must be made to canter.

As the day wore on the sky turned slate gray, a hue akin to the rocky face of the coastal undercliffs. He rode at pace through a frosty countryside of fallow fields, low stone walls, and tiny villages, much like his own. Occasionally he passed dull-looking peasants, trudging on foot or riding lethargic mules. He was mindful of thieves but in truth his only possessions of value were the horse itself and the few small coins that Josephus had given him for the journey.

He arrived in Tisbury just before sundown. It was a prosperous town with several large timber houses and a multitude of neat cottages lining a broad street. On a central green, sheep huddled in the gloom. He rode past a small wooden church, a solitary structure on the edge of the green, which stood cold and dark. Beside it was a small burial ground with signs of a fresh grave. He quickly crossed himself. The air was filled with smoky hearth fires, and Ubertus was distracted from the burial mound by the delicious odors of charred meat and burning fat everywhere.

Today had been market day, and there were still carts and produce stalls in the square not yet removed because their owners remained in the tavern drinking and throwing dice. Ubertus dismounted at the tavern door. A boy took notice and offered to hold his reins. For one of his coins, the boy led the horse away for a bucket of oats and a trough of water.

Ubertus entered the warm crowded tavern and his senses were assaulted by a din of drunken voices and the smells of stale ale, sweating bodies, and piss. He stood before the blazing peat fire, revived his cramped hands and called out in his thick Italian accent for a jug of wine. Since it was a market town, the men of Tisbury were well-used to strangers, and they received him with cheerful curiosity. A group of men called him to their table and he fell into an animated conversation about where he hailed from and why he had come to town.

It took Ubertus under an hour to pour three jugs of wine down his throat and obtain the knowledge he had been sent to discover.

Sister Magdalena usually walked through the abbey grounds at a deliberate pace, not too slowly, as that would be wasteful of time, but not too speedily, as that would create the impression that something on this earth was more important than the contemplation of God.

Today she ran, clutching something in her hand.

A few days of warmer air had thinned the snow to a patchy shell, and the paths were well-trampled and no longer slippery.

In the Scriptorium, Josephus and Paulinus sat alone in silence. They had dismissed the copyists so they could meet privately with Ubertus, who had returned from his mission, cold and exhausted.

Ubertus was no longer there, having been sent back to his village with a grim thanks and a benediction.

His report was simple and sobering.

On the eighteenth day of December, three days earlier, a child was born in the town of Tisbury to Wuffa the tanner and his wife Eanfled.

The child's name was Sigbert.

While neither would openly admit it, they were not shocked by the news. They half expected to hear as much since it was scarcely possible that the fantastic circumstances of a mute boy born to a dead mother who could, without tuition, write names and dates, could grow more fantastic.

When Ubertus was gone, Paulinus had said to Josephus, "The boy was the seventh son, of this there can be no doubt. He has a profound power."

"Is it for good or evil?" Josephus asked shakily.

Paulinus looked at his friend, puckered his mouth but did not answer.

Without warning, Sister Magdalena burst in.

"Brother Otto told me you were here," she said, breathing heavily and slamming the door behind her.

Josephus and Paulinus exchanged conspiratorial glances. "Indeed we are, Sister," Josephus said. "Is there something troubling you?"

"This!" She thrust her hand forward. There was a rolled parchment in her fist. "One of the sisters found this in the children's dormitory under the pallet of Octavus's bed. He has stolen it from the Scriptorium, I have no doubt. Can you confirm it?"

Josephus unrolled the parchment and inspected it along with Paulinus.

Kal ba Lakna   *21 12 782 Natus*

Flavius de Napoli   *21 12 782 Natus*

CИМЕОН *21 12 782 Natus*

ימלח *21 12 782 Mors*

Juan de Madrid   *21 12 782 Natus*

Josephus looked up from the first page. It was written in Octavus's tight scrawl.

"That one is in Hebrew, I recognize the script," Paulinus whispered to him, pointing at one of the entries. "I do not know the origin of the one above it."

"Well?" the sister demanded. "Can you confirm the boy has stolen this?"

"Please sit, Sister," Josephus sighed.

"I do not wish to sit, Prior, I wish to know the truth and then I wish to severely punish this boy."

"I beg you to sit."

She reluctantly sat upon one of the copying benches.

"The parchment was certainly stolen," Josephus began.

"The wicked boy! But what is this text? It seems a strange listing."

"It contains names," Josephus said.

"In more than a single language," Paulinus added.

"What is its purpose and why is Oswyn included?" she asked suspiciously.

"Oswyn?" Josephus asked.

"The second page, the second page!" she said.

Josephus looked at the second sheet.

Oswyn of Vectis 21 12 782 Mors

The blood drained from Josephus's face. "My God!"

Paulinus rose and turned away to hide his expression of alarm.

"Which of the brothers wrote this?" Magdalena demanded to know.

"None of them, Sister," Josephus said.

"Then who wrote it?"

"The boy, Octavus."

Josephus lost count of the number of times Sister Magdalena crossed herself as he and Paulinus told her what they knew of Octavus and his miraculous ability. Finally, when they were done and there was no more to be told, the three of them exchanged nervous looks.

"Surely this is the work of the Devil," Magdalena said, breaking the quiet.

Paulinus said, "There is an alternative explanation."

"And that is?" she asked.

"The work of the Lord." Paulinus chose his words carefully. "Surely, there can be no doubt that the Lord chooses when to bring a child into this world and when to reclaim a soul to his bosom. God knows all. He knows when a simple man calls out to him in prayer, he knows when a sparrow falls from the sky. This boy, who is unlike all others in the manner of his birth and his countenance, how do we know he is not a vessel of the Lord to record the comings and goings of God's children?"

"But he may be the seventh son of a seventh son!" Magdalena hissed.

"Yes, we know of the beliefs concerning such a being. But who has met such a man before? And who has met one born on the seventh day of the seventh month of the year 777? We cannot presume to know that his powers have an evil purpose."

"I, for one, cannot see an evil consequence of the boy's powers," Josephus said hopefully.

Magdalena's demeanor changed from fear to anger. "If what you say is true, we know that our dear abbot will die on this very day. I pray to the Lord that this is not so. How can you say that this is not evil?" She rose and snatched up the parchment pages. "I will not hold secrets from the abbot. He must hear of this, and he—and he alone—must decide on the boy's fate."

She was determined, and neither Paulinus or Josephus were inclined to dissuade Sister Magdalena from her actions.

The three of them approached Oswyn after None, the mid-afternoon prayer, and accompanied him to his chambers in the Chapter House. There, in the dimming light of a wintry afternoon, the embers of his fire glowing amber, they told him their tale as each tried to study his pinched face, which because of his deformity angled down toward his table.

He listened. He studied the parchments, pausing for a moment to reflect on his own name. He asked questions and considered the responses. Then he signaled that the caucus was over by striking his fist on the table once.

"I cannot see good coming of this," he said. "At worst, it is the hand of the Devil. At best, it is a severe distraction to the religious life of this community. We are here to serve God with all our heart and all our might. This boy will divert us from our mission. You must cast him out."

At that, Magdalena suppressed a show of satisfaction.

Josephus cleared his dry throat. "His father will not take him back. There is no place for him to go."

"That is not our concern," the abbot said. "Send him away."

"It is cold," Josephus implored. "He will not survive the night."

"The Lord will provide for him and decide his fate," the abbot said. "Now, leave me to contemplate my own."

It was left to Josephus to do the deed, and after sundown he dutifully led the boy by the hand to the front gate of the abbey. A kind young sister had put heavy socks on his feet and wrapped him in an extra shirt and a small cloak. A cutting wind off the sea was pushing the temperature to the freezing point.

Josephus unlatched the gate and swung it open. They were hit squarely by a strong cold gust. The prior gently nudged the boy forward. "You must leave us, Octavus. But do not fear, God will protect you."

The boy did not turn to look back but faced the dark void of night with his immutable blank stare. It broke the prior's heart to treat one of God's creatures harshly, so harshly that he was likely condemning the child to a freezing death. And not an ordinary child but one with an extraordinary gift that, if Paulinus was correct, came not from the depths of Hell but perhaps from the realm of Heaven. But Josephus was an obedient servant, his first allegiance to God, whose opinion on this matter was not apparent to him, and his next allegiance to his abbot, whose opinion was clear as a windowpane.

Josephus shuddered and closed the gate behind him.

The bell rang for Vespers. The congregation assembled in the Sanctuary. Sister Magdalena held her lute to her chest and basked in her victory over Josephus, whom she scorned for his softness.

Paulinus's mind swirled with theological ideas about Octavus—whether his powers were gift or curse.

Josephus's eyes stung with salty tears at the thought of the frail little boy alone in the cold and dark. He felt intense guilt at his own warmth and comfort. Yet Oswyn, he was sure, was correct on one notion: the boy was indeed a distraction from his duties of prayer and servitude.

They waited for the shuffling steps of the abbot, which failed to materialize. Josephus could see the brothers and sisters shifting nervously, all of them keenly aware of Oswyn's punctuality.

After a few minutes Josephus became alarmed and whispered to Paulinus, "We must check on the abbot." All eyes followed them as they left. Whispers filled the Sanctuary, but Magdalena put a stop to them with a finger to her lips and a loud *shush*.

Oswyn's chamber was cold and dark, the untended fire

nearly spent. They found him curled and bent on his bed, fully dressed in his robes, his skin as cool as the room air. In his right hand he clutched the parchment upon which his name was written.

"Merciful God!" Josephus cried.

"The prophesy—" Paulinus muttered, falling to his knees.

The two men mouthed quick prayers over Oswyn's body, then rose.

"The bishop must be informed," Paulinus said.

Josephus nodded. "I will send a messenger to Dorchester in the morning."

"Until the bishop says otherwise, you must lead this abbey, my friend."

Josephus crossed himself, digging his finger into his chest as he made the sign. "Go tell Sister Magdalena and ask her to begin Vespers. I will be there shortly, but first there is something I must do."

Josephus ran through the darkness to the abbey gate, his chest heaving with exertion. He pushed it open and it squeaked on its hinges.

The boy was not there.

He ran down the path, frantically calling his name.

There was a small shape by the road.

Octavus had not gone far. He was sitting quietly in the frigid night, shivering at the edge of a field. Josephus tenderly picked him up in his arms and carried him back toward the gate.

"You can stay, boy," he said. "God wants you to stay."

Will started flirting at sea level and was still going strong at 34,000 feet. The flight attendant was his type, a big shapely girl with pouty lips and dirty blond hair. A wisp of it kept falling in front of one eye and she was constantly and absently brushing it aside. After a while he began to imagine lying beside her naked, brushing it aside himself. A little wave of guilt inexplicably washed over him when Nancy intruded into his thoughts, proper and reproachful. What was she doing mucking up his fantasies? He willfully fought back and reverted to the stewardess.

He had followed standard TSA security procedures for checking onto the US Airways flight with his service weapon. He was preboarded in coach and had settled into an aisle seat over the wing. Darla, the stewardess, immediately liked the looks of the brawny guy in a sport coat and khakis and draped herself over the cross aisle seat.

"Hey, FBI," she chirped, knowing as much because of the security procedures he'd undergone.

"Hey yourself."

"Get you something to drink before we get invaded?"

"Do I smell coffee?"

"Coming up," she said. "We've got an air marshal in 7C today, but you're way bigger than he is."

"You want to tell him I'm here?"

"He already knows."

Later, during the beverage service, she seemed to lightly

brush his shoulder or his arm whenever she passed. Maybe it was his imagination, he thought as he drifted to sleep, lulled by the low rumble of the engines. Or maybe not.

He awoke with a startle, pleasantly disorientated. There were green crop fields stretching to the horizon so he knew they were somewhere over the middle of the country. Loud angry voices were coming from the rear near the lavs. He undid his seat belt, turned around and identified the problem: three young Brits spanning a row, drinking buddies in full lager-lout mode, getting prelubed for their Vegas holiday. Ruddy-faced, they were gesticulating like a three-headed monster at a willowy male flight attendant who had cut off their flow of beer. As alarmed passengers looked on, the Brit nearest the aisle—a taut bundle of muscle and tendon—rose up and stood eyeball-to-eyeball with the crew member and shouted emphatically, "You heard my mate! He wants another fuckin' drink!"

Darla quickly moved up the aisle to assist her colleague, deliberately seeking out Will's eyes as she flew by. The air marshal in 7C held his seat, standard operating procedure, watching the cockpit, on guard for a diversion. He was a young guy, blanched with nerves, sucking it up. Probably his first real incident, Will thought, leaning into the aisle, studying him.

Then, a sickening thud, skull on skull, a Glaswegian kiss. "That's what ya get, ya fuckin' bastard!" the assailant screamed. "Ya want another one?" Will missed the act but saw the aftermath.

The head butt opened the attendant's scalp and knocked him yelping to his knees. Darla involuntarily let out a short shriek at the sight of flowing blood.

The air marshal and Will rose as one, locked onto each other and started to perform like a team that had drilled repeatedly together. The marshal stood in the aisle, drew his weapon and called out, "Federal agents! Sit down and place your hands on the seat in front of you!"

Will showed his ID and slowly advanced toward the rear holding the badge above his head.

"Oh what tha fuck is this, then?" the Brit called out as he saw Will closing. "We're just trying to get our hols started, mate."

Darla helped the bleeding attendant to his feet and led him forward, scooting by Will, who gave her a reassuring wink. When he was five rows from the troublemakers he halted and spoke slowly and calmly. "Take your seat immediately and place your hands on top of your head. You are under arrest. Your vacation is over." Then the staccato punctuation mark, "Mate."

His friends implored him to back off but the man would not stand down, crying now with rage and fear, cornered, his jugulars distended purple. "I will not!" he kept repeating. "I will not!"

Will pocketed his badge and unholstered his gun, double-checking the engaged safety. At this, the passengers became terrified; an obese woman with an infant started blubbering, which started a chain reaction throughout the cabin. Will tried to erase the drowsiness from his face and look as bad-ass as possible. "This is your last opportunity to end this well. Sit down and put your hands on your head."

"Or what?" the man taunted, his nose thick with mucus. "You going to shoot me and put a hole through the bleedin' plane?"

"We use special ammo," Will said, lying through his teeth. "The round'll just rattle around inside your head and turn your brain into pudding." An expert shot who had spent his youth picking off fox squirrels in the Panhandle brush, at this range he could place a round anywhere he wanted within a few millimeters, but it would exit, all right.

The man was speechless.

"You've got five seconds," Will announced, elevating the pistol from a chest shot to a head shot. "I honestly don't care if I pull the trigger at this point. You've already given me a week of paperwork."

One of his friends cried out, "For fuck's sake, Sean, sit down!" and tugged his companion by the tail of his polo shirt. Sean hesitated for a few long seconds then let himself be pulled onto his seat, where he meekly raised his hands over his head.

"Good decision," Will told him.

Darla rushed up the aisle with a handful of plastic wrist restraints, and with the help of other passengers, the three friends were cuffed. Will lowered his weapon and slid it back under his coat then called out to the marshal, "We're clear back here." Breathing heavily, he lumbered back to his seat to the accompaniment of thunderous applause from the entire cabin. He wondered if he'd be able to get back to sleep.

The taxi pulled away from the curb. Even though it was evening, the desert heat was still stunning, and Will welcomed the frosty interior.

"Where to?" the cabbie asked.

"Who do you think's got the better room?" Will asked.

Darla pushed at his ribs playfully. "An airline room or a government one, it's probably the same." She leaned in and whispered, "But honey, I don't think we're going to notice."

They were looping around the perimeter of McCarran heading toward the Strip. Parked next to a remote hangar, Will noticed a cluster of three white 737s, unmarked except for red body stripes. "What airline is that?" he asked Darla.

"That's the Area 51 shuttle," she replied. "They're military planes."

"You're joking."

The cabbie needed to participate. "She ain't kidding. It's the worst-kept secret in Vegas. We got hundreds of government scientists who commute there every day. They got alien space ships they're trying to make work, that's what I hear."

Will chuckled. "I'm sure whatever it is, it's a waste of taxpayer money. Believe it or not, I think I know a guy who works there."

Nelson Elder presided over a culture of fitness. He vigorously exercised every morning and expected members of his senior management team to do likewise. "No one wants to see a fat insurance guy," he'd tell them, least of all him. He had a gold-plated prejudice against the unfit that bordered on revulsion, a vestige of growing up poor in Bakersfield, California, where poverty and obesity commingled in his hardscrabble mobile home park. He didn't hire obese people, and if he insured them, he made damn sure they paid hefty risk-adjusted premiums.

His bronzed skin still tingled from his three-mile run and stinging steam shower, and as he sat in his corner office, with its fine view of chocolate-brown mountains and an aquamarine finger of Lake Mead, he felt as well physically as a sixty-one-year-old man could. His tailored suit form-fitted his tight frame and his athletic heart beat slowly. Yet mentally he was in turmoil, and his cup of herbal tea was doing little to settle him.

Bertram Myers, Desert Life's CFO, was at his door panting heavily and sweating like a racehorse. He was twenty years younger than his boss, his hair wiry and black, but he was a lesser athlete.

"Good run?" Elder asked.

"Excellent, thanks," Myers answered. "Had yours yet?"

"You bet."

"How come you're in so early?"

"F.B. fucking I. Remember?"

"Jesus, I forgot. I'm going to hop in the shower. Want me to sit in?"

"No, I'll handle it," Elder said.

"You worried? You look worried."

"I'm not worried. I think it is what it is."

Myers agreed. "Exactly, it is what it is."

Will had a short cab ride to the Desert Life headquarters in Henderson, a bedroom town south of Vegas near Lake Mead. To him, Elder looked like something out of central casting, a prototypical silver-fox CEO, easy with his wealth and station. The executive leaned back in his chair and attempted to lower Will's expectations. "As I said on the phone, Special Agent Piper, I'm not sure if I can help you. This may be a long trip for a short meeting."

"Don't worry about that, sir," Will replied. "I had to come out here anyway."

"I saw in the news that you'd made an arrest in New York."

"I'm not at liberty to comment about an ongoing investigation," Will said, "but I think you can assume if I thought the case was wrapped up, I probably wouldn't have come out here. I wonder if you could tell me about your relationship with David Swisher?"

According to Elder, there wasn't all that much to tell. They had met six years earlier during one of Elder's frequent visits to New York to meet with investors. At the time, HSBC was one of multiple banks courting Desert Life as a client, and Swisher, a senior managing director at the bank, was a rainmaker. Elder had gone to HSBC's headquarters, where Swisher led a pitch team.

Swisher followed-up aggressively by telephone and e-mail over the next year and his perseverance paid off. When Desert Life decided to place a bond offering in 2003 to fund an acquisition, Elder chose HSBC to lead the underwriting syndicate.

Will asked if Swisher had personally traveled to Las Vegas as part of that process.

Elder was certain he had not. He had a firm recollection that the company visits were handled by more junior bankers. Apart from the closing dinner in New York, the two men didn't see each other again.

Had they communicated over the years?

Elder recalled an occasional phone call here and there.

And when was the last?

A good year ago. Nothing recent. They were on each other's corporate holiday card lists but this was hardly an active relationship. When he read about Swisher's murder, Elder said, he had of course been shocked.

Will's line of questioning was interrupted by his Beethoven

ring tone. He apologized and switched off the phone, but not before recognizing the caller ID number.

Why the hell was Laura calling?

He picked up his train of thought and fired off a list of follow-up questions. Had Swisher ever talked about a Las Vegas connection? Friends? Business contacts? Had he ever mentioned gambling or personal debts? Had he ever shared any aspect of his personal life? Did Elder know if he had any enemies?

The answer to all these was no. Elder wanted Will to understand that his relationship with Swisher was superficial, transient and transactional. He wished he could be more helpful but plainly he could not.

Will felt his disappointment rise like bile. The interview was going nowhere, another Doomsday dead end. Yet there was something niggling about Elder's demeanor, a small discordant something. Was there a note of tension in his throat, a touch of glibness? Will didn't know where his next question came from—maybe it sprung from a well of intuition. "Tell me, Mr. Elder, how's your business doing?"

Elder hesitated for more than an imperceptible moment, a long enough pause for Will to conclude that he'd struck a nerve. "Well, business is very good. Why do you ask?"

"No reason, just curious. Let me ask you: most insurance companies are in places like Hartford, New York, major cities. Why Las Vegas, why Henderson?"

"Our roots are here," Elder replied. "I built this company brick by brick. Right out of college, I started as an agent in a little brokerage in Henderson, about a mile from this office. We had six employees. I bought the place from the owner when he retired and renamed it Desert Life. We now have over eight thousand employees, coast-to-coast."

"That's very impressive. You must be very proud."

"Thank you, I am."

"And the insurance business, you say, is good."

That tiny hesitation again. "Well, everybody needs insurance. There's a lot of competition out there and the regulatory environment can be a challenge sometimes, but we've got a strong business."

As he listened, Will noticed a leather pen holder on the desk, chock full of black and red Pentel pens.

He couldn't help himself. "Could I borrow one of your pens?" he asked, pointing. "A black one."

"Sure," Elder replied, puzzled.

It was an ultrafine point. Well, well.

He reached into his briefcase and pulled out a sheet of paper in a clear plastic cover, a Xerox copy of the front and back of Swisher's postcard. "Could you take a look at this?"

Elder took the sheet and retrieved his reading glasses. "Chilling," he said.

"See the postmark?"

"May eighteenth."

"Were you in Las Vegas on the eighteenth?"

Elder was palpably irritated by the question. "I have no idea, but I'd be happy to have my assistant check for you."

"Great. How many times have you been to New York in the past six weeks?"

Elder frowned and replied testily, "Zero."

"I see," Will said. He pointed to the photocopy. "Could I get that back, please?"

Elder returned the sheet, and Will thought, Hey, buddy, for what it's worth, I've got your fingerprints.

After Will departed, Bertram Myers wandered in and sat down in the still warm chair. "How'd it go?" he asked his boss.

"As advertised. He was focused on David Swisher's murder. He wanted to know where I was the day his post-card was mailed from Las Vegas."

"You're joking!"

"No I am not."

"I had no idea you were a serial killer, Nelson."

Elder loosened his tightly knotted Hermes tie. He was starting to relax. "Watch out, Bert, you may be next."

"So that was it? He didn't ask a single troubling question?"

"Not one. I don't know why I was worried."

"You said you weren't."

"I lied."

Will left Henderson to spend the rest of the day working out of the FBI field office in North Las Vegas before his scheduled return to New York on the red-eye. Local agents had been working up unidentified fingerprints on Doomsday postcards. By cross-tabbing with prints taken from postal workers at the Las Vegas Main Office they managed to ID a few latents. He had them throw Elder's prints into the mix then settled into the conference room to read the newspaper and wait for the analysis. When his stomach started rumbling he took a walk down Lake Mead Boulevard to look for a sandwich shop.

The heat was blistering. Doffing his jacket and rolling up his shirtsleeves didn't help much so he ducked into the first place he found, a quiet, pleasantly air-conditioned Quiznos manned by a crew of desultory workers. While he waited at a table for his sub to toast he called his voice mail and cycled through the messages.

The final one set him off. He cursed out loud, drawing a dirty look from the manager. A snot-nosed voice informed him his cable was about to be cut off. He was three months overdue and unless he paid today he'd be coming home to a test pattern.

He tried to remember the last time he'd paid any of his household bills and couldn't. He visualized the large stack of unopened mail on his kitchenette counter—he needed this like head lice.

He'd have to call Nancy; he owed her one anyway.

"Greetings from Sin City," he said.

She was cool.

"What's going on with Camacho?" he asked.

"His diary checked out. He couldn't have done the other murders."

"No surprise, I guess."

"Nope. How was your interview with Nelson Elder?"

"Is he our killer? I seriously doubt it. Is there something fishy about him? Yeah, definitely."

"Fishy?"

"I got a sense he was hiding something."

"Anything solid?"

"He had Pentel ultrafines on his desk."

"Get a warrant," she said, bone dry.

"Well, I'll check him out." Then, sheepishly, he asked her to help with his little cable problem. He had a spare key in his office. Could she stop by his apartment, pick up the overdue bill, and give him a call so he could take care of it with a credit card?

Not a problem, she told him.

"Thanks. And one more thing." He felt he had to say it: "I want to apologize for the other night. I got pretty loaded."

He heard her taking a breath. "It's okay."

He knew it wasn't but what more could he say? When he hung up, he looked at his watch. He had hours to kill before his red-eye back to New York. He wasn't a gambler so there was no tug toward the casinos. Darla was long gone by now. He could get loaded, but he could do that anywhere. Then something occurred to him that made him half smile. He opened his phone to make another call.

Nancy tensed up as soon as she opened the door to Will's apartment.

There was music.

An open travel bag was in the living room.

She called out. "Hello?"

The shower was running.

Louder. "Hello?"

The water stopped and she heard a voice from the bathroom. "Hello?"

A wet young woman hesitantly emerged wrapped in a bath towel. She was in her early twenties, blond, lissome with a prepossessing naturalness. Puddles were forming around her perfect, small feet. Awfully young, Nancy bitterly thought, and she was blindsided by her initial reaction to the stranger—a tug of jealousy.

"Oh, hi," the woman said. "I'm Laura."

"I'm Nancy."

There was an uncomfortably long pause until, "Will's not here."

"I know. He asked me to pick something up for him."

"Go ahead, I'll be right out," Laura said, retreating into the bathroom.

Nancy tried to find the cable bill and get out before the woman reemerged but was too slow and Laura was too fast. She was barefoot in jeans and a T-shirt, her hair in a towel turban. The kitchenette was uncomfortably small for the two of them.

"Cable bill," Nancy said weakly.

"He sucks at ADL," Laura said, then at Nancy's incomprehension, added, "Activities of daily living."

"He's been pretty busy," Nancy said in his defense.

"And you know him—how?" Laura asked, fishing.

"We work together." Nancy steeled herself for her next response—no, I'm not his secretary.

Instead, surprisingly, "You're an agent?"

"Yeah." She mimicked Laura. "And you know him—how?"

"He's my dad."

An hour later they were still talking. Laura was drinking wine, Nancy, iced tap water, two women with a maddening bond—Will Piper.

Once their roles were clarified they took to each other. Nancy seemed relieved the woman wasn't Will's girlfriend; Laura seemed relieved her father had an ostensibly normal female partner. Laura had taken the train up from Washington that morning for a hastily arranged meeting in Manhattan. When she couldn't reach her father to ask if she could stay the night, she decided he was probably out of pocket and let herself in with her own key.

Laura was shy at first but the second glass of wine uncorked an agreeable volubility. Only six years separated them and they quickly found common ground beyond Will. Unlike her father, it seemed to Nancy that Laura was a culture hound who rivaled her own knowledge of art and music. They shared a favorite museum, the Met; a favorite opera, *La Boheme*; a favorite painter, Monet.

Spooky, they agreed, but fun.

Laura was two years out of college, doing part-time office work to support herself. She lived in Georgetown with her boyfriend, a grad student in journalism at American University. At a tender age, she was on the verge of crossing what she considered to be a profound threshold. A small, but prestigious publisher was seriously considering her first novel. Although she had written since puberty, an English teacher in high school starchily upbraided her not to call herself a writer until her work was in print. She desperately wanted to call herself a writer.

Laura was insecure and self-conscious but her friends and mentors had urged her on. Her book was publishable, she'd been told, so naively she sent the manuscript, unsolicited and unagented, to a dozen publishers then proceeded to write the screenplay version because she saw it as a film too. Time passed and she became acclimated to heavy packages at her door, the boomeranged manuscript plus a rejection letter—nine, ten, eleven times—but the twelfth never arrived. Finally, a call instead, from Elevation Press in New York, expressing interest and wondering if, absent a commitment, she'd make some changes and resubmit. She readily agreed and did a rewrite in accordance with their notes. The day before, she'd received an e-mail from the editor, inviting her to their offices, a nerve-wracking but auspicious sign.

Nancy found Laura a fascination, a glimpse into an alternative life. Lipinskis weren't writers or artists, they were shopkeepers or accountants, or dentists or FBI agents. And she was interested in how Will's DNA could possibly have produced this untainted charming creature. The answer had to be maternal.

In fact, Laura's mother—Will's first wife, Melanie—wrote poetry and taught creative writing at a community college in Florida. The marriage, Laura told her, had lasted just long enough for her conception, birth, and second birthday party, before Will smashed it into smithereens. Growing up, the words "your father" were spat as epithets.

He was a ghost. She heard about his life secondhand, capturing snippets from her mother and aunts. She pictured him from the wedding album, blue-eyed, large and smiling, locked in time. He left the sheriff's department. He joined the FBI. He remarried. He divorced again. He was a drinker. He was a womanizer. He was a bastard whose only saving grace was paying child support. And he never so much as called or sent a card along the way.

One day Laura saw him on the news being interviewed about some ghastly serial killer. She saw the name Will Piper on the TV screen, recognized the blue eyes and the squared-off jaw, and the fifteen-year-old girl cried a river. She began to write short stories about him, or at least what she imagined him to be. And in college, emancipated from her mother's influence, she did some detective work and found him in New York City. Since then they'd had a relationship, of sorts, quasifilial and tentative. He was the inspiration for her novel.

Nancy asked its title.

"*The Wrecking Ball*," Laura replied.

Nancy laughed. "The shoe fits, I guess."

"He *is* a wrecking ball, but so are booze, genes, and destiny. I mean Dad's father and mother were both alcoholics. Maybe he couldn't escape it." She poured herself another glass of wine and waved it in a toast. By now her speech was a little heavy. "Maybe I can't either."

Nelson Elder was arriving at the foot of the driveway of his home, a six-bedroom mansion at The Hills, in Summerlin, when his mobile phone rang. The caller ID registered PRIVATE CALLER. He answered and pulled the large Mercedes up to one of the garage bays.

"Mr. Elder?"

"Yes, who is this?"

The caller's voice was pinched with tension, almost squeaky. "We met a few months ago at the Constellation. My name is Peter Benedict."

"I'm sorry, I don't recall."

"I was the one who caught the blackjack counters."

"Yes! I remember! The computer guy." Strange, Elder thought. "Did I give you my cell phone number?"

"You did," Mark lied. There wasn't a phone number in the world he couldn't grab. "Is it okay?"

"Sure. How can I help you?"

"Well, actually, sir, I'd like to help you."

"How so?"

"Your company is in trouble, Mr. Elder, but I can save it."

Mark was breathing rapidly and visibly shaking. His cell phone was on the kitchen table, still warm from his cheek. Each step of his plan had taxed him, but this was the first requiring human interaction, and his terror was slow to dissipate. Nelson Elder would meet with him. One more chess move and the game was his.

Then his doorbell jolted him into the next level of autonomic overdrive. He rarely had unannounced visitors, and in fear he almost bolted for his bedroom. He calmed himself and hesitantly went to the door and opened it a crack.

"Will?" he asked incredulously. "What are you doing here?"

Will stood there with a big easy smile on his face. "Weren't expecting me, were you?"

Will could see that Mark was unsteady, like a tower of playing cards trying to maintain a composure. "No. I wasn't."

"Hey, look, I was in town on business and thought I'd look you up. Is this a bad time?"

"No. It's fine," Mark said mechanically. "I just wasn't expecting anybody. Would you like to come in?"

"Sure. For a few minutes, anyway. I've got a little time to kill before I head to the airport."

Will followed him to the living room, reading tension and discomfort in his old roomie's stiff gait and high voice. He couldn't help profiling the guy. It wasn't a parlor trick—he always had the knack, the ability to figure out someone's feelings, conflicts, and motivations with lightning speed. As a child, he'd used his natural acumen to fashion a protected triangulated space between two alcoholic parents, saying and doing the right things in the right aliquots to satisfy their neediness and preserve some measure of balance and stability in the household.

He'd always wielded his talent to his advantage. In his personal life, he used it in a Dale Carnegie way to win friends and influence people. The women in his life would say he used it to manipulate the hell out of them. And in his career, it had given him a tangible edge over the criminals who populated his world.

Will wondered what was making Mark so uncomfortable—a phobic, misanthropic kind of personality disorder or something more specific to his visit?

He sat down on an unyielding sofa and sought to put him at ease. "You know, after we saw each other at the reunion, I kind of felt bad I hadn't gone to the effort to look you up all these years."

Mark sat across from him, mute, with tightly crossed legs.

"So, I hardly ever come out to Vegas—this is just a one-nighter—and on my way to the hotel yesterday someone pointed out the Area 51 shuttle and I thought of you."

"Really?" Mark asked with a rasp. "Why's that?"

"That's where you sort of implied you worked, no?"

"Did I? I don't recall saying that."

Will remembered Mark's odd demeanor when the subject of Area 51 came up at the reunion dinner. This looked like a no-go zone. In fact he didn't care, one way or the other. Mark clearly had a high-level security clearance and took it seriously. Good for him. "Well, whatever. It doesn't matter to me where you work, it just triggered an association and I decided to drop in, that's all."

Mark continued to look skeptical. "How'd you find me? I'm not listed."

"Don't I know. I've got to admit it—I queried an FBI database in the local office when 411 didn't do the trick. You weren't on the radar screen, buddy. Must have an interesting job! So I called Zeckendorf to see if he had your number. He didn't, but you must've given him your address so his wife could mail you that picture." He waved at the reunion photo on the table. "I put mine on the coffee table too. I guess we're just a couple of sentimental guys. Say, you wouldn't have anything to drink, would you?"

Will saw that Mark was breathing easier. He'd broken the ice. The guy probably had a social anxiety disorder and needed time to warm up.

"What would you like?" Mark asked.

"Got scotch?"

"Sorry, only beer."

"When in Rome."

When Mark went to the kitchen, Will stood up and out of curiosity had a look around. The living room was sparsely furnished with characterless modern things that could have been in the lobby of a public space. Everything was neat, with no clutter and also no feminizing touches. He knew that decorating style cold. The shiny chrome bookcase was filled with academic-type computer and software books arranged precisely by height so the rows topped off as straight as possible.

On the white lacquered desk, next to a closed laptop computer, was a short stack of two thin manuscripts bound in brass brads. He glanced at the cover page of the one on top: *Counters: a screenplay by Peter Benedict, WGA #4235567.* Who's Peter Benedict? he wondered, Mark's nom de plume or some other guy? Beside the screenplays there were two black pens. He almost laughed out loud. Pentel ultrafines. The little peckers were everywhere. He was back on the sofa when Mark returned with the beers.

"In Cambridge, didn't you mention you did some writing?" Will asked.

"I do."

"Those screenplays yours?" he asked, pointing.

Mark nodded and gulped.

"My daughter's something of a writer too. What do you write about?"

Mark started tentatively but progressively relaxed as he talked about his most recent script. By the time Will downed the beer, he'd heard all about casinos and card-counting and Hollywood and talent agents. For a reticent guy, this was almost a blue-streak topic. During his second beer, he got a taste of Mark's postcollege, pre-Vegas life, a barren landscape of few personal bonds and endless computer work. During the third beer, Will reciprocated with details about his own past, sour marriages, busted relationships and all, and Mark listened in fascination, with a growing amazement that the golden boy's life, which he had assumed was perfect, was anything but. At the same time, creeping pangs of guilt were making Will uneasy.

After taking a leak, Will returned to the living room and announced he had to be going, but before he did, he wanted to get something off his chest. "I've got to apologize to you."

"For what?"

"When I look back on freshman year, I realize I was a jerk. I should have helped you out more, gotten Alex to leave you alone. I was a dumb-ass and I'm sorry." He didn't mention the duct-taping incident; he didn't have to.

Mark involuntarily teared up and looked profoundly embarrassed. "I—"

"You don't have to say anything. I don't want to cause any discomfort."

Mark sniffed. "No, look, I appreciate it. I don't think we really knew each other."

"True enough." Will dug his hand in his pockets for the car keys. "So, thanks for the beers and the chat. I've got to hit it."

Mark inhaled and finally said, "I think I know why you're in town. I saw you on TV."

"Yeah, the Doomsday case. The Vegas connection. Sure."

"I've watched you on TV for years. And read all the magazine articles."

"Yeah, I've had my fill of media stuff."

"It must be exciting."

"Believe me, it's not."

"How's it going? The investigation, I mean."

"I've got to tell you, it's a pain up my butt. I didn't want any part of it. I was just trying to ease on down retirement road."

"Are you making any progress?"

"You're obviously a guy who can keep a secret. Here's one: we don't have a fucking clue."

Mark looked weary when he said, "I don't think you're going to catch the guy."

Will squinted at him strangely. "Why do you say that?"

"I don't know. What I've read about it, he sounds like he's pretty clever."

"No, no, no. I'll catch him. I always do."

The call from Peter Benedict rattled Elder. It was deeply unsettling to receive an offer to help Desert Life from a man he had met once in a casino. And he was almost certain he hadn't given out his mobile number. Add to that the FBI's sudden interest in him and his company, and this was shaping up to be a worrisome weekend. During times of trouble he preferred to be in his headquarters with his people surrounding him, a general among his troops. He thought nothing of pulling in his executive team during a crisis to work on Saturdays and Sundays but needed to deal with this situation alone. Even Bert Myers, his confidant and consigliore, would have to be blacked-out until he knew what he was dealing with.

Only he and Myers knew the extent of Desert Life's problems because the two of them were the sole architects of a scheme to get the company out of its financial hole. Undoubtedly, the correct adjective to describe the scheme was "fraudulent," but Elder preferred to think of it as "aggressive." The plan was in its early stages, but unfortunately it wasn't working yet. In fact, it was backfiring and the hole was getting deeper. In desperation, they had decided to shift some cash from their reserves to artificially boost profits for the last quarter and shore up the stock price.

Dangerous ground, the path to Hell, or at least prison.

They knew it, but in for a penny, in for a pound. And God willing, Elder thought, things would turn around in the next quarter. It had to. He had built this company with his own two hands. It was his life's work and his one true love. It meant more to him than his arid country club wife or his dissolute offspring and it had to be saved, so if this Peter Benedict character had a viable idea, then he was obligated to hear it.

The backbone of Desert Life's business was life insurance. The company was the largest underwriter of life insurance policies west of the Mississippi. Elder had cut his teeth in the business as a life insurance man. The steady actuarial predictability of forecasting death rates had always attracted him. If you tried to predict an individual's time to death and put money on it, you'd be wrong too often to make a consistent profit. To get around trying to figure out an individual's risk, insurers relied instead on the "law of large numbers" and employed armies of actuaries and statisticians to conduct analyses on past performance to help predict the future. While no one could calculate what premium you'd have to charge one individual to make money, you could predict with confidence the economics of insuring, say, thirty-five-year-old male nonsmokers with negative drug screens and a family history of heart disease.

Still, profit margins were tight. For every dollar Desert Life took in as premiums, thirty cents went to expenses, most went to cover losses, and the little left over was profit. Profits in the insurance game came two ways: underwriting profits and investment income.

Insurance companies were huge investors, putting billions of dollars into play every day. The returns from those investments were the cornerstone of their business. Some companies even underwrote to a loss—taking a dollar of premium and expecting to pay more than a dollar in losses and expenses but hoping to make it up in investment income. Elder disdained that strategy but his appetite for investment returns was large.

Desert Life's problems were growth-related. Over the years, as he'd enlarged the business and expanded his empire through acquisitions, he diversified away from dependence on life insurance. He branched out into homeowners and auto insurance for individuals and property, casualty and liability insurance for businesses.

For years business boomed, but then the worm turned.

"Hurricanes, goddamn hurricanes," he'd grumble out loud, even when he was alone. One after another, they slammed into Florida and the Gulf coast and beat the stuffing out of his profits. His surplus reserves—the funds available to pay out future claims—were falling to red-flag levels. State and federal insurance regulators were taking notice and so was Wall Street. His stock was nose-diving and that was turning his life into something out of Dante's *Inferno*.

Bert Myers, financial genius, to the rescue.

Myers wasn't an insurance guy; he had a background in investment banking. Elder had brought him in a few years earlier to help with their acquisition strategy. As far as corporate finance types went, he was a very sharp knife in a very large drawer, one of the smartest guys on the Street.

Faced with dwindling profits, Myers hatched a plan. He couldn't control Mother Nature and all those damage claims against the company but he could boost their investment returns by "wandering over the line," as he put it. Government regulators, not to mention their own internal charter, imposed strict restrictions on the kinds of investments they could make, mostly low-return, nonrisky forays in the bond market and conservative investments in mortgages, consumer loans, and real estate.

They couldn't take their precious reserves and bet them up the road on the roulette tables. But Myers had his eye on a hedge fund run by some math whizzes in Connecticut who had reaped enormous returns by correctly betting on international currency fluctuations. The fund, International Advisory Partners, was off-the-chart from a risk perspective, and investing in it was not an option for a company like Desert Life. But once Elder signed off on the scheme, Myers set up a dummy real estate partnership, ostensibly meeting the Desert Life risk profile, and passed a billion plus in reserves into IAP, hoping for outsized returns to repair their profit statements.

Myer's timing was not good. IAP used Desert Life's cash infusion to bet that the yen would fall relative to the dollar—and didn't the Japanese finance minister have to mess things up by making an adverse statement about Japanese monetary policy?

Their first quarter: down fourteen percent on their investment. The IAP guys were insisting that this was an anomaly and their strategy was sound. Myers just needed to hang on and everything would come out roses. So, in the full desert heat, their palms were sweating but they were holding on as tightly as they could.

Elder decided to meet Peter Benedict on a Sunday morning to keep it low-key and far away from his office. A down-market waffle house in North Las Vegas seemed like a venue his employees or friends were unlikely to frequent, and with the smell of maple syrup in his nostrils he sat and waited in an interior booth, dressed in white poplin golf trousers and a thin orange cashmere sweater. He wasn't sure he remembered what the man looked like and he scanned each patron.

Mark arrived a few minutes late, an unassuming presence in jeans and his ubiquitous Lakers cap, carrying a manila envelope. He spotted Elder first, steeled himself, and made his way to the booth. Elder rose and extended his hand, "Hello, Peter, nice to see you again."

Mark was shy, uncomfortable. Elder's culture demanded some small talk but it was painful for Mark. Blackjack was their only known common ground so Elder chatted about cards for a few minutes before insisting they order some breakfast. Mark became distracted by the fluttering in his chest, which he worried might be turning into something pathological. He sipped ice water and tried to control his breathing but his heart raced. Should he get up and leave?

It was too late for that.

The statutory small talk ended and Elder got down to it. The pleasantries done, his tone was flinty: "So, Peter, tell me why you think my company is in trouble?"

Mark had no formal finance background but he had taught himself how to read financial statements in Silicon Valley. He'd begun by dissecting his own data security company's SEC filings then moved on to other high-tech companies, looking for good investments. When he came across an accounting concept he didn't understand, he read about it until he had amassed a body of knowledge a CPA would envy. His mind had so much horsepower, he found the logic and the mathematics underpinning accountancy trivial.

Now, in a constricted voice, he began rattling mechanically through all the subtle anomalies in Desert Life's last 10-Q: the quarterly financial report filed with the government. He had detected faint footprints of fraud that no one on Wall Street had noticed. He even guessed correctly that the company might be trawling in prohibited waters for high-yield returns.

Elder listened with a queasy fascination.

When Mark was done, Elder cut into a waffle, took a small bite and quietly chewed. When he swallowed, he said, "I'm not commenting whether you're right or wrong. Suppose you just tell me how you think you can help Desert Life."

Peter took the manila envelope he'd been keeping on his lap and handed it across the table. He said nothing but it was clear to the older man that the envelope was to be opened. Inside were a bunch of newspaper clippings.

All of them were about the Doomsday Killer.

"What the hell is this?" Elder asked.

"It's the way to save your company," Mark almost whispered. The moment was upon him and he felt woozy.

Then the moment seemed to slip away.

Elder reacted viscerally and started to get up. "What are you, some kind of a sicko? For your information, I know one of the victims!"

"Which one?" Mark croaked.

"David Swisher." He reached for his wallet.

Mark mustered his courage and said, "You should sit down. He wasn't a victim."

"What do you mean?"

"Please sit down and listen to me."

Elder complied. "I've got to tell you, I don't like where this conversation is going. You've got a minute to explain yourself or I'm out of here, understand?"

"Well, he *was* a victim, I guess. He just wasn't a victim of the Doomsday Killer."

"How do you know that?"

"Because there is no Doomsday Killer."

Abbot Josephus caught sight of himself in the reflection of one of the long windows of the Chapter House. It was black outside, but the candles indoors had not yet been smothered so the window had the quality of a reflecting glass.

He had a bulging middle and fleshy jowls and he was the only adult male in the community who was not tonsured, nor could he be, since he was completely bald.

A young monk, an Iberian with dark hair and a beard as dense as bear fur, knocked and entered with a candle snuffer. He bowed slightly and began his task.

"Good evening, Father." His accent was thick as honey.

"Good evening, José."

The abbot favored José above all of the younger brothers because of his intellect, his skill as a manuscript illustrator, and his good humor. He was seldom gloomy, and when he became amused, his laugh reminded the older man of the laughter he had heard many years earlier booming from the mouth of his friend Matthias, the blacksmith who had forged the abbey bell.

"How is the night air?" the abbot asked.

"It is fragrant, Father, and filled with cricket-song."

With the Chapter House dark. José left two candles burning in the abbot's chamber, one on his study table, the other by his bedside, and bade his superior good night. Alone, Josephus knelt by his bed and prayed the same prayer he had uttered since the day he became abbot: "Dear Lord, please bless this humble servant who strives to honor you each and every day and give me the strength to be the shepherd of this abbey and to serve your ends. And bless your vessel, Octavus, who toils endlessly to fulfill your divine mission, for you command his hand just as you command our hearts and minds. Amen."

Then Josephus blew out the last candle and climbed into his bed.

When the Bishop of Dorchester asked his new abbot whom he wanted to serve as prior, Josephus was quick to suggest Sister Magdalena. To be sure, there was no one better suited for the task. Her sense of organization and duty were unsurpassed among the ranks of the ministers. But Josephus had another motive, which had always made him uneasy. He needed her cooperation to protect the mission he believed Octavus was meant to accomplish.

She was the first Prioress of Vectis, and she prayed eagerly to be forgiven for the pride she felt every day. Josephus allowed her to attend to all details of the administration of the abbey, just as he had for Oswyn, and he listened patiently to her daily reports on the abuses and transgressions she ferreted out so energetically. Vectis, he acknowledged, was certainly more efficient and regimented than under his reign as prior. Yes, there was perhaps more grumbling over small matters, but he deigned to intervene only when he perceived Magdalena's actions excessive or cruel.

Instead he concentrated his attentions on prayer, the completion of the abbey's construction, and, of course, the boy, Octavus.

The latter two preoccupations intersected at the Scriptorium. Upon Oswyn's death, Josephus revisited the plans for the new Scriptorium and decided it must be even grander, since he fervently believed that the holy books and texts produced at Vectis were vital work for the betterment of mankind. He foresaw a future where ever more monks might produce more manuscripts, and the abbey and all Christendom would be elevated by their efforts.

Furthermore, he wanted a private chamber to be constructed, an inner sanctorum within the building where Octavus could work unimpeded. It was to be a special, protected place where he could transcribe the names that brewed inside him and poured onto the page as ale from a tapped barrel.

The cellar of the Scriptorium was dark and cool, perfect for the storage of large sheets of vellum and jars of ink but also well-suited for a boy who had no desire to play in the sunshine or walk in a meadow. A walled-off room was built in one end of the cellar, and there, behind a latched door, Octavus lived his life in perpetual candlelit darkness. His sole motivation was to sit on his stool, lean into his writing desk, and furiously dip his quill over and over and over again and scribble onto parchment until he collapsed in fatigue and had to be carried to his bed.

Because of his zeal for his vocation, Octavus rarely slept more than a few hours a day and would always wake without prompting, seemingly renewed. Whenever Paulinus first entered the Scriptorium in the morning, the boy was already hard at work. A young sister or novice would bring him his meals, dutifully avoiding contact with his handiwork, then empty his chamber pot and bring fresh tallow candles. Paulinus would collect the precious finished pages and bind them into heavy, thick, hide-covered books when there were sufficient numbers.

As Octavus grew from a small boy to a young man, his body elongated as if a baker had been pulling on warm dough. His appendages were spindly, almost rubbery, and his complexion, like bread dough, was pallid, without a trace of color. Even his lips were bleached out, with only the lightest tinge of pink. Had Paulinus not seen drops of crimson ooze from parchment cuts on his fingers, he would have supposed the lad was bloodless.

Unlike most boys, who upon maturation lose their delicate faces, Octavus's jaw did not go square and his nose did not spread. He maintained a boyish physiognomy that defied explanation, but then again, his very existence defied explanation. His fine hair remained bright ginger. Every month or so, Paulinus would summon the barber to trim his locks while he wrote, or better yet, while he slept, and clumps of carrot-colored hair would litter the floor until one of the girls who attended him swept them up.

The girls who, under oaths of secrecy, were permitted to feed him and dispose of his waste, were in awe of his stone-silent beauty and his absolute concentration, although one boldly mischievous novice, a fifteen-year-old named Mary, would sometimes make unsuccessful attempts to attract his gaze by dropping a goblet or clattering a plate.

However, nothing could distract Octavus from his work. The names rushed from his quill to the page in the hundreds, thousands, tens of thousands.

Paulinus and Josephus would often stand over him in a kind of reverie, watching the frantic scratching of his quill. While many entries were of the Roman alphabet, many were not. Paulinus recognized Arabic, Aramaic, and Hebraic scripts, but there were others he could not decipher. The boy's pace was furious, defying the absence of tension or urgency in his countenance. When the quill dulled, Paulinus would substitute another, so the lad could keep his letters tight and small. He packed his pages so densely that a finished page was more black than white. And when a page was done, he would turn it over and keep writing, drawing on some innate sense of parsimony or efficiency. Only when both sides were filled would Octavus reach for a clean sheet. Paulinus, arthritic and with a perpetually knotted stomach, would inspect each completed page, nervously wondering whether he might spot a name of particular interest: Paulinus of Vectis, for example.

Sometimes Paulinus and Josephus talked about how marvelous it would be to ask the lad what he thought about his life's work and for him to offer a cogent explanation. But they might as well have wished for a cow to explain what its existence meant to her. Octavus never met their gaze, never responded to their words, never showed emotion, never spoke. Over the years, the two aging monks often discussed the purpose of

Octavus's industry in a biblical context. God, the omniscient and eternal, knows all things of the past and the present, but also of the future, they both agreed. All of the events of the world are surely predetermined by dint of God's vision, and the Creator had apparently chosen the miraculously born Octavus as his living quill to record what was to be.

Paulinus possessed a copy of the thirteen books written by St. Augustine, his *Confessions*. The monks at Vectis held these volumes in high esteem since Augustine was a spiritual beacon to them, second only to St. Benedict. Josephus and Paulinus pored over the volumes and could almost hear the venerable saint speaking to them through time in this passage: *God decides the eternal destinations of each person. Their fate follows according to God's choice.*

Wasn't Octavus manifest proof of that assertion?

At first Josephus stored the leather-bound books in a rack against a wall in Octavus's chamber. By the time the boy was eight he had filled ten bulky books and Josephus had a second rack built. As he grew older, his hand grew faster, and in recent years he was producing some ten books a year. When the total number of volumes exceeded seventy and threatened to crowd out his chamber, Josephus decided the books must have their own place.

The abbot diverted workmen from other abbey construction projects to begin an excavation at the far side of the Scriptorium cellar, opposite Octavus's chamber. The copyists who labored in the main hall above grumbled about the muffled pick-axing and shoveling but Octavus was unfazed by the racket and pressed on.

In time Josephus had a library for Octavus's growing collection, a cool, dry, stone-lined vault. Ubertus personally supervised the masonry work, aware that his son was behind the closed door but completely uninterested in laying eyes upon the boy. He belonged to God now, not to him.

Josephus maintained a strict code of secrecy around Octavus. Only Paulinus and Magdalena knew the nature of his work, and outside this inner circle, only the few girls who tended him had direct contact. Of course, in a small community such as the abbey, there were whispered rumors about mysterious texts and sacred rituals involving the young man whom most had not seen since he was a little boy. However, Josephus was so loved and respected that no one questioned the piety and correctness of his actions. There were many things in this world the inhabitants of Vectis did not understand and this was just another one of them. They trusted God and Josephus to keep them safe and show them the correct path to holiness.

The seventh of July was Octavus's eighteenth birthday.

He began the day by relieving himself in the corner and marching straight to his writing desk for his first ink dip. He continued writing at the precise spot on the page where he had left off. Several large candles that burned even as he slept rested in heavy, forged stands and bathed the desk in flickering yellow light. He blinked to moisten his sandy eyes and set to work.

A new name. Mors. Then another name. Natus. And on and on.

In the early morning, Mary, the novice, knocked and, without waiting for a response she knew would never come, entered his chamber. She was a local girl who hailed from the Normandy-facing southern part of Vectis. Her father was a farmer with too many mouths to feed who hoped his earnest daughter would fare better as a servant of God than an impoverished wheat thresher. This was her fourth summer at the abbey. Sister Magdalena thought her a keen lass, quick to learn her prayers but a tad too high-spirited for her liking. She was mirthful and given to playful behavior with her fellow novices, such as hiding a sandal or placing an acorn in a bed. Unless her decorum improved, Magdalena was hesitant to admit her to the order.

Mary brought a light meal on a tray, brown bread and a slab of bacon. Unlike the other girls, who were fearful and never addressed Octavus, she would jabber away as if he were a normal young man. Now, she stood in front of his desk to try to get him to look at her. Her chestnut hair was still long and flowing and it spilled from under her veil. If she became a sister, her hair would be cut short, something she wished for but nonetheless dreaded. She was tall and big-boned, gangly like a yearling, pretty, with perpetually blush-apple cheeks.

"Well, Octavus, it's a fine summer morning up there, wouldn't you like to know."

She put the tray on his desk. Sometimes he would not even touch his food but she knew he had a fondness for bacon. He put his quill down and started chomping at the bread and meat. "You know why you've got bacon today?" she asked. He ate greedily, staring at the plate. "It's because it is your birthday, that's why!" she exclaimed. "You're eighteen years old! If you want to take a good rest today and put down your quill and take a walk in the sunshine, I'll let them know and I'm sure they'll let you."

He finished the food and immediately started writing again, his fingers rubbing grease on the parchment. For the two years she had catered for him, she'd grown increasingly intrigued by the boy. She had imagined that she alone would one day unlock his tongue and get him to speak his secrets. And she had convinced herself that there was something significant about his eighteenth birthday, as if the passage to manhood would break the spell and let this strangely beautiful youth enter the fraternity of man.

"You didn't even know it was your birthday, did you?" she said with frustration. She taunted him. "Seventh of July. Everyone knows when you were born because you're special, aren't you?"

She reached under her linen smock and pulled out a small bundle secreted there. It was the size of an apple, wrapped in a bit of cloth and tied with a thin strip of leather.

"I've got a present for you, Octavus," she said in singsong.

She was behind his chair and reached around him, putting the package on top of his page, forcing him to stop. He stared at the package with the same blankness he reserved for everything.

"Unwrap it," she urged.

He continued to stare.

"All right, then, I'll do it for you!"

She leaned over his back, encircled his thin torso with her sturdy arms and began to untie the parcel. It was a round golden cake that stained the cloth with sweet goo.

"Look! It's a honey cake! I made it myself, just for you!"

She was pressing against him.

Perhaps he felt the sensation of her firm small breasts against his thin shirt. Perhaps he felt the warm skin of her upper arm brush his cheek. Perhaps he smelled a female musk from her pubescent body or the warm gusts from her mouth as she talked.

He dropped his quill and let his hand drop to his lap. He was breathing hard and appeared to be in some kind of distress. Frightened, Mary took a few steps backward.

She could not see what he was doing, but he seemed to be grabbing at himself as if stung by a bee. She heard small animal-like noises whistling through his teeth.

Abruptly, he stood up and turned. She gasped and felt her knees go weak.

His trousers were open and in his hand he held a huge, erect cock, pinker than any flesh on his body.

He lurched toward her, tripping on his leggings as he clamped onto her breasts with his long delicate fingers, like tentacles with suckers.

Both of them fell to the dirt floor.

She was far stronger than Octavus but the shock had made her weak as a kitten. Instinctively, he pulled up her smock and exposed her creamy thighs. He was between her legs, pushing hard against her. His head was draped over her shoulder, his forehead pressed to the ground. He was making his quick little whistling noises. She was a worldly girl; she knew what was happening to her.

"Christ the Lord, have mercy on me!" she cried over and over.

By the time José, the Iberian monk, heard the screams and rushed down the stairs from his copy desk in the main gallery, Mary was seated against the wall softly crying, her smock stained red with blood, and Octavus was back at his desk, his trousers around his ankles, his quill flying over the page.

It was sticky and steamy, a high-humidity afternoon where the heat radiating off the pavement seemed like a punishment. New Yorkers tread on hot-plate sidewalks, rubber soles softening, limbs heavy with the effort of walking through what seemed gruel. Will's polo shirt clung to his chest as he lugged a couple of heavy plastic grocery bags bulging with the fixings for a party.

He cracked a beer, lit a burner, and sliced an onion while the saucepan heated. The sizzle of the onions and the sweet smoke filling the kitchenette pleased him. He hadn't smelled home cooking in a long while and couldn't remember when he'd last used the stove. Probably in the Jennifer era, but everything about that relationship had gone hazy.

The ground beef was browning nicely when the doorbell rang. Nancy had an apple pie and a melting tub of frozen yogurt and looked relaxed in hip-hugger jeans and a short sleeveless blouse.

Will felt relaxed, and she noticed. His face was softer than usual, his jaw less clenched, his shoulders less rounded. He grinned at her.

"You look *happy*," she said with some surprise .

He took the bag from her and spontaneously bent to deliver a peck on the cheek, the gesture taking both of them by surprise.

He quickly took a step back and she made a blushing recovery by sniffing at the spicy cumin and chili-pepper haze and making a joke about undiscovered culinary skills.

While he stirred the saucepan, she set his table then called out, "Did you get her anything?"

He hesitated, his mind grinding on the question. "No," he said finally. "Should I have?"

"Yes!"

"What?"

"How should I know! You're her father."

He went quiet, his mood turning sooty.

"Let me run out and get some flowers," she offered.

"Thanks," he said, nodding to himself. "She likes flowers." It was a guess—he had a memory of a toddler with a bunch of freshly picked daisies in her chubby hand. "I'm sure she likes flowers."

The past few weeks had been drudgery. The substance of the larger case against Luis Camacho eroded away, leaving only one count of murder. Hard as they pressed, they couldn't make a single other Doomsday case stick to him; in fact, they couldn't come close. They had painstakingly mapped him, reconstructing every day of his life for the past three months. Luis worked steadily and reliably, jetting back and forth to Las Vegas two to three times a week. He was mainly domesticated, spending most nights in New York at his lover's house. But he also had the instincts of a tomcat, drifting to clubs and gay bars when his partner was tired or otherwise occupied, zealously pursuing liaisons. John Pepperdine was a low-energy monogamous sort, while Luis Camacho had sexual energy that burned like magnesium. There wasn't any doubt that his fiery temper had led to murder, but John, it appeared, was his only victim.

And the killings had stopped: good news for everyone still drawing air, bad news for the investigation, which could only rehash the same tired clues. Then one day Will had a Eureka moment, of sorts. What if John Pepperdine had been the intended ninth victim of the Doomsday Killer but Luis Camacho had struck first in an ordinary crime of passion?

Maybe Luis's Las Vegas connection was a classic red herring. What if the real Doomsday Killer was there on City Island that day, on the other side of the police tape, watching, bemused that someone else had committed the crime? Then, to bedevil the authorities, what if he had gone into hiatus, letting them stew, sowing the seeds of confusion and frustration?

Will obtained subpoenas for the news organizations that had been on Minnieford Avenue that warm bloody evening, and over the course of several days he and Nancy pored over hours of videotape and hundreds of digital images looking for another dark-skinned man of medium height and build who might have been lurking at the crime scene. They came up empty, but Will thought it was still a viable hypothesis.

Today's celebration was a welcome respite from all that. Will dumped a box of Uncle Ben's into boiling water and opened another beer. The doorbell rang again. He hoped it was Nancy with the flowers, and it was, but both she and Laura were there together, gabby and happy like girlfriends. Behind them stood a young man, tall, whippet-thin, with intelligent, darting eyes and a mound of curly brown hair.

Will grabbed the bouquet from his partner and sheepishly handed it to Laura. "Congratulations, kiddo."

"You shouldn't have," Laura joked.

"I didn't," he said quickly.

"Dad, this is Greg."

The two men checked out each other's grip with hand-shakes.

"Pleased to meet you, sir."

"Same here. Weren't expecting you but I'm pleased to finally meet you, Greg."

"He came for moral support," Laura said. "He's like that."

She pecked her father's cheek as she passed, put her bag down on the sofa and unzipped a side pocket. Triumphantly, she waved a contract from Elevation Press in the air. "Signed, sealed, delivered!"

"Can I call you a writer now?" Will asked.

A tear formed and she nodded.

He quickly turned away and retreated into the kitchenette. "Let me get the bubbly before you get all blubbery."

Laura whispered to Nancy, "He so doesn't like it when you get emotional."

"I've noticed," Nancy said.

Over steaming bowls of chili, Will toasted for the umpteenth time and seemed to take pleasure in the fact that all of them were swigging champagne. He fetched another bottle and continued to pour. Nancy mildly protested but let him continue until the froth overflowed and wet her fingers. "I almost never drink, but this is tasty," she said.

"Everyone's got to drink at this party," Will said firmly. "You a drinking man, Greg?"

"In moderation."

"I excessively drink in moderation," Will joked, catching a sharp look from his daughter. "I thought journalists were big boozers."

"We come in all stripes."

"You going to come in the striped model that follows me around news conferences?"

"I want to do print journalism. Investigative reporting."

Laura chimed in, "Greg believes that investigative journalism is the most effective way to tackle social and political problems."

"Do you?" Will asked with a jab to his words. Sanctimony always raised his hackles.

"I do," Greg replied, equally prickly.

"Okay, I now pronounce you . . . " Laura said lightly, to head off a problem.

Will pressed. "How's the job landscape look for investigative journalism?"

"Not great. I'm doing an internship at the *Washington Post*. Obviously, I'd love to get a gig there. If you ever want to pass me a tip, here's my card." He was half kidding.

Will slipped it into his shirt pocket. "I used to date a gal at the *Washington Post*." He snorted. "It wouldn't help your chances to use me as a reference."

Laura wanted to change the subject. "So, you want to hear about my meeting?"

"Absolutely, give me details."

She slurped through the champagne foam. "It was so great," she cooed. "My editor, Jennifer Ryan, who's a real sweetheart, spent almost half an hour telling me how much she liked the changes I'd made and how it only needed a few tweaks, etcetera, etcetera, and then she told me we were going up to the fourth floor to meet with Mathew Bryce Williams, who's the publisher. It's an old town house, so beautiful, and Mathew's office is dark and filled with antiques, like some kind of English club, you know, and he's an older guy, like Dad's age, but way more distinguished—"

"Hey!" Will howled.

"Well, he is!" she continued. "He's like a caricature of an upper-class Brit but he was urbane and charming and—you're not going to believe this—he offered me sherry from a crystal decanter which he served in little crystal glasses. It was so perfect. And then he went on and on about how much he loved my writing—he called my style 'lean and spare with the muscularity of a fresh young voice.'" She spoke his words with a mock English accent. "Can you believe he said that?"

"Did he say anything about how much you're going to make?" Will asked.

"No! I wasn't going to ruin the moment with a crass discussion about money."

"Well, you're not going to retire on what they're paying up front. Is she, Greg, unless there's a lot of dough in investigative journalism?"

The young man wouldn't take the bait.

"It's a small publisher, Dad! They only do like ten books a year."

"Are you doing a book tour?" Nancy asked.

"I don't know yet but it's not like it's going to be some huge book. It's literary fiction, not a pulp novel."

Nancy wanted to know when she could read it.

"The galleys should be out in a few months. I'll send you a copy. Want to read it, Dad?"

He stared at her. "I don't know, do I?"

"I think you'll survive."

"Not every day you get called a wrecking ball—especially by your daughter," he said ruefully.

"It's a novel. It's not you. It's inspired by you."

Will raised his glass. "Here's to inspirational men."

They clinked glasses again.

"Did you read it, Greg?" Will asked.

"I did. It's superb."

"So you know more about me than I know about you." Will was getting looser and louder. "Maybe her next book'll be about you."

The comment made Laura say acidly, "You know, you really ought to read it. I've turned it into a screenplay— how's that for hopeful? I'll leave a copy. It's a quicker read. You'll get the idea."

Laura and Greg left soon after dinner to catch a train back to Washington. Nancy stayed behind to help clean up. The evening was too pleasant to cut short, and Will had shaken off his irritability and seemed relaxed and mellow, an altogether different man from the coiled spring she encountered every day on the job.

Outside, the light was bleaching out and the traffic noises were fading, except for the occasional wail of a Bellevue ambulance. They worked side by side in the little kitchenette, washing and drying, both swaying with the afterglow of the champagne. Will was already on the scotch. Both of them were happily out of their routine, and the domestic simplicity of doing dishes was soothing.

It wasn't planned—Will would reflect on it later—but instead of reaching for the next plate, he reached for her ass and started rubbing it gently in little circles. In retrospect, he should have seen it coming.

She had cheekbones now and an hour-glass shape and,

damn it, he would say if asked, looks mattered to him. But even more, her personality had molded under his tutelage. She was calmer, less gung-ho and caffeinated, and to his amusement, some of his cynicism had rubbed off. There was the occasional pleasant whiff of sarcasm emanating form her mouth. The insufferable Girl Scout was gone and in her place was a woman who no longer jangled his nerve endings. Quite the opposite.

Her hands were in soapy water. She kept them there, closed her eyes for a moment and didn't say or do anything.

He turned her toward him and she had to figure out what to do with her hands. She finally placed them wet on his shoulders and said, "Do you think this is a good idea?"

"No, do you?"

"Nope."

He kissed her and liked the way her lips felt and the way her jaw softened. He cupped her bottom with both palms and felt the smooth denim. His boozy head got hazy with desire and he pressed against her.

"The housekeeper came today. I've got clean sheets," he whispered.

"You know how to romance a girl." She wanted this to happen, he could tell.

He led her by a slippery hand to the bedroom, flopped on the bedspread and pulled her on top.

He was kissing her blood-warm neck, feeling under her blouse, when she said, "We're going to regret this. It's against all—"

He covered her lips with his mouth then pulled back to say, "Look, if you really don't want to, we can roll the clock back a few minutes and finish the dishes."

She kissed him, the first one that was hers to give. She said, "I hate doing dishes."

When they left the bedroom, it was dark and the living room was eerily quiet, just the hum of the air conditioner and the low whoosh of distant traffic on the FDR Drive. He had given her a clean white dress shirt to put on, something he'd done before with new women. They seemed to like the feeling of starch against bare skin and all the iconic imagery of the ritual. She was no different. The shirt swallowed her up and covered her prudishly. She sat on the sofa and drew her knees up to her chest. The skin that showed was cool and mottled like alabaster.

"Want a drink?" he asked.

"I think I've had quite enough tonight."

"You sorry?"

"Should be, but I'm not." Her face was still tinged pink. He thought she looked prettier than he had ever seen her, but also older, more womanly. "I kind of thought this might happen," she said.

"For how long?"

"The beginning."

"Really! Why?"

"A combination of your reputation and mine."

"I didn't know you had one too."

"It's a different sort of reputation," she sighed. "Good girl, safe choices, never rocking the boat. I think I've secretly wanted the boat to capsize, to see what it felt like."

He smiled. "From wrecking ball to shipwreck. Spot the common theme?"

"You're a bad boy, Will Piper. Good girls secretly like bad boys, didn't you know?"

His head was clearer, almost flat sober. "We're going to have to hide this, you know."

"I know."

"I mean, your career and my retirement."

"I *know*, Will! I should go."

"You don't have to."

"Thank you but I don't think you really want a sleep-over." Before he could respond, she touched the cover of Laura's script on the coffee table. "You going to read it?" she asked.

"I don't know. Maybe." Then, "Probably."

"I think she wants you to."

* * *

When he was alone, he poured a scotch, sat on the sofa and turned on the table lamp. The brightness of the bulb stung his eyes. He stared at his daughter's screenplay, the image of the lightbulb scorching the cover. As the image receded it looked for all the world like a sinister smiley face staring back at him. It dared him to pick up the script. He took the dare and muttered, "Fucking wrecking ball."

He'd never read a screenplay before. Its shiny brass brads reminded him of the last time he'd laid eyes on one, a month earlier at Mark Shackleton's house. He turned the cover page and waded in—the format confused him with all the interior/exterior jazz.

After a few pages he had to start over, but then he got into the swing of it. Apparently, the character he inspired was named Jack, a man whose sparse description seemed to fit him to a tee: a brawny man in his forties, a sandy-haired product of the South with an easy manner and a hard edge.

Unsurprisingly, Jack was a high-functioning alcoholic and womanizer. He was in a new relationship with Marie, a sculptress who knew better than to let a man like him into her life but was powerless to resist him. Jack, it seemed, had left a trail of women in his wake, and—painfully to Will— one of them was a daughter, a young woman named Vicki. Jack was haunted by flashbacks of Amelia, an emotionally frail woman whom he had beaten to a metaphysical pulp before she set herself free with vodka and carbon monoxide. Amelia—a thinly veiled homage to Melanie, Will's first wife and Laura's mother—was a woman who found the waters of life too difficult and complicated to navigate. Throughout the script, she appeared to him, cherry red from the poison, rebuking him about his cruelty to Marie.

Midway through the script, Will found himself too sober to continue, so he poured a fresh three fingers. He waited for the drink to anesthetize him then carried on till the bitter end, to Marie's suicide, witnessed by the sobbing presence of Amelia, and to Vicki's redemptive decision to leave her own abusive relationship and choose a kinder, though less passionate man. And Jack? He moved on to Sarah, Marie's cousin, who he met at her funeral, the wrecking ball still swinging away.

When he put the script down, he wondered why he wasn't crying.

So this was how his daughter saw him. Was he that grotesque?

He thought about his ex-wives, multiple girlfriends, the conga line of one-nighters, and now Nancy. Most of them pretty nice gals. He thought about his daughter, a good egg tainted by the sulfurous bad-egg smell of her father. He thought about—

Suddenly, his introspection braked to a screeching halt. He grabbed at the script and opened it to a random page.

"Son of a bitch!"

The screenplay font.

It was Courier 12 point, the same as the Doomsday post-cards.

He had forgotten his initial puzzlement at the postcard font, an old standby from the days of typewriters but a more uncommon choice in the computer/printer age. Times New Roman, Garamond, Arial, Helvetica—these were the new standards in the world of pull-down menus.

He jumped onto the Internet and had his answer. Courier 12 was the mandatory font for screenplays, completely de rigueur. If you submitted a script to a producer in another format you'd be laughed out of town. Another tidbit: it was also widely used by computer programmers to write source code.

A mental vision slammed into his thoughts. A couple of screenplays authored by "Peter Benedict" and a few black Pentel pens sat on a white desk near a bookcase filled with computer programming books. Mark Shackleton's voice-over completed the imagery: "I don't think you're going to catch the guy."

He spent a short while contemplating the associations, odd as they were, before dismissing as absurd the notion there might be a connection between the Doomsday case and his college roommate. Schackleton, the grown-up nerd, running around New York, stabbing, shooting, sowing mayhem! Please!

Still, the postcard font was an unplumbed clue—he strongly felt it now—and he knew that to ignore one of his hunches would be foolhardy, especially when otherwise they were at a complete dead end.

He grabbed his cell phone and excitedly texted Nancy: *U and I are going to be reading scripts. Doomie may be a screenwriter.*

She felt the smooth, cool fourteen-carat links of the wrist-band and ran her fingertip over the rough border of diamonds around the narrow rectangular watch face.

"I like this one," she murmured.

"Excellent choice, madame," the jeweler said. "This Harry Winston is a popular choice. It's called the 'Avenue Lady.'"

The name made her laugh. "Hear what it's called?" she asked her companion.

"Yep."

"Isn't that perfect!"

"How much?" he asked.

The jeweler looked him in the eye. If the man had been Japanese or Korean or an Arab, he'd have known the sale was in the bag. As it was, Americans in khakis and baseball caps were a tough call. "I can sell it to sir today for $24,000."

Her eyes widened. This was the most expensive one. Still, she *loved* it, and let him know by nervously touching the bare skin of his forearm.

"We'll take it," he said without hesitation.

"Very good, sir. How would sir like to pay?"

"Just put it on my room. We're staying in the Piazza Suite."

The jeweler would have to pop into the back room to confirm the sale but he was feeling solid. The suite was one of their best, fourteen-hundred square feet of marble and opulence, with a spa and sunken living room.

She was wearing the watch when they left the shop. The sky over St. Mark's Square was perfectly baby blue with

just the right assortment of fluffy cumulus clouds. A gondola ferrying a rigid, unsmiling Swiss couple glided by. The
gondolier launched into song to stir up some emotion in his
charges, and his rich voice echoed off the dome. Everything
was perfect, her companion thought. The non-Mediterranean
temperature, the absence of brackish smells from real
canals, and no pigeons. He hated the dirty birds ever since
his parents had taken him to the authentic St. Mark's Square
as a shy and sensitive boy and a tourist lobbed a handful of
bread crumbs near his feet. The pigeon swarm nightmar-
ishly overwhelmed him, and even as an adult he recoiled
when he saw flapping wings.

She was wearing the watch as they strolled arm in arm
through the lobby of the Venetian Hotel.

She was wearing the watch in the elevator, cocking her
hand at an angle to catch the attention of the three ladies
riding with them.

And she was wearing the watch and nothing else up in the
suite when she gave him the best sex he'd ever had.

He let her call him Mark now, and instead of Lydia, she let
him use her real name, Kerry. Kerry Hightower.

She was from Nitro, West Virginia, a river town founded
at the turn of the century around a gunpowder plant. It was
a gritty place notable for little except that Clark Gable once
worked there as a telephone repairman. Growing up poor,
she watched old Clark Gable movies and dreamed of becoming a Hollywood actress.

In junior high she discovered her acting skills were not
abundant but she doggedly tried out for every school play
and community production, landing small supporting roles
only because she was so earnest and attractive. But in high
school she discovered a higher talent. She loved sex, was
extremely good at it, and was completely and charmingly
uninhibited. In a revelation, she settled on a new amalgam-
ated calling: she decided she would become a porn star.

A fellow cheerleader, two years older, had moved to Las
Vegas and was working as a card dealer. To Kerry, Vegas

was nine-tenths on the way to California, where, as she understood it, the adult film business flourished. A week after graduation from Nitro High, she bought a one-way ticket to Nevada and moved in with her old chum. Life there wasn't easy, but her sunny disposition kept her afloat. She bopped around from one low-paying job to another until she landed, if not on her feet, on her back at an escort agency.

When she'd met Mark at the Constellation, she was on her fourth agency in three years, finally accumulating a little money. She only worked for higher-end outfits where her non-pierced, nontattooed, girl-next-door persona was valued. Most of the men she dated were nice enough fellows—she could count the number of times on one hand when she felt abused or threatened. She never fell for any of her customers—they were johns, after all—but Mark was different.

From the start she found him nerdy and sweet with no macho pretenses. He was wicked smart too, and his job at Area 51 drove her crazy with curiosity because, when she was ten, she was certain she'd seen a flying saucer one summer night, darting high over the Kanawha River, as bright as a jar of lightning bugs collected on the riverbank.

And in the past few weeks, he had dropped the pseudonym and started buying up all of her time and lavishing presents on her. She was starting to feel more like a girlfriend and less like a call girl. He was getting more self-assured by the day, and while he was never going to be Clark Gable, he was beginning to grow on her.

She was unaware that with $5 million sitting high and dry in an offshore bank account, he was feeling more confident about the accomplishments of Mark Shackleton. Peter Benedict was gone. He wasn't needed anymore.

Even the bathrooms in the suite had flat-screen TVs. Mark got out of the shower and started toweling himself. There was a cable channel on. He wasn't paying attention until he heard the word Doomsday and looked up to see Will Piper on a replay of the weekly FBI press conference, standing tall at a podium speaking into a crop of microphones. The sight of Will on TV always made his heart race. He reached for his toothbrush without taking his eyes off the screen and began brushing his teeth.

The last time he'd seen Will at a media briefing, he looked lackluster and dispirited. The postcards and killings had stopped and the wall-to-wall coverage was no longer sustainable. The long unsolved case had drained the public and law enforcement alike. But he seemed more energized today. The old intensity was back. Mark pushed the volume button.

"I can say this," Will was saying. "We are pursuing some new leads and I remain completely confident we will catch the killer."

That irritated Mark and he said, "Oh, bullshit! Give it up, man," before turning off the TV.

Kerry was snoozing on the bed, naked underneath a thin sheet. Mark cinched his bathrobe and retrieved his laptop from his briefcase in the suite's sunken living room. He went online and saw he had an e-mail from Nelson Elder. Elder's list was longer than usual—business was good. It took Mark the better part of half an hour to complete the job and reply via his secure portal.

He went back to the bedroom. Kerry was stirring. She waved her adorned wrist in the air and said something about how great it would be to have a matching necklace. She threw off the sheet and sweetly beckoned him with a finger.

At that precise moment, Will and Nancy were having the opposite of sex. They were sitting at Will's office plowing through a mind-numbing mountain of bad screenplays, completely unsure of the object of their exercise.

"Why were you so confident at the news conference?" she asked him.

"Did I overdo it?" he asked sleepily.

"Oh, yeah. Big-time. I mean, what do we have here?"

Will had to shrug. "A wild goose chase is better than doing nothing."

"You should've told the press that. What are you going to say next week?"

"Next week's a week away."

The wild goose chase almost didn't happen. Will's initial call to the Writers Guild of America was a disaster. They lit into him about the Patriot Act and vowed to fight till Hell froze over to prevent the government from getting its mitts on a single script in its archives. "We're not looking for terrorists," he had protested, "just a demented serial killer." But the WGA was not going to give in without a fight, so he got his superiors to sign off on a subpoena.

Screenwriters, Will learned, were a squirrelly lot, paranoid about producers, studios, and especially other writers ripping them off. The WGA gave them a modicum of comfort and protection by registering their scripts and storing them electronically or in hard copy in case proof of ownership was ever required. You didn't have to be a guild member—any amateur hack could register his script. All you did was send a fee and a copy of the screenplay and you were done. There were West Coast and East Coast chapters of the WGA. Over fifty thousand scripts a year were registered with WGA West alone, a tidy little business for the guild.

The Department of Justice had a tricky time with the probable cause section of the subpoena. It was "fanciful," Will was told but they'd give it the old college try. The FBI ultimately succeeded at the Ninth District Court of Appeals because the government agreed to whittle down its request so it was less of a fishing expedition. They'd only get three years' worth of scripts from Las Vegas and a halo of Nevada zip codes, and the writers' names and addresses would be suppressed. If any "leads" were developed from this universe of material, the government would have to go back with fresh probable cause to obtain the writer's identity.

The scripts started pouring in, mostly on data disks but also in boxes of printed material. The FBI clerical staff in New York went into printer overdrive, and eventually Will's office looked like a caricature of the mail room at a Hollywood talent agency, film scripts everywhere. When the task was done, there were 1,621 Nevada-pedigreed screenplays sitting on the twenty-third floor of the Federal Building.

Without a road map, Will and Nancy couldn't skim too hastily. Still, they quickly found a rhythm and were able to slog through a script in about fifteen minutes, carefully reading the first few pages to get the gist, then flipping and scanning the rest. They steeled themselves for a slow, laborious process, hoping to wrap up the task within one painful month. Their strategy was to look for the obvious: plots about serial killers, references to postcards, but they had to stay vigilant for the nonobvious—characters or situations that simply struck a responsive chord.

The pace was unsustainable. They got headaches. They got irritable and snapped at each other all day then retreated to Will's apartment to make cranky love in the evenings. They needed frequent walks to clear their heads. What really made them crazy was that the vast majority of scripts were complete and utter crap, incomprehensible or ridiculous or boring to the extreme. On the third or fourth day of the exercise, Will perked up when he picked up a script called *Counters* and declared excitedly, "You're not going to believe this, but I know the guy who wrote this."

"How?"

"He was my freshman roommate in college."

"That's interesting," she said, uninterested.

He read it much more thoroughly than the others, which set him back an hour, and when he put it down he thought, Don't give up your day job, buddy.

At three in the afternoon Will made a notation into his database about a piece of dreck concerning a race of aliens who came to Earth to beat the casinos, and grabbed the next one in his pile.

He gently kicked Nancy's knee with the tip of his loafer.

"Hey," he said.

"Hey," she replied.

"Suicidal?"

"I'm already dead," she answered. Her eyes were pink and arid. "What's your point?"

His next one was titled *The 7:44 to Chicago*. He read a few pages and groused, "Christ. I think I read this one a few days ago. Terrorists on a train. What the fuck?"

"Check the submission date," she suggested. "I've had a few with multiple submissions. Writer changes it and spends another twenty bucks to register it again."

He punched the title into his database. "When you're right, you're right. This one's a later draft. I rated it zero out of ten for relevance. I can't read it again."

"Suit yourself."

He started to close the script then stopped himself. Something caught his eye, a character name, and he began frantically paging forward, then sat upright, flipping faster and faster.

Nancy noticed something was up. "What?" she asked.

"Gimme a second, gimme a second."

She watched him make frantic notes, and whenever she interrupted to ask what he had, he replied, "Would you please just wait a second?"

"Will, this isn't fair!" she demanded.

He finally put the script down. "I've got to find the earlier draft. Could I have missed this? Quick, help me find it, it's called *The 7:44 to Chicago*. Check the Monday stack while I check Tuesday."

She crouched on the floor near the windows and found it a few minutes later, deep in a pile. "I don't know why you don't tell me what's going on," she complained.

He grabbed it out of her hands. In seconds he was shaking with excitement. "Good Lord," he said softly. "He changed the names from the earlier draft. It's about a group of strangers who get blown up by terrorists on a train from Chicago to L.A. Look at their last names!"

She took the script and started reading. The names of the strangers floated off the page: Drake, Napolitano, Swisher, Covic, Pepperdine, Santiago, Kohler, Lopez, Robertson.

The Doomsday victims. All of them.

There was nothing she could say.

"The second draft was registered April 1, 2009, seven weeks before the first murder," Will said, kneading his hands. "April Fool's Day—ha, fucking ha. This guy planned it out and advertised it in advance in a goddamned screenplay. We need an emergency order to get his name."

He wanted to envelop her, lift her off the ground and swing her in a circle by her waist, but he settled for a high five.

"We've got you, asshole," he said. "And your script pretty much sucks too."

Will would remember the next twenty-four hours the way one remembered a tornado—emotions rising in anticipation of the impact, the blurred and deafening strike, the swath of destruction, and afterward the eerie calm and hopelessness at the loss.

The Ninth Circuit granted the government's subpoena and the WGA unmasked the writer's personal data.

He was at his PC when his inbox was dinged by an e-mail from the Assistant U.S. Attorney running the subpoena. It was forwarded from the WGA with the subject line: *Response to US Gov v. WGA West re. WGA Script #4277304*.

For the rest of his life he would remember the way he felt when he read that e-mail.

In complete and lawful response to the afore-referenced proceedings, the registered author of WGA Script #4277304 is Peter Benedict, P.O. Box 385, Spring Valley, Nevada.

Nancy came into his office and saw him frozen like marble at his screen.

She drew close until he could feel her breath against his neck. "What's wrong?"

"I know him."

"What do you mean, you know him?"

"It's my college roommate." The image of the scripts on Shackleton's neat white desk rushed back in, his insistent words, *I don't think you're going to catch the guy,* his palpable unease at his spontaneous visit and—one more detail! "The fucking pens."

"Sorry?"

Will was shaking his head in lamentation. "He had black ultrafine Pentels on his desk. It was all there."

"How can it be your roommate? This doesn't make any sense, Will!"

"Jesus," he moaned. "I think Doomsday was aimed at me."

Will's fingers danced over his keyboard as he feverishly hopped from one federal and state database to another. As he hunted, he repeatedly thought, Who are you, Mark? Who are you really?

Information started hitting his screen—Shackleton's DOB, his social, some old parking tickets in California—but there were maddening gaps and shrouds of obscurity. His photo was blacked-out on his Nevada driver's license record, there weren't any credit reports, mortgages, educational or employment records. There were no criminal or civil proceedings. No property tax records. He wasn't in the IRS database!

"He's completely off the fucking grid," Will told Nancy. "Protected species. I've seen this once or twice but it's rare as hell."

"What's our move?" she asked.

"We're getting on a plane this afternoon." She'd never heard him sound as agitated. "We're going to make this bust ourselves. Go start the paperwork with Sue, right away. We'll need a federal arrest warrant from the U.S. Attorney in Nevada."

She brushed her fingers against the back fringe of his hair. "I'll make the arrangements."

A couple of hours later a car was waiting to take them to the airport. Will finished packing his briefcase. He checked his watch and wondered why Nancy was late. Even under his subversive watch, she had retained the virtue of punctuality.

Then he heard those clicking high-heeled steps of Sue Sanchez approaching fast and his stomach tightened in a Pavlovian way.

He looked up and saw her taut, strained face at his door, her eyes off-the-chart wild. She had something to say but the words weren't coming out fast enough for him.

"Susan. What? I've got a plane to catch."

"No you don't."

"Sorry?"

"Benjamin just got a call from Washington. You're off the case. Lipinski too."

"What!"

"Permanently. Permanently off." She was almost hyperventilating.

"And why the fuck is that, Susan?"

"I have no idea." He could see she was telling the truth. She was borderline hysterical, fighting to stay professional.

"What about the arrest?"

"I don't know anything and Ronald told me not to ask any questions. This is way above my pay grade. Something huge is going on."

"This is bullshit. We've got the killer!"

"I don't know what to say."

"Where's Nancy?"

"I sent her home. They don't want you two partnering up anymore."

"And why is that?"

"I don't know, Will! Orders!"

"And what am I supposed to do now?"

She was mournfully apologetic, the official face of something she didn't understand.

"Nothing. They want you to stand down and do nothing. As far as you're concerned, it's over."

When the baby was born, Mary refused to name it. She did not feel it was hers. Octavus had crudely placed it inside her and she could only watch her body grow heavy as its time neared and endure the pain of its birth just as she had endured the act of its procreation.

She suckled it because her breasts were full and she was required to do so, but would not look at its indifferent lips as it fed nor stroke its hair the way most mothers did when an infant was sucking at her teat.

After her violation, she was moved from the Sister's Dormitory to the Hospicium. There, she was segregated from the prying eyes and gossip of the novices and sisters and would gestate in the relative anonymity of the guesthouse, where visitors to the abbey were unaware of her shame. She was well-fed and permitted to take walks and work in a vegetable garden until the fullness of her term made her waddle and puff. However, all who knew her were saddened by the change in her disposition, the loss of her sparkle and humor, the dullness that prevailed. Even Prioress Magdalena secretly lamented the alterations to her temperament and the loss of youthful color from her formerly ruddy cheeks. The lass could never be admitted to the order now. How could she? Nor could she return to her village on the far side of the island—her kin would have nothing to do with her, a debased woman. She was in limbo, like an unbaptized child, neither evil nor graced.

When the baby was born and they all saw its bright ginger hair, its milky skin, and its apathetic countenance, the abbot and Paulinus deduced that Mary was a vessel, perhaps a divine one, who was owed nurturing and protection in much the same way the way the child had to be nurtured and protected.

This was no virgin birth, but the mother's name was Mary and the child was special.

A week after the baby was born, Magdalena visited Mary and found her lying in bed, staring vacantly into the air. The baby was still, in its cradle on the floor.

"Well, have you a name for him yet?" the prioress asked.

"No, Sister."

"Do you intend to name the child?"

"I do not know," she answered listlessly.

"Every child must have a name," Magdalena declared sternly. "I shall name it then. He will be Primus, the first child of Octavus."

Primus was now in his fourth year. Lost in his own world, he wandered the Hospicium and its environs, pale as cream, never straying far, never interested in objects or people. Like Octavus, he was mute and expressionless, with small green eyes. Every so often Paulinus would come, take him by the hand and lead him to the Scriptorium, where they would descend the stairs to his father's chamber. Paulinus would watch them as he might study heavenly bodies, looking for signs, but they were indifferent to one another. Octavus would continue to furiously write, the boy would move dreamily around the room, not bumping into anything but not seeing either. The quills did not interest him, nor the ink, the parchment, and the scribbles that emanated from Octavus's hand.

Paulinus would report back to Josephus, "The boy has shown no inclinations," and the two old men would shrug at each other and shuffle off for prayer.

It was a crisp autumn afternoon with a snap to the air. The waning sun was the color of marigold petals. Josephus was gingerly walking the abbey grounds, deep in meditation, silently praying for God's love and salvation.

Salvation was much on his mind. For weeks he had noticed that his urine first turned brown and now cherry red and his hearty appetite had vanished. His skin was becoming slack and tawny and the whites of his eyes were muddy. When he rose from kneeling prayer he felt like he was floating on waves and had to hold on for balance. He did not need to consult with the barber surgeon nor Paulinus. He knew he was dying.

Oswyn never saw the completion of the abbey reconstruction, nor would he, he reckoned, but the church, the Scriptorium, and the Chapter House were done and work was progressing on the dormitories. But more important, Octavus's library was on his mind. He could never truly fathom its purpose and he'd stopped trying to make sense of it. He simply knew these things:

It existed.

It was divine.

One day Christ would reveal its purpose.

It must be protected.

It must be allowed to grow.

Yet, as he watched the blood drain slowly from him with every passage of his water, he feared for the mission. Who would guard and defend his library when he was gone?

In the distance he saw Primus sitting in the dirt of the guest vegetable garden, a barren, harvested plot beside the Hospicium. The boy was alone, which was not unusual since his mother was inattentive. He had not seen him for a while and was now curious enough to spy on him.

The boy was nearly the age of Octavus when Josephus first took him in, and the resemblance was uncanny. The same reddish hair, the same bloodless complexion, the same twiglike body.

When Josephus was thirty paces away he stopped in his tracks and felt his heart race and his head swim. If he had not taken to using a walking staff he might have stumbled. The boy had a stick and was holding it in his hand. Then, before Josephus's eyes, he began using it to scrape the dirt in large swirling motions.

He was writing, Josephus was certain of it.

Josephus struggled to get through None prayers. After the congregation dispersed, he tapped three people on the shoulder and pulled them to a corner of the nave. There, he huddled with Paulinus, Magdalena, and José, who had been included in his inner circle ever since the young monk discovered the rape. Josephus had never regretted his decision to open up to the Iberian, who was calm and wise and discreet to a fault. And the abbot, the prioress, and the astronomer, who all were growing old, appreciated José's strength and vigor.

"The boy has begun to write," Josephus whispered. Even at a whisper, his voice echoed in the cavernous nave. They crossed themselves. "José, bring the boy to Octavus's chamber."

They sat the boy on the floor next to his father. Octavus took no notice of him nor any of the others who had invaded his sanctum. Magdalena had shunned Octavus since the atrocity, and even with the passage of time she recoiled at his sight. She no longer allowed her girls to tend him—those tasks were now delegated to young male novices. She kept as far away from his writing table as she could, half worried he might spring up and violate her too.

José placed a large sheet of vellum before Primus and surrounded it with a semicircle of candles.

"Give him a dipped quill," Paulinus rasped.

José dangled a quill in front of the boy as one might tempt a cat to pounce upon a feather. A drop of ink fell and splashed the page.

The boy suddenly reached out, grabbed the quill with his tiny right fist and put the tip onto the page.

He moved his hand in circles. The quill loudly scraped the parchment.

The letters were large and clumsy but clear enough to decipher.

V-a-a-s-c-o

"Vaasco," Paulinus said when the last letter was written.

S-u-a-r-i-z

"Vaasco Suariz," José intoned. "Portuguese *nombre*."

Then numbers also sprang childlike from the juvenile hand.

8 6 800 Mors

"The eighth day of Junius, 800," Paulinus said.

Josephus said, "Please, José, check Octavus's current page. What year is he recording?"

José stood over Octavus's shoulder and studied the page. "His last entry is the seventh day of Junius, 800!"

"Dear Jesus!" Josephus exclaimed. "The two of them are connected as one!"

The four ministers tried to read each other in the dancing candlelight.

"I know what you are thinking," Magdalena said, "and I cannot abide by it."

"How can you know, Prioress, when I myself do not," Josephus answered.

"Search your soul, Josephus," she said skeptically. "I am certain you know your own mind."

Paulinus threw up his hands. "You are both talking in riddles. Can an old man not expect to know of what you are speaking?"

Josephus rose slowly to avoid wooziness. "Come, let us leave the boy with Octavus for a short while. No harm will come of him. I would have my three friends join me upstairs where we might have a prayerful discussion."

* * *

It was warmer and more comfortable than in the damp cellar. Josephus had them sit at copy desks, Josephus facing Magdalena, Paulinus facing José.

He recounted the night of Octavus's birth and each remarkable milestone in the youth's history. To be sure, they all knew these details, but Josephus had never before laid out an oral history and they were sure he had a purpose for doing so now. He then turned to the briefer though no less remarkable history of Primus, including the events that had just transpired.

"Can any of us doubt," Josephus asked, "that we have a sacred obligation to preserve and sustain this divine work? For reasons which we may never know, God has entrusted us, His servants at Vectis Abbey, to be the keepers of these miraculous texts. He has endowed this youth, Octavus, born in miraculous circumstances, with the power—nay, the imperative—to chronicle the entry and passage of all the souls entering and departing from this Earth. Man's destiny is thus laid bare. The texts are a testament to the power and omniscience of the Creator, and we are humbled by the love and care He has for His children." A tear formed and started to slide down his face. "Octavus is but one special though surely mortal being. I have wondered, and so have you, how the enormity of his task might be perpetuated. We now have our answer."

He paused and noted their solemn nods.

"I am dying."

"No!" José protested, showing the concern a son might have for a father.

"Yes, it is true. I am quite sure that none of you are too shocked. You have only to look at me to know that I am gravely ill."

Paulinus reached out to touch his wrist and Magdalena wrung her hands.

"And Paulinus, will you not acknowledge that you have seen the name Josephus of Vectis entered in one of the books?"

Paulinus answered through parched lips, "I have."

"And you know my date certain?"

"I do."

"It is soon?"

"It is."

"It is not tomorrow, I trust," he jested.

"It is not."

"Excellent," he said, lightly tapping his fingertips together. "It is my duty to prepare for the future, not only for the abbey, but for Octavus and the Library. So here, tonight, I declare that I will send for the bishop and beseech him, upon my passing, to elevate Sister Magdalena to Abbess of Vectis and Brother José to prior. Brother Paulinus, dear friend, you will continue to serve them as you have done so faithfully for me."

Magdalena bowed her head deeply to hide the thin smile she could scarcely suppress. Paulinus and José were mute with grief.

"And I have one further declaration," Josephus continued. "Tonight we are forming a new order within Vectis, a secret and holy order for the protection and preservation of the Library. We four are the founding members, which will henceforth be known as the Order of the Names. Let us pray."

He led them in deep prayer, and when he was done they rose as one.

Josephus touched Magdalena on her bony shoulder. "When Vespers is complete, we will do what must be done. Will you do this willingly?"

The old woman hesitated and silently prayed to the Holy Mother. Josephus was waiting for her response. "I will," she said.

After Vespers, Josephus retired to his room to meditate. He knew what was transpiring but did not wish to witness the events personally. His resolve was strong but he remained at the core a kind, gentle soul with no stomach for this kind of business.

He knew that as he bowed his head in prayer, Magdalena and José were leading Mary from the Hospicium down the dark path to the Scriptorium. He knew she would be softly weeping. He knew the weeping would turn to loud sobbing when they pulled her by the hand down the stairs into the cellar. And he knew the sobs would turn to screams when Paulinus opened the door to Octavus's chamber and José bodily forced her through the threshold then latched the door behind her.

Reggie Saunders was having a roll in the hay, as he called it, with Laurel Barnes, the buxom wife of Wing Commander Julian Barnes, in the middle of the wing commander's four-poster bed. He was enjoying himself a great deal. It was a grand country house with a grand master bedroom, a nice little fire to take the chill off, and an appreciative Mrs. Barnes, who had grown accustomed to faring for herself during her husband's war hiatus.

Reggie was a florid, burly fellow with a manly beer belly. A childish smile and impossibly large shoulders were the one-two punch that matted all sorts of women, the present one included. Concealed by his impishness and gabby affability was a moral compass that was broken. The arrow pointed in one direction only, toward Reggie Saunders. He always felt the world owed him for his existence, and his successful navigation of the World War with eyes, limbs, and genitals intact was a sign to him that a grateful nation should continue to provide for his needs be they financial or sensual. Laws of the Crown and societal mores were approximate guide posts in his world, things to consider perhaps, then ignore.

His army war service started nasty and inconvenient as a staff sergeant in Montgomery's Eighth Army trying to dislodge Rommel from Tobruk. After too long in the desert, he wheedled a transfer in 1944 from North Africa to liberated France to a regiment tasked with recovering and cataloguing Nazi art loot.

His boss was the nicest gentlemen he had ever met, a Cambridge don whose idea of commanding men was to ask them politely whether they might be able to help him with this or that. Incredibly, the army had gotten it right with Major Geoffrey Atwood, finding a job for the Professor of Archaeology and Antiquities that actually suited his skills rather than dangerously and ineffectively sticking him somewhere with a map, field glasses, and large guns.

Saunders's job mainly consisted of ordering a squad of lads to shift heavy wooden crates out of basements and transport them to other basements. He never shared a sense of moral outrage at the German's takings. He found their thievery quite understandable under the circumstances. In fact, under his watch a knick-knack or two made it through his hands in exchange for a few quid, and why not? Postwar, he wandered from job to job, doing a bit of construction here and there, absconding when necessary from romantic entanglements. When Atwood rang to see if he'd be interested in a little adventure on the Isle of Wight, he was in between engagements and replied, "Blow in my ear, boss, and I'll follow you anywhere."

Now, Reggie was pounding away, pleasantly lost in a sea of pink flesh that smelled of talc and lavender. The lady of the house was making little cooing sounds that sent him drifting to the aviary at Kew Gardens where he was brought as a young boy for a bit of natural culture. He soon reeled his mind back to the moment. The vinegar stroke was coming, and a job worth doing was a job worth doing well, his granddad had always said. Then he heard something mechanical, a throaty rumble.

Years of night patrol in the Libyan and Moroccan deserts had trained his ears, a survival skill he was drawing on one more time.

"Don't stop, Reggie!" Mrs. Barnes moaned.

"Hang on a sec, petal. Ya hear that?"

"I don't hear anything."

"The motor." It wasn't a servant's car, not this one. He

could tell it was a thoroughbred. "You sure hubby's not due?"

"I told you. He's in London." She grabbed his buttocks and tried to get him going again.

"Someone's coming, luv, and it's not the bloody postman."

He left the bed naked and parted the nearest curtains. A pair of headlights pierced the darkness.

Rolling up to the front, crunching the gravel drive, was a cherry Invicta, a rare beauty so distinctive, he recognized it as soon as the entryway lanterns hit it.

"Who d'ya know drives a red Invicta?" he asked.

He might as well have asked, Did you hear that Satan was at the front door?

She leapt out of bed, grabbing at her underthings, making high-pitched sounds of fear and alarm.

"That would be the wing commander's vehicle," Reggie said fatalistically, shrugging his big shoulders. "I'll be off now, luv. Ta-ta."

He hopped into his trousers and gathered his other clothes to his chest as he flew down the rear stairs into the kitchen. He was through the servants' back door just as the wing commander was entering the reception hall, merrily calling out to his wife, "Hi ho! Guess who's home a day early!"

Reggie finished dressing in the garden and started to shiver straight away. While the previous week had been unseasonably warm, a mass of cold air from the north was hammering the thermometer. He had met up with the missus outside the pub and she had driven them to the house. Now he was stranded at least six miles from the camp and there was no flippin' way, he thought, he was going to hoof it.

He tiptoed around to the front. The 1930 Invicta was radiating heat. Its cabin was deep, like a bathtub with fluted red-leather seats. The keys were dangling in the ignition. His analytical process was uncomplicated: I'm cold, the automobile is warm, I'll just borrow it to nip down the road. He hopped in and turned the key. The 140-horsepower Lagonda engine roared to life, too loud. A second later he panicked. Where the hell was the gear lever? He moved his hands all over, feeling for it. The front door of the house flew open.

Then he remembered: it was a bleeding automatic transmission, the first one in Britain! He pushed the accelerator and the transmission performed smoothly. The car sped forward, spraying gravel. In the rearview mirror he caught sight of an angry middle-aged man pumping his balled-up fists into the air. The engine drowned out whatever he was shouting.

"Same to you, mate," Reggie called out. "Thanks for your motor and thanks for your missus."

He ditched the Invicta at the pub in Fishbourne and fast-walked the final mile, whistling in the dark and rubbing his hands for warmth. A log fire supercharged with paraffin was blazing at the camp and it helped him find his way. A dense cloud cover diffused the moonlight, turning the night sky the color of gray flannel. The vapors from the fire hurtled upward thick and black like depraved harpies, and Reginald followed their ascendancy until he lost them against the looming spire of the cathedral of Vectis Abbey.

A door to one of the dilapidated caravans opened as Reggie was nearing the fire to warm himself. A lanky young man called out, "Gawd! Will you look who's come back! Reg's been booted!"

"I left of my own bloody accord, mate," Reggie replied curtly. "Any food about?"

"Tin of beans I should think."

"Well, toss one out then, I'm famished after me shag."

The young man guffawed but the word had a magical quality because every one of the four caravan doors opened and their inhabitants spilled out to hear more. Even Geoffrey Atwood emerged from the boss's caravan, wearing a heavy woolen turtleneck, thoughtfully puffing on a pipe. "Did someone say shag?"

"You lot aren't expecting me to kiss and tell?"

"Yes please," the lanky young man, Dennis Spencer, said salaciously. He was a pimply first-year at Cambridge, young enough to have skirted national service.

There were four others, three men and a woman, all of them from Atwood's department. Martin Bancroft and Timothy Brown, like Spencer, were undergraduates, albeit mature students who had returned from the war to complete their tolled degrees. Martin had never left England. He had been stationed in London as an intelligence officer. Timothy had been a radar man on a naval frigate operating mainly in the Baltic. Both of them were giddy to be back at Cambridge and over-the-moon at the prospect of a bit of fieldwork.

Ernest Murray was older, in his thirties, currently wrapping up his D. Phil. in Antiquities, which he hurriedly abandoned when the Germans invaded Poland. He had seen heavy action in Indochina, which left him painfully diffident. Somehow, Anglo-Saxon archaeology didn't seem as relevant to him anymore, and he couldn't fathom what he wanted to do with the rest of his life.

The only woman in the party was Beatrice Slade, a lecturer in Medieval History and Atwood's academic confidante who had pretty much run his department during the war. She was a tough wisecracking fireplug of a lady, openly lesbian, famously so. She and Reggie were essentially incompatible human beings. When her back was turned he crudely mocked her sexuality, and when his was turned she did the same to him.

"Ah, we're all up and about," Atwood said, blinking at the stinging fire. "Shall we have a coffee while Reg tells us his tale?"

"I'll brew a pot, Prof," Timothy offered.

"So what happened then, Reg?" Martin asked. "Figured you'd be kippin' in a feather bed tonight, not back here in the rust bucket."

"Had a spot of bother, mate," he replied. "Nothing I couldn't handle." He rolled a cigarette and licked the paper.

"Nothing you couldn't handle?" Beatrice asked mockingly. "Stymied because she wanted to go again?" At that she swung her hips like a burlesque queen and all of them, even Atwood, began to howl at his expense.

"Very funny, very amusing," Reggie said. "Her husband came home on the early side and I had to remove my person from the premises forthwith to avoid an unpleasant encounter."

"I say, Mr. Saunders," Dennis said with mock respect to his elder, "was your arse clothed or unclothed during this removal?"

They erupted again. Atwood took a few puffs of his pipe and said pensively, "That's a rather unpleasant mental image."

The morning was wintry with a few flakes of snow; the ground looked like it had been lightly salted. Ernest was an excellent caterer and managed to do a full-cooked breakfast for seven on two gas rings. They sat around the fire on milk crates, bundled in layers of wool, fortifying themselves with steaming mugs of sweet tea. Crunching into a triangle of fired bread dipped into yolk, Atwood looked across the frigid field at the icy sea and remarked, "Who's idea was it to excavate in January?"

It would have been better if it were a warm summer morning or a crisp autumn one, but it was utterly fantastic to all of them to be here in any season, in any conditions. Only yesterday, it seemed, they were in the thick of war, dreaming about how blissful it would be to do a bit of archaeology on a peaceful island. So the instant Atwood received a £300 grant from the British Museum to resume his excavations at Vectis, he hastily organized a dig, winter be damned.

Reggie was the pit boss. He checked his watch, stood up, and with his best sergeant major voice shouted, "All right, lads, let's get a move on! We've got a lot of dirt to shift today."

Timothy pointed at Beatrice in an exaggerated way and mouthed the question, *Lads?*

"You're right," Reggie said, gathering his gear, "I apologize. She's too bloody old for me to be calling her a lad."

"Sod off, you pathetic wanker," she said.

Atwood's dig was in a corner of the abbey grounds far from the main complex of buildings. The lord abbot, Dom William

Scott Lawlor, a soft-spoken cleric with a passion for history, was kind enough to let the Cambridge party camp within the complex. In return, Atwood invited him to stroll by for progress reports, and on the previous Saturday, Lawlor had even appeared in blue jeans and anorak to spend an hour scraping a square meter with a trowel.

The diggers marched across the field from the campground while the cathedral bells chimed for 9:00 A.M. mass and Terce. Seagulls swooped and complained overhead, and in the distance the steel-blue waves of the Solent churned. To the east the cathedral spire looked magnificent against the bright sky. Across the fields, tiny figures, monks in dark robes, filed from their dorms to the church. Atwood watched them, squinting into the sunshine, marveling at their time-lessness. If he had been standing on the same spot a thousand years earlier, would the scene have looked much different?

The excavation site was neatly laid out with pegs and twine. It covered an area of forty by thirty meters, rich brown earth with grass and topsoil peeled away. From a distance it was clear that the entire site was in a depression, about a meter lower than the surrounding field. It was this hollow that attracted Atwood's interest before the war when he surveyed the abbey grounds. Surely there had been an activity of some sort on this spot. But why so remote from the main abbey complex?

In two brief excavations in 1938 and 1939, Atwood had dug test trenches and found evidence of a stone foundation and bits of twelfth but mainly thirteenth century pottery. As the war raged on his thoughts often returned to Vectis. Why the blazes had a thirteenth century structure been built there, isolated as it was from the heart of the abbey? Was its purpose clerical or secular? The abbey library had no mention of the building in its archives. He was resigned to the fact that Hitler had to be defeated before he could tackle the mystery.

On the south side of the site, facing seaward, Atwood was digging his main trench, a cutting thirty meters long, four wide, and now three meters deep. Reggie, a good man with heavy machinery, had started the trench with a mechanical digger, and now the whole team was down in the deep cutting doing spade and bucket work. They were following what was left of the southern wall of the structure down to the foundation to see if they could find an occupation level.

Atwood and Ernest Murray were in the southwest corner of the cutting, cleaning the wall with trowels to take photographs of the section.

"This level here," Atwood said, pointing to an irregular band of black soil running across the section, "see how it follows the top of the wall? There was a fire."

"Accidental or deliberate?" Ernest asked.

Atwood sucked on his pipe. "Always difficult to say. It's possible it was set deliberately as part of a ritual."

Ernest furrowed his brow. "For what purpose? This wasn't exactly a pagan site. It was contemporaneous with the abbey within the abbey perimeter!"

"Excellent point, Ernest. Are you sure you don't want to pursue a career in archaeology after all?"

The younger man shrugged. "I dunno."

"Well, while you're pondering your fate, let's snap these pictures and begin excavating down another half meter or so. We can't be far off the floor."

Atwood assigned the three undergraduates to the southwest corner to take the trench deeper. Beatrice sat at a portable table near the cutting, cataloguing pottery shards, and Atwood took Ernest and Reggie to the northwest corner of the site to start a small trench in an attempt to find the other end of the foundation wall. As the morning progressed it became noticeably warmer and the diggers started peeling off layers until they were down to their shirts.

At lunchtime Atwood wandered over to the deep trench and remarked, "What's this? Is that another wall there?"

"I think so," Dennis said eagerly. "We were going to fetch you."

They had exposed the top of a thinner stone wall running parallel and about two meters from the main foundation.

"See? There's a gap in it, Professor," Timothy offered. "Could a door have been there?"

"Well, perhaps. Possibly so," Atwood said, climbing down a ladder. "I wonder, could you take this area down a bit," he said, pointing to some dirt. "If the interior wall extends to the outer wall in a perpendicular fashion, I would say we've got a small room. Wouldn't that be nice?"

The three young men got on their knees to start troweling. Dennis worked near the outer wall, Martin near the interior wall, Timothy in the middle. Within a few minutes they had all made clinking contact with stone.

"You were right, Professor!" Martin said.

"Well, I have been at this for a few years. You get a feel for this type of thing." He was pleased with himself and lit his pipe in celebration. "After lunch let's dig down to the level of the floor and see if we can find what this little room was for?"

The young men rushed their lunch, eager to find the floor. They wolfed down cheese sandwiches and lemon squash and hopped back into the pit.

"You're not impressing anyone, ya bloody brown-nosers!" Reggie shouted after them as he reclined on a mound of dirt and lit a roll-up.

"Shut your gob, Reg," Beatrice said. "Leave 'em be. And roll us a fag too."

An hour later the young men called to the others. The three undergrads were standing around the boundaries of the small room, looking impressed with themselves.

"We've found the floor, everyone!" Dennis exclaimed.

Exposed for view was a surface of smooth dark stones, expertly shaped to join to one another in a continuous surface. But Atwood's eye was drawn to another feature. "What's this?" he asked, and climbed down to take a closer look.

In the southwest corner of the small room was a larger stone, which appeared to be out of place. The floor stones were bluestone. This larger one was a large limestone block, about two meters by a meter and a half and quite thick. It protruded almost a foot higher than the level of the floor and had irregular edges.

"Any thoughts?" Atwood asked his people as he scraped around its edges with his trowel.

"Doesn't look like it belongs, does it?" Beatrice said.

Ernest took some pictures. "Someone went to a lot of trouble to haul that in."

"We should try to shift it," Atwood said. "Reg, who would you say has the strongest back?"

"That would be Beatrice," Reggie replied.

"Fuck off, Reg," the woman said. "Let's see some of that famous muscle power."

Reggie got a crowbar and tried to get an edge under a lip of limestone. He used a rock as a fulcrum but the block still wouldn't budge. Sweating, he declared, "Right! I'm getting the bloody digger."

It took an hour for Reggie to use the mechanical digger to make its own ramp to get down low enough to safely reach the block.

When he was in position, close enough to reach the rock with the bucket and far enough from the edge of the cutting to avoid a cave-in, he called out from the cab to say he was ready. Over the sputter of the diesel engine, the bells were pealing for the None service.

Reggie nudged the teeth of the bucket against an edge of limestone and caught hold on his first pass. He curled the bucket toward its arm and the stone block lifted.

"Hang on!" Atwood shouted. Reggie froze the action. "Get a crowbar in there!"

Martin jumped in and slid the iron bar into the gap between the limestone and the flooring stones. He leaned into the bar but couldn't lever it an inch. "Too heavy!" he shouted.

With Martin applying steady pressure, Reggie moved the bucket again and the stone slid a foot, then another. Martin guided it with the crowbar and when it shifted enough to be stable waved his arms like a crazy man. "Stop! Stop! Come here! Come here!"

Reggie killed the engine and all of them scrambled into the pit.

Dennis saw it first. "Bloody hell!"

Timothy shook his head. "Would you look at that!"

While the rest of them stared, agog, Reggie relit a dog end he had saved in his shirt pocket and took a deep drag of tobacco. "Fuck me. Is that supposed to be there, Prof?"

Atwood stroked his thinning head of hair in wonder and simply said, "We're going to need some light."

They were staring into a deep black hole, and the oblique rays of the afternoon sun were revealing what appeared to be stone stairs descending into the earth.

Dennis ran back to the camp to retrieve every battery-powered flashlight he could find. He returned, red-faced and huffing, and passed them around.

Reggie was feeling protective of his old boss so he insisted on going first. He'd cleared a few of Rommel's underground bunkers in his day and knew his way around a tight space. The rest of them followed the big man in single file, with Beatrice, stripped of her usual bravado, timidly taking up the rear.

When they had all successfully navigated the tightly spiraled stairway that plunged, by Atwood's estimate, an incredible forty to fifty feet straight into the earth, they found themselves huddled in a room not much larger than two London taxicabs. The air was stagnant, and Martin, who was prone to claustrophobia, immediately felt desperate. "It's a bit close down here," he whimpered.

They were all moving their flashlights around and the beams intersected like searchlights during the blitz.

Reggie was the first to realize there was a door. "Hallo! What're you doing here?" He studied the worm-holed surface with his flashlight. A huge iron key protruded from a gaping key hole.

Atwood set his light on it and said, "In for a penny, in for a pound. You game?"

Young Dennis crept up close. "Absolutely!"

"All right then," Atwood said. "Your honor, Reggie."

From her squashed position in the rear, Beatrice couldn't see what was happening. "What? What are we doing?" Her voice was strained.

"We're opening a ruddy big door," Timothy explained.

"Well, hurry up," Martin insisted, "or I'm going back up. I can't breathe."

Reggie turned the key and they heard the clunk of a mechanism. He pressed his palm against the cool wooden surface but the door wouldn't move. It resisted his efforts until he put the full weight of his shoulder into it.

It slowly creaked open.

They shuffled through as if they were on a chain gang, and all of them started sweeping the new space with their beams.

This room was larger than the first, much larger.

Their minds assembled the scrambled stroboscopic images into something cohesive, but seeing wasn't tantamount to believing, at least at first.

No one dared to speak.

They were in a high-domed chamber the size of a conference hall or a small theater. The air was cool, dry and stale. The floor and walls were fashioned from large blocks of stones. Atwood took note of these structural features, but it was a long wooden table and bench that jolted him. He moved his light over it from left to right and estimated that the table was over twenty feet long. He moved closer until his thighs touched it. He shone his light on its surface. There was an earthenware pot, the size of a teacup, with a black residue. Further down the bench there was a second pot, a third, a fourth.

Could it be?

It occurred to Atwood to cast his beam beyond the table.

There was another table. And behind it another. And another. And another.

His mind reeled. "I believe I know what this is."

"I'm all ears, Prof," Reggie said in a low voice. "What the bloody hell is it?"

"It's a scriptorium. An underground scriptorium. Simply amazing."

"If I knew what that meant," Reggie said, sounding irritated, "I'd know what this is, wouldn't I."

Beatrice explained with awe, "It's where monks copied manuscripts. If I'm not mistaken, it's the first subterranean one ever discovered."

"You are not mistaken," Atwood said.

Dennis was reaching for an ink pot but Atwood stopped him. "Don't touch. Everything must be photographed in situ, exactly as we find it."

"Sorry," Dennis said. "Do you think we'll find any manuscripts down here?"

"Wouldn't that be marvelous," Atwood said, his voice trailing off. "But I wouldn't count on it."

They decided to split into two parties to explore the boundaries of the chamber. Ernest took the three undergraduates to the right, and Atwood led Reggie and Beatrice to the left. "Careful as you go," Atwood warned.

He counted each row of tables as he passed, and when he'd counted fifteen, saw that Reggie was casting his light on another large door at the rear of the room. "Fancy going through there?" Reggie asked.

"Why not?" Atwood answered. "However, nothing can top this."

"It's probably the bloody water closet," Beatrice joked nervously.

They were practically pressing against Reggie as he lifted the weighty latch and pulled the door open.

All at once they shone their flashlights in.

Atwood gasped.

He felt faint and literally had to sit down on the stone floor. His eyes began to well up.

Reggie and Beatrice held onto each other for support, two opposites attracting for the first time.

From a distant corner they heard the others urgently shouting, "Professor, come here. We've found a catacombs!"

"There's hundreds of skeletons, maybe thousands!"

"Goes on forever!"

Atwood couldn't answer. Reggie took a few steps back to make sure his boss was all right. He leaned over, helped the older man to his feet and boomed out in his loudest military baritone, "Sod the skeletons, you lot! You'd all better come over here 'cause you're not going to bloody believe what we've got ourselves into."

Atwood's first thought was that he was dead, that he had inhaled some toxic vapors and died. He wasn't a religious man but this had to be some sort of otherworldly experience.

No, this was real. If the first chamber was the size of a theater, the second was the size of an airline hangar. To his left, a mere ten feet from the door, was a vast wooden case, filled with enormous leather-bound volumes. To his right was an identical stack, and in between the two was a corridor just wide enough for a man to pass. Atwood recovered his senses and traced one stack with his flashlight to understand its dimensions. It was about fifty feet long, some thirty feet high, and consisted of twenty shelves. He did a rapid count of the number of books on just one shelf: about 150.

All of his nerve endings tingled as he wandered into the central corridor. To both sides were huge bookcases, identical to the first pair, and they seemed to go on and on into the darkness.

"Shitload of books in here," Reggie said.

Somehow, Atwood had hoped that the first words spoken on the occasion of one of the great discoveries in the history of archaeology might have been more profound. Had Carter, at the mouth of Tutankhamen's tomb heard, "Shitload of stuff in here, mate?" Nevertheless, he had to agree.

"I should say so."

He violated his own no-touch rule and put his pointer finger softly against the spine of one book on an eye-level shelf at the end of the third stack. The leather was firm and in excellent preservation. He carefully wiggled it out.

It was heavy, at least the heft of a five-pound bag of flour, about eighteen inches long, twelve inches wide, five inches thick. The leather was cool, shiny, unadorned by any markings on the covers but in the spine he saw a large, clear number deeply tooled into the leather: 833. The parchments were rough-cut, slightly uneven. There had to be two thousand pages.

Reggie and Beatrice were by his side. Both aimed their lights on the book he cradled in the crook of his arm. He gently opened it to a random page.

It was a list. Names, by the look of the three columns across a page, some sixty names per column. In front of each name was a date, all of them *23 1 833*. Following each name was the word *Mors* or *Natus*. "It's some kind of registry," Atwood whispered. He turned the page—more of the same. An endless list. "Have you any thoughts on this, Bea?" he asked.

"Looks like it's a record of births and deaths, like any medieval parish church might keep," she replied.

"Rather a lot of them, wouldn't you say?" Atwood said, sending his beam down the long central corridor.

The others had caught up and were murmuring at the library entrance. Atwood called back to them to stay put for the moment. He failed to notice that Reggie had started down the corridor, deeper into the chamber.

"How old would you say this vault is?" Atwood asked Beatrice.

"Well, judging from the stone work, the door construction, and the lock hardware, I'd have to say eleventh, maybe twelfth century. I'd hazard a guess we're the first living souls to breathe this air in about eight hundred years."

From a hundred feet away Reggie's voice echoed out to them. "If bossy-boots is so bloody smart then how come I've got a book here what got dates in it for the sixth of May 1467?"

They needed a generator. Despite their fevered excitement, Atwood decided it was too hazardous to do further exploration in the dark. They retraced their steps and emerged into the late afternoon glare, then hurriedly covered the opening to the spiral stairs with planks and a tarp, then an inch of dirt so the casual observer like Abbot Lawlor would notice nothing. Atwood admonished them. "No one is to speak a word of this to anyone. Anyone!"

They returned to their camp and Reggie took a couple of the lads to find a generator somewhere on the island. Atwood holed up in his caravan to furiously make an entry into his notebook, and the rest of them talked among themselves in hushed tones over a simmering lamb stew.

After sundown, the van returned. They had found a builder in Newport who hired them a portable generator. They also procured several hundred feet of electrical line and a crate of lightbulbs.

Reggie opened up the back of the van for the professor's inspection. "Reginald delivereth," he declared proudly.

"He always seems to," Atwood said, patting the big man on the back.

"This is big, isn't it, boss?"

Atwood was subdued; the experience of writing his diary left him nervously deflated. "You always dream of finding something very important. Something that changes the land-scape, as it were. Well, old man, I fear this might be too big."

"How d'ya mean?"

"I don't know, Reg. I must tell you, I have a bad feeling."

They spent the entire next morning firing up the generator and stringing the underground structures with incandescent lights. Atwood decided that photography was the first order of business, so he deployed Timothy and Martin to shoot the scriptorium chamber, Ernest and Dennis to shoot the catacombs, and he and Beatrice photographed the library. Flashbulbs popped incessantly, and their ozone smell per-meated the musty air. Reggie acted as roving electrician, laying wire, tinkering with misbehaving bulbs, and tending the generator, which chugged away aboveground.

By mid-afternoon they had discovered that the vast library

was only the first of two. At the rear of the first chamber was a second one, presumably built, they reckoned, at a later date when space was exhausted. The second vault was as enormous as the first, 150 feet square, at least thirty feet in height. There were sixty pairs of long, tall bookcases in each chamber, each pair separated by a narrow central passage. Most of the stacks were crammed with thick tomes, except for a few cases at the back of the second room, which were empty.

After they had done a cursory exploration of the boundaries of the vaults, Atwood did a rough calculation in his notebook and showed the numbers to Beatrice. "Bloody hell!" she said. "Are these right?"

"I'm not a mathematician, but I believe they are."

The library contained nearly 700,000 volumes.

"That would make this one of the ten largest libraries in Britain," Beatrice said.

"And I dare say, the most interesting. So, shall we make a stab at why medieval monks—if that's who they were—were rather compulsively writing down names and dates from the future?" He clapped his notebook shut and the sound of it echoed for a couple of beats.

"I didn't get much sleep thinking about that," Beatrice admitted.

"Nor I. Follow me."

He led her into the second room. They hadn't strung wire very far into this chamber, and Beatrice stayed close to him, both of them following the sickly yellow light cast from his flashlight. They plunged deeply into the dark stacks, where he stopped and tapped on a spine: 1806.

He moved to another row. "Ah, getting closer, 1870." He kept going, glancing at the dates on the spines until finally, "Here we go, 1895, a very good year."

"Why?" she asked.

"Year I was born. Let's see. Move that light closer, would you? No, need to go a bit earlier, this one starts in September."

He put the book back and tried a few adjacent ones till he exclaimed, "Aha! January, 1895. It was my birthday a fortnight ago, you know. Here we go, January fourteenth, lots of names. Gosh! This thing has every language under the sun! There's Chinese, Arabic, English, of course, Spanish . . . Is that Finnish?—I believe that's Swahili, if I'm not mistaken." His finger moved an inch over the columns until it stopped. "By God, Beatrice! Look here! 'Geoffrey Phillip Atwood 14 1 1895 Natus.' There I am! There I bloody am! How in Hades did they know that Geoffrey Phillip Atwood was going to be born on January 14, 1895?"

Her voice was frigid. "There is no rational explanation for this, Geoffrey."

"Other than they were awfully clever buggers, wouldn't you say? I'll venture they're the ones in the catacombs. Special treatment for clever buggers. Not going to bury their special lads up in the regular cemetery. Come on, let's find something more recent, shall we?"

They hunted for a while in the second chamber. Suddenly, Atwood stopped so abruptly that Beatrice bumped him from behind. He let out a low whistle. "Look at this, Beatrice!"

He shined the flashlight beam on a heap of cloth on the ground near the end of a row, a mass of brown and black material, like a load of laundry. They cautiously drew closer until they were looking down on it, shocked by the sight of a fully clothed skeleton lying on its back.

The large straw-colored skull had traces of leathery flesh and some strands of dark hair where the scalp had been. A flat black cap lay next to it. The occipital bone was caved in with a deeply depressed skull fracture, and the stones underneath were rust-stained with ancient blood. The clothing was male: a black, padded, high-collared doublet; brown knee breeches; black hose loose on long bones; leather boots. The body lay on top of a long black cloak, trimmed at the collar with ratty fur.

"This fellow is clearly not medieval," Atwood mumbled.

Beatrice was already kneeling, taking a closer look. "Elizabethan, I'd say."

"Are you sure?"

There was a purple silk pouch hanging from the skeleton's belt, embroidered with the letters J.C. She poked at it with her index finger then gently forced the dry purse strings open, tipping silver coins onto her palm. They were shillings and threepence. Atwood moved his beam closer. The rather masculine profile of Elizabeth I was on the obverse. Beatrice flipped the coin over, and above the coat of arms was crisply stamped: 1581.

"Yeah, I'm sure," she whispered. "What do you suppose he's doing here, Geoffrey?"

"I rather think that today's going to produce more questions than answers," he responded pensively. His eyes wandered to the stacks above the body. "Look! The nearest books are dated 1581! Surely, no coincidence. We'll come back to our friend later with the camera gear but let's finish our quest first."

They carefully skirted the skeleton and carried on through the stacks until Atwood found what he was looking for.

Fortunately, the 1947 volumes were within arm's reach, since they had no ladder.

He swept the cases with his beam and exclaimed, "I've found it! Here's where 1947 starts." He excitedly pulled down volumes until he triumphantly declared, "Today! January thirty-first!"

They sat together on the cold floor, squeezed between the racks, and let the heavy book straddle their laps so that one-half was resting on one of her thighs and one half on his. They scanned page after page of densely-packed names. *Natus, Mors, Mors, Natus.*

Atwood lost count of the number of pages turned, fifty, sixty, seventy.

Then he saw it, moments before she did: *Reginald William Saunders Mors.*

The diggers had made the Cunning Man in Fishbourne their local. They could walk to the inn from the excavation site, the beer was cheap, and the landlord let them pay a penny per head to use the bathtub in the guest wing. The pub sign, a leering man crouching over a stream catching a trout with his bare hands, never failed to elicit a smile, but not this evening. The diggers sat alone at a long table in the smoky public bar, moodily avoiding the locals.

Reggie checked his timepiece and tried to make light of the matter. "This round's on me if I can borrow a couple of quid. Pay you back tomorrow, Beatrice."

She reached into her purse and tossed him a few bills. "Here you go, you big gorilla. You'll be here to pay me back."

He snatched the bank notes. "What do you think, Prof? Is it curtains for old Reg?"

"I'll be the first to admit it, I'm foxed by all of this," Atwood said, rapidly downing the remaining quarter pint of his beer. He was on his third, which was more than his usual, and his head was swimming. All of them were drinking at a clip and their words were getting slushy.

"Well, if this is my last night on earth, I'm going out with a gut full of best bitter," Reggie said. "Same again for everyone?"

He gathered the empty pint mugs by their handles and carried them to the bar. When he was out of earshot Dennis leaned in and whispered to the group, "No one actually believes this rubbish, do they?"

Martin shook his head. "If it's rubbish, how come the prof's birth date was in one of the books?"

"Yeah, how come?" Timothy chimed in.

"There has to be a scientific explanation," Beatrice said.

"Does there?" Atwood asked. "Why does everything have to fit into a neat scientific package?"

"Geoffrey!" she exclaimed. "Coming from you? Dr. Empiricism? When was the last time you went to church?"

"Can't remember. Excavated quite a few old ones." He had the dazed look of a newly minted drunk. "Where's my beer gone?" He looked up and saw Reggie at the bar. "Oh, there he is. Good man. Survived Rommel. Hope he survives Vectis."

Ernest was thoughtful. He wasn't as tipsy as the rest. "We

need to do some tests," he said. "We need to look up more people we know or perhaps historical figures to verify their dates."

"Just the approach," Atwood said, hammering a beer mat with his hand. "Using the scientific method to prove that science is rubbish."

"And if all the dates are right?" Dennis asked. "Then what?"

"Then we turn this over to scary little blokes who do scary little things in scary little offices in Whitehall," Atwood replied.

"Ministry of Defense," Ernest said quietly.

"Why them?" Beatrice asked.

"Who else?" Atwood asked. "The press? The Pope?" Reggie was waiting for the publican to pull the last of the pints. "We're dying of thirst here!" Atwood called to him.

"Just coming, boss," Reggie said.

Julian Barnes came through the door, his great coat open and flapping. No one was more surprised than the local men, who knew who he was but had never seen him in a pub, let alone this one. He had an unpleasant kind of bearing, a snotty blend of entitlement and pomposity. His hair was slicked back, his moustache perfectly carved. He was small and ferretlike.

One of the locals, a union man who despised his lot, said sarcastically, "The wing commander's got us confused with the Conservative party offices. Down the road on the left, Squire!"

Barnes ignored him. "Tell me where I can find Reginald Saunders!" he boomed out in a round oratorical tone.

The archaeologists snapped their heads in attention.

Reggie was still at the bar, about to deliver the poured pints. He was a dart's toss from the pompous little man. "Who wants to know?" he asked, straightening himself to his full, intimidating height.

"Are you Reginald Saunders?" Barnes demanded officiously.

"Who the hell are you, mate?"

"I repeat my question, are you Saunders?"

"Yeah, I'm Saunders. Have you got business with me?"

The small man swallowed hard. "I believe you know my wife."

"I also know your motor, guv. Toss-up which I prefer."

With that, the wing commander pulled a silver pistol from his pocket and shot Reggie through his forehead before anyone could say or do anything.

Following his audience with Winston Churchill, Geoffrey Atwood was driven back to Hampshire in a covered army transit lorry. Beside him on the wooden bench was an impassive young captain, who only spoke when spoken to. The destination was a wartime base where the army still maintained a large barracks and training ground, and where Atwood and his group had been detained.

At the onset of the journey Atwood had asked him, "Why can't I be released here in London?"

"My instructions are to return you to Aldershot."

"Why is that, if I may ask?"

"Those are my instructions."

Atwood had been in the army long enough to know an immovable object when he saw one, so he saved his breath. He supposed solicitors were drawing up secrecy agreements and that all would be well.

As the van squeaked and bucked on its worn suspension, he tried to think pleasant thoughts about his wife and his children, who would be overjoyed at his return. He thought about a good meal, a hot bath, and resuming his reassuringly pedestrian academic duties. Vectis would by necessity disappear down a deep well, his notes and photographs confiscated, his memories expunged, practically speaking. He imagined he might have furtive chats with Beatrice over a glass of sherry in his rooms at the museum, but their heavy-handed confinement had achieved its desired effect: he was scared. Far more scared than ever during the war.

When he returned to the locked barracks, it was night-time and his comrades surrounded him like photographers swarming a film star. A pale, dispirited lot, they had lost weight and were irritable, fed up, and ill with worry. Beatrice was housed separately from the men but was allowed to stay with them during the day in a common room where their minders brought them colorless army grub. Martin, Timothy, and Dennis played hand after dreary hand of gin rummy, Beatrice fumed and swore at the guards, and Ernest sat in the corner stroking his hands in an agitated, depressive state.

They had all pinned their hopes on Atwood's foray to London, and now that he was back, demanded to know every detail. They listened, rapt, as he recounted his conversation with Major General Stuart and applauded and wept when he told them their release was imminent. It was only a matter of working through government secrecy agreements for signature. Even Ernest perked up and pulled his chair closer, the tension in his jaw slackening.

"You know what I'm going to do when I get back to Cambridge?" Dennis asked.

"We're not interested, Dennis," Martin said, shutting him up.

"I'm going to take a bath, put on clean clothes, go to the jazz club and introduce myself to loose women."

"He said we're not interested," Timothy said.

They spent the next morning waiting impatiently for news of their release. At lunchtime an army private entered with a tray and laid it on a communal table. He was a dull humorless lad whom Beatrice loved to torture. "Here, you dimwitted wanker," she said. "Get us a couple of bottles of wine. We're going home today."

"I'll have to check, miss."

"You do that, sonny. And check to see if your brains have spilled out your ears."

Major General Stuart picked up his ringing phone at his office in Aldershot. It was a call from London. The muscles of his hard face, fixed with disdain, didn't move. The exchange was short, to the point. There was no need for exposition or clarification. He signed off with a "Yes, sir," and pushed his chair away from his desk to carry out his orders.

The lunch was unappetizing but they were hungry and eager. Over stale rolls and glutinous spaghetti, Atwood, a man of great descriptive powers, told them everything he could recall about Churchill's famed underground bunker. Midway through their meal the private returned with two uncorked bottles of wine.

"As I live and breathe!" Beatrice exclaimed. "Private Wanker came through for us!" The lad put the bottles down and left without a word.

Atwood did the honors, pouring the wine into tumblers. "I would like to propose a toast," he said, turning serious. "Alas, we will never be able to speak again of what we found at Vectis, but our experience has forged among us an eternal bond that cannot be torn asunder. To our dear friend, Reggie Saunders, and to our bloody freedom!"

They clinked glasses and gulped the wine.

Beatrice made a face. "Not from the officers' mess, I shouldn't think."

Dennis started seizing first, perhaps because he was the smallest and lightest. Then Beatrice and Atwood. In seconds all of them had slumped off their chairs and were convulsing and gurgling on the floor, bloody tongues clamped between teeth, eyes rolling, fists clenched.

Major General Stuart came in when it was over and wearily surveyed the sorry landscape. He was bone-tired of death but there was no more obedient soldier in His Majesty's Army.

He sighed. There was heavy lifting to do and it would be a long day.

The general led a small contingent of trusted men back to the Isle of Wight. Atwood's excavation site had been cordoned off and the cutting covered by a large field headquarters tent, shielding it from view.

Abbot Lawlor had been told by a military man that Atwood's party discovered some unexploded ordnance in their trench and were evacuated to the mainland for safety. In the intervening twelve days, a steady flow of army transit lorries were ferried to the island by Royal Navy barges, and one by one the heavy vehicles rumbled up to the tent. Squaddies who had no idea of the significance of what they were handling did the backbreaking work around the clock of hauling wooden crates out of the ground.

The general entered the library vaults, the clop of his boots reverberating sharply. The rooms were stripped bare, row after row of towering empty bookcases. He stepped over the Elizabethan skeleton with complete disinterest. Another man might have tried to imagine what transpired there, tried to understand how it was possible, tried to wrestle with the philosophical vastness of it all. Stuart was not that man, which perhaps made him ideal for the job. He only wanted to return to London in time to get to his club for a scotch whiskey and a rare beefsteak.

When his walk-through was done, he would pay a visit to the abbot and commiserate about the terrible mistake the army had made: that they'd believed they had cleared all the ordnance before allowing Atwood's group to return. Unfortunately, it seems they missed a German five-hundred-pounder.

Perhaps a mass in their honor would be appropriate, they would somberly agree.

Stuart had the area cleared and let his demo man finish the wiring. When the percussion bombs went off, the ground shook seismically and tons of medieval stones collapsed in on their own weight.

Deep within the pancaked catacombs, the remains of Geoffrey Atwood, Beatrice Slade, Ernest Murray, Dennis Spencer, Martin Bancroft, and Timothy Brown would lie for eternity beside the bones of generations of ginger-haired scribes whose ancient books were packed into a convoy of olive-green lorries streaming toward a U.S. Air Force base in Lakenheath, Suffolk, for immediate transport to Washington.

July 29, 2009
New York City

Will's hangover was so mild it almost didn't qualify as one. It was more like a light case of the flu that could be cleared up in an hour by a couple of Tylenol.

The night before, he figured he'd drop off the deep end, bump along the bottom for a good long time and not surface until he was nearly drowned. But a couple of drinks into his planned bender he got angry, angry enough to rev down the self-pity and keep the flow of scotch at a steady state where his input matched his metabolism. He leveled off and engaged in largely rational thought for much of the night instead of the usual volatile nonsense that masqueraded as logic, quickly forgotten. During this functional interlude, he called Nancy and arranged to meet early.

He was already at one of the Starbucks near Grand Central, drinking a venti, when she arrived. She looked worse than him.

"Good commute?" he quipped.

He thought she wanted to cry and half considered giving her a hug, but that would have been a first—a public show of affection.

"I got a nonfat latte for you," he said, sliding the cup. "It's still hot." That nugget set her off. Tears started flowing. "It's only a cup of coffee," he said.

"I know. Thanks." She took a sip then asked the question: "What happened?"

She leaned in over the small table to hear his reply. The store was packed with customers, noisy with chatter and explosions of the milk steamer.

She looked young and vulnerable and he reflexively touched her hand. She misinterpreted the gesture.

"Do you think they found out about us?" she asked.

"No! This has nothing to do with that."

"How do you know?"

"They haul your ass to H.R. and tell you. Believe me, I know."

"Then, what?"

"It's not us, it's the case." He drank some coffee, glancing at each face that came through the door.

"They don't want us to arrest Shackleton," she said, reading his mind.

"That's what it looks like."

"Why would they block the capture of a serial killer?"

"Great question." He massaged his forehead and eyes wearily. "It's because he's special cargo."

She looked quizzical.

He dropped his voice. "When is someone taken off the grid? Federal witness? Covert activity? Black ops? Whatever it is, the screen goes dark and he's a nonperson. He said he worked for the feds. Area 51, whatever that is, or some such bull crap. This smells of one part of the government—us—bumping up against another part of the government, and we lost."

"Are you saying that officials in some federal agency decided to let a killer walk?" She was incredulous.

"I'm not saying anything. But yeah, it's possible. Depends how important he is. Or maybe, if there's some justice, he's dealt with quietly."

"But we'd never know," she said.

"We'd never know."

She finished her latte and rummaged her purse for a compact to fix her makeup. "So that's it? We're done?"

He watched her remove the streaks. "You're done. I'm not done."

His squared-off jaw was set in a classic pose of truculence, but there was also a serenity, the troubling kind when someone perched on a ledge has decided to jump.

"You're going back to the office," he said. "They'll have new work for you. I hear Mueller's coming back. Maybe they'll team you up again. You'll go on and have a great career because you're one heck of an agent."

"Will—" she blurted.

"No, hear me out, please," he said. "This is personal. I don't know how or why Shackleton killed these people but I do know he did this to rub my face in this dung heap of a case. It's got to be a part—maybe a big part—of his motivation. What's going to happen to me is what's supposed to happen. I'm not a company man anymore. Haven't been one for years. The whole idea of minding my fucking p's and q's to coast through to retirement has been bullshit." He was venting now, but the public space was keeping him from really broadcasting. "Screw the twenty and screw the pension. I'll find a job somewhere. I don't need a lot to get by."

She put her compact down. It looked like she'd have to redo her makeup again.

"God, Nancy, don't cry!" he whispered. "This isn't about us. Us is great. This is the best male-female thing I've had in a long time, maybe ever, if you want the truth. Apart from being smart and sexy, you're the most self-sufficient woman I've ever been with."

"That's a compliment?"

"From me? It's huge. You're not needy like one hundred percent of my exes. You're comfortable with your own life, which makes me comfortable with mine. I'm not going to find that again."

"Then why blow it up?"

"Wasn't my intent, obviously. I've got to find Shackleton."

"You're off the case!"

"I'm putting myself back on. One way or another it's going to get me booted. I know how they think. They won't tolerate the insubordination. Look, when I'm a mall security guard in Pensacola, maybe you can get a transfer down there. I don't know what they've got for art museums but we'll figure out ways to get you some culture."

She dabbed her eyes. "Do you have a plan at least?"

"It's not a very sophisticated one. I already called in sick. Sue'll be relieved she won't have to deal with me today. I'm booked on a flight to Vegas later this morning. I'm going to find him and make him talk."

"And I'm supposed to go back to work like nothing's happened."

"Yes and no." He pulled two cell phones from his briefcase. "They're going to be all over me as soon as they realize I'm off the reservation. It's possible they'll put a tap on you. Take one of these prepaids. We'll use them to talk to each other. Unless they get our numbers, they're untraceable. I'll need eyes and ears, but if you think for a second you're compromising yourself, we're going to pull the plug. And give Laura a call. Tell her something that puts her at ease. Okay?"

She took one of the phones. It was already damp from the brief time in his clutch. "Okay."

Mark was dreaming about lines of software code. They were forming faster than he could type, as fast as he could think. Each line was spare, perfect in a minimalist way, without an extraneous character. A floating slate was filling fast with something wonderful. It was a fabulous dream, and he was appalled that it was being zapped by ring tones.

It jarred him that his boss, Rebecca Rosenberg, was on his mobile. He was in bed with a beautiful woman in a magnificent suite in the Venetian Hotel and the Jersey voice of his troll-like supervisor was stomach-churning.

"How are you?" she asked.

"I'm fine. What's up?" It wasn't lost on him that she had never called like this before.

"I'm sorry to bother you on your vacation. Where are you?"

They could find out if they wanted from his mobile signal so he didn't lie. "In Vegas."

"Okay, so I know it's a real imposition, but we've got a code problem that no one can fix. The lambda HITS went down and the watchers are freaking out."

"Did you try rebooting it?" he asked blearily.

"A million times. It looks like the code got corrupted."

"How?"

"No one can figure it out. You're its daddy. You'd be doing me a big favor by coming in tomorrow."

"I'm on vacation!"

"I know, I'm sorry to have to call you but if you do this for us, I'll get you three extra vacation days, and if you finish the job in half a day, we'll get you Lear-jetted back to McCarran at lunchtime. So what do you say? Deal?"

He shook his head in disbelief. "Yeah. I'll do it."

He tossed the phone onto the bed. Kerry was still sound asleep. Something was fishy. He had covered his tracks so flawlessly, he was certain the Desert Life business was undetectable. He just had to bide his time, wait a month or two before starting the voluntary resignation process. He'd tell them he'd met a girl, that they were going to get married and live on the East Coast. They'd gnash their teeth and lecture him about mutual commitments, the length of time it took to recruit and train him, the difficulty in finding a replacement. They'd appeal to his patriotism. He'd hang tough. This wasn't slavery. They had to let him go. On his way out the door, they'd give him a good hard scrub and find nothing. They'd watch him for years, maybe forever, as they did with all past employees, but so be it. They could watch him all they wanted.

When Rosenberg hung up, the watchers took their earpieces out and nodded their approval. Malcolm Frazier, their chief, was there too, stiff-necked with an inanimate face and a wrestler's body. He told her, "That was good."

"If you think he's a security risk, why don't you pick him up today?" she asked.

"We don't think he's a security risk, we know he is," Frazier said gruffly. "We'd prefer to do this in a controlled environment. We'll confirm he's in Nevada. We've got people over at his house. We'll keep tabs on his mobile signal. If we think he's going to be a no-show tomorrow, we'll move."

"I'm sure you know your jobs," Rosenberg said. The air in her office was permeated with the scent of large athletic men.

"Yes, Dr. Rosenberg, we do."

On his way to the airport it began to drizzle and the taxi's wiper blades beat like a metronome keeping time for an adagio. Will slumped in the backseat, and when he nodded off, his chin came to rest on his shoulder. He awoke on the LaGuardia service road with a sore neck and told the driver he wanted US Airways.

His tan suit was speckled with raindrops. He caught the ticket agent's name, Vicki, from her name tag and engaged her in small talk while he presented his ID and federal carry license. He absently watched her as she typed, a chunky, simple girl with long brown hair clipped into a pony tail, an unlikely nemesis.

The terminal was awash in gray light, a clinically sterile concourse with little pedestrian traffic since it was mid-morning. That made it easy for him to scan the hall and isolate persons of interest. His antennae were up and he was tense. Nobody but Nancy knew he was taking a walk on the wild side but he felt conspicuous anyway, like he had a sign around his neck. The passengers waiting for check-in up and down the hall looked legit, and there were two uniformed cops chatting near the ATM machine at the far end.

He had an hour to kill. He'd grab a bite and buy a paperback. When he was airborne he'd be able to relax for a few hours, unless Darla was working this leg, in which case he'd have to wrestle with the quandary of cheating on Nancy, though he was pretty sure he might succumb to the "what happens in Vegas, stays in Vegas" slogan. He hadn't thought about the big blonde for a while, but now he was having a hard time getting her out of his thoughts. For a full-bodied gal, she had the tiniest, most weightless lingerie—

Vicki was stalling, he realized. She was shuffling a few papers, staring at her terminal with frightened eyes.

"Everything okay?" he asked.

"Yeah. The screen's frozen. It'll clear."

The cops by the ATM were looking his way, talking into their radios.

Will snatched up his IDs from the counter. "Vicki, let's finish this up later. I've got to hit the restroom."

"But . . ."

He sprinted. The cops were a good sixty yards away and the floors were slippery. He had a quick shot straight out the door to the curb, and he was out of the building in three seconds. He didn't look back. His only chance was to move and think faster than the cops following him. A black Town Car was dropping off a passenger. The driver was about to pull away when Will opened the back door and plunged through it, tossing his travel bag onto the seat.

"Hey! I can't pick up here!" The driver was in his sixties with a Russian accent.

"It's okay!" Will said. "I'm a federal agent." He flashed his badge. "Drive. Please."

The driver grumbled in Russian but smoothly accelerated. Will pretended to search through his bag, a ruse to lower his head. He heard shouts in the distance. Had they made him? Did they get the tag number? His heart was pounding.

"I could get fired," the driver said.

"I'm sorry. I'm on a case."

"FBI?" the Russian asked.

"Yes, sir."

"I got son in Afghanistan, where you want to go?"

Will quickly ran through scenarios. "Marine Air Terminal."

"Only other side of airport?"

"You're a great help. Yeah, only there." He switched off his mobile phone and tossed it in his bag, swapping it for the bulkier prepaid.

The driver wouldn't take any money. Will got out and looked around: moment of truth. Everything looked normal, no blue lights, no pursuers. He immediately joined the short taxi rank in front of the terminal and hopped into a yellow cab. When it drove off he used his prepaid phone to call Nancy and fill her in. The two of them urgently hatched a small plan.

He figured they'd be motivated and resourced, so he had to put on a good effort, multiple transfers, zigzags. He had the first taxi drop him off on Queens Boulevard, where he stopped at a Chase Bank and withdrew a few grand in cash from his account and hailed another cab. The next stop was 125th Street in Manhattan, where he boarded a Metro North commuter to White Plains.

It was early afternoon and he was hungry. The rain had stopped and the air was fresher and more breathable than earlier. The sky was brightening and his bag wasn't heavy so he set off on foot in search of food. He found a small Italian restaurant on Mamaroneck Avenue and holed up at a table away from the window for a languorous three-course time-killer. He stopped himself from ordering a third beer and switched to soda for his main course of lasagna. When he was done he paid in cash, let his belt out a notch and walked into the sunshine.

The public library was nearby. It was a grand municipal building, some architect's concept of neoclassical design. He checked his bag at the front desk, but because there was no metal detector, he kept his weapon in its shoulder holster and found a quiet spot at a long table at the far end of the air-conditioned central reading room.

He suddenly felt conspicuous. Of the two dozen people in the room, he was the only one wearing a suit and the only one with a clean table space. The large room was library quiet, with an occasional cough and the scuff of a chair leg on the floor. He removed his tie, stuffed it into a jacket pocket, and set off to find a book to kill the time.

He wasn't much of a reader and he wasn't sure he remembered the last time he wandered the stacks of a library— probably at college, probably chasing a girl rather than a book. Despite the drama of the day, he was postprandial and drowsy and his legs were heavy. He weaved through claustrophobic rows of tall metal bookcases and inhaled the stale cardboard smell. Thousands of book titles blurred into one another and his brain started getting fuzzy. He had an overwhelming desire to curl up in a dark corner and take a nap, and was on the brink of going fully numb when he snapped back to alertness.

He was being watched.

He sensed it first, then heard footsteps, to his left in a parallel row. He turned in time to see a heel disappearing at the end of the stacks. He touched his holster through his jacket then hurried to the end of his row and made two quick rights. The row was empty. He listened, thought he heard something farther along, and crept quietly in that direction, another two rows toward the center of the room. When he wheeled round the corner, he saw a man scuttling away from him. "Hey!" he called out.

The man stopped and turned. He was obese, with an unruly speckled black beard, and was dressed as if it were winter, in hiking boots, a moth-holed sweater, and a parka. His upper cheeks were pocked and irritated and his nose was bulbous and textured like an orange peel. He had wire-rim glasses with a thrift-shop pedigree. Even though he was in his fifties, he had the petulance of a child caught doing something wrong.

Will approached him cautiously. "Were you following me?"

"No."

"I think you were."

"I was following you," he admitted.

Will relaxed. The man wasn't a threat. He pegged him as a schizophrenic, nonviolent, controlled. "Why were you following me?"

"To help you find a book." There was no modulation. Every word had the same tone and emphasis as the last, each one delivered with complete earnestness.

"Well, friend, I can use the help. I'm not big on libraries."

The man smiled and showed a mouthful of bad teeth. "I love the library."

"Okay, you can help me find a book. My name is Will."

"I'm Donny."

"Hello, Donny. You lead, I'll follow."

Donny joyfully hurried through the stacks like a rat who had mastered a maze. He led Will to a corner then down two flights of stairs to a basement floor where he burrowed deeply into the new level with a sense of purpose. They passed a library assistant, an older woman pushing a cart of books, who smiled slyly, pleased that Donny had found a willing playmate.

"You must have a really good book for me, Donny," Will called out to him.

"I got a really good book for you."

With plenty of time on his hands, Will found the escapade diverting. The man he was chasing had all the hallmarks of chronic schizophrenia with maybe a touch of retardation thrown in, and by the look of him, was on big-time meds. Deep in a library subbasement, he was in Donny's house playing Donny's game, but he didn't mind.

Finally, Donny stopped midway down an aisle and reached over his head for a large book with a worn cover. He needed both sweaty hands to wriggle it free before offering it to Will.

The Holy Bible.

"The Bible?" Will said with a fair bit of surprise. "I've got to tell you, Donny, I'm not much of a Bible reader. You read the Bible?"

Donny looked down at his boots and shook his head. "I don't read it."

"But you think I should?"

"You should read it."

"Any other books I ought to be reading?"

"Yes. One other book."

He scooted off again, Will following, lugging the eight-pound Bible under his arm, pushed up against his holstered gun. His mother, a meek Baptist who endured his son of a bitch father for thirty-seven years, read the Bible incessantly, and just then he cloyingly remembered an image of her at the kitchen table, reading her Bible, holding onto it for dear life, her lower lip trembling, while his old man, drunk in the living room, cursed her out at the top of his lungs. And she plumbed the Bible for personal forgiveness when she too turned to the bottle for release. He wouldn't be reading the Bible anytime soon.

"The next book going to be as profound as this one?" Will asked.

"Yes. It's going to be a good book for you to read."

He couldn't wait.

They went down another flight of stairs to the lowest level, an area that didn't look like it saw a lot of foot traffic. Donny suddenly stopped on a dime and dropped to his knees at a shelf filled with older leather-bound books. He triumphantly pulled one out. "This is a good one for you."

Will was keen to see it. What, in this poor soul's view of the world, would match the Bible? He braced himself for a revelatory moment.

NY State Municipal Code—1951.

He put the Bible down to examine the new book. As advertised, it was page after page of municipal codes with a heavy emphasis on permitted uses of land. It was probably a minimum of half a century since anyone had touched the volume. "Well, this sure is profound, Donny."

"Yep. It's a good book."

"You picked both these books randomly, didn't you?"

He nodded his head vigorously. "They were random, Will."

At five-thirty he was sound asleep in the reading room with his head comfortably perched on the Bible and the Municipal Code. He felt a tug on his sleeve, looked up and saw Nancy standing over him. "Hi."

She was checking out his reading material. "Don't ask," he pleaded.

Outside, they sat in her car talking. He figured if he was going to be taken down, it would have happened already. It looked like no one had connected the dots.

She told him that back in the office all hell was breaking loose. She wasn't in the loop but the news was spreading fluidly within the agency. Will's name had been added to the TSA's no-fly list and his check-in attempt at LaGuardia had triggered multiagency pandemonium. Sue Sanchez was feverish—she'd spent all day behind closed doors with the brass, emerging only to bark a few orders and generally be a pain in the ass. They'd questioned Nancy a few times about her knowledge of Will's actions and intent but seemed satisfied that she didn't know anything. Sue was almost apologetic at having forced Nancy to work with him on the Doomsday case and assured her repeatedly that she wouldn't be stained by the association.

Will sighed deeply. "Well, I'm grounded. I can't fly, I can't rent a car, I can't use a credit card. If I try to get on a train or a bus I'll get picked up at Penn Station or the Port Authority." He stared out the passenger-side window, then put a hand on her thigh and patted it playfully. "I'll have to steal a car, I guess."

"You're absolutely right. You're going to steal a car." She started the motor and left the parking lot.

They argued all the way to her house. He didn't want to involve her parents, but Nancy insisted. "I want them to meet you."

He wanted to know why.

"They've heard all about you. They've seen you on TV." She paused before finishing, "They know about us."

"Tell me you didn't tell your parents you're having an affair with your partner who's almost twice your age."

"We're a close family. And you're not twice my age."

The Lipinski abode was a compact 1930s brick house with a steeply pitched slate roof on a stubby dead-end street across from Nancy's old high school, its flower beds brimming with cascades of orange and red roses that made it look like the structure was being consumed by fire.

Joe Lipinski was in the backyard, a small man, shirtless

with baggy shorts. There were sprouts of silky-white hair everywhere—sparse on his sunburned scalp, tufted on his chest. His round, impish cheeks were the fleshiest part of his body. He was kneeling on the grass, pruning a rosebush, but shot up with a youthful spring to his legs and yelled, "Hey! It's the Pied Piper! Welcome to Casa Lipinski!"

"You have a beautiful garden, sir," Will offered.

"Don't sir me, Joe me. But thanks. You like roses?"

"Sure I do."

Joe reached for a small bud, pruned it off and held it out. "For your button hole. Put it in his button hole, Nancy."

She blushed but complied, threading it in place.

"There!" Joe exclaimed. "Now you two kids can go to the prom. C'mon. Let's get out of the sun. Your mother's got dinner almost ready."

"I don't want to put you out," Will protested.

Joe dismissed him with a what-are-you-talking about look and winked at his daughter.

The house was warm because Joe didn't believe in air-conditioning. It was a period piece, unchanged since moving day, 1974. The kitchen and bathrooms had been updated in the sixties but that was it. Small rooms with thick mushy carpets and worn lumpy furniture, a first-generation escape to the suburbs.

Mary Lipinski was in the kitchen, which was fragrant from simmering pots. She was a pretty woman who hadn't let herself go, although, Will noted, she was on the thick-hipped side. He had an unpleasant habit of divining what his girlfriends might look like in twenty years, as if he'd ever had a relationship that lasted more than twenty months. Still, she had a tight, youthful face, lovely shoulder-length brown hair, a firm bosom, and nice calves. Not bad for her late fifties, early sixties.

Joe was a CPA and Mary was a bookkeeper. They had met at General Foods, where he was an accountant, about ten years her senior, and she was a secretary in the tax department. At first he commuted up from Queens; she was a local girl from White Plains. When they married, they bought this small house on Anthony Road just a mile away from the headquarters. Years later, after the company was acquired by Kraft, the White Plains operation was closed down and Joe took a buyout. He decided to open up his own tax business, and Mary took a job at a Ford dealer doing their books. Nancy was their only daughter, and they were thrilled she was back in her old room.

"So that's us, the modern day Joseph and Mary," Joe said, concluding a brief family history and passing Will a plate of string beans. A Verdi opera was softly playing on the Bose radio. Will was lulled into a contented state by the food, the music, and the plain conversation. This was the kind of wholesome shit he never provided for his daughter, he thought wistfully. A glass of wine or beer would have been nice but it appeared the Lipinskis weren't serving. Joe was zeroing in on the punch line: "We're just like the originals, but this one here, she was no immaculate conception!"

"Dad!" Nancy protested.

"Would you like another piece of chicken, Will?" Mary asked.

"Yes ma'am, I would, thank you."

"Nancy tells me you spent the afternoon in our fine public library," Joe said.

"I did. I came across a real character there."

Mary grimaced. "Donny Golden," she said.

"You know him?" Will asked.

"Everyone knows Donny," Nancy answered.

"Tell Will how you know him, Mary," Joe prodded.

"Believe it or not, Will, Donny and I went to high school together."

"She was his girlfriend!" Joe shouted gleefully.

"We dated once! It's such a sad story. He was the most handsome boy, from a nice Jewish family. He went off to college, normal and healthy, and got very sick during his freshman year. Some say it was drugs, some say it was just when he developed his mental problem. He spent years in institutions. He lives in some kind of supervised house downtown and spends all his time in the library. He's harmless but it's painful to see him. I won't go there."

"He doesn't have such a bad life," Joe said. "No pressures. He's oblivious to all the bad things in the world."

"I think it's sad too," Nancy said, picking at her food. "I saw his yearbook pictures. He was really cute."

Mary sighed. "Who knew what fate had in store for him? Who ever knows?"

Suddenly, Joe turned serious. "So, Will, tell us what's in store for you. I hear there's some funny business going on. I'm concerned for you, certainly, but as a father, I'm very concerned for my daughter."

"Will can't talk about an ongoing investigation, Dad."

"No, listen, I hear you, Joe. I've got some things I've got to do but I don't want Nancy getting caught up in this. She's got a brilliant career ahead of her."

"I'd rather she was doing something less dangerous than the FBI," her mother said, chiming what sounded like a constant refrain.

Nancy made a face and Joe dismissed his wife's worry with a wave. "I understand you were close to making an arrest but both of you were yanked off the investigation. How does something like this happen in the United States of America? When my parents were in Poland, these things happened all the time. But here?"

"I want to find that out. Nancy and I put a lot of time into this case, and there are victims who don't have a voice."

"Well, you do what you have to do. You seem like a nice fellow. And Nancy is quite fond of you. That means you're going to be in my prayers."

The opera was over and the station was doing a news summary. None of them would have paid any attention if Will's name weren't mentioned:

"And in other news, the New York Office of the Federal Bureau of Investigation has filed an arrest warrant for one of their own. Special Agent Will Piper is wanted for questioning for irregularities and possible criminal wrongdoing related to the investigation of the Doomsday serial killer. Piper, a nearly twenty-year veteran of law enforcement, is best known for being the public face of the still-unsolved Doomsday case. His whereabouts are unknown and he is considered armed and potentially dangerous. If a member of the public has any information, please contact local police authorities or the FBI."

Will grimly stood up and put his jacket back on. He fingered the rosebud in the lapel. "Joe and Mary, thank you for dinner and thank you for your hospitality. I've got to be going."

There wasn't much city-bound traffic this time of day. They had stopped first at a convenience store on Rosedale Avenue, where Nancy hopped out to buy provisions while Will fidgeted in her car. Two bags of groceries were on the backseat, but no, she had said emphatically, she would not buy him booze.

Now they were cruising on the Hutch and the Whitestone Bridge was coming up. He reminded her to call his daughter, then fell silent and watched the sun turn the Long Island Sound burnt orange.

Nancy's grandparents' house was on a quiet street of postage-stamp-sized homes in Forest Hills. Her grandfather was in a nursing home with Alzheimer's. Her grandmother was visiting a niece in Florida for a respite. Granddad's old Ford Taurus was in the one-car lock-up garage behind the house; in case they found a cure, Nancy joked darkly. They arrived at dusk and parked out front. The garage keys were under a brick, the car keys in the garage under a paint can. The rest was up to him.

He leaned over and kissed her and they held each other for a long while, like a couple at a drive-in.

"Maybe we should go inside," Will exhaled.

She playfully rapped his forehead with her knuckles. "I'm not sneaking into my grandma's house to have sex!"

"Bad idea?"

"Very bad. Besides, you'll get sleepy."

"That wouldn't be good."

"No it wouldn't. Call me every step of the way, okay?"

"Okay."

"Will you be safe?"

"I'll be safe."

"Promise?

"I promise."

"There's something I didn't tell you about work today," she said, kissing him one last time. "John Mueller was back in for a few hours. Sue's putting us together to work on the Brooklyn bank robberies. I talked to him for a while, and do you know what?"

"What?"

"I think he's an asshole."

He laughed, gave her a thumbs-up, and opened his door. "Then my work here is done."

Mark fretted. Why had he agreed to come in off his vacation?

He wasn't quick enough on his feet or strong enough to stand up for himself—he was always a lapdog for parents, teachers, bosses—always too eager to please, too scared to disappoint. He didn't want to leave the hotel and burst the delicious bubble he and Kerry were inhabiting.

She was in the bathroom, getting ready. They had a superior night planned: dinner at Rubochon's at the MGM Mansion, a little blackjack, then drinks back in the Venetian at the Tao Beach Club. He'd have to leave early and go straight to the airport, and he probably wouldn't feel too brilliant come dawn, but what was he going to do now? If he was a no-show he'd raise all sorts of alarms.

He was already dressed for the night and restless, so he logged onto the Net via the hotel's high-speed service. He shook his head: another e-mail from Elder. The man was sucking him dry, but a deal was a deal. Maybe he'd priced himself too low at $5 million. Maybe he'd just have to hit him up for another five in a few months. What was the guy going to do? Say no?

Working through Elder's new list, Malcolm Frazier's group was on Alpha Alert: shifts on cots and cold food. Moody sorts to begin with, they were in a despicable state over the prospect of a night away from wives and girlfriends. Frazier had even forced Rebecca Rosenberg to stay overnight, a first. She was beside herself over the whole situation, completely in tatters.

He pointed at his monitor with irritation. "Look. He's on that encrypted portal again. Why the Christ can't you break that? I mean how long is it going to take you to break that? We don't even know who's on the other end."

Rosenberg shot daggers at him. She was following the identical traffic on her screen. "He's one of the best computer security scientists in the country!"

"Well, you're his boss, so break the goddamned code, will you? How's it going to look if we have to farm this out to the NSA? You're supposed to be the best, remember?"

She shrieked with frustration, making the men in the room jump. "Mark Shackleton is the best! I sign his time cards! Just shut up and let me work!"

Mark was almost done with his e-mail when the bathroom door opened a crack and he heard a muffled, "I'll be ready soon!" in her lilting twang.

"I wish I didn't have to go back to work tomorrow," he said over the sound of the TV.

"Me too."

He hit the mute button; she liked to talk from inside the bathroom. "Maybe we can rebook for next weekend."

"That would be great." The faucet ran for a second then stopped. "You know what would also be great?"

He logged off and slipped the computer back in its case. "What would also be great?"

"To go to L.A. next weekend, you and me. I mean, we

both want to live there. Now that you've come into all this money, you can quit your stupid UFO job and be a movie writer full-time and I can quit my stupid escort job and my stupid vasectomy job and be an actress, maybe a real one. We can go house hunting next weekend. Whaddya say? I think it'd be fun."

Will Piper's face was plastered all over the plasma screen. Christ, Mark thought, second time in two days! He unmuted the set.

"Did you hear me? Wouldn't it be fun?"

"Hang on a second, Kerry, I'll be right with you!" He watched the news item in horror. It felt like a boa constrictor had wrapped itself around his chest and was squeezing the breath out of him. Yesterday he saw this guy boasting about new leads, and today he was a fugitive? And it was a coincidence he was being called in from vacation? Two hundred IQ points started rowing in the same direction. "Fuck, fuck, fuck, fuck, fuck—"

"What'd you say, honey?"

"Be right with you!" His hands were shaking like he had malaria as he reached back into his case for his laptop.

He never wanted to do this; a lot of Area 51 people were tempted—that's what the watchers were for, that's what his algorithms were for—but he wasn't like the others. He was an it-is-what-it-is kind of guy. Now he desperately needed to know. He entered his password and logged onto the pirated U.S. database stored on his hard drive. He had to work fast. If he stopped to think about what he was doing, he was going to balk.

He started entering names.

Kerry came out of the bathroom, dressed to the nines in a slinky red dress with her new watch gleaming on her wrist. "Mark! What's the matter?" His computer was snapped shut on his lap but he was bawling like an infant, big chest-sucking sobs and torrents of tears. She knelt down and threw her arms around him. "Are you okay, honey?"

He shook his head.

"What happened?"

He had to think fast. "I got an e-mail. My aunt died."

"Oh, sweetie, I'm so sorry!" He stood up, wobbly—no, more than wobbly, in a near faint. She rose with him and gave him a giant hug, which prevented him from falling back down. "Was it unexpected?"

He nodded and tried to wipe his face dry with his hand. She got him a tissue, rushed back to his side and daubed him dry like a mother tending a helpless child. "Look, I've got an idea," he said robotically. "Let's go to L.A. tonight. Right now. We'll drive. My car's overheating. We'll take yours. We'll buy a house tomorrow, okay? In the Hollywood Hills. A lot of writers and actors live there. Okay? Can you pack?"

She stared at him, worried and perplexed. "Are you sure you want to go right now, Mark? You've just had a shock. Maybe we should wait till the morning."

He stamped his foot and shouted in a juvenile fit. "No! I don't want to wait! I want to go now!"

She backed away a step. "Why the big rush, honey?" He was scaring her.

He almost started crying again but was able to stop himself. Sniffing hard through blocked nostrils, he packed up his laptop and turned his cell phone off. " 'Cause life's too short, Kerry. It's too fucking short."

Their room overlooked Rodeo Drive. Mark stood at the window in a hotel bathrobe and through parted curtains mournfully watched luxury cars take the turn off Wilshire onto Rodeo. The sun wasn't high enough to burn off the morning haze, but it looked like it was going to be a perfect day. The suite on the fourteenth floor of the Beverly Wilshire Hotel cost $2,500 for the night, paid for in cash to make it a little harder for the watchers. But who was he kidding? He looked into her handbag to check Kerry's mobile phone. He had switched it off while she was driving and it was still off. She would be on their radar already, but he was playing for time. Precious time.

They arrived late, after a long drive through the desert during which neither of them spoke much. There wasn't time to plan things but he wanted everything to be perfect. His mind drifted back to when he was seven, waking up before his parents and rushing to make them breakfast for the first time in his life, pouring out cereal, slicing a banana, and carefully balancing the bowls and cutlery and little glasses of OJ on a tray that he proudly presented to them in bed. He'd wanted everything to be perfect that day, and when he succeeded, he solicited their praise for weeks. If he kept his wits, he could succeed today too.

They had champagne and steaks when they arrived. More champagne was on its way for brunch, with crepes and strawberries. A Realtor would meet them in the lobby in an hour for an afternoon of house-hunting. He wanted her to be happy.

"Kerry?"

She moved under the sheets and he called her name again, a bit louder.

"Hi," she answered into the pillow.

"Brunch is coming, with mimosas."

"Didn't we just eat?"

"Ages ago. Want to get up now?"

"Okay. Did you tell them you weren't going into work?"

"They know."

"Mark?"

"Uh-huh?"

"You were acting kind of weird last night."

"I know."

"Will you act normal today?"

"I will."

"Are we really going to buy a house today?"

"If you see one you like."

She propped herself up and showed her face, which was brightly illuminated by her smile. "Well, my day's starting pretty nice. Come over here and I'll start yours off nice too."

Will drove all night and now was cruising on flat land through Ohio, going for broke, driving fast into the dawn and hoping he'd skip through unscathed, avoiding speed traps and unmarked staties. He knew he couldn't make it all the way without sleeping. He'd have to pick his spots, Motel 6 kinds of places near the highway, where he'd pay cash and pick up four hours here, six there—no more than that. He wanted to be in Vegas by Friday night and ruin this motherfucker's weekend.

He couldn't recall the last time he'd pulled an all-nighter, especially an alcohol-free one, and it didn't feel good. He had cravings for booze, for sleep, and for something to squelch his anger and indignation. His hands were cramped from gripping the wheel too hard, his right ankle sore because the old Taurus didn't have cruise control. His eyes were red and dry. His bladder ached from the last large coffee. The only thing giving him any solace was the red Lipinski rosebud, succulent and healthy, stuck into a plastic water bottle in the cup holder.

In the middle of the night, Malcolm Frazier left his Operations Center and took a walk to clear his head. The last piece of news was unbelievable, he thought. Un-fucking-believable. This abomination happened on his watch. If he survived this—if *they* survived this—he'd be testifying at closed Pentagon hearings till he was a hundred.

They'd gone into crisis mode the moment Shackleton switched his cell phone off and the beacon was lost. A team converged on the Venetian but he was gone, his Corvette still in the valet lot, the bill unsettled.

What followed was a very dark hour until they were able to turn things around. He had been with a woman, an attractive brunette whom the concierge recognized as an escort he'd seen around the hotel. They accessed Shackleton's mobile phone records and found dozens of calls to a Kerry Hightower, who fit the woman's description.

Hightower's phone was pinging towers along I-15 west-bound until the signal went dead fifteen miles west of Barstow. It looked like L.A. was a likely destination. They fed the description of her car and its tag number to the CHP and local sheriff departments but wouldn't know until an after-action investigation that her Toyota had been in the shop and she was driving a loaner.

Rebecca Rosenberg was eating her third postmidnight candy bar when she suddenly blasted through Shackleton's encryption and almost choked on a gob of caramel. She peeled out of her lab, ran clumsily down the hall to the Operations Center, and burst into the scrum of watchers, her white-girl version of a sixties Afro bouncing on her shoulders.

"He's been passing DOD's to a company!" she gasped.

Frazier was at his terminal. He swiveled toward her and

looked like he wanted to throw up. This was as bad as it got.
"The fuck you say. You sure?"

"Hundred percent."

"What kind of company?"

It got worse. "Life insurance."

The corridors of the Primary Research Lab were empty,
which magnified the echo-chamber effect. To relieve tension, Malcolm Frazier coughed to play with the acoustic
bounciness. Shouting or yodeling wouldn't have been digni-
fied even if no one was listening. During the day, as Chief of
NTS-51 Operational Security, he roamed the underground
with a cocky swagger that intimidated the rank and file. He
liked being feared and had no regrets that his watchers were
universally hated. That meant they were doing their jobs.
Without fear, how was order to be maintained? The tempta-
tion to exploit the asset was simply too great for the geeks.
He had contempt for them, and always felt a rush of superi-
ority when he saw them in the strip 'n' scan, fat and puffy
or thin and weak, never fit and well-muscled like his lot.
Shackleton, he recalled, was one of the thin and weak ones,
snappable like a plank of balsa wood.

He gravitated to the special elevator and called it up with
an access key. The descent was so smooth it was almost imperceptible, and when he emerged he was the only soul on
the Vault level. His motion would trigger a monitor and one
of his men would be watching, but he was permitted to be
there, he knew the entry codes, and he was one of the few
authorized to pass through the heavy steel doors.

The power of the Vault was visceral. Frazier felt his back
straighten as if an iron rod had been rammed through his
spine. His chest swelled and his senses heightened, his depth
perception—even in the subdued cool-blue light—so acute
he was almost seeing in 3-D. Some men felt tiny in the vastness of the place, but the Vault made him feel large and
powerful. Tonight, in the midst of the most serious security
breech in the history of Area 51, he needed to be there.

He stepped into the chilled dehumidified atmosphere. Five feet, ten, twenty, a hundred. He wasn't planning to walk its full length; he didn't have the time. He went far enough to fully experience the magnitude of its domed ceiling and stadium dimensions. He let the fingertips of his right hand brush one of the bindings. Strictly speaking, contact was not allowed, but he wasn't exactly pulling it off the shelf—it was just an affirmation.

The leather was smooth and cool, the color of mottled buckskin. Tooled onto the spine was the year: 1863. There were rows of 1863s. The Civil War. And Lord knew what else was going on in the rest of the world. He wasn't an historian.

At one side of the Vault a narrow stairway led to a catwalk where one could take in the full panorama. He went there and climbed to the top. There were thousands of gunmetal-gray bookcases stretching into the distance, nearly 700,000 thick leather books, over 240 billion inscribed names. The only way to get your mind around these numbers, he was convinced, was to stand there and take it in with your own eyes. All the information had long been stored on disks, and if you were one of the geeks, you were impressed with all the terabits of data or some such bullshit, but there was no substitute for actually being in the Library. He grabbed the railing, leaned into it and breathed slow, deep breaths.

Nelson Elder was having a pretty good morning. He was at his favorite table in the company cafeteria tucking into an egg-white omelet and the morning paper. He was energized from a good run, a good steam shower, and renewed confidence in the future. Of all the things in his life that affected his mood, the single biggest factor was the Desert Life stock quote. In the last month the stock was up 7.2 percent, rising a full 1.5 percent the day before on an analyst upgrade. It was too early for this craziness with Peter Benedict to affect his bottom line, but he could predict with mathematical certainty that denying coverage to life insurance applicants with an impending date of death, and risk-adjusting the premiums for those with an intermediate death horizon, would turn his company into a cash machine.

To top that off, Bert Myer's walk on the wild side with his Connecticut hedge fund was turning the corner, with double-digit yields in July. Elder translated his bullishness into a new, more aggressive tone with investors and research analysts, and the Street was taking notice. The sentiment on Desert Life was shifting.

He didn't care how this odd-duck Benedict had access to his magical database or where it came from or how it was even possible. A moral philosopher, he wasn't. He only cared about Desert Life, and now he had an edge that none of his competitors could ever match. He had paid Benedict $5 million out of his own pocket to avoid his auditors picking up a corporate transaction and asking questions. He already had enough worries about Bert's hedge fund adventure.

But it was money well spent. The value of his personal stock holdings had appreciated by $10 million, a damned good return on investment in one month! He would keep his own counsel on the Benedict business. No one knew, even Bert. It was too bizarre and too dangerous. He had enough trouble explaining to his head of underwriting why he needed to receive a daily nationwide list of all new life insurance applicants.

Bert saw him eating alone and came by grinning and wagging a finger. "I know your secret, Nelson!"

That startled the older man. "What are you talking about?" he asked sternly.

"You're ditching us this afternoon and playing golf."

Elder exhaled and smiled. "How'd you know?"

"I know everything around here," the CFO boasted.

"Not everything. I've got a couple of things up my sleeves."

"You got my bonus up there too?"

"You keep the high yields coming and you'll be buying an island in a couple of years. Want to join me for breakfast?"

"Can't. Budget meeting. Who're you playing with?"

"It's a charity thing over at the Wynn. I don't even know who's in my four."

"Well, enjoy yourself. You deserve it."

Elder winked at him. "You're right. I do."

Nancy couldn't concentrate on the bank robbery file. She turned a page only to realize that none of it registered and she had to go back and read it again. She had a meeting with John Mueller later in the morning, and he was expecting some kind of briefing. Every few minutes she compulsively opened the browser and searched the Web for new articles on Will, but the same AP story was being recycled around the world. Finally, she couldn't wait any longer.

Sue Sanchez saw her in the hall and hailed her from a distance. Sue was among the last people Nancy wanted to see but she couldn't very well pretend she hadn't noticed her.

The strain on Sue's face was remarkable. The corner of her left eye was twitching and there was a quaver in her voice. "Nancy," she said, drawing so close it made her uncomfortable. "Has he tried to contact you?"

Nancy made sure her handbag was closed and zippered. "You asked me last night. The answer's still no."

"I have to ask. He was your partner. Partners get close." The statement made Nancy nervous, and Sue picked up on it and backtracked. "I don't mean close in that way. You know, bonding, friendship."

"He hasn't called or e-mailed. Besides, you'd know if he had," she blurted out.

"I haven't authorized a tap on him or you!" Sue insisted. "If we were doing a tap I'd be aware of it. I'm his superior!"

"Sue, I know a lot less than you do about what's going on, but would you really be shocked if some other agencies were calling the shots?"

Sue looked hurt and defensive. "I don't know what you're talking about." Nancy shrugged, and Sue recovered her composure, "Where are you going?"

"To the drugstore. Need anything?" Nancy said, moving toward the elevator bank.

"No. I'm fine." She didn't sound convincing.

Nancy walked five blocks before reaching into her bag for the prepaid phone. She checked one more time for tags and punched the number.

He picked up on the second ring. "Joe's Tacos."

"Sounds appetizing," she said.

"I'm glad you called." He sounded bone weary. "I was getting lonely."

"Where are you?"

"Someplace as flat as a pool table."

"Can you be more specific?"

"Sign says Indiana."

"You didn't go all night, did you?"

"I believe I did."

"You've got to get some sleep!"

"Uh-huh."

"When?"

"I'm looking for a place as we speak. Did you talk to Laura?"

"I wanted to see how you were first."

"Tell her I'm fine. Tell her not to be worried."

"She'll be worried. I'm worried."

"What's going on in the office?"

"Sue looks like shit. Everyone's got their doors closed."

"I heard about me on the radio all night. They're playing this large."

"If they've got a dragnet out on you, what are they doing with Shackleton?"

"I guess the chances of finding him with his feet up on his porch aren't too high."

"What then?"

"I'm going to use my years of skills and resourcefulness."

"What does that mean?"

"It means I'm going to wing it." He went quiet and then said, "You know, I was thinking."

"About what?"

"About you."

"What about me?"

There was another long pause, the whooshing sound of an eighteen-wheeler passing. "I think I'm in love with you."

She closed her eyes, and when she opened them she was still in lower Manhattan. "Come on, Will, why are you saying something like that? Sleep deprivation?"

"Nope. I mean it."

"Please find a motel and get some sleep."

"That's all you have to say?"

"No. I think I might love you too."

Greg Davis was waiting for the kettle to boil. His relationship with Laura Piper was only a year and a half old and they were facing their first significant crisis as a couple. He wanted to step up to the plate and be a great guy and a supportive boyfriend, and in his family you dealt with a crisis by brewing tea.

Their apartment was tiny, with minimal light and no views, but they'd rather have a garret in Georgetown than a nicer place in a soulless suburb. She had finally fallen asleep at 2:00 A.M., but as soon as she awoke, she turned the TV back on, saw the crawl on the screen informing that her father remained at large and began crying again.

"Do you want regular or herbal?" he called out.

He heard sobs. "Herbal."

He brought her a cup and sat beside her on the bed.

"I tried calling him again," she said weakly.

"Home and cell?"

"Voice mail." He was still in his boxers. "You'll be late," she said.

"I'm calling in."

"Why?"

"To stay with you. I'm not leaving you alone."

She wrapped her arms around him, and his shoulder got wet from her tears. "Why are you so good to me?"

"What kind of question is that?"

His cell phone began to vibrate and move on the bed table. He lunged for it before it fell off the edge. It read: UNKNOWN CALLER.

A woman was asking for him.

"This is Greg."

"It's Nancy Lipinski, Greg. We met at Will's apartment."

"Jesus! Nancy! Hello!" He whispered to Laura, "Your dad's partner," and she sat bolt upright. "How'd you get my number?"

"I work for the FBI, Greg."

"Yeah. I see that," he said. "Are you calling about Will?"

"Yes. Is Laura there?"

"She is. Why'd you call me?"

"Laura's phones could be tapped."

"Christ, what did Will do?"

"Am I talking to his daughter's boyfriend or a journalist?" Nancy asked.

He hesitated then looked at Laura's pleading eyes. "Her boyfriend."

"He's in a lot of trouble but he didn't do anything wrong. We got too close to something and he's not backing down. I need you to promise me you'll keep this confidential."

"Okay," he assured her, "you're off the record."

"Put Laura on. He wants her to know he's all right."

The Realtor was a platinum blonde entering her Botox years. She talked a mile a minute and bonded with Kerry in an instant. The two of them were yapping away in the front of the big Mercedes while Mark sat in the back, anesthetized, his legs straddling his briefcase.

He was aware on some level that there was chatter going on and that they were passing cars and people and shops along Santa Monica Boulevard, that it was cool in the sedan and hot and sunny outside the tinted windows, and that there were two clashing perfumes in the cabin and a metallic taste in his mouth and a throbbing behind his eyes, but each sense existed in its own dimension. He was no more than a series of unlinked sensors. His mind wasn't processing and integrating the data. He was somewhere else, lost.

Kerry's squeal penetrated his veil. "Mark! Gina's asking you a question!"

"Sorry, what?"

The Realtor said, "I was asking about your time frame."

"Soon," he said softly. "Very soon."

"That's great! We can really use that as leverage. And you said you wanted a cash deal?"

"That's right."

"I mean, you guys are so totally with it!" the Realtor gushed. "I get out-of-towners coming in and all they want to see is Beverly Hills or Bel Air or Brentwood—the three B's—but you guys are so smart and focused. I mean, did you know that the Hollywood Hills in your price range with your aggressive attitude is the single best luxury value in L.A.? We're going to have a great afternoon!"

He didn't respond and the two women picked up their conversation and left him alone again. When the car began its climb into the mountain range, he felt his back pushing against the seat. He closed his eyes and was in the rear of his father's car, driving into the White Mountains to their rental cabin in Pinkham Notch. His father and mother were droning on about something or other and he was on his own with the numbers swimming in his head, trying to arrange them into a theorem proof. When the theorem yielded and QED started flashing in his mind, he was suffused with a gush of joy he wished he could summon now.

The Mercedes snaked up narrow winding roads and houses hidden by gates and hedges. It came to a stop behind one of the ubiquitous landscaping trucks they had been passing, and when Mark opened his door he was blasted by furnace heat and the roar of a leaf blower. Kerry sprinted to the gate clutching a listing sheet, looking like a skipping child.

The Realtor told Mark, "She is so cute! You guys better pace yourself. I've got a lot of appointments lined up!"

* * *

Frazier was motoring on black coffee and adrenaline, and if he could persuade someone in medical to give him amphetamines, he'd throw those on board too. The facility was in normal day-mode, filled to the gills with employees doing their regular geek jobs. He, on the other hand, was doing something irregular and unprecedented, juggling an internal investigation and three field ops simultaneously while briefing his masters in Washington every few minutes.

One field team was in New York, pursuing the Will Piper angle; the second was in Los Angeles, in if-and-when mode, in case Mark Shackleton materialized in California; the third in Las Vegas, working the Nelson Elder situation. All his men were ex-military. Some had served in CIA field ops in the Middle East. All of them were effective sons of bitches, performing coolly despite the impotent panic in the Pentagon.

He was feeling better about Rebecca Rosenberg, although her eating habits disgusted him and spoke to a lack of personal discipline. He watched her gorge on nougat and caramel all night, and she seemed to be getting lumpier in front of his eyes. Her trash bin was filled with wrappers and she was ugly as hell, but he was concluding with grudging admiration that she wasn't just a geek supervisor but a damned good geek in her own right. She was breaking through Shackleton's defenses stone by stone and laying it all out in the open.

"Look at this," she said when he swung by. "More Peter Benedict stuff. He used to have a credit line under that name at the Constellation Casino, and there's a Peter Benedict Visa card."

"Any interesting charges on it?"

"He hardly used it but there were a few transactions with the Writers Guild of America. For screenplay registration or something."

"Jesus, a fucking writer. Can you get ahold of them?"

"You mean hack them off their server? Yeah, probably. There's something else."

"Hit me."

"A month ago he set up an account in the Caymans. It got

kicked off with a $5 million wire transfer from Nelson G. Elder."

"Fuck me." He needed to call DeCorso, the Las Vegas team leader.

"He's probably the best programmer the lab's ever had," she marveled. "A wolf watching the chickens."

"How'd he get the data out?"

"I don't know yet."

"Every employee's going to have to be rescreened," he said. "Forensically."

"I know."

"Including you."

She gave him a sour-ball look and handed him a dollar. "Be a dear and get me another candy bar."

"After I call the goddamn Secretary."

Harris Lester, Secretary of the Navy, had an office suite at the Pentagon deep in C Ring, about as far removed from fresh air as any of the complex's interior spaces. His path to the highly political position was fairly typical—navy service during Vietnam, years in the Maryland Legislature, three-term congressman, Senior VP Northrop Grumman Mission Systems Division, and finally, a year and a half ago, appointment by the newly elected President as Secretary of the Navy.

He was a precise, risk-averse type of bureaucrat who disdained surprises in his personal and professional life, so he reacted with a mix of shock and irritation when his boss, the Secretary of Defense, personally briefed him on Area 51.

"Is this some kind of fraternity initiation, Mr. Secretary?"

"Do I look like a goddamn frat boy?" the SecDef had barked. "This is the real deal, and by tradition it belongs to the navy, so it belongs to you, and God help you if there's a leak under your tenure."

Lester's shirt was so starched it crackled when he sat down at his desk. He smoothed his black and silver striped tie, then ran his hand over what was left of his hair to get the strands all going in the right direction, before reaching for his rimless reading glasses. His assistant came over the intercom before he could crack his first folder. "I've got Malcolm Frazier calling from Groom Lake, Mr. Secretary. Do you want to take him?"

He could almost feel the acid squirting into his stomach. These calls were killing him but they couldn't be delegated. This was his issue and these were his decisions. He glanced at the clock: it was the middle of the night out there. The usual time for nightmares.

The Mercedes arrived at their last appointment in the late afternoon, pulling into a semicircular drive at a Mediterranean-style property.

"I think this is going to be the one!" the Realtor exclaimed with boundless energy. "I've saved the best for last."

Kerry was dazed but happy. She checked her hair with her compact and said dreamily, "I loved all of them."

Mark dragged himself behind them. A prissy looking listing agent was waiting, tapping his watch in admonition.

Mark was reminded to check his own.

Nelson Elder was making the loop with a marketing VP from the Wynn organization, the city fire commissioner, and the CEO of a local medical device company. He was a fair golfer, a fourteen-handicapper, but he was having an outstanding round, which was tipping him toward elation. He made the turn at forty-one, the best nine he'd shot in years.

The freshly sprinkled Bermuda fairways were the color of moist emeralds in the brown desert. The bent-grass greens were rolling true, and blessedly, he could do no wrong. Even though there was water galore on the course, he was keeping the ball straight and dry. The sun was dancing off the glassy surface of the Wynn Hotel, which towered over the country club, and as he lounged in his cart sipping a bottle of iced tea, listening to an artificial brook flowing and gurgling, he felt more satisfied and tranquil than he had in a very long while.

* * *

The Mediterranean villa on Hollyridge Drive was making Kerry crazy. She ran from room to glorious room—designer kitchen, step-down living room, formal dining room, library, media room, wine cellar, huge master suite with three other bedrooms—saying, "Oh, my God! Oh, my God!" and the Realtor at her heels cooing, "Didn't I tell you! It's all redone. Look at the details!"

Mark didn't have the stomach for it. Under the suspicious gaze of the listing agent, he headed for the patio and sat down beside the sparkling water of the vanishing pool. The patio was flanked by manzanita bushes, and hummingbirds flitted on delicate baby-blue flowers. The vast canyon stretched below, the grid of streets indistinct in the afternoon light.

Over his shoulder, above the roofline, high on a distant ridge, the tops of the letters of the Hollywood sign were visible. This is what he'd wanted, he thought ruefully, what he dreamed he'd be doing when he made it as a writer, sitting by his pool, in the hills, under the sign. He just thought it would last longer than five minutes.

Kerry rushed out the French doors and almost wept at the view. "Mark, I love this one so much. I love it, I love it, I love it!"

"She loves it," the Realtor added, coming up behind.

"How much?" Mark asked woodenly.

"They're asking three-four, and I think that's a good price. There's a million-five in renovations . . . "

"We'll take it." He was expressionless.

"Mark!" Kerry screamed. She threw her arms around his neck and kissed him a dozen times.

"Well, you've made two women extremely happy," the Realtor said greedily. "Kerry tells me you're a writer. I think you're going to write a lot of great scripts sitting right beside this gorgeous pool! I'm going to submit your offer and call you tonight at your hotel!"

Kerry was snapping photos with her cell-phone camera. It didn't sink in right away, but when Mark realized what was happening he sprang up and snatched it out of her hand.

"Did you take any pictures before?"

"No! Why?"

"You turned the phone on just now?"

"Yes! What's the big deal?"

He hit the off button. "You're low on power. Mine's dead. I'm trying to conserve in case we need to make a call." He handed it back to her.

"Okay, silly." She looked at him reproachfully, as if to say: *Don't be acting weird again.* "Come and look inside with me! I'm so happy!"

Frazier was dozing at his desk when one of his men tapped him on his shoulder. He awoke with a thick snort.

"We got a ping from Hightower's phone. It was on and off, real quick."

"Where are they?"

"East Hollywood Hills."

Frazier clawed his unshaven cheek. "Okay, we caught a break. Maybe we'll get a second one. What's DeCorso's status?"

"He's in position, waiting for authorization."

Frazier closed his eyes again. "Wake me up when the Pentagon calls back."

Elder was lining up his drive on the eighteenth hole. Back-dropping the green was a thirty-seven-foot-high waterfall, a magnificent way to finish a round. "What do you think," he asked the Wynn exec. "Driver?"

"Oh yeah, let the big dog play, Nelson. You've been crushing it all day."

"You know, if I par this, it'll be the best round I ever shot."

Hearing this, the fire captain and the CEO edged a little closer to check out the ball path.

"For Christ's sake! Don't jinx yourself!" the Wynn guy yelped.

Elder's backswing was slow and flawless, and at the top of the arc—a moment before a bullet ripped through his skull, splattering the foursome with blood and brains—it occurred to him that life was extremely good.

DeCorso confirmed the kill through his sniper scope, then efficiently broke the weapon down, tossed it in a suit bag, and exited the eleventh floor hotel room with its desirable view of the pristine golf course.

When they got back to their suite, Kerry wanted to make love, but he couldn't bring himself to do it. He begged off, blaming the sun, and retreated to take a shower. She kept nattering through the door, too excited to stop talking, while he let the powerful shower drown out the sound of his crying.

The Realtor had told Kerry that Cut, the restaurant in their hotel, was to die for, a comment that made him wince. She pleaded to go there for dinner, and anything she wanted, he was going to give her, though his fervent desire was to hide in their room.

She looked stunning in her red dress, and when they made their entry, heads turned to see if she was a celebrity. Mark carried his briefcase, so the betting-man scenario was an actress meeting her agent or lawyer. This skinny fellow was surely too homely to be her date, unless, of course, he was filthy rich.

They were seated at a window table under a massive skylight, which by dessert time would bring the moonlight flooding into the room.

She wanted to talk of nothing but the house. It was a dream come true—no, more than that, because, she exclaimed, she never dreamed such a place even existed. It was so high up it felt like being in a spaceship, like the UFO she'd seen as a girl. She was like a kid with her questions: when was he going to quit his job, when were they going to move, what kind of furniture would they buy, when should she start acting lessons, when was he going to start writing again? He would shrug or answer monosyllabically and stare out the window, and she'd race to the next thought.

Suddenly she stopped talking, which made him look up.

"Why are you so sad?" she asked.

"I'm not."

"Yes you are."

"No, I'm not."

She didn't look convinced but let it pass and said, "Well, I'm happy. This is the best day of my whole life. If I hadn't met you, I'd be—well, I wouldn't be here! Thank you, Mark Shackleton."

She blew him a kittenish kiss that broke through and made him smile. "That's better!" she purred.

Her phone rang from inside her bag.

"Your phone!" he said. "Why is it on?" He scared her with his panicky expression.

"Gina needed a number if they accepted our offer." She was fumbling for it. "That's probably her!"

"How long has it been on!" he moaned.

"I don't know. A few hours. Don't worry, the battery's fine." She clicked ANSWER. "Hello?" She looked disappointed and confused. "It's for you!" she said, handing it to him.

He caught his breath and held it to his ear. The voice was male, authoritative, cruel. "Listen to me, Shackleton. This is Malcolm Frazier. I want you to walk out of the restaurant and go back to your room and wait for the watchers to pick you up. I'm sure you checked the database. Today is not your day. It was Nelson Elder's day and he's gone. It's Kerry Hightower's day. It's not your day. But that doesn't mean we can't hurt you badly and make you wish that it were. We need to find out how you did it. This doesn't have to be hard."

"She doesn't know anything," Mark said in a pleading whisper, turning his body away.

"It doesn't matter what you say. It's her day. So, stand up and leave, right now. Do you understand me, Mark?"

He didn't respond for several heartbeats.

"Mark?"

He shut the phone and pushed his chair back.

"What's the matter?" she asked.

"It's nothing." He was breathing hard. His face was twisted.

"Is it about your auntie?"

"Yes. I've got to go to the bathroom. I'll be right back." He fought to keep himself together, unable to look at her.

"My poor baby," she said soothingly. "I'm worried about you. I want you to be as happy as me. You hurry back to your Kerry-bear, okay?"

He picked up his briefcase and walked away, a man to the gallows, small shuffling steps, head bowed. As he reached the lobby he heard the sound of breaking glass followed by two full agonizing seconds of silence, then piercing female screams and thunderous male shouts.

The restaurant and lobby were a whir of bodies, running, scrambling, pushing. Mark kept walking like a zombie straight out the Wilshire entrance, where a car was idling at the curb, waiting for the valet. The parking attendant wanted to see what was going on in the lobby and made for the revolving doors.

Without giving it any thought, Mark automatically got in the driver's seat of the idling car and drove off into the warm Beverly Hills evening, trying to see through his tears.

．

Marilyn Monroe had stayed there, and Liz Taylor, Fred Astaire, Jack Nicholson, Nicole Kidman, Brad Pitt, Johnny Depp, and others whom he forgot because he wasn't paying attention to the bellman who could see he wanted to be alone and watched him leave quickly without the customary grand tour.

To the bellman, the guest looked confused and disheveled. His only bag was a briefcase. But they got all types of rich druggies and eccentrics, and for a tip, the mumbling fellow had stripped a hundred off a wad so it was all good.

Mark woke up, disoriented after a deep sleep, but despite the cannon fire in his head, he quickly snapped to reality and closed his eyes again in despair. He was aware of a few sounds: the low hum of an air conditioner, a bird chirping outside the window, his hair rubbing between the cotton sheets and his ear. He felt the downward draft from a ceiling fan. His mouth was so desiccated, there didn't seem to be a molecule of moisture to lubricate his tongue.

It was the kind of suite that provided guests with quart-sized bottles of premium liquor. On the desk was a half-empty vodka bottle, strong effective medicine for his memory problem—he'd drunk one glass after another until he stopped remembering. Apparently, he'd undressed and turned off the lights, some basic reflex intact.

The filtered light coming through the living room door was infusing color into the pastel decor. A palette of peach, mauve, and sage came into focus. Kerry would have loved this place, he thought, rolling his face into the down pillow.

He had driven the purloined car only a few blocks when he decided he was too tired to run. He pulled over, parked on a quiet residential stretch of North Crescent, got out and drifted aimlessly without a plan. He was too numb to realize he was more conspicuous in Beverly Hills as a pedestrian than as a driver of a stolen BMW. Some period of time passed. He found himself staring at a chartreuse sign with three-dimensional white script letters popping out.

The Beverly Hills Hotel.

He looked up at a pink confection of a building set back in a verdant garden. He found himself walking up the drive, wandering into Reception, asking what rooms they had, and taking the most expensive, a grand bungalow with a storied history that he paid for with a fistful of cash.

He stumbled out of bed, too dehydrated to urinate, chugged an entire bottle of water then sat back down on the bed to think. His computerlike mind was gooey and overheated. He wasn't used to struggling to answer a mental problem. This was a decision tree analysis: each action had possible outcomes, each outcome triggered new potential actions.

How hard was it? *Concentrate!*

He ran the gamut of possibilities from running and hiding, living off his remaining cash for as long as he could, to giving himself up to Frazier immediately. Today wasn't his day, or tomorrow: he was BTH, so he knew he wasn't going to be murdered or go off the deep end as a suicide. But that didn't mean Frazier wouldn't make good on his threat to hurt him, and best case, he'd spend the rest of his life in a dark solitary hole.

He started to cry again. Was it for Kerry or for fucking up so miserably? Why couldn't he have been content with things as they were? He held his throbbing temples in his hands and rocked himself. His life hadn't been that bad, had it? Why did he think he needed money and fame? Here he was in a temple of money and fame, the best bungalow at the Beverly Hills Hotel, and big fucking deal: it was only a couple of rooms with furniture and some appliances. He had all that stuff already. Mark Shackleton: *he* wasn't a bad guy. He had a sense of proportion. It was that fucker, Peter Benedict, that grasping striver, who'd gotten him into trouble. He's the one who should be punished, not me, Mark thought, taking a small step toward insanity.

He felt compelled to turn on the TV. In a span of five minutes three of the news stories were about him.

An insurance executive had been killed on a Las Vegas golf course by a sniper.

Will Piper, the FBI agent in charge of the Doomsday investigation, remained a fugitive from justice.

In local news, a diner at a Wolfgang Puck restaurant was shot in the head through a window by an unknown assailant still at large.

He started sobbing again at the sight of Kerry's body, barely filling out a medical examiner's bag.

He knew he couldn't let Frazier have him. The chiseled man with dead eyes petrified him. He'd always been scared of the watchers, and that was before he knew they were cold-blooded killers.

He decided only one person could help him.

He needed a pay phone.

It was a task that almost defeated him because twenty-first century Beverly Hills was bereft of public phones and he was on foot. The hotel probably had one but he needed to find a place that wouldn't lead them right to his door.

He walked for the better part of an hour, getting sweaty, until he finally found one in a sandwich shop on North Beverly. It was in between breakfast and lunch and the place was not crowded. He felt like he was being watched by the few patrons, but it was imaginary. He melted into the drab hall near the restrooms and the back door. He'd changed a twenty back at the hotel, so armed with a pocketful of quarters, he rang the first of his numbers and got voice mail. He hung up without leaving a message.

Then the second—voice mail again.

Finally the last number. He held his breath.

A woman answered on the second ring. "Hello?"

He hesitated before he spoke. "Is this Laura Piper?" Mark asked.

"Yes. Who's this?" Her apprehension was palpable.

"My name is Mark Shackleton. I'm the man your father is looking for."

"Omigod, the killer!"

"No! Please, I'm not! You have to tell him that I didn't kill anybody."

Nancy was driving John Mueller to Brooklyn to interview one of the bank managers in the borough's recent robbery spree. There was overwhelming surveillance and eyewitness evidence to indicate that the same two Middle Eastern–looking men were involved in all five jobs, and the Terrorism Task Force was breathing down the neck of the Major Crimes Division to see if there was a terrorism angle.

Nancy was unhappy about the second-guessing, but her partner was undisturbed.

"You can't take these cases lightly," he said. "Learn that lesson early in your career. We are in a global war on terror and I think it's completely appropriate to treat these perps as terrorists till proven otherwise."

"They're just bank robbers who happen to look Muslim. There's nothing to indicate they're political," she insisted.

"You're wrong once, you've got the blood of thousands of Americans on your hands. If I had stayed on the Doomsday case, I would have pursued the possibility of terrorism there too."

"There wasn't any terror connection, John."

"You don't know that. Case isn't closed, unless I missed something. Is it closed yet?"

She gritted her teeth. "No, John, it's not closed."

He hadn't brought it up yet but this was his opening. "What the heck is Will doing anyway?"

"I believe he thinks he's doing his job."

"There's always one right way to do things and multiple wrong ways—Will consistently finds one of the wrong ways," he pontificated. "I'm glad I'm here to get your training back on the straight and narrow."

When he wasn't looking, she rolled her eyes. She was already agitated, and he was making things worse. The day began with a disturbing news story about the sniper-killing of Nelson Elder, surely a coincidence, but she was powerless to check into it—she was off the case.

Will might have gotten the news on the car radio or a motel TV, and anyway, she didn't want to call and take the chance of waking him during one of his rest breaks. She'd have to wait for him to reach out to her.

Just as she was pulling into the bank parking lot in Flatbush, her prepaid phone rang. She hurriedly unlatched her seat belt and scrambled out of the SUV to get far enough away to be out of Mueller's range when she answered.

"Will!"

"It's Laura." She sounded wild.

"Laura! What's the matter?"

"Mark Shackleton just called me. He wants to meet Dad."

Will was climbing, which felt good to him because it felt different. He was ragged from fighting hypnotically flat terrain, and the I-40 gradient through the Sandia Mountains was helping his mood. Back in Plainfield, Indiana, he'd caught six hours at a Days Inn, but that was eighteen hours ago. Without another rest soon he'd nod off and crash.

When he stopped, he'd call Nancy. He'd heard about Elder's murder on the radio and wanted to see if she knew anything. It was making him crazy, but there were a lot of things agitating him, including his forced abstinence. He was jittery, humoring himself in a silly voice:

"Maybe you've got a drinking problem, Willie.

"Hey, screw you, the only problem I've got is that I haven't had a drink.

"I rest my case.

"Take your case and shove it up your ass."

And he was agitated over what he'd told Nancy the day before, the love business. Had he meant it? Was it fatigue and loneliness speaking? Did she mean what *she* said? Now that he'd uncorked the love word, he would have to deal with it.

Maybe sooner rather than later—the phone was ringing.

"Hey, I'm glad you called."

"Where are you?" Nancy asked.

"The great state of New Mexico." There were traffic noises on her side. "You on the street?"

"Broadway. Friday traffic. I've got something to tell you, Will."

"About Nelson Elder, right? I heard it on the news. It's driving me nuts."

"He called Laura."

Will was confused. "Who called?"

"Mark Shackleton."

The line went quiet.

"Will?"

"That son of a bitch called my daughter?" he seethed.

"He said he tried your other numbers. Laura was the only way. He wants to meet."

"He can turn himself in anywhere."

"He's scared. You're the only one he says he can trust."

"I'm less than six hundred miles from Vegas. He can trust me to fuck him up for calling Laura."

"He's not in Las Vegas. He's in L.A."

"Christ, another three hundred miles. What else did he say?"

"He says he didn't kill anyone."

"Unbelievable. Anything else?"

"He says he's sorry."

"Where do I find him?"

"He wants you to go to a coffee shop in Beverly Hills to-morrow morning at ten. I've got the address."

"He's going to be there?"

"That's what he said."

"Okay, if I keep going at this clip and take an eight-hour nap somewhere, I've got plenty of time to have a cup of coffee with my old buddy."

"I'm worried about you."

"I'll stop for a rest. My butt's sore but I'm okay. Your grandmother's car wasn't built for comfort or speed."

He was happy he could make her laugh.

"Listen, Nancy, about what I said yesterday—"

"Let's wait until this is over," she offered. "We ought to talk about it when we're together."

"Okay," he readily agreed. "Keep your phone charged. You're my lifeline. Give me the address."

Frazier hadn't gone home since the start of the crisis, and he hadn't let his men leave the Ops Center either. There was no end in sight; the pressure from Washington was intense and everyone was frustrated. They had Shackleton within their grasp, he lambasted his people, but an untrained piece of shit had somehow managed to slip the grasp of some of the best tactical ops men in the country. Frazier's rear end was on the line and he didn't like it being there.

"We need a gym down here," one of his men groused.

"It's not a spa," Frazier spat out.

"Maybe a speed bag. We could hang it in the corner," another one piped up from his terminal.

"You want to punch something, come over here and take a shot at me," Frazier growled.

"I just want to find the asshole and go home," the first man said.

Frazier corrected him. "We've got two assholes, our guy and the FBI turd. We need both of them."

A Pentagon line rang and the speed-bag man answered and started taking notes. Frazier could tell from his body language that something was up.

"Malcolm, we got something. The DIA tappers picked up a call to Agent Piper's daughter."

"From who?" Frazier asked.

"Shackleton."

"Fuck me . . . "

"They're downloading the intercept. We should have it in a couple of minutes. Shackleton wants to meet Piper at a coffee shop in Beverly Hills tomorrow morning."

Frazier clapped his hands together in triumph and yelled, "Two birds with one fucking stone! Thank you, Lord!" He started thinking. "Any outbound calls? How's she passing the info?"

"No calls from her home line or her cell since this one."

"Okay, she's in Georgetown, right? Get a bead on all public phones in a two-mile radius of where she lives and check them for recent calls to other pay phones or prepaid cells. And find out if she has a roommate or a boyfriend and get their numbers and call logs. I want to see a crosshair over Piper's forehead."

It was evening in Los Angeles and the heat was starting to dissipate. Mark remained in his bungalow all day with a Do Not Disturb sign on the door. He vowed to do penance for Kerry by fasting but got light-headed in the afternoon and broke into the assortment of salty snacks and cookies at the bar. In any event, he reasoned, what happened to her was meant to happen, so he wasn't really to blame, was he? The thought made him feel a little better, and he opened a beer. He drank two more in rapid succession, then started on the vodka.

His bungalow had its own private courtyard hidden behind salmon-colored walls inscribed with faux Italianate arches. He ventured out with the bottle, sat on a lounger and reclined. The air was fragrant with the exotic aromas of the tropical garden flowers. He let himself sleep, and when he awoke the sky was black and it had become chilly. He shivered in the night air and never felt more alone.

The Mojave desert was 112 degrees in the early hours of Saturday morning, and Will thought he might spontaneously incinerate when he pulled the car off the road and emerged for a pee. He prayed the old Taurus would start up again, and it did. He'd make it to Beverly Hills with time to spare.

In the Area 51 Ops Center, Frazier was watching Will's electronic signature as a yellow dot on a satellite-view map. His last cell phone ping was off a Verizon tower five miles west of Needles on I-40. Frazier liked to limit operational variables and eliminate surprises—the digital hawk-eye view was comforting.

Traditional shoe-leather work led them to Will's prepaid phone. A Defense Intelligence Agency team in Washington established that Laura's apartment was rented by a man named Greg Davis. On Friday night Davis's mobile phone had received and placed calls from a T-Mobile prepaid phone located in White Plains, New York. That T-Mobile phone had only made and received calls from one other number since it was activated, a number corresponding to another T-Mobile prepaid phone moving west through Arizona on Friday night.

It was a trivial leap to Will's FBI partner, Nancy Lipinski, who lived in White Plains. The DIA tappers put both prepaid lines under surveillance and Frazier had it all, wrapped in ribbon in a bow, like a Christmas present. His men would be at Sal and Tony's Coffee Shop for a nice Saturday breakfast, and in the meantime he'd watch Will's yellow dot moving westward at eighty miles per hour and count down the hours till the misery was over.

Will rolled into Beverly Hills just before seven in the morning and did a drive-by of the coffee shop. North Beverly Drive was devoid of traffic—at this hour the whole city had the feel of a sleepy small town. He parked on a parallel street, Canon, set the alarm on his phone to nine-thirty, and promptly fell asleep.

When the alarm went off the street was bustling and the car had grown uncomfortably warm. His first order of business was finding a public restroom to do some morning ablutions. There was a gas station a block away. He grabbed his overnight bag, got out of the car and heard a sound, his prepaid phone clattering onto the sidewalk. He swore at himself, picked it up and stuffed it back in his pants.

At that moment Will's screen blip at the Area 51 Ops Center went dark. Frazier was alerted and did a caustic rant before calming down and concluding, "It'll be okay. He's in our box. In a half hour this'll be history."

Sal and Tony's Coffee Shop was popular. A mix of locals and tourists crammed the tables and booths. It smelled of pancake batter, coffee, and hash, and when Will arrived a few minutes early, his ears were assaulted by loud conversations.

The hostess greeted him with a gravelly cigarette voice: "How're you doing, honey? You a single?"

"I'm meeting someone." He looked around. "I don't think he's here yet." Shackleton was supposed to be at the back door near the pay phone at ten.

"Shouldn't be too long. We'll have you seated in a couple of minutes."

"I need to use your phone," he said.

"I'll find you."

From the back of the restaurant, Will studied the room, jumping from table to table, profiling the customers. There was an elderly man with a cane, and his wife—locals. Four smartly dressed young men—salesmen. Three pale flabby women with Rodeo Drive visors—tourists. Six Korean women—tourists. A father with a six-year-old son—divorce visitation. A strung-out young couple in their twenties in tattered jeans—locals. Two middle-aged men and a woman with Verizon shirts—workers.

And then there was a table of four in the middle of the room that made his palms clammy. Four men in their thirties, cut from the same piece of cloth. Clean-cut, recent haircuts, fit—he could tell from their necks they were lifters. All of them were trying too hard to appear casual in loose shirts and khakis, forcing the pass-the-hash-browns banter. One of them had his fanny pack laid on the table.

None of them looked his way, and he pretended not to look at them. He shuffled his feet and waited by the phone, keeping them in his peripheral field. Agency boys; which agency, he didn't know. Everything told him to abort, to walk out the back door and keep going, but then what? He had to find Shackleton and this was the only way. He'd have to deal with the lifters. He felt the weight of his gun against his ribs every time he breathed.

Frazier felt a spark of electricity coursing through his body when Will Piper appeared on his monitor. The fanny pack was being manipulated by one of the men to track him, and the monitor showed him standing up against a wall beside a pay phone.

"Okay, DeCorso, that's good," Frazier said into his headset mic. "I've got him." He clenched his jaw. He wanted to see the screen fill with the second target, he wanted to fire out the go order and to watch his men take both of them down and bundle them up for special delivery.

Will explored his options. He did his best imitation of a casual saunter and entered the men's room for a look-see. There were no windows. He splashed some cold water on his face and wiped himself dry. It was still a few minutes before ten. He left the men's room and headed straight out the back door. He wanted to see if any of the men made a move, but more important, he wanted to scope out his environs. There was an alleyway running between Beverly and Canon that serviced the buildings on both streets. He saw the back entrances of a bookstore, a drugstore, a beauty salon, a shoe store, and a bank all within a stone's throw. To his left the alley opened up into a parking lot servicing one of the commercial buildings on Canon. There were foot routes that would take him north, south, east, or west. He felt a little less trapped and went back inside.

"There you are!" the hostess called out from the front, startling him. "I got your table."

The table for two was near the window, but the view to the phone was unimpeded. It was 10:00 A.M.. The men at the middle table were getting more coffee.

DeCorso, the team leader, had a buzz cut, heavy black eyebrows, and thick hairy forearms. Frazier was complaining into DeCorso's earpiece, "It's time. Where the fuck is Shackleton?"

On his monitor Frazier watched Will pouring coffee from a carafe and stirring in cream.

Five minutes passed.

Will was hungry, so he ordered.

Ten minutes.

He wolfed down eggs and bacon. The men in the middle were lingering.

At ten-fifteen he was beginning to think that Shackleton was playing him. Three cups of coffee had taken their toll— he got up to use the men's room. The only other person inside was the old man with his cane, moving like a snail. When Will was done, he left and noticed the bulletin board beside the pay phone. It was a paper quilt of business cards, apartment-for-rent flyers, lost cats. He'd seen the board earlier but it hadn't registered.

It was staring him in the face!

A three-by-five-inch card, the size of a postcard.

A hand-drawn coffin, the Doomsday coffin, and the words: *Bev Hills Hotel, Bung 7.*

Will swallowed hard and acted on pure impulse.

He snatched the card and dashed out the back door into the alleyway.

Frazier reacted before the men on the scene, "He's taking off! Goddamn it, he's taking off!"

The men jumped up and pursued but got hung up when the old man leaving the restroom blocked their way. It was impossible to watch the video images since the camera bag was jostling up and down, but Frazier saw the old man in some frames and screamed, "Don't slow down! He'll get away!"

DeCorso lifted the man in a bear grip and deposited him

back in the men's room while his colleagues rushed to the door. When they hit the alleyway it was empty. On DeCorso's orders, two went right, two went left.

They frantically searched, scouring the alley, running through stores and buildings on Beverly and Cañon, checking under parked cars. Frazier was screaming so much into DeCorso's earpiece that the man begged him, "Malcolm, please calm down. I can't operate with all the yelling."

Will was in a bathroom stall in the Via Veneto Hair Salon, one door away from the coffee shop. He stayed put for over ten minutes, half standing on the toilet, his gun drawn. Someone entered shortly after he arrived but left without using the facilities. He exhaled and maintained his uncomfortable pose.

He couldn't stay there all day and someone was bound to use the toilet, so he left the bathroom and quietly slipped into the salon, where a half-dozen pretty hairdressers were working away on customers and chatting. It looked like a female-only type of shop and he was way out of place.

"Hi!" one of the hairdressers said, surprised. She had severely short blond hair and a micro-mini stretched over strawberry tights. "Didn't see you."

"You do walk-ins?" Will asked.

"Not usually," the girl said, but she liked his looks and wondered if he might be famous. "Do I know you?" she asked.

"Not yet, but if you give me a haircut you will," he teased. "You do men?"

She was smitten. "I'll do you myself," she gushed. "I had a cancellation anyway."

"I don't want to sit near the window and I want you to take your time. I'm not in a rush."

"You've got a lot of demands, don't you?" She laughed. "Well, I will take good care of you, Mr. Bossy Man! You sit right there and I'll get you a cup of coffee or tea."

An hour later Will had four things: a good haircut, a manicure, the girl's phone number, and his freedom. He asked for a cab and when he saw it standing on Cañon gave her a big tip, sprang into the backseat and sank low. As it pulled away, he felt he'd made a clean escape. He ripped up the slip with the phone number and let the fragments flutter out the window. He'd have to tell Nancy about this act, certifiable proof of his commitment.

Bungalow 7 had a peach-colored door. Will rang the bell. There was a Do Not Disturb tag on the handle and a fresh Saturday paper. He'd slipped his Glock into his waistband for fast access and let his right hand brush against its rough grip.

The peephole darkened for a second then the handle moved. The door opened and the two men looked at each other.

"Hello, Will. You found my message."

Will was shocked at how haggard and old Mark appeared, almost unrecognizable. He stepped back to let his visitor in. The door closed on its own, leaving them in the semidarkness of the shade-drawn room.

"Hello, Mark."

Mark saw the butt of Will's pistol between his parted jacket. "You don't need a gun."

"Don't I?"

Mark sank onto an armchair by the fireplace, too weak to stand. Will went for the sofa. He was tired too.

"The coffee shop was staked out."

Mark's eyes bulged. "They didn't follow you, did they?"

"I think we're good. For now."

"They must've tapped my call to your daughter. I knew you'd be mad and I'm sorry. It was the only way."

"Who are they?"

"The people I work for."

"First tell me this: what if I hadn't seen your card?"

Mark shrugged. "When you're in my business you rely on fate."

"What business is that, Mark? Tell me what business you're in."

"The library business."

* * *

Frazier was inconsolable. The operation was blown to hell and he couldn't think of one thing to do except shriek like a banshee. When his throat became too raw to continue, he hoarsely ordered his men to hold their positions and continue their apparently futile search until he told them otherwise. If he'd been there, this wouldn't have happened, he brooded. He thought he had professionals. DeCorso was a good operative but clearly a failure as a field leader, and who would take the blame for that? He kept his headset glued to his skull and slowly walked through the empty corridors of Area 51, muttering, "Failure is not a fucking option," then rode the elevator topside so he could feel hot sun on his body.

Mark was hushed and confessional at times, alternatively tearful, boastful, and arrogant, occasionally irritated by questions he considered repetitive or naive. Will maintained an even, professional tone though he struggled at times to retain his composure in the face of what he was hearing.

Will set things in motion with a simple question: "Did you send the Doomsday postcards?"

"Yes."

"But you didn't kill the victims."

"I never left Nevada. I'm not a killer. I know why you think there was a killer. That's what I wanted you and everyone else to think."

"Then how did these people die?"

"Murders, accidents, suicides, natural causes—the same things that kill any random group of people."

"You're saying there was no single killer?"

"That's what I'm saying. That's the truth."

"You didn't hire or induce anyone to commit these murders?"

"No! Some of them were murders, I'm sure, but *you* know in your heart that not all of them were. Don't you?"

"A few of them have problems," Will admitted. He thought of Milos Covic and his window plunge, Marco Napolitano and the needle in his arm, Clive Robertson and his nosedive.

Will's eyes narrowed. "If you're telling me the truth, then how in hell did you know in advance these people were going to die?"

Mark's sly smile unnerved him. He'd interviewed a lot of psychotics, and his I-know-something-you-don't-know grin was straight out of a schizophrenic's playbook. But he knew that Mark wasn't crazy. "Area 51."

"What about it? What's the relevance?"

"I work there."

Will was testy now. "Okay, I pretty much got that. Spill it! You said you were in the library business."

"There's a library at Area 51."

He was being forced to drag it out of him, question by question. "Tell me about this library."

"It was built in the late 1940s by Harry Truman. After World War Two, the British found an underground complex near a monastery on the Isle of Wight, Vectis Abbey. It contained hundreds of thousands of books."

"What kind of books?"

"Books dating back to the Middle Ages. They contained names, Will, billions—over two hundred billion names."

"Whose names?"

"Everyone who's ever lived."

Will shook his head. He was treading water, feeling like he was about to go under. "I'm sorry, I'm not following you."

"Since the beginning of time, there've been just under one hundred billion people who've ever lived on the planet. These books started listing every birth and every death since the eighth century. They chronicle over twelve hundred years of human life and death on earth."

"How?" Will was angry. Was this guy a sicko after all?

"Anger is a common reaction. Most people get angry when they're told about the Library because it challenges everything we think we know. Actually, Will, no one has a clue about the how part or the why. There's been sixty-two years of debate and no one knows. It would have taken hundreds of monks at a time, if that's what they were, writing continuously for over five hundred years to physically write down all these names, one for each birth, one for each death. They're listed by date, the earlier ones in the Julian calendar, the later ones in the Gregorian calendar. Each name is written in its native language with a simple notation in Latin—birth or death. That's all there is. No commentary, no explanation. How did they do it? Religious types say they were channeling God. Maybe they were clairvoyants who saw the future. Maybe they were from outer space. Believe me, no one has any idea! All we know is that it was a monumental task. Think about it: the numbers have been accelerating over the centuries. but just today, August 1, 2009, there are 350,000 people who will be born and 150,000 will die. Each name written with pen and ink. Then tomorrow's names and the day after, and the day after that. For twelve hundred years! They must have been like machines."

"You know I can't believe any of this," Will said quietly.

"If you give me a day, I can prove it. I can pull up a list of everyone who's going to die in Los Angeles tomorrow. Or New York, or Miami. Or anywhere."

"I don't have a day." Will got up and started aggressively pacing. "I can't believe I'm even giving you the right time of day." He angrily swore and demanded, "Go online and look up the Panama City, Florida, *News Herald*. Look at today's obituaries and see if you've got them on your goddamned list."

"The local paper's outside the door? Wouldn't that be easier?"

"Maybe you've already looked at it!"

"You think this is an elaborate setup?"

"Maybe it is."

Mark looked troubled. "I can't go online."

"Okay, this is bullshit!" Will shouted. "I knew this was bullshit."

"If I log my computer onto the Web, they'll locate us in a few minutes. I won't do it."

Will looked around the room in frustration and spotted a keyboard in the TV cabinet. "What's that?" he asked.

Mark smiled. "Hotel Internet access. I didn't notice that."

"So, you can do it?"

"I'm a computer scientist. I think I can figure it out."

"I thought you said you were a librarian."

Mark ignored him. In a minute he had the newspaper's website on the TV screen.

"Hometown paper, right?" Mark said.

"You know it is."

Mark took out his laptop and booted it up.

While he was logging on, Will pounced on an inconsistency. "Wait a minute! You said these books only had names and dates. But then you said you could sort them by city. How?"

"That's an enormous part of what we do at Area 51. Without geographical correlates, the data is useless. We have access to virtually every digital and analog database in the world, birth records, phone records, bank records, marital records, employment records, utilities, land deeds, taxes, insurance, you name it. There are 6.6 billion people in the world. We have some form of address identifiers, if only the country or province, on ninety-four percent of them. Very nearly a hundred percent in North America and Europe." He looked up. "I've got this encrypted. Just so you know, it needs a password, which I'm not going to give you. I need insurance you'll protect me."

"From whom?"

"The same people who're after you. We call them the watchers. Area 51 security. Okay, I'm on. Take the keyboard."

"Go into the bedroom," Will ordered. "I don't want you seeing the dates."

"You don't trust me."

"You're right, I don't."

Will spent several minutes calling out names of the recently deceased in Panama City. He mixed in names from the archives with people who died the day before. To his astonishment, Mark was shouting back the correct date of death every time. Finally, Will called him back in and complained, "Come on!

This is like a Vegas lounge act and you're like one of those mentalists. How are you doing this?"

"I told you the truth. If you think I'm pulling a fast one, you'll have to wait till tomorrow. I'll give you ten people in L.A. who're going to die today. You check the obits tomorrow."

Mark then proceeded to dictate ten names, dates, and addresses. Will took them down on a hotel notepad and moodily stuffed the sheet in his pocket. But he immediately pulled it out and said defiantly, "I'm not waiting until tomorrow!" He dug his phone out of his pants and saw it was dead—the battery had gotten dislodged when it fell onto the sidewalk. He reseated it and the phone came alive again. Mark watched with amusement as Will called information to get the phone numbers.

Will swore out loud each time he got voice mail or a no pickup. Someone answered the seventh number on the list. "Hello, this is Larry Jackson returning Ora LeCeille Dunn's call," Will said. He was listening and pacing. "Yes, she called me last week. We have a mutual acquaintance." He was listening again but now he was slumping onto the sofa. "I'm sorry, when was that? This morning? It was unexpected? I'm very sorry to hear the news. My condolences."

Mark opened his arms expansively. "Do you believe me now?"

Frazier's headset got noisy again. "Malcolm, Piper's phone is back on the grid. He's somewhere in the 9600 block of Sunset."

Frazier started sprinting back toward the Ops Center on an upward climb of his personal roller coaster.

Will got up and surveyed the bar. There was a fifth of Johnnie Walker Black. He opened it and poured a measure into a whiskey glass. "Want one?"

"It's too early."

"Is it?" He pounded back a shot and let it work through his system. "How many people know about this?"

"I don't know exactly. Between Nevada and Washington, I'd guess a thousand."

"Who runs it? Who's in charge?"

"It's a navy operation. I'm pretty sure the President and some cabinet members are in the know, some Pentagon and Homeland Security people, but the highest-ranking person I'm positive about is the Secretary of the Navy because I've seen him copied on memos."

"Why the navy?" Will asked, bemused.

"I don't know. It was set up like that from the beginning."

"This has been under wraps for sixty years? The government's not that good."

"They kill leakers," Mark said bitterly.

"What's the point? What do they do with it?"

"Research. Planning. Resource allocation. The CIA and military have used it as a tool since the early fifties. They feel they can't *not* use it, since it's there. We can predict events, even if we can't alter outcomes, at least fatal outcomes. If you can predict large events you can plan around them, budget for them, set policy, maybe soften their blow. Area 51 predicted the Korean War, the Chinese purges under Mao, the Vietnam War, Pol Pot in Cambodia, the Gulf wars, famines in Africa. We can usually spot big plane crashes, natural disasters like floods and tsunamis. We had 9/11 nailed."

Will was dazed. "But we couldn't do anything about it?"

"Like I said, these outcomes can't be changed. We didn't know how the attacks were going to happen or who was going to be responsible, though rightly or wrongly, we had ideas. I think that's why we were so quick to go into attack mode against Iraq. It was all gamed out in advance."

"Jesus."

"We've got supercomputers grinding data around the clock, looking for worldwide patterns." He leaned in and lowered his voice. "I can tell you with certainty that 200,000 people will die in China on February 9, 2013, but I can't tell you why. People are working on that right now. In 2025— March twenty-fifth, to be precise—over a million people will die in India and Pakistan. That's a paradigm changer but it's too far away for anyone to focus on it."

"Why Nevada?"

"The Library was taken there after the Air Force flew it from England to Washington. A nuclear-proof vault was built under the desert. It took twenty years to transcribe all the post-1947 material and get it digital. Before they were computerized, the books were precious. Now, they're pretty much ceremonial. It's amazing to see it, but the actual Library doesn't have much of a purpose anymore. As to why Nevada, it was remote and protectable. Truman laid down a smoke screen in 1947 by concocting the Roswell UFO story and letting the public believe that Area 51 was built for UFO research. They couldn't hide the existence of the lab because of all the people who work there, but they hid its purpose. A lot of dumb-asses still believe the UFO crap."

Will was about to take another hit of scotch but realized it was affecting him more than he wanted. Getting sloshed wasn't a good option right now. "What do *you* do there?" he asked.

"Database security. We have the most secure servers in the world. We're hack proof and leak-proof, from the inside and out, or at least we were."

"You breached your own systems."

"I'm the only one who could have done it," he boasted.

"How?"

"It was pure simplicity. Memory stick up my butt. I beat the watchers, those fuckers. They can't have the public knowing about the Library. Can you imagine what the world would be like? Everyone would be paralyzed if they knew the day they were going to die—or their wife, or parents, or children or friends. Our analysts think that society, as we know it, would be altered permanently. Whole segments of the population might just fuck off and say, 'What's the point?' Criminals might commit more crimes if they knew they weren't going to be killed. You can envision some pretty nasty scenarios. The funny thing is, it's just births and deaths. There's nothing in the data about how people live their lives, nothing about quality. All that's extrapolation."

Will raised his voice. "Then why did you do it? Why the postcards?"

Mark knew the question was coming. Will could see it. His lower lip quivered like a child about to be disciplined. "I wanted to—" He broke down, sobbing and choking.

"You wanted to what?"

"I wanted to make my life better. I wanted to be some-one—different." He dissolved in tears again.

The man was pathetic, but Will controlled his ire. "Go on, I'm listening."

Mark got a tissue and blew his nose. "I didn't want to be a drone stuck in a lab my whole life. I see rich people at the casinos and I ask myself, why them? I'm a million times smarter. Why not me? But I never catch a break. None of the companies I went to work for after MIT exploded. No Microsofts, no Googles. I made a few bucks on stock options but the whole dot-com thing passed me by. Then I screwed up by going to work for the government. Once the sexiness of Area 51 wears off, it's just a low-paying computer job in an underground bunker. I tried to sell my screenplays—I told you I'm a writer—and they were rejected. So, I decided I could change my life by leaking only a little data."

"So this is about money? Is that it?"

Mark nodded but added, "Not money for the sake of money—for the change that goes along with it."

"How were you going to make money off of Doomsday?"

Mark's frown turned into a triumphant smile. "I already did! Big money!"

"Enlighten me, Mark. I'm not as sharp as you."

Mark didn't pick up on his facetiousness—he took it as a compliment and launched into an explanation, slow and pa-tient at first then increasingly pressured. "Okay, here's how I conceived it—and I've got to say that it played out exactly as I planned. I needed a demonstration of what I could deliver. I needed credibility. I needed to be able to get people's attention. The way to do that is to get the media involved, am I right? And what would satisfy all these criteria? Doomsday! I thought the name was brilliant, by the way. I wanted the world to think there was a serial killer who was warning his victims. So I picked a random group of nine people in New York from the database. Okay, I see the look in your eyes, and maybe this was a crime at some level, but obviously I didn't kill anybody. But once the case really took off in the media, I was able to instantly capture the attention of the man I needed to reach— Nelson Elder." He tripped on Will's expression. "What? You know him?"

Will was shaking his head in amazement. "Yeah, I know him. I hear he's dead."

"They killed him." He whispered, "And Kerry."

"I'm sorry, who?"

"They killed my girlfriend!" Mark cried, then lowered his voice again. "She didn't know anything. They didn't have to do that. And the thing is, I could have looked both of them up early on. By the time I thought to do it . . . "

The lightbulb went off in Will's head, a delayed reaction. "Jesus! Nelson Elder—life insurance!"

Mark nodded. "I met him at a casino. He was a nice guy. Then I found out his company was in trouble, and what better way to help a life insurance company than tell them when people are going to die? That was my big idea. He saw it right away."

"How much?"

"Money?"

"Yeah, money."

"Five million dollars."

"You gave away the crown jewels for a lousy five million?"

"No! It was very discreet. He gave me names, I gave him dates. That was it. It was a good deal for everyone. I kept the database. Nobody's got it but me."

"The whole thing?"

"Just the United States. Desert Life only does business in the U.S. The whole database was too big to steal."

Will was swimming in a stew of information overload and raging emotions. "There's a little more to this, an extra little wrinkle, isn't there?"

Mark was silent, fidgeting with his hands.

"You wanted to stick it to me, didn't you? You chose New York for your charade because that's my patch. You wanted me to eat shit. Didn't you?"

Mark hung his head in childlike contrition. "I've always been jealous," he whispered. "When we roomed together, I mean, I never knew anyone like you in high school. Everything you did worked out great. Everything I did . . . " His voice trailed off to nothing. "When I saw you last year, it reopened things."

"We were just freshman roommates, Mark. Nine months together, when we were kids. We were very different people."

Mark made a forlorn admission, choking back emotion. "I was hoping you'd want to room with me after freshman year. You helped them. You helped them tape me to my bed."

Will's skin crawled. The man was pathetic. Nothing about his actions or intentions had a trace of nobility. It was all about self-loathing, self-pity, and infantile urges wrapped in a surfeit of IQ points. Okay, the kid had been traumatized, and okay, he'd always felt guilty about his role, but it was an innocent college prank, for Christ's sake! The man holed up in this hotel room was loathsome and dangerous, and he had to quash a powerful desire to lay him out with a blow to his sharp, thin jaw.

In one fell swoop this pitiable creature had turned his own life on its ear. He didn't want to be involved with any of this. All he'd wanted was to retire and be left alone. But it was obvious that once you knew about the Library, things could never be the same. He needed to think, but first he needed to survive.

"Tell me something, Mark, did you look me up?" he said confrontationally. "Do I get taken out today?" As he waited for the answer, he thought, If it's yes, who gives a shit? What do I have to live for anyway? I'll only screw up Nancy's life the way I screwed up everyone else's. Bring it on!

"No. Me neither. We're both BTH."

"What does that mean?"

"Beyond the horizon. The books stop in 2027. Area 51 had a life expectancy of eighty years."

"Why do they stop?"

"We don't know. There was evidence of a fire at the monastery. Natural disaster? Something political? Religious? There's no way of knowing. It's just a fact."

"So, I live past 2027," Will said wistfully.

"I do too," Mark reminded him. "Can I ask *you* a question?"

"Okay."

"Did you figure out it was me? Is that why they're looking for you too?"

"I did. I nailed your ass."

"How?" Will could see how badly he wanted to know. "I'm sure I didn't leave any tracks."

"I found your screenplay in the WGA registry. First draft, bunch of uninteresting character names. Second draft, bunch of very interesting names. You had to tell somebody, didn't you? Even if it was a private joke."

Mark was astonished. "What gave you the idea?"

"The font on the postcards. It's not used that much these days unless you're writing screenplays."

Mark sputtered, "I had no idea."

"Of what?"

"That you were that smart."

As Frazier sat in front of his terminal, he willed himself into a state of optimism. They had Will's cell phone blip on the screen again, his men were in proximity, and he reminded himself that none of his operatives were going to die today and neither was Shackleton or Piper. The inescapable conclusion was that the operation was going to be smooth and that both men would be reeled in for interrogation. What happened to them afterward was clearly not going to be up to him. They were BTH, so he imagined they'd be defanged one way or another. He didn't much care.

His optimism was shaken by DeCorso. "Malcolm, here's the story," he heard through his headset. "This is a hotel, the Beverly Hills Hotel. It's got a few hundred rooms on twelve acres. The beacon we've got is accurate to about three hundred yards. We don't have the manpower to box him in and search the hotel."

"For fuck's sake," Frazier said. "Can't we boost the signal somehow?"

One of the Ops Center techs answered without looking up from his screen, "Call his phone. If he answers, we can triangulate him to fifty feet."

Frazier's mouth curled into a Cheshire smile. "You fucking all-star. I'm going to buy you a case of beer." He reached for a phone and hit the button for an outside line.

Will's prepaid phone rang. He thought of Nancy. He wanted to hear her voice, and didn't pay attention to the caller ID tag: OUT OF AREA. "Hello?" No one answered. "Nancy?" Nothing.

He hung up.

"Who was it?" Mark asked.

"I don't like it," Will answered. He looked at his phone, grimaced and turned it off. "I think we should leave. Get your stuff."

Mark looked scared. "Where are we going?"

"I don't know yet. Somewhere out of L.A. They know I'm here so they know you're here. We'll get a cab to my car and start driving. Couple of smart guys, we should be able to figure something out."

Mark stooped to pack his laptop away. Will was towering over him. "What?" Mark said, alarmed.

"I'm taking your briefcase."

"Why?"

Will gave him a brawn over brains look. "Because I want it. I'm not asking again. And I want your password."

"No! You'll ditch me."

"I won't do that."

"How do I know?"

The slender man looked so frightened and vulnerable that Will took pity on him for the first time. "Because I'm giving you my word. Look, if both of us have the password, it increases the chance I can use it as leverage to get you back if we get split up. It's the right move."

"Pythagoras."

"Come again?"

"The Greek mathematician, Pythagoras."

"Does that have some significance?"

Before Mark could answer, Will heard a scraping sound from the patio and drew his pistol.

The front door and the patio door blew in simultaneously.

The room was suddenly full of men.

For a participant, close-quarter firefights seem to last forever, but to an external observer like Frazier, who had an audio feed, it was over in under ten seconds.

DeCorso saw Will's weapon and started shooting. The first round buzzed past Will's ear.

Will dived onto the tangerine carpet and returned fire from a low angle, aiming at chests and abdomens, big body masses, jerking his trigger as fast as he could. He'd only fired his weapon in action once before, at a very bad highway stop in Florida, his second year as a deputy sheriff. Two men went down that day. They were easier to hit than fox squirrels.

DeCorso fell first, causing a moment of disarray among his men. The watchers' guns were fitted with silencers, so the bullets didn't pop, but thwacked into wood, furniture, and flesh. In contrast, Will's gun boomed every time he pulled the trigger, and Frazier winced at each one, eighteen blasts, till the room fell silent.

By then, it was filled with caustic blue fumes and the tart smell of gunpowder. Will could hear a tinny voice yelling hysterically into a headset that was lying on the floor, separated from its man.

Everywhere, the primary color of blood was clashing with the suite's pastel hues. Four intruders were on the floor, two moaning, two silent. Will rose to his knees, then halt-ingly stood on rubbery legs. He didn't feel any pain but had heard that adrenaline could temporarily mask even a seri-ous wound. He checked himself for blood, but he was clean. Then he saw Mark's feet behind the sofa and scrambled to help him up.

Christ, he thought when he saw him. Christ. There was a hole in his head the size of a wine cork, bubbling with blood and brain matter, and he was gurgling and oozing secretions from his mouth.

He was BTH?

Will shuddered at the thought of this poor son of a bitch living like this for at least another eighteen years, then grabbed Mark's briefcase and bolted out the door.

Will tried to be invisible. People were rushing past him, heading toward the bungalow. Two sprinting hotel security guards in blue blazers elbowed him off the path. He kept walking slowly, impassively, in the opposite direction through the hotel gardens, a man with a briefcase shaking inside his suit.

As the doors to the main building closed behind him, he heard muffled shouts from the bungalow area. All hell was about to break loose. Sirens were approaching; response times are fast in ritzy zips, he thought. He needed to make a snap decision. He could try to make it to his car or stay put and hide in plain sight. The tactic had worked at the beauty salon so he decided to try it again, and besides, he was too unsteady to do much more.

The front desk was in turmoil. Guests were reporting gunshots, security protocols were being enacted. He briskly strode past overwrought employees and angled toward the elevators, where he hopped on a waiting car and randomly pressed the third-floor button.

The corridor was empty except for a service cart in front of a room halfway down the hall. He peeked into the partially open door of Room 315 and saw a housekeeper vacuuming.

"Hello!" he called out as blithely as he could.

The maid smiled at him, "Hello, sir. I'll be finishing soon." There were bags, a man's clothes in the closet.

"I'm back early from a meeting," Will said. "I've got to make a call."

"No problem, sir. Just call housekeeping when you like and I can come back."

He was alone.

Looking out the garden-facing window, he saw police and paramedics. He slumped on the side chair and closed his eyes. He didn't know how much time he had—he needed to think.

Will was back on the fishing boat with his father, Phillip Weston Piper, who was silently baiting a line. He'd always thought it a grand-sounding name for a man with rough hands and sun-beaten skin who made his living arresting drunks and ticketing speeders. His grandfather had been a social studies teacher in a Pensacola junior high school with high hopes for his newborn son and thought a posh name would give him a leg up in the world. It was a nonfactor. His father grew up to be a fun-hunting carouser and booze hound who drank his way through life and was a miserable bully of a husband who subjected his mother to a constant fusillade of abuse.

But he was a halfway decent father, taciturn to the extreme, though Will always sensed that he was making the effort to do the right thing for his son. Maybe their relationship would have been better if he'd known in advance that his father was going to die during his senior year at college. Maybe then he would have made the first move and engaged the man in a conversation to find out what he thought of his life, his family, his son. But that conversation was buried with Phillip Weston Piper, and now he had to go through life without it.

Will never thought much about religion or philosophy. His business was, in effect, the death business, and his approach to the investigation of murders was fact-based. Some people lived, others died—wrong place, wrong time. There was a terrible randomness to it.

His mother had been a church woman, and when he visited, he dutifully accompanied her to the First Baptist Church in Panama City. She was mourned there when cancer took her. He had heard his fill of will-of-God talk and divine plans. He'd read about Calvinism and predestination in school. All this was hokum, he always thought. Chaos and randomness ruled the world. There was no master plan.

Apparently, he'd been wrong.

He opened his eyes and looked over his shoulder. The entire Beverly Hills police force was down in the garden. More EMTs and paramedics were arriving. He reached for the laptop and opened it. It was in sleep mode. When it resumed, the log-on window to Shackleton's database demanded a password. Will misspelled Pythagoras three times before getting it right. So much for his Harvard education.

There was a search screen: enter name, enter DOB, enter DOD, enter city, enter zip code, enter street address. It was all very user-friendly. He typed his own name and his DOB, and the computer told him: BTH. Fine, he thought, confirmed. Hopefully not BTH the way Mark Shackleton was BTH, but he had at least eighteen years in him, a lifetime.

The next entries wouldn't be so easy. He hesitated, considered shutting the computer down, but there were more sirens, more shouts from the garden. He inhaled sharply then typed, *Laura Jean Piper, 7-8-1984,* then hit the Enter key.

BTH

He exhaled, and silently mouthed, *Thank God.*

Then he inhaled again and typed, *Nancy Lipinski, White Plains, NY,* and hit Enter.

BTH

One more to solidify his plan: *Jim Zeckendorf, Weston, Massachusetts.*

BTH

That's all I want to know, that's all I need to know, he thought. He was trembling.

As he sat there, the logic seemed inescapable. He, his

daughter, and Nancy were going to survive despite the operatives who were tasked to kill in order to keep Area 51 secret. That meant he was going to take an action that prevented their deaths.

It was madness! Take free will and throw it out the window, he thought. He was being carried downstream by the River of Destiny. He was not the master of his fate, the captain of his soul.

He was crying now, for the first time since the day his father died.

While trauma teams were transporting the wounded from the bungalow to waiting ambulances, Will was at the desk in Room 315, composing a letter on hotel stationary. He finished and reread it. There was a blank he needed to fill in before dropping it in a mailbox.

The beautiful Saturday afternoon in Beverly Hills was marred by the noise and diesel stench of dozens of emergency service vehicles and news vans spewing fumes up and down Sunset Boulevard. He walked past them, head down, and hailed a taxi.

"Hell's going on here?" the driver asked him.

"Damned if I know," Will answered.

"Where to?"

"Take me to any kind of computer store, the L.A. public library, and a post office. In that order. This is extra." He reached over the seat and dropped a hundred dollars in the driver's lap.

"You want it, mister, you got it," the cabbie said enthusiastically.

At a Radio Shack, Will bought a memory stick. Back in the taxi, he quickly copied Mark's database onto the device and tucked it into his breast pocket.

He had the taxi wait outside the Central Library, a white art deco palace near Pershing Square in downtown L.A. After a stop at the information desk, he headed deep into the bowels of the stacks. In the raw fluorescence of a sublevel, in a basement area that rarely saw foot traffic, he thought about crazy Donny and quietly thanked him for giving him the idea of a perfect hiding place.

An entire case was devoted to the thick, musty, decades-old volumes of Los Angeles County municipal codes. When he was certain no one was about, he reached on tiptoes for the highest shelf and wriggled out the 1947 volume, a hefty book that slid heavily onto his outstretched palm.

Nineteen forty-seven. A small touch of irony on a grim day. The book smelled old and unused, and unless something went terribly wrong, he was confident he would be the last person to handle it for a very long time. He opened it to the middle. The binding over the spine splayed an inch, forming the pocket he used to deeply insert the memory stick. When he closed the tome, the binding stretched and creaked, the sliver of hardware swallowed up, well-concealed.

His next stop was a quick one, the nearest post office, where he purchased a stamp and dropped the completed letter into the first-class slot. It was addressed to Jim Zeckendorf at his Boston law firm. There was an envelope within an envelope. The cover letter began:

Jim, I'm sorry to get you involved in something complicated but I need your help. If I don't personally contact you by the first Tuesday of every month for the foreseeable future, I want you to open the sealed envelope and follow the instructions.

Back in the taxi, he told the driver, "Okay, last stop. Take me to Grauman's Chinese Theater."

"You don't hit me as the tourist type," the driver said.

"I like crowds."

The Hollywood sidewalk was thick with tourists and hawkers. Will stood on the square of cement inscribed, TO SID, MANY HAPPY TRAILS, ROY ROGERS AND TRIGGER, complete with handprints, footprints, and horse-shoe prints. He fished the phone out of his pocket and turned it on.

She picked up quickly, as if she'd been holding the phone, waiting for it to ring.

"Jesus, Will, are you okay?"

"I've had a heck of a day, Nancy. How are you?"

"Worried sick. Did you find him?"

"Yeah, but I can't talk. We're being monitored."

"Are you safe?"

"I'm covered. I'll be fine."

"What can I do?"

"Wait for me, and tell me again that you love me."

"I love you."

He hung up and got a number from information. With tenacity, he jawboned his way up the line until he was one step away from speaking to his target. He cut through the officiousness of the staffer. "Yeah, this is Special Agent Will Piper of the FBI. Tell the Secretary of the Navy I'm on the line. Tell him I was with Mark Shackleton earlier today. Tell him I know all about Area 51. And tell him he has one minute to pick up the phone."

Baldwin, Abbot of Vectis, knelt in troubled prayer at the foot of the holiest tomb in the abbey.

Between the pillars separating the nave from the aisles, the memorial slab was set into the stone floor. The smooth flat stones were freezing cold, and through his vestments, Baldwin's knees were going numb. Still, he stayed down, concentrating on his plaintive prayers he offered over the corpus of St. Josephus, patron saint of Vectis Abbey.

The tomb of Josephus was a favorite place of prayer and meditation inside Vectis Cathedral, the splendid high-spired edifice that had been erected on the site of the old abbey church. The slab of blue stone that marked his tomb was simply inscribed with the deeply chiseled: *Saint Josephus, Anno Domini 800.*

In the five hundred years since the death of Josephus, Vectis Abbey had undergone profound changes. The boundaries of the abbey were vastly expanded by the annexation of surrounding fields and meadows. A high stone wall and portcullis now surrounded the site as protection against the French pirates who preyed on the island and the Wessex coast. The cathedral, one of the finest in Britain, pierced the sky with its tapering, graceful tower. Over thirty substantial stone buildings, including dormitories, Chapter House, kitchens, refectory, cellerage, buttery, infirmary, Hospicium, Scriptorium, warming rooms, brewery, abbot house, and stables, were connected to one another with covered walkways and internal passages. The cloisters, yards, and vegetable gardens were ample and well-proportioned. There was a large cemetery. A farm with a grain mill and piggery occupied a far parcel. All told, the abbey supported almost six hundred inhabitants, in essence making it the second largest town on the island. It was a prosperous beacon of Christendom, rivaling Westminster, Canterbury, and Salisbury in prominence.

The island itself had also grown in population and prospered. Following the conquest of Britain by William, Duke of Normandy, at the Battle of Hastings in 1066, the island came under Norman control and fully slipped its pagan Scandinavian bonds. The archaic Roman name, Vectis, was abandoned, and the Normans began to call it the Isle of Wight. William gifted the island to his friend William fitzOsbern, who became the first Lord of the Isle of Wight. Under the protection of William the Conqueror and future British monarchs, the island became a rich, well-fortified bastion against the French. From the squat, strong Carisbrooke Castle at the center, a succession of Lords of the Isle of Wight exercised feudal rule and forged an ecclesiastical alliance with the monks of Vectis Abbey, their spiritual neighbors.

The last Lord of the Isle of Wight was, in actuality, not a lord but a lady, Countess Isabella de Fortibus, who acquired the lordship when her brother died in 1262. From her land holdings and the maritime taxes she collected, the sour, homely Isabella became the wealthiest woman in Britain. Because she was lonely, rich, and pious, Edgar, the previous Abbot of Vectis—and later, Baldwin, the present abbot—unctuously courted her and bestowed on her their most solicitous prayers and finest illuminated manuscripts. In return, Isabella donated generously to the abbey and became its principal patron.

In 1293, Baldwin was personally summoned to her death bed in Carisbrooke, where in her drafty bedchamber she weakly informed him that she had sold the isle to King Edward for six thousand marks, thus transferring control to the Crown. He would have to seek patronage elsewhere, she told him dismissively. As she took her last breath, he grudgingly blessed her.

The four years since Isabella's death had been challenging for Baldwin. Decades of dependence on the woman had left the abbey unprepared for the future. The population at Vectis had grown so large that it was no longer self-sufficient and external funds were constantly required. Baldwin was forced to frequently travel off the island, like a beggar, courting earls and lords, bishops and cardinals. He was not a political creature like Edgar, his predecessor, a man with easy approachability, beloved by his ministers, children, even dogs! Baldwin was fishlike, cool and slippery, an efficient administrator with a passion for ledgers as great as his love for God, but with correspondingly little love of his fellow man. His idea of bliss was a peaceful afternoon alone in his rooms with his books. However, happiness and peace were abstract concepts of late.

There was trouble brewing.

Deep underground.

Baldwin said a special prayer to Josephus and arose to seek out his prior for urgent consultation.

Luke, son of Archibald, a boot maker from London, was the youngest monk at Vectis. He was a strapping twenty-year-old with the physique of a soldier more than of a servant of God. His father was mystified and disappointed that his eldest son would choose religion over a brick oven, but he could no sooner stop his strong-willed boy than he could stop bread from rising. Young Luke, when an urchin, had fallen under the kindly sphere of his parish priest and since then never wanted more from life than to devote himself to Christ.

The total immersion of monastic life appealed to him especially. He had long heard tales from the priests of the isolated beauty of Vectis Abbey, and at age seventeen made his way south to the Isle of Wight, using his last coppers to buy a ferryboat passage. During the crossing, he watched the steep, concave cliffs of the island looming large and stared in awe at the cathedral spire on the horizon, a stone finger pointing to Heaven, he reckoned. He prayed with all his might that this would be a journey without return.

Following a long hike through the rich countryside, Luke presented himself at the portcullis and humbly begged admittance. Prior Felix, a burly Breton, as dark as Luke was fair, recognized his earnestness and took him in. After four years of toil as an oblate and then a lay brother, Luke was ordained a minister of God, and every day since then his heart brimmed with jubilation. His perpetually broad smile made his fellow brothers and sisters mirthful, and some would go out of their way to walk past him just for a glimpse of his sweet face.

Within days of Luke's arrival at Vectis, he began to hear whispered rumors about the crypts from the longer-serving novices. There was a subterranean world at the abbey, it was said. There were strange beings underground and strange doings. Rituals. Perversions. A secret society, the Order of the Names.

This was rubbish, Luke had thought, a rite of initiation for young men with fanciful imaginations. He would concentrate on his duties and his education and not allow himself to be drawn into such nonsense.

Yet there was no denying that a complex of buildings was out of bounds to him and his fellows. In a far corner of the abbey beyond the monk's cemetery there was a simple unadorned timber building the size of a small chapel, which was connected to a long low building some referred to as the outer kitchen. Out of curiosity, Luke had periodically wandered close enough to sneak peeks of comings and goings. He had witnessed grain, vegetable, meat, and milk deliveries. He had seen the same group of brothers regularly entering and leaving, and on more than one occasion, young women escorted into the chapel-sized building.

He was young and inexperienced and satisfied that there were things in this world he was not expected or entitled to understand. He would not allow himself to be distracted from his intimacy with God, which was growing stronger every day he spent within the walls of the monastery.

* * *

Luke's perfectly balanced and harmonious existence came to an end on a late October day. The morning had begun unseasonably warm and sunny but turned cool and rainy as the edge of a storm brushed the isle. He was taking a meditative walk on the abbey grounds, and as the wind whipped up and the rain started pelting down, he hugged the perimeter wall to shield himself. His path took him to the far side of the sisters' dormitory, where he could see young women hurrying outside to collect the wash.

A particularly strong gust plucked a child's shirt from a hemp line and launched it into the air, where the wind played with it awhile before depositing the cloth on the grass a short distance from Luke. As he sprinted for it he saw a girl break from her colleagues and run across the field to retrieve it too. Her veil pulled away as she ran, revealing long flowing hair the color of bee's honey.

She is not a sister, Luke thought, for her hair would be shorn. She was lissome with the grace of a young deer and just as skittish when she realized she was about to make to make contact with him. Stopping short, she let Luke reach the shirt as she held back. He snatched it up and waved it in the rain, his smile as huge as ever. "I have it for you!" he called out.

He had never seen a face as beautiful as hers, a perfect chin, high cheeks, green-blue eyes, moist lips, and skin the luminescence of a pearl he once saw on the hand of a fine lady in London.

Elizabeth was no more than sixteen, a vision of youth and purity. She was from Newport, sold by her father into indentured servitude at age nine to serve in the household of Countess Isabella at Carisbrooke. Isabella, in turn, bequeathed her two years later to Vectis as a gift to the abbey. Sister Sabeline had personally chosen Elizabeth from a group of girls on the offer. She'd held the girl's chin between her thumb and forefinger and declared that this one would be suitable for the monastery.

"Thank you," Elizabeth told Luke as he approached her, her voice sounding to him like a small bell, light and high.

"I am sorry it has become soaked." He gave the shirt to her. Even though their hands did not touch, he felt an energy pass between them. He made sure no one was looking before asking, "What is your name?"

"Elizabeth."

"I am Brother Luke."

"I know. I have seen you."

"You have?"

She looked down. "I must get back," she said, and she ran off.

He watched her glide away from him, and from that moment on she began competing in Luke's thoughts with Jesus Christ, his Lord and Savior.

He made a practice of passing behind the sisters' dormitory during his constitutionals, and somehow she always seemed to appear, if only to slap a garment on the washing stone or empty a bucket. When he caught sight of her, his smile would broaden and she would nod back and let the corners of her mouth curl toward her ears. They would never speak, but this did not diminish the pleasure of these encounters, and as soon as one would end he started to think about the next.

Surely, this behavior was wrong, he thought, and surely his musings were impure. But he had never felt this way about another person and was utterly powerless to block her from his mind. He repented and repented repeatedly, but kept ruminating on an insane urge to touch her silky skin with his palms, a preoccupation that was strongest when he lay alone in his bed, struggling to quiet the ache in his loins.

Luke began to hate himself, and his self-loathing wiped the perpetual smile from his face. His soul was tortured and he became another somber-faced monk moving slowly through the monastery.

He knew exactly what he deserved—to be punished, if not in this world then in the next.

As Abbot Baldwin was completing his prayers at the shrine of Josephus, Luke was strolling past the sisters' dormitory, wishing to catch a glimpse of Elizabeth. It was a cold crystalline morning and the discomfort of the blistering wind against his exposed skin stoked his masochism. The yard behind the dormitory was empty, and he could only hope his movements were being followed from one of the small windows that lined the steep-roofed building.

He was not disappointed. As he came closer, a door opened and she emerged wrapped in a long brown cloak. He had been holding his breath; when he saw her, he let out a puff of air that condensed and formed an ephemeral cloud. He thought she looked so lovely, he would slow down to prolong the moment, perhaps allowing himself to drift a bit nearer than usual, near enough to see the flutter of her eyelashes.

Then something quite extraordinary happened.

She walked straight toward him, stopping him dead in his tracks. She kept coming until she was only an arm's length away. He wondered whether this was a dream, but when he saw that she was crying and felt the warm air of her sobs pulsing against his neck, he knew it was real. He was too shocked to check for spies. "Elizabeth! What is the matter?"

"Sister Sabeline told me I am to be next," she said, choking and sputtering.

"Next? Next for what?"

"For the crypts. I am to be taken to the crypts! Please help me, Luke!"

He wanted to reach out to comfort her but knew that would be unpardonable. "I do not know what you speak of. What is to happen in the crypts?"

"You do not know?" she asked.

"No! Tell me!"

"Not here. Not now!" she sobbed. "Can we meet tonight? After you have done Vespers?"

"Where?"

"I don't know!" she cried. "Not here! Quickly! Sister Sabeline will find me!"

He thought quick, panicky thoughts. "All right. The stables. After Vespers. Meet me there if you are able."

"I will. I must flee. God bless you, Luke."

* * *

Baldwin paced nervously around his prior, Felix, who was seated on a chair with a horsehair cushion. Ordinarily this would have been a comfortable setting—the abbot's private receiving room, a nice radiating fire, a chalice of wine on a soft chair—but Felix was certainly not comfortable. Baldwin was flitting about like a fly in a hot room, and his anxiety was contagious. He was a man of wholly ordinary looks and proportions, without any physical manifestations of his holy position such as outward serenity or a wise countenance. Had he not worn the ermine-festooned robe and ornate crucifix of abbot, he would be mistaken for any village tradesman or merchant.

"I have prayed for answers, yet I have none," Baldwin pouted. "Can you not shed light on this dark matter?"

"I cannot, Father," Felix said in his thick-tongued Breton accent.

"Then we must have a meeting of the council."

The Council of the Order of the Names had not been convened for many years. Felix struggled to remember the last time—it was nearly twenty years earlier, he believed, when decisions had to be made concerning the last great Library expansion. He was a young man then, a scholar and bookbinder who had sought out Vectis because of its famous Scriptorium. Because of his intelligence, skills, and probity, Baldwin, who was prior in those days, inducted him into the Order.

Baldwin led the None Office inside the cathedral, the mellow song of his congregation filling the Sanctuary. He followed the prescribed order of service by rote and allowed his mind to drift to the crypts during the droning chants. None began with the Deus in Adjutorium, followed by the None hymn, Psalms 125, 126, and 127, a versicle, the Kyrie, the Pater, the Oratorio, and the concluding seventeenth prayer of St. Benedict. When it was done, he exited the Sanctuary first and listened for the select footsteps of members of the Order following him to the adjoining Chapter House, a polygonal building with a sharply peaked roof.

At the table sat Felix; Brother Bartholomew, the grizzled old monk who led the Scriptorium; Brother Gabriel, the sharp-tongued astronomer; Brother Edward, the surgeon, who presided over the infirmary; Brother Thomas, the fat drowsy keeper of the Cellarium and the Buttery; and Sister Sabeline, Mother Superior of all the sisters, a proud middle-aged woman of aristocratic blood.

"Who can tell me the current state of affairs within the Library?" Baldwin demanded, referring to the monks who labored there.

They had all visited recently, driven by uneasy curiosity, but no one had more intimate knowledge than Bartholomew, who spent much of his life underground and even assumed the physical characteristics of a vole. He had a pointy face, an aversion to light, and made small quick movements with his scrawny arms to emphasize his speech. "Something is troubling them," he began. "I have watched them for many years." He sighed. "Many years, indeed, and this is the closest I have ever seen to emotion."

Gabriel chimed in. "I agree with our brother. These are not typical displays of emotions that any one of us might experience—joy, anger, tiredness, hunger—but an unsettling sense of something being out of order."

"What specifically are they doing that is different from their usual practices?" Baldwin asked thoughtfully.

Felix leaned forward. "I would say their sense of purpose seems somehow diminished."

"Yes!" Bartholomew agreed.

"Over the years, we have always marveled at their infallible industry," Felix continued. "Their toil is unimaginable. They work until they collapse and when they awake after brief respite, they are rejuvenated and begin anew. Their pauses for food, drink, and nature are fleeting. But now . . . "

"Now they are getting lazy, like me!" Brother Thomas guffawed.

"Hardly lazy," the surgeon interjected. Brother Edward had a long thin beard, which he stroked obsessively. "I would say they have grown somewhat apathetic. The pace of their work is slower, more measured, their hands move sluggishly, their sleep periods are longer. They linger at their food."

"It is an apathy," Bartholomew agreed. "They are as they have always been, but you are correct, there is a certain apathy."

"Is there anything else?" Baldwin asked.

Sister Sabeline fingered the edge of her veil. "Last week one of them did not rise to the occasion."

"Astonishing!" Thomas exclaimed.

"Has this occurred again?" Gabriel asked.

She shook her head. "There has not been an opportune time. However, tomorrow I am bringing a pretty girl called Elizabeth. I will inform you of the outcome."

"Do so," the abbot said. "And keep me informed about this—apathy."

Bartholomew carefully made his way down the steep spiraling stairs leading from the small chapel-sized building to the crypts. There were torches set at intervals along the stairwell that were bright enough for most, but his eyes were failing after a lifetime of reading manuscripts by candles. He felt for the edge of each stair with his right sandal before dropping his left foot onto the next.

The winding of the stairs was so tight, and he turned so many times on himself, that he was dizzy by the time he reached the bottom. Every time he descended these stairs and entered the crypts, he marveled at the engineering and building skills of his predecessors who had burrowed so deeply into the earth in the eleventh century.

He unlocked the enormous door with the heavy black iron key he kept on his belt. Since he was small and light he had to lean into it with all his strength. It swung on its hinges and he entered the Hall of the Writers.

Though he had entered the hall thousands of times since he was first initiated into the Order of the Names as a young abbey scholar with a quizzical nature, he never ceased to pause in amazement and wonder at the sight of it.

Now, Bartholomew looked out on a crop of pale-skinned, ginger-haired men and boys, each one grasping a quill, dipping and writing, dipping and writing, producing a din of scratching as if hundreds of rats were trying to claw into barrels of grain. Some were old men, some young boys, but despite their ages, they all looked uncannily similar to one another. Every face was as blank as the next, green eyes boring into sheets of white parchment.

The writers faced the front of the cavern, seated shoulder by shoulder at their long tables. The chamber had a domed ceiling that was plastered and whitewashed. The dome was specially designed by the eleventh century architect, Brother Bertram, to reflect the candles and increase their luminosity, and every few decades the plaster was whitewashed anew to counter the soot.

There were up to ten writers at each of fifteen tables stretching to the rear of the chamber. Most of the tables were fully occupied, but there were scattered gaps. The reason for the gaps was apparent because the edge of the chamber was lined with cotlike beds, some of which were occupied by sleepers.

Bartholomew walked among the rows, stopping to peer over a shoulder here, a shoulder there. All seemed in order. The main door leading from the stairwell opened. Young brothers were bringing in pots of food.

At the rear of the chamber, Bartholomew opened another heavy door. He lit a torch from a candle that was always kept by the door and entered the first of two interconnected pitch-dark rooms, each one dwarfing the Hall of the Writers.

The library was a magnificent construction, cool dry vaults so vast they seemed, in torchlight, to have no physical boundaries. He passed through the narrow center corridor of the first vault and inhaled the rich earthy smell of the cowhide covers. He liked to periodically check that no burrowing rodents or nesting insects had penetrated the stone-lined fortress, and would have made his usual thorough inspection of the entire library had he not heard a commotion behind him.

One of the young brothers, a monk named Alfonso, was calling for his companions.

Bartholomew ran back to the hall and saw him kneeling behind the fourth table from the front with two of his fellow monks. A pot of stew was spilled on the floor and Bartholomew almost slipped on it.

"What is wrong?" the old man called to Alfonso.

None of the writers were affected by the disturbance. They remained occupied as if nothing had happened. But at Alfonso's knees there was a puddle of blood and a stream of crimson flowing from the eye of one of the ginger-heads, a quill thrust through his left eye deep into his brain matter.

"Jesus Christ Our Savior!" Bartholomew exclaimed at the sight. "Who did this!"

"No one!" Alfonso cried. The young Spaniard was shaking like a cold wet dog. "I saw him do it to himself. I was serving stew. He did it to himself!"

The Order of the Names convened again that day. No one had ever seen or heard of such an event and there was no oral history. Certainly, writers were born and writers died from old age. In this way they were like all mortal men, save for the fact that they never recorded their own births or deaths. But this death was entirely different. The fellow was young and had no sign of disease. Brother Edward, the surgeon, had confirmed this. Bartholomew had examined the last entry on the man's last page and there was nothing at all remarkable about it. It was simply one more name that happened to be in Chinese characters, by Bartholomew's reckoning.

It was clear this was suicide, an inexplicable abomination for any man. They discussed long into the night what actions they should take but there were no ready answers. Gabriel wondered if the body should be taken above the ground and burned, but there was dissent. A writer had never been treated so, and they were loath to break ancient traditions. Finally, Baldwin decided he should be placed inside the crypts that honey-combed the earth alongside the

Hall of Writers. Generations of writers lay in repose within these catacombs, and this wretched soul would be accorded the same fate.

When Felix returned to the underground chamber with strong, young brothers to aid in the burial, he noticed that the writers were even more sluggish and listless, with a greater number than usual asleep on their cots.

It was almost as if they were in mourning.

The horses shuffled and whinnied when Luke came into the stables. It was black and cold and he was frightened by his own boldness for even being there. "Hello?" he called out in a half whisper. "Is anybody here?"

A small voice answered, "I'm here, Luke. At the end."

He used the slice of moonlight coming through the open stable door to find her. Elizabeth was in the stall of a large bay mare, huddling beside its belly for warmth.

"Thank you for coming," she said. "I am afraid." She wasn't crying anymore. It was too cold for that.

"You are freezing," he said.

"Am I?" She held out her hand for him to touch. He did so with trepidation, but when he felt her alabaster wrist, he encircled it with his hand and would not let go.

"Yes. You are."

"Will you kiss me, Luke?"

"I cannot!"

"Please."

"Why do you torture me? You know I cannot. I have taken my vows! Besides, I came to hear your plight. You spoke of crypts." He let go and pulled away.

"Please do not be angry at me. I am to be taken to the crypts tomorrow."

"For what purpose?"

"They want me to lay with a man, something I have never done," she cried. "Other girls have suffered this fate. I have met them. They have borne babies that are taken from them when they are suckled. Some girls are used as birth mothers again and again until they lose their minds. Please do not let this happen to me!"

"This cannot be true!" Luke exclaimed. "This is a place of God!"

"It is the truth. There are secrets at Vectis. Have you not heard the stories?"

"I have heard many things but I have seen nothing with my own eyes. I believe what I see."

"But you believe in God," she said. "And you have not seen Him."

"That is different!" he protested. "I do not need to see Him. I feel His presence."

She was growing desperate. She composed herself and reached for his hand, which in the unguarded moment he allowed her to grasp. "Please, Luke, lie down with me, here in the straw."

She carried his hand to her bosom and pressed it there. He felt the firm flesh through her cloak, and his ears filled with rushing blood. He wanted to close his palm around the sweet globe, and for a moment he almost did. Then he regained his senses and recoiled, banging into the side of the stall.

Her eyes were wild. "Please, Luke, do not go! If you lie with me, they will not take me to the crypts. I will be of no use to them."

"And what would happen to me!" he hissed. "I would be cast out! I will not do this. I am a man of God! Please, I must leave you now!"

As he ran from the stables he could hear Elizabeth's soft wails mixing discordantly with the neighing of disturbed horses.

Storm clouds lay so low and heavy over the island that the transition from darkness to dawn seemed slight. Luke lay awake all through the night, fitful and troubled. At Lauds, it was almost impossible to concentrate on his hymns and psalms, and in the brief interval before he was obliged to return to the cathedral for the Prime Office, he rushed through his chores.

Finally he could bear it no more. He quietly approached his superior, Brother Martin, clutching his stomach and asking for permission to forgo Prime and attend the infirmary.

Permission granted, he put up his hood and chose a circuitous route to the forbidden buildings. He picked a large maple tree on a nearby knoll, close enough to watch but far enough to conceal himself. From that vantage point, he stood guard in the raw gray mist.

He heard the bells ring for Prime.

No one came or left the chapel-sized building.

He heard the bells ring again to signify the end of the Office.

All was quiet. He wondered how long he could pass unnoticed and what the consequence of his subterfuge would be. He would accept his punishment but was hopeful that God would treat him with a small measure of love and understanding for his pitiful frailties.

The bark was rough on his cheek. Consumed with fatigue, he dozed briefly but awoke with a start when his skin chafed on the jagged surface.

He saw her coming down the path, led by Sister Sabeline as if towed by a rope. Even from a distance he could tell she was crying.

At least this part of her tale was true.

The two women disappeared through the front door of the chapel.

His pulse quickened. He clenched his fists and softly beat them against the tree trunk. He prayed for guidance.

But he did nothing.

Elizabeth felt she was in a dream the moment she entered the chapel and began her descent underground. Years later, looking back, her mind would never allow her to retain the details of what she was about to see, and as an old lady she would sit alone by the fire and try to decide whether any of it had been real.

The chapel itself was an empty space with a blue-stone floor. There were low stone walls but the structure was mainly timber-framed with a steeply pitched shingled roof. The only interior decoration was a gilded wooden crucifix affixed to the wall above an oaken door at the rear.

Sister Sabeline pulled her through the door and led her down the steep stairway that bored into the earth.

At the threshold to the Hall of the Writers, Elizabeth squinted into the dim cavern and tried to make sense of what she saw. Wide-eyed, she stared at Sabeline, but the woman's icy rebuke was, "Hold your tongue, girl."

None of the writers seemed to take notice as Sabeline dragged her in front of them one by one, row by row, until one man raised his ginger head from a page and looked at the girl. He was perhaps eighteen or nineteen. Elizabeth noticed that three spindly fingers on his right hand were stained black with ink. She thought she heard a low grunt come out of his puny chest.

Sabeline yanked the horrified girl away. At the end of the row, Sabeline pulled her toward an archway into a black void. Elizabeth thought it must surely be the gate to Hell. As she passed through it, she turned her head and saw the grunting young man rise from his table.

The void was the entrance to the catacombs. If the first room smelled like misery, the second room smelled like death. Elizabeth choked and gagged at the stench. There were yellow skeletons with bits of adherent flesh piled like firewood in the recesses of the walls. Sabeline held out a candle, and everywhere the light splashed Elizabeth saw grotesque skulls with jaws agape. She prayed she would fall into unconsciousness, but woefully remained sensate.

They were not alone. Someone was beside her. She whirled around to see the dumb blank face and green eyes of the young man blocking the passageway. Sabeline withdrew, her sleeve brushing the leg bones of a corpse, its dry bones clattering together musically. Then, holding the candle high, the nun and watched from a short distance.

Elizabeth was panting like an animal. She could have fled, deeper into the catacombs, but was too afraid. The ginger-haired man stood inches away, his arms limp by his sides. Seconds passed. Sabeline called to him in frustration, "I have brought this girl for you!"

Nothing happened.

More time passed and the nun demanded, "Touch her!"

Elizabeth braced herself for the touch of what seemed a living skeleton and closed her eyes. She felt a hand on her shoulder, but strangely, it did not repulse her. It was reassuring. She heard Sister Sabeline shrieking, "What are you doing here! What are you doing!"

She opened her eyes and, magically, the face she saw was Luke's. The pale, ginger-haired youth man was on the ground, picking himself up from the spot where Luke had roughly shoved him.

"Brother Luke, leave us!" Sabeline screamed. "You have violated a sacred place!"

"I will not leave without this girl," Luke said defiantly. "How can this be sacred? All I see is evil."

"You do not understand!" the nun roared.

From the hall, they heard a sudden pandemonium.

Heavy thuds.

Crashes.

Flopping. Thrashing.

The ginger-haired youth turned away and walked toward the noise.

"What is happening?" Luke asked.

Sabeline did not answer. She took her candle and rushed toward the hall, leaving them alone in the pitch-dark.

"Are you safe?" Luke asked Elizabeth tenderly. He was still touching her shoulder, and she realized he had never let go.

"You came for me," she whispered.

He helped her find her way from the darkness into the light, into the hall.

It was no longer the Hall of the Writers.

It was the Hall of the Dead.

The only living soul was Sabeline, whose shoes were soaked with blood. She aimlessly walked among a sea of bodies, draped on the tables and cots, crumpled in piles on the ground, a mass of lifelessness and quivering involuntary twitching. She had a sick, glassy expression and could only mutter, "My God, my God, my God, my God," over and over, in the cadence of a chant.

The floor and tables and chairs of the chamber were slowly being coated with the blood spurting from the quill-pierced eyes of almost 150 ginger-haired men and boys.

Luke led Elizabeth by her hand through the carnage. He had the presence of mind to glance at the parchments that lay on the writing tables, some of them blotting up puddles of blood. What curiosity or survival instinct prompted him to snatch up one of the sheets as he fled? That would be something he would contemplate for years to come.

They ran up the precarious stairs, through the chapel, and out into the mist and rain. They kept running until they were a mile from the abbey gate. Only then did they stop to soothe their burning lungs and listen to the cathedral bells pealing in alarm.

The navy operated a single G-V, the C-37A, a luxury, high-performance business jet favored by the Secretary of the Navy for his personal travel. The twin Rolls-Royce turbofans put out neck-snapping thrust on its steep-angle takeoff, and out its windows, in seconds, the endless incandescence of the Los Angeles night disappeared behind sheets of low clouds.

Harris Lester was running on caffeine after a stressful, time-zone-stretched day that had begun before dawn in his Fairfax, Virginia, home and included stops at the Pentagon, Andrews Air Force Base, and LAX. After a brief layover in L.A., it was wheels up again for the return flight to Washington. His facial tone was slack and unhealthy and his breath was stale. The only things about him that were crisp and fresh were his dress shirt and pressed tie, and they looked like they had just been unwrapped from Brooks Brothers tissue paper.

There were only three people in the passenger cabin, a paneled interior configured in club style, with pairs of plush dark blue leather seats facing each other over smooth teakwood tables. Lester and Malcolm Frazier, whose chiseled block of a face was contorted into an immutable grimace, were staring at the man seated across from Lester, who clutched his armrest with one hand and a cut-crystal glass of scotch with the other.

Will was bone-weary but the most relaxed person on board. He had played his cards, and it appeared he had the winning hand.

Hours earlier he had been scooped off the street in Hollywood by Frazier and a team of watchers who were jetted in from Groom Lake to make the pickup. They bundled him into a black Tahoe and sped off to a private aviation terminal at the airport, where they kept him on ice, uninterrogated, in a conference room until Lester arrived. Will had the distinct impression that Frazier would have preferred to kill him outright, or at least inflict a punishing dose of pain; he supposed if someone had shot up one of his FBI teams, he'd have wanted to do the same. But he could also tell that Frazier was a soldier, and good soldiers obeyed orders.

Now, Frazier opened Shackleton's laptop and after a few keystrokes he spat out, "What's his password?"

"Pythagoras," Will answered.

Frazier sighed. "Fucking egghead. "P-I?"

"P-Y," Will said sadly.

Then, in seconds, "It's here as advertised, Mr. Secretary."

"How can we be sure you made a copy, Agent Piper?" Lester asked.

Will pulled a receipt from his wallet and tossed it on the table. "Radio Shack memory stick, bought today, postincident."

"So we know you stashed it somewhere in the city," Frazier said contemptuously.

"It's a big city. On the other hand, I could have dropped it in the mail. Or, I could have given it to someone who may or may not have known what it was. In any event, I can guarantee you that if I don't regularly and frequently make personal contact with one or more unnamed parties, the memory stick will be sent to the media." He forced his mouth into a thin smile. "So, gentlemen, don't fuck with me or anyone I care about."

Lester massaged his temples. "I know what you're saying and why you're saying it, but you don't really want this ever to get out, do you?"

Will put his glass down and watched its sweaty bottom make a wet ring on the wood. "If I wanted that, I would have sent it to the papers myself. It's not for me to say whether the public should know. Who the hell am I? I wish *I* never learned about it. I haven't had a chance to give it a lot of thought but just knowing it's there changes—everything." He suddenly chuckled, punch drunk.

"What's funny?" Lester asked.

"For a guy named Will, the concept of free will is kind of important." On a dime, he turned serious again. "Look, I don't know if free will even exists now. It's all laid out in advance, right? Nothing's going to change if your name comes up. Am I right?"

"You got that right," Frazier said bitterly. "Otherwise you'd be in a thirty-thousand-foot free fall as we speak."

Will let the man's venom slide off him. "You've lived with this. Doesn't it affect the way you go about your life?"

"Of course it does," Lester snapped. "It's a burden. I've got a son, Agent Piper, my youngest boy. He's twenty-two and he's got cystic fibrosis. We all know he's not going to have a normal life expectancy, we accept that. But do you think I like knowing that the date of his death is set in stone? Do you think I want to know that day, or have him know? Of course not!"

Frazier had a different take, one that left Will chilled to the bone: "For me, it makes things easier. I knew that Kerry Hightower and Nelson Elder were going to die when they did. All I did was pull the trigger. I sleep okay."

Will shook his head and had another drink. "Therein lies the problem, don't you think? What the hell would the world be like if it was out there and everyone thought like you?"

The high-pitched whine of the engines was the only sound until Lester gave a politician's answer. "That's why we go to the lengths we do to keep the Library a secret. We've had a remarkable track record for over six decades, thanks to the work of dedicated men like Frazier here. We only mine the data for geopolitical and national security purposes. We don't willy-nilly make person-specific queries unless there's an overriding security reason. We are responsible stewards of this miraculous resource. There have been minor—I'd say trivial—breaches and indiscretions in the past that have been dealt with surgically. This Shackleton affair is the first catastrophic breech in Area 51's history. I hope you understand that."

Will nodded and leaned as far forward as the table would allow. He bore into the Secretary. "I understand completely. I also understand leverage. If you ever get your hands on my copy of the database, you'll stick me in the deepest hole you can dig, and to be on the safe side, you'll make sure everyone I'm close to disappears too. You know it, I know it. I'm just protecting myself. I'm not a theologian or a philosopher. I'm not interested in big moral issues, okay? I didn't ask to get involved in your world, but it happened, because thirty years ago I was randomly assigned to be Mark Shackleton's roommate! All I want is to be left alone, retire, and live my puny little life until at least 2027. Your big adversary is a good old country boy who just wants to go fishing." He reclined and watched Lester's sagging face fixed in a passive frieze. "Which one of you boys wants to freshen my drink?"

Back in Washington, he was voluntarily held for a two-day debriefing by Frazier and a group of sweethearts from the DIA who made Frazier seem like a humanitarian. They got him to regurgitate everything he knew about the affair, everything the whereabouts of the memory stick.

When they were done with him, he agreed to execute the same daunting confidentiality agreement that all Area 51 employees had to sign, and he was released, free and clear, into the waiting arms of his brethren at the FBI.

The FBI director ordered that he not be required to undergo further agency questioning or file a report on the last days of the Doomsday investigation. Sue Sanchez, flummoxed and clueless, offered him a package—paid administrative leave until he had his twenty years, then full retirement. He accepted the deal with a smile, and on her way out he gave her a playful pat on the bottom, and winked when she turned in anger.

*   *   *

Will sat back and listened to the dinner table conversation with quiet satisfaction. There was a domestic feel about it, something traditional and archetypal that put his internal rhythms in harmony. There hadn't been many Piper family dinners when he was growing up, nor could he recall them during the brief time he provided his daughter with a nuclear family.

He slowly chewed his steak and listened to the repartee. His apartment was a pleasant wreck, piled with moving boxes, suitcases, women's clothing, new pieces of furniture, and bric-a-brac.

Laura tried to refill his wine but he put his hand over the glass to stop her.

"Are you feeling, okay, Dad?" she joked.

"I'm pacing myself," he said smugly.

"He's definitely cut down," Nancy said.

He shrugged. "The new me. Same as the old me but slightly lower blood alcohol levels."

"Do you feel better for it?" Greg asked.

"Off the record?"

"Yes, sir, off the record."

"Yeah, I do. Go figure. What's up with the book, Laura?"

"All systems go. I'm waiting on the galleys and preparing myself for a life of fame and fortune."

"As long as you're happy, I'm okay with whatever the future's got in store for you. Both of you."

Greg lowered his eyes, nonplussed by the kindness. The reporter in him still had a burning curiosity about the Doomsday case. He had asked Laura the questions out loud, rehearsing them in case he got the nerve to try to interview Will, but knew the subject was taboo. He seriously doubted he'd ever be told, even if he became Will Piper's his son-in-law.

Why had Will been removed from the investigation and declared a fugitive? Why had the case faded from official discussion with no arrests and no resolution? Why had Will been rehabilitated and gently put out to pasture?

Instead he asked, "So what's in store for you, Will? You going to do a little fishing, put your feet up awhile?"

"No way!" Nancy interjected. "Now that I've moved in, Will's going to be taking in plays, museums, galleries, good restaurants, you name it."

"I thought you hated New York, Dad."

"I'm already here. Might as well give it a try. Us retirees got to keep our minds active while the women folk solve bank robberies."

Later, when they were leaving, Will gave his daughter a kiss on the cheek and pulled her out of Greg's earshot. "You know, I like your guy. I wanted to tell you that. Hold onto him."

He knew for a fact that Greg Davis was BTH.

Will lay on the bed watching Nancy personalize his bedroom with pictures, a jewelry box, a stuffed bear.

"You okay with this?" she asked.

"It looks nice."

"I mean, okay with us? Was this a good idea?"

"I think it was." He patted the mattress. "When you're done redecorating you should come here and check out your new bed."

"I've slept in it before," she said, and giggled.

"Yeah, but this is different. It's communal property now."

"In that case, I'll take the window half," she said.

"You know, I think you're my type."

"What type is that?"

"Smart, sexy, sassy, pretty much all the s's."

She crawled beside him and cuddled up, and he wrapped his arms around her. He'd told her about the Library. It was something he had to share with one person in his life, and the secret glued them together.

"In L.A., I looked up something else on Shackleton's computer," he said softly.

"Do I want to know?"

"On May 12, 2010, a child is born named Phillip Weston Piper. That's nine months from now. That's our son."

She blinked a few times then kissed his face.

He returned the kiss and said, "I've got a pretty good feeling about the future."

The hem of the abbot's white robe was soaked with blood. Each time he stooped to touch a cold forehead or make the sign of the cross over a supine body, his garment got bloodier.

Prior Felix was at Baldwin's side, supporting him by the arm so the abbot wouldn't tumble on the blood-slicked stones. They made their rounds through the carnage, pausing over each ginger-haired writer to check for signs of life, but there were none. The only other beating heart in the Hall of the Writers belonged to old Bartholomew, who was making his own grim inspection at the opposite end of the chamber. Baldwin had sent Sister Sabeline away because her hysterical crying was unnerving and preventing him from collecting his thoughts.

"They are dead," Baldwin said. "All dead. Why in God's name has this happened?"

Bartholomew was systematically going from row to row, stepping carefully over and around bodies, trying to keep his footing. For a very old man, he was moving briskly from one station to another, plucking manuscript pages off the table and making a stack of them in his hand.

He made his way to Baldwin clutching a ream of parchments.

"Look," the old man said. "Look!"

He laid the pages down.

Baldwin picked up one and read it.

Then the next, and the next. He fanned the pages out on the table to see more of them quickly.

Each page carried the date 9 February 2027, with the identical inscription.

"*Finis Dierum*," Baldwin said. "End of Days."

Felix trembled. "So this is when the end will come."

Bartholomew half smiled at the revelation. "Their work was done."

Baldwin gathered up the pages and held them to his breast. "Our work is not yet done, brothers. They must be laid to rest in the crypt. Then I will say a mass in their honor. The Library must be sealed and the chapel must be burned. The world is not ready."

Felix and Bartholomew quickly nodded in agreement as the abbot turned to leave.

"The year 2027 is far in the future," Baldwin said wearily. "At least, mankind has a very long time to prepare for the End of Days."

Acknowledgments

I'm not sure this book would have seen the light of day without the intercession of Steve Kasdin, of the Sandra Dijkstra Literary Agency, who took a shine to my letter in his query pile and helped shape the manuscript into its final form. He's very popular in the Cooper family. Thanks too for the soul-lifting encouragement from my early readers, Gunilla Lacoche, Megan Murphy, Allison Tobia, and George Tobia, my friend and lawyer. I'm also delighted to be part of the HarperCollins family under the experienced wing of my delightful editor, Lyssa Keusch. Finally, a big shout-out to my wife, Tessa, and my son, Shane, who gave their support every step of the way.

KEEP READING FOR AN EXCERPT FROM

Book of Souls,

THE THRILLING SEQUEL TO

Library of the Dead

Toby reached his hand into the inside pocket of his form-fitted Chester Barrie suit and extracted his thin white cotton specimen gloves. Decades earlier, his boss had steered him to his Savile Row tailor and ever since, he had clothed himself in the best fabrics he could afford. Clothes mattered, and so did grooming. His bristling moustache was always perfectly trimmed and visits to his barber every Tuesday lunchtime kept his grey-tinged hair unfailingly neat.

He slid on the gloves like a surgeon and hovered over the first exposed binding. 'Right. Let's see what we have.'

The top row of spines revealed a matched set. He plucked out the first book. 'Ah! All six volumes of Freeman's *History of the Norman Conquest of England*, 1877–1879, if I recall.' He opened the cloth cover to the title page. 'Excellent! First edition. Is it a matched set?'

'All firsts, Toby.'

'Good, good. They should go for six to eight hundred. You often get mixed sets, you know.'

He laid out all six books carefully, taking note of their condition before diving back into the crate. 'Here's something a bit older.' It was a fine old Latin Bible, Antwerp, 1653, with a rich worn calf binding and gilt ridges on the spine. 'This is nice,' he cooed. 'I'd say one fifty to two hundred.'

He was less enthusiastic about the next several volumes, some later editions of Ruskin and Fielding in dodgy condition, but he grew quite excited at Fraser's *Journal of a Tour Through Part of the Snowy Range of the Himala Mountains, and to the Source of the Rivers Jumna and Ganges*, 1820, a pristine first. 'I haven't seen one of these in this state for years! Marvellous! Three thousand, easily. My spirits are lifting. Tell me, there wouldn't be any incunabula in the collection?'

From the perplexed expression on the youth's face, Toby knew he was tapping a dry hole. 'Incunabula? European printed books? Pre-1501? Ring a bell?'

The young man was clearly stung by Toby's irritability and he flushed in embarrassment. 'Oh, right. Sorry. No incunabula whatsoever. There *was* something on the oldish side, but it was handwritten.' He pointed helpfully into the crate. 'There it is. His granddaughter wasn't keen on parting with it.'

'Whose granddaughter?'

'Lord Cantwell's. She had an unbelievable body.'

'We don't, as a habit, make reference to our clients' bodies,' Toby said sternly, reaching for the broad spine of the book.

It was remarkably heavy; he needed two hands to securely drag it out and lay it on the table.

Even before he opened it, he felt his pulse race and the moisture evaporate from his mouth. There was something about this large, dense book that spoke loudly to his instincts. The bindings were smooth old calf-leather, mottled, the color of good milk chocolate. It had a faintly fruited smell, redolent of ancient mould and damp. The dimensions were prodigious, eighteen inches long, twelve inches wide and a good five inches thick: a couple of thousand pages, to be sure. As to weight, he imagined hoisting a two-kilo bag of sugar. This was much heavier. The only markings were on the spine, a large, simple hand-tooled engraving, incised deeply into the leather: 1527.

He was surprised, in a detached way, to see his right hand trembling when he reached out to lift the cover. The spine was supple from use. No creaking. There was a plain unadorned creamy endpaper glued onto the hide. There was no frontispiece, no title page. The first page of the book, the color of butter, roughly uneven to the touch, began without exposition, racing into a closely spaced handwritten scrawl. Quill and black ink. Columns and rows. At least a hundred names and dates. He blinked in a large amount of visual information before turning the page. And another. And another. He skipped to the middle. Checked several pages towards the end. Then the last page. He tried to do a quick mental calculation, but because there was no pagination, he was only guessing—there must have been well over a hundred thousand listed names from front to back.

'Remarkable,' he whispered.